Never Wake

Gabrielle Goldsby

Quest Books

Nederland, Texas

ISBN 978-1-932300-61-1

First Printing 2006

9 8 7 6 5 4 3 2 1

Cover design by Donna Pawlowski

Published by:

Regal Crest Enterprises, LLC
4700 Highway 365, Suite A
PMB 210
Port Arthur, Texas 77642

Find us on the World Wide Web at
http://www.regalcrest.biz

Printed in the United States of America

Acknowledgments

I would like to thank the wonderful fans, editors, beta readers, and authors who attended the inaugural GCLS convention in New Orleans in 2005. Your kind words of encouragement about the first of several drafts of this novel will always be appreciated. Here's to many more GCLS conventions to come.

I must thank Mecheal for being my sounding board and my first reader for so many years.

I would be remiss if I didn't thank Lori Lake. You have single handedly been responsible for some of my best work. You have shown more confidence in my ability then even I, at times. Thank you for both pushing me out of my comfort zone and for pulling me out of the fire just when I need it.

Last but not least, I want to thank my editor, Jane Vollbrecht. I have always believed that everything happens for a reason. Working with you has been one of the best experiences of my life. Thank you for the quote that will hang on my story board until your advice comes naturally:

"Remember to smile. Remember to have fun."
-Jane Vollbrecht

For Melissa.
Forever will never be long enough

Prologue

MAYBE DWIGHT FEELS bad about that last beating.

Seconds after the thought came to Reba, she dismissed it. She'd stopped believing Dwight had a heart the day he put her out on the stroll.

What a dumb ass she had been. Fresh off the bus from Vidor, Texas, she had fallen in love with him the moment she laid eyes on his perfect white teeth. He had, she thought, rescued her from sleeping in homeless shelters. She had thought herself in love, despite the fact that all they ever did together was have sex. When he'd said he needed her to do him a favor, she had jumped at the chance to do something for him. When he'd told her what it was, she had hesitated. When Dwight's "favor" walked into the hotel room and started to undress, she had closed her eyes through the whole thing. She had been closing her eyes ever since.

How long had it been? Reba frowned; her eyes clinched tight against any possible light that might make her feel obligated to get out of bed. Not quite four years. Dwight had beaten her from the start. Still, she hadn't begun hating him until he had moved the others into her house.

Her house. Reba's mouth twisted. She'd believed him when he had told her he had purchased the house for her. She should have known. She should have known from the very beginning that a house that large, that far outside of town, even with its overgrown garden and peeling paint, could never be hers. She should have known what that house was when she first saw it. Her prison.

IT'S FUNNY WHAT the mind is capable of. Her mind, had fooled her into believing that Dwight had realized what he had been asking her to do was wrong. He had then bought her a huge, old house and left her to make it into a home for them. Her days were spent digging up the weeds in the garden; her nights and evenings exploring the house and transforming her bedroom into her sanctuary. Those were the happiest three weeks of her life. Her delusion had been so thorough that she had begun to think that Dwight hadn't been ignoring her when she talked about settling down. Maybe he had heard her when she spoke of having kids together. But like everything else in Reba's life, that fantasy wouldn't last either.

He brought the first of them to the house—was it Tawny, Keri or Bambi? It didn't matter. Once *they* came, she could no longer fool herself into thinking that she and Dwight were anything but hunter and prey, owner and slave, guard and prisoner.

After the other girls arrived, Dwight no longer felt the need to pretend kindness. Indeed, he had told her on several occasions that she was free to go any time she wanted. He had all the girls he needed, and if she left, it would just make room for a younger, prettier girl.

Dwight was good with his fists, but his words were capable of drawing blood, too. "Go on a diet 'fore I have to offer two-for-one specials. Not sure why anyone would pay for that." And Reba's personal favorite," Go suck that prick's dick."

Reba remembered hearing the latter before she led Sammy Shit-face into her sanctuary. He would have been her last John for the day. She had hoped Sammy would be done fast so that she could get a hot bath and clean sheets spritzed with the apple linen spray she had bought from Bed, Bath, and Beyond on their last trip to Portland. She wanted alone time. *He* wanted something so nasty that the word *no* was out of her mouth before he could finish speaking.

No. She would never have guessed how good one word could feel on her lips. She smiled even now, lying in this darkness, too scared to move for fear of stirring up pain.

She had never seen Dwight as furious as he had been when Sammy Shit-face scurried out of the room complaining that she had refused him. But even when Dwight's big diamond ring was driving toward her nose, she'd felt the slightest thrill. She had said no. It was her body. Hers, damn it, and she refused to let it be used as a fucking toilet.

Reba took a cautious sniff. The scent of stale sex always made her nauseous, which is why she kept a set of clean sheets stashed on the top shelf of her closet. She knew for a fact that some of the other girls didn't bother changing their sheets for days on end. *Dirty bitches!* She looked forward to her nighttime ritual of removing the soiled sheets and replacing them with clean, fragrant ones after her last client. But she hadn't had time to duck the blow, let alone have the strength to change her sheets afterward. She should have smelled the stink of fat, pasty-assed men with pumpkin tummies and pricks the size of Vienna sausages, but it wasn't there. Reba frowned again; neither was the scent of Tide with a touch of Downey.

Reba pressed the sheet to her nose and inhaled. No scent. Maybe one of the girls had changed her sheets while she was out cold. Yeah right, that would be a cold day in hell. But what difference did it make? As long as she didn't have to lay in stink, she should be happy.

Reba curled on to her side. No pain. Dwight must be losing his touch. Cool blue light crept between the door and the carpet. A fan clicked on somewhere and a chilly draft drifted over Reba's skin. Now that was odd. Dwight was a stickler for energy conservation. Or, to be more accurate, he would much rather spend three hundred dollars on a new tie than pay PGE one dime more than he had to. Any girl crazy enough to turn on the air conditioner would no doubt get herself a well-earned vacation. That was the one good thing about taking a beating from Dwight. It meant you got a break from having to fuck anyone with a hundred bucks. The length of time off depended on how fast a healer you were. Even clients who like it rough don't like bruised goods.

Reba flipped onto her back. She didn't remember ever seeing an air conditioner and she had explored the house from roof to basement. It had to be early morning. Otherwise some thoughtless bitch would have slammed a cabinet door or yelled something to someone standing two feet away from her by now.

Her room was too dark to make out the old lounger that she had found in the attic, nor could she see the picture that she had picked up at Saturday market for thirteen dollars and a smile.

Reba blinked into the darkness and squinted in the direction of the cheap digital clock she'd had for years. Another blink confirmed that she wasn't wearing her contacts. She *always* slept in her contacts. She had this fear that she would wake up one night with the house on fire and she wouldn't be able to see well enough to get out on her own. Lord knew none of those heifers would slow down long enough to help her—unless it was to put a foot in her ass on their way out the door.

Funny how she had nightmares about dying in fires when death by Dwight's hand was more probable. She snorted, and the sound ricocheted around the room as if she lay in a tunnel. Unease crept into the room like the bluish tinted light peeking beneath her door. All the rooms in the house had taupe-colored carpet and paisley pink and purple wallpaper. The other girls resented the fact that because Reba had moved in first, she had been able to pick the biggest room and the least gaudy furnishings. What she hadn't liked, she had swapped out.

Her room, when not occupied by some heavy-breathing tub of bacon drippings, had become her most favorite place in the world. Someone had to have removed her thick carpeting or at least some of her furnishings for the room to sound so hollow. *Leave it to a pack of hookers to steal your shit while you're in a fucking coma.* Reba's anger seeped from her body as fast as it flared.

I'm getting too old for this shit. I need to retire before Dwight retires me first. Dwight's voice cut unbidden through the darkness. "Can't teach an old ho' new tricks." She remembered how he cackled at the joke as if he had written it himself. He *was*, however, the originator of such doozies as, "Anyone with a name like Reba is gonna turn out to be a hooker or a country singer, and we all know *our* Reba can't sing a tanch." What the fuck did "tanch" mean anyway? She'd tried looking it up in one of the old dictionaries in the attic once, but hadn't found it. She had to admit Dwight was right when he said Reba was a name made for a hooker. She could count on hearing that one at least once a month. That and "You're a stupid, good-for-nothing ____." She had begun to believe he was right. That she was good for nothing. It's not like he was the first one to say it. Her momma had said it so many times she had begun to accept it as a truth.

She had her doubts about it now, though. How could that be true? Everyone was good for at least one thing, right? Hell, when she set her mind to something she was damn near unstoppable. Hadn't she been the first girl in her senior class to get out of Vidor, even though all of them claimed they would?

To hear Momma tell it, you'd have thought Nicole was the first to leave, but she wasn't. Nicole was still in pigtails and K-mart jeans when Reba waved goodbye from a Greyhound bus headed as far as two hundred dollars could take her.

She imagined Momma as she bragged to her neighbor. "My youngest daughter, Nicole, got me this here from Paris. Nicole travels all over the world for her flight attendant job, you know?"

Flight attendant – more like a glorified waitress, Reba thought. But a glorified waitress could afford to go home for visits in a rent-a-car as Nicole did, according to Momma. A glorified waitress could also afford to send home money as Nicole often did.

Reba furrowed her brow and squinted at the light glowing beneath her door. A nightlight plugged into the dangling electrical socket in the hall had been one of Dwight's few concessions.

The twins, Bambi and Keri, had one of those daddies who liked to sneak into their kid's room to "say goodnight" once the house was dark and mommy was asleep. So Dwight allowed them to leave a small light on in their rooms and the night light in the hall after they went to bed, even though Reba was sure it was a fire hazard. It wasn't out of kindness. Clients don't care for girls with bags under their eyes.

But why was it blue? She had lain awake enough nights glaring at that light intruding into her room to know that it should be orange – no, not quite orange – it was more of a gold, but definitely not blue. Reba glared at the space between the floor and door and pushed the blankets down to her waist. The light went off and then reappeared again.

Was someone out there playing with the switch or...there, it happened again. What the hell? Reba pushed her comforter—no, not a comforter, more like a thin blanket and sheet—down and swung her legs over the side of the bed. *Too high to be my bed.*

Once again, the blue light was interrupted by darkness before reappearing. It happened two more times before it came to her. Momma had once let her and Nicole take in a stray dog. She had lost interest in having a pet within a week; Nicole even faster. The dog was left chained to an old clothes-line pole in the back yard. After about a year, it began pacing back and forth, its head hung low and swaying opposite to the rest of the body. She and Nicole began to fear that dog. Feeding it became Momma's form of punishment and reward. The child on Momma's shit list, often Reba, would have to feed the dog most often. The favorite, more times than not Nicole, would watch with a malicious grin as the other got as close as she had to before dropping a tin pie dish in front of the animal and high-tailing it back into the house. At some point the dog had begun to pace at all hours of the night, his shadow casting dark splashes across their bedroom curtains like an accusing spirit. Perhaps it was guilt, but both she and Nicole would wake up screaming, until Momma had one of her male friends take the dog away. This interruption of light reminded her of that dog. Someone was pacing, right outside her door.

No, this was not her door. Where the fuck was she?

Reba stood up, her hands out in front of her. She was wearing some kind of light gown. She always slept in a thick granny gown because the old house was drafty, even in the summer. Reba's outstretched fingers stumbled across the top of a metal chair that was almost too heavy for her to lift without making a sound, but she did.

She was not in the house, and whoever stood outside that door was doing his damnedest not to make any noise.

Reba couldn't explain how she knew it, but evil was waiting out there. What was he waiting for? Why hadn't he come in and killed her in her sleep?

The chair was becoming heavy and Reba had started lowering it to the floor when it came to her. He—and for some odd reason she knew it was a he—was waiting for something. Just like that dog was waiting for his meal. She wanted to believe she was overreacting. Maybe he was just giving her a chance to wake up. Maybe... No, Reba had never been accused of having great luck. Someone or something was out there listening, and at any moment, he was going to come through that door. *If I'm wrong—God, please let me be wrong—I'll just feel stupid. If I'm wrong, I'll call Momma and ask her if I can come home. Was Vidor that bad? Hell, maybe Nicole could get me one of those flight attendant jobs.*

The pacing stopped and fright made Reba's breathing short. She held up the chair with renewed strength. She was going home. She was going home to Vidor.

You better be ready, motherfucker, she thought, *because I am.* She tightened her grasp on the chair and blood rushed into her forearms and shoulders.

"Bring it on," she whispered as the smallest amount of hot bile settled in the back of her throat.

Chapter One

THE SCREAM WAS cut off moments after Troy Nanson awakened. She wasn't frightened. She didn't even open her eyes. In fact, *hearing* the scream comforted her. It meant that the silent nightmares—her constant bedmate for the last sixteen month—were over, at least for now. As usual, she couldn't remember the nightmare, but she didn't need to. She knew who and what haunted her. She also knew why.

Guilt—familiar, thick and cloying—always followed her nightmares, but this time there was something else. She was uncomfortable. She often awoke on her back, but her muscles felt stiff and sore, as if she had been lying in one position for too long.

I'm going to be late. The thought should have galvanized her into action, but it didn't. She kept her dry, gritty eyes closed. It wasn't unusual for her to cry during the night and awaken with her lids sealed shut.

What *was* unusual was how quiet the room was. For the last sixteen months she had slept in her living room because that's where her TV was. She would fall asleep to the sound of some stupid sitcom and awaken to an even more stupid infomercial. She had learned that awakening in the middle of the night to complete silence could be just as frightening as a sudden noise.

It wasn't just the lack of noise. She hadn't tried to move yet, but the bed she was lying on felt narrow, too narrow to be her own and too comfortable to be her living room couch. She forced her tear-crusted eyelids open.

"Where...? She sat up, and pain cleaved through her head and spread like spilled wine throughout her body. "Shit," she said. A lightening bolt of pain shot through her temples and pushed her toward unconsciousness. She closed her eyes against it, but not before they confirmed what she already knew. These walls were not shit brown.

"DO YOU KNOW how long I went to school? How much money my parents paid for those schools, so that Joe Harmon, who I bet hasn't worked a day in his life, could throw shit on me because I wouldn't give him a prescription for a drug that he doesn't need?"

Emma considered responding. She *did* know how long Dr. Edwards had gone to school and she could guess how much that schooling had cost. But the warning glare from her assistant, Dana, was all the confirmation Emma needed to keep quiet. A response, any response at this point, would not be appreciated and could cost her more than she could afford to pay.

Dr. Edwards waited a split second longer than Emma was comfortable with before continuing her rant. "You name one experienced physician that would be willing to put up with this kind of shit."

Emma made the mistake of looking at Dana, who was doing her best to look stern. The thin tether she had on her emotions broke, and she began to laugh. Dr. Edwards' body stiffened, much as it had two weeks before when Emma dreamed she had bent her over her desk and shoved her hand down her pants. Dr. Edwards' expression had been a lot more pleasant to gaze at in the dream.

The smell emanating from her lab coat pushed all thoughts of the fantasy right out the window along with any hopes Emma had of salvaging their relationship. "I'm sorry. I'm so sorry," she said between hiccupping laughs. "I don't know what's wrong with me."

She looked over Dr. Edwards' shoulder in the hopes that Dana would bail her out, but her assistant was already walking away—no doubt to start sketching out an ad to be posted at all the medical schools in the area. Volunteers were plentiful, but as Dr. Edwards had already pointed out, there weren't many experienced physicians willing to deal with working at a free clinic.

"I've had an offer from the Columbia River Clinic," she said with stiff-necked dignity. "I'll be taking it." She turned, her back ram-rod straight, and walked toward the front door.

Emma gulped down her last guffaw and jogged after her. "Wait, Dr. Edwards...Sharon, listen. I shouldn't have laughed, but you have to admit..."

Dr. Edwards whirled around. Her face had darkened and her voice and mouth were tight with anger. "I will not work one minute longer with...with those people."

Emma's laughter felt like a brittle memory. She had been attracted to this woman. Her lack of a sense of humor had been a minor detail until now. "What do you mean, 'those people'?"

"The people who live in this neighborhood," she bit out, and looked toward the waiting room where, at any given time, poor single mothers, drug dealers, and gang bangers could be sitting inches away from each other. Her grandmother's dream had been that no one be turned away. That included sometimes violent drug abusers like Joe Harmon.

"My grandmother opened this clinic in this neighborhood *because* people like Mr. Harmon live here." Emma tried to soften her tone. "When you came to work here, you said you became a doctor to help people."

A look of pity crossed Dr. Edwards' face. "Poor people aren't the only ones who need good health care, Emma."

"That's not what I'm saying. Sharon, please, you know there are already hundreds of physicians with addresses across the river. The people who need your help the most don't live over there."

Dr. Edwards started to cross her arms in front of her chest, but stopped because she was still wearing her soiled lab coat. Her hands fell to her sides and Emma sensed that she was wasting time for both of them. Dr. Edwards had already made up her mind. Or rather Joe Harmon had made it up for her.

"You know, you should try living in the real world, because that kind of mindless sentimentality died in the sixties. Do you think these people care that this clinic has to struggle to make ends meet each month? Or that your grandmother—and now you—have to pay out-of-pocket for things they take for granted? NO, all they care about is getting their free Vicodin and the fact that they had to wait two hours to see a doctor, who by the way, is the same doctor who would be making six figures while seeing half the number of patients anywhere else in the city."

"Are you that doctor?" Emma asked. *Please say no. Please say no.*

"I'm the doctor who wants to hear a thank you sometimes. I'm the doctor who doesn't want to have to worry about my safety every time I'm alone with a patient."

The answer, though not unexpected, left Emma feeling deflated.

Dr. Edwards' tone softened. "I'm sorry if I'm leaving you in a lurch."

Emma shook her head and tried for a smile. A lurch, as Dr. Edwards had put it, didn't quite cover it. It would be hard, if not impossible, to replace her. But Emma was disappointed for other reasons. There had been chemistry between them. No, it was more than just chemistry—Emma had a sixth sense about feelings. And she could sense that Dr. Edwards shared her physical attraction.

Dana liked to tease Emma about her narcissistic infatuation with Dr. Edwards, but it was more than that. Even though they shared similar features, curly dark brown hair, olive skin, and blue eyes—the resemblance ended there, as far as Emma was concerned. Dr. Edwards had a power and confidence that Emma could only dream of having, and she had been—dreaming of having her, that is, several times and in many different erotic positions.

"Look," Dr. Edwards said, "maybe we could get together for drinks one night. I'd hate to think we couldn't still be friends." She leaned closer and Emma caught a whiff of something foul and moved back without thinking.

"Uh, yeah, I'll give you a call," Emma said, but they both knew she wouldn't.

Dr. Edwards nodded, turned, and stalked toward the front door. She stopped, and Emma waited, hoping that she had read her wrong and that her heart-felt words had made a delayed impact. Dr. Edwards took off the soiled lab coat and pushed it through the door of the metal trash bin, identification badge and all.

Emma closed her eyes, and by the time she had opened them, Dr. Sharon Edwards was gone and she had a huge problem.

"Ida, why in the hell did you leave this place to *me*?" she said, and trudged toward Dana's office.

Dana was sitting behind her desk, reading from a yellow legal pad, a pencil clenched between her teeth. She did not look up as Emma slumped into the rickety visitor's chair across from her.

"She gone?" Dana asked around the pencil in her mouth.

Emma nodded and then because Dana wasn't looking at her, said, "Yeah, she's gone."

"She ask you out, at least?"

Emma shrugged. "I said I'd call her."

"And will you?"

"No, I don't think so."

Dana looked calm, but the splintering sound coming from the pencil gripped between her teeth would have given away her frustration to even someone less intuitive than Emma.

"She said some pretty mean things out there, Dana." Emma felt like she was fifteen and being reprimanded for something over which she had no control.

"Give the woman some slack; she had a shitty day."

Emma couldn't keep the side of her mouth from quaking at that comment. Dana glared at her until the urge to laugh faded away. Dana began to laugh and Emma joined her. The laughter was temporary relief from the stress they had both been under since Ida's death a year ago.

"You're getting too good with those looks," Emma said.

"I learned from the best."

'The best' had been Emma's grandmother. Ida could wither the backbone of known gang members with that look. Emma had seen it on several occasions. Joe Harmon would not have dared throw fecal matter on anyone during Dr. Ida Glass' watch.

Ida had given up a lucrative partnership in Salem, Oregon to move to Portland to open the clinic. It had been her life's work. Although Emma had always planned to help her grandmother, Ida's sudden death from a heart defect left Emma with a decision to make. Either she could keep the clinic open or she could close it and leave the hundreds of people they helped each month with no place to go.

The decision hadn't been a hard one. Now here she was, thirty-one years old, and expected to run the largest charity clinic in the city. She couldn't even keep the talent.

"I must not be that good because you laughed in that poor woman's face."

"I don't know what wrong with me," Emma said. "I couldn't stop laughing at her. I think I'm just tired."

"Do you—think she'll call you after she's calmed down?"

The question was worded too casually. What Dana wanted to ask was if Emma "sensed" whether Sharon was still interested in her. Dana was the only non-family member who knew about the ability Emma and Ida shared. And it made her uncomfortable. Because of Dana's reaction, Emma had made a vow to keep the ability to herself until she met the person she would spend the rest of her life with. That person would have to be strong enough to accept her and her special ability.

"No, nothing other than her anger and embarrassment. But that's to be expected, I guess." Dana looked up from her legal pad and Emma saw the look of sadness in her eyes.

"I wish that could have worked out for you," she said.

Emma smiled. "I do, too. In more ways than one, but that thing between us was just physical."

"Dr. Phil says that attraction is the first step in many relationships."

"I thought your husband asked you to stop watching that show."

Dana sniffed. "He did, but he's not the boss of me."

Emma grinned. Dana and her husband were very religious people. Because of that, it had taken Emma years to tell Dana that she was a lesbian. Dana had already suspected as much and had no issues with it. In fact, almost every other week, she still demanded to know when Emma was going to settle down. The only strain between them had come when Dana found out that Emma, like Ida, could sometimes pick up on other people's feelings. Ida called it being hyper-aware, but even though Dana had never said so, Emma knew Dana felt like it was eavesdropping—an invasion of privacy. Emma didn't disagree, but it wasn't something she could just turn off.

"What do you think of this?" Dana pushed the legal pad across the desk. Emma read the ad for a new physician. Her stomach lurched at the figure Dana had written. Although the figure was low for a qualified doctor, it would require her to go to the drastic measure of asking her parents to help make end meet until the grant came through for the following year. Her grandmother had been a very capable physician, not to mention a phenomenal fund raiser. Emma was neither of those.

Emma ground the heel of her palm between her eyebrows. "I think we'll be lucky if we get a doctor with any experience at all."

"I thought you were going to ask one of the doctors to prescribe something for that."

Emma shook her head. "Nah, nothing much works except sleep."

"You going to call them"

Emma stood, her feet and back protesting all the way. 'Them' was the code name for her parents. "Yeah, I'll have to, but not tonight. Tonight, I'm going to go home, take a hot bath, maybe eat a little something, and get in bed with a good book. And if I'm lucky Dr. Edwards—a more socially-conscious Dr. Edwards—will come and ravish me in my dreams. See you tomorrow."

"Girl, you're a nut," Dana said, and her laughter followed Emma to the office door. "Try not to worry about it tonight. Something will come through for us, it always does."

Emma held up her hand and waved it without looking back. Something always did come through for her grandmother. But for Emma, it seemed like it was one setback after another, and now she would have to swallow her pride and go running to her parents for the bail out.

She remembered she had forgotten to exchange her lab coat for her Columbia jacket, but decided she would pick it up the following morning. She was just too exhausted to go back for it. She pushed through the front door, imagining the look of I-told-you-so on her mother's face as Emma explained why she would be needing a small loan—one she could never pay back—to keep the clinic open another year.

Emma let out a frustrated breath. Worrying about the impending conversation was making her head hurt more. *This has got to be the suckiest day in recorded history.* She stopped in front of her 1982 Mercedes Benz and hunted around in her backpack for her keys.

The car was a gas guzzler. All conversations with her mother began and ended with, "Why don't you trade that tank in for something with better gas mileage, maybe a hybrid or something? You look like a child in it, anyway." She had to agree with her mother there. The car didn't fit her, but it was yet another part of her grandmother that she couldn't bear to part with.

By the time she found her keys, her shivering and the throbbing in her head made it difficult to fit the key in the door lock. She turned it, first one way and then the other. "Damn it, not again," she said under her breath. She tried it two more times but the lock didn't budge. This was the second time since she'd inherited the car that she'd had frozen door locks. She would have to slide through the passenger side. She turned to do just that when a blinding pain shot from the back of her head to the front.

She stumbled, dropped her bag, and turned around. Her hand went to the warm area at the back of her head. Even before she brought her hand around to see it, she smelled the blood. Working in the clinic for so many years had given her a cast-iron stomach, but her stomach lurched now as she stared at her blood covered hand.

A man—a shaky, shadow of a figure—stood in front of her wearing what looked like a large rain poncho. He was holding something in his hand. A bottle? A brick? What was it? She squinted into the darkness trying to make it out. For reasons she didn't comprehend, it seemed important that she know what he'd hit her with.

The back of her neck tingled and her legs felt numb. How many times had she been hit? She should have known. She should have sensed...

Her eyes were still glued to the object in the dark figure's hand and, almost as if a microphone were zeroed in on it, she heard her own blood as it dripped from the brick onto the ground.

"No," she said with her hand out in front of her. *This can't be happening. It's a nightmare, Emma—just a nightmare.*

"All you had to do was give me a little something," he said.

"Give you..." Her words were slurred, but in the instant before Joe Harmon hit her again, it unfolded behind her closed eyelids like a movie projected on a white screen. She saw Sharon tossing her lab coat into the trash as she walked out the door and she saw herself as she walked into the parking lot wearing her own white lab coat. In the dim light, she and Sharon would be hard to tell apart. But *why* hadn't she sensed danger before she walked into the darkened parking lot?

She was hit twice more before she lost count and had to block out the sound.

"Wake up, Emma..." The voice was too calm. Was it her grandmother's? No, it can't be. She's dead.

"Just wake up now. Open your eyes."

"Emma? Wake up!"

Chapter Two

NICKEL-COLORED LIGHT spilled through the blinds and onto the floor. By the time Troy admitted to herself that no one would be coming to check on her, it had pooled like mercury in the center of the room. She thought she might have slept after trying to sit up earlier, but it was possible that she had fainted from the pain.

When she'd moved out of her foster home on her eighteenth birthday, she had spent half of the five-hundred-dollar check from the State of Oregon on a deposit for her two-room cottage and a can of "oops paint" from The Home Improvement Co-op. The label on the top of the can had said sunflower yellow, but the paint inside was the color of a Hershey chocolate bar, or as Patricia liked to call it 'shit brown.' Troy had painted the walls twice. Always in that same color pallet. She couldn't bring herself to change it to something more cheery.

But these walls were painted institution white. It felt like a hospital, but she couldn't be sure. There were no decorative pictures and no medical equipment, just a bed and a chair. Fear, anxiety, and desolation flooded over her. Now, this she was familiar with. Something had happened to her. She didn't know what. The last thing she remembered was visiting Patricia, but her memory went blank after that.

She flexed her toes first, followed by her calves, thighs, back, biceps, and hands. One by one, she assessed each body part until she was certain that, although sore in places, everything seemed to be in good working order. She tried to convince herself to try to get up again, but the memory of the pain kept her shackled to the bed. *Come on, Troy, you can't just lie here.* The truth was she wouldn't have minded just lying there. Someone would remember to check on her soon. But until they did, she wouldn't be expected to hold a conversation, or work, or even look like she was interested in what the world was doing around her.

But the truth was she couldn't afford to stay in this bed any longer that she already had. She was a private contractor, responsible for purchasing her own health insurance. Therefore, she had none. She couldn't afford the premiums; she didn't know of any bike messengers who could.

She'd been lucky—at least the other messengers thought she was. Troy knew it was more than just luck. She obeyed the traffic laws—for the most part—and she knew Portland like the back of her hand. Still, even with being smart, careful, and yes, maybe a little bit lucky, she had been doored twice when careless people had swung open car doors in her path.

"All right, enough of this," she said aloud. "Time to get out of here before Raife sends out a search party." She eased up on her elbows, wincing ahead of time against the pain. It did come, but it was already ebbing away, like the tail end of a bad hangover.

Good. She sat up with her head resting on the headboard for a few minutes longer until a new ache in her shoulder blade and neck told her it was time to sit all the way up. She did so cautiously. Her back was a little stiff, but it often got that way when she lay in one position for too long. She also felt a little feverish. But none of that was unbearable. The last thing she remembered was riding home after work, but nothing after that.

She seemed to be fine, but if some idiot had doored her again, or if someone had walked out into her path, it was no telling how her bike had fared. If Dite was a goner, then she would be out of work for God knew how long until she could cobble together another bike. *Which means you better stop the meter on this hospital bill right now, Troy Nanson.*

Galvanized, she swung her legs over the side of the bed and stretched, first her toes, then her calves until she felt confident enough to stand. The carpet was a gray, rough, low-pile industrial—the type used in public places because it didn't show stains. She clutched the headboard and tried not to think about the substances hospitals would want to hide with dark carpets. The muscles in her quads and calves quivered from the effort of holding her weight. What the hell had they given her? Her legs were her livelihood. They were capable of giving her upwards of seventy miles per day, if she asked them to. They just needed to give her a few feet now. She took one step toward the door and then another.

Her legs felt stronger with every step she took. Whatever she had been given was wearing off a lot faster than she would have expected. She hesitated and put her hand on the door. She pushed through the door and peered out into the fluorescent light of the hallway. There were two doors to her left and three to her right. At the end of the corridor was a red exit sign.

Unease caused her to glance behind her once before entering the hall. She was very tempted to peek into some of the rooms along the way but decided not to. There would be someone at the front desk and she would explain that she felt much better and would like to check herself out. As for the bill—if they were lucky and reasonable, with the interest, she'd have them paid off in about thirty years. She almost snickered but didn't quite make it.

She rounded a corner and found herself in a small waiting room, half of which was taken up by a crescent shaped front desk. The desk and the small room behind it were empty.

The clock on the wall confirmed that it was eleven o'clock, which felt wrong to Troy. But, regardless of the time she could think of no reason a hospital would go un-staffed...unless... Troy walked toward a set of double doors marked "Conference Room." Of course. How many times had she walked into the deserted lobby of an office because there was some kind of meeting? That's why she couldn't find anyone; they were all in a meeting or something. "That's just too damn bad," she said, and ordered her sore muscles to move.

The door swung open with so little effort that she almost fell into the room. *Oh no,* she thought to herself as the first balloon caught her eye. A *HAPPY BIRTHDAY* banner hung from the ceiling and a cake stood uncut on a table that looked identical to the one she had lain across during her last pap smear. Paper plates, napkins, and forks sat in neat little undisturbed piles. Five people—three women, two men—sat with their backs toward her. Their bodies were too still.

"Excuse me?" Troy expected them to turn and look at her embarrassed or angry, but no one moved. Troy tried again. "Hey, look, I don't mean to interrupt, but there's no one out front..." She stopped speaking because none of the five people sitting in front of her responded. Dread crept along her back and over her shoulders. "Hello?" This time, Troy heard the fear—the soft pleading in her own voice. *Please be all right. I don't do dead very well.* Troy walked part way around the couch, half expecting to see perfect bullet holes in each of the silent people's foreheads. Her anxiety eased as no such wound appeared. Her footsteps faltered, and she became aware of two things at the same time. There was a half-full bottle of vodka sitting next to the punch bowl and an unopened present sitting on one of the women's laps was moving in unison with her ample breast. She was breathing. They all were. Anger bloomed in Troy's chest.

Drunk! They were all drunk. Fuck these people. She'd be damned if she would pay for this kind of care. Troy pushed through the door and padded barefoot toward the desk. Her intention was to leave a note, but a pair of scrubs still wrapped in the dry cleaning bag caught her attention. She snatched them off the hanger, and with one last angry look toward the conference room, she headed toward the front door.

The parking lot's lone light washed out the colors of a late-model Lexus, a classic VW, a Ford Explorer, and a small Toyota truck. Frigid air pushed through the scrubs as if they were gossamer.

"Damn, why didn't I get some shoes while I was in there stealing shit?" Her eyes settled on a bike rack half hidden in shadow. She frowned against the dull ache in her head and hobbled closer to the bike rack.

He bike was yellow, brown, and burgundy depending on what side you approached from. She would have to walk around the other side to see the burgundy, but she knew it would be there, the same way she knew the tires would be white-walled before she got close enough to see them. This bike looked like it was held together with bungee cords and well placed strips of duct tape. Electrical tape was wrapped around the handlebars for the grip and the color contrast. All of it was for show, for those few occasions when the clock left her no time to lock Dite up and she needed to move faster than carrying her on her shoulder would allow. No one would steal a bike that looked like that, and if they did, they would be spotted before they got more than a few miles away. Dite was one of a kind. Troy reached her bike. Her hand hovered over the seat. She didn't need to touch it to know that it was Dite, but she did touch the seat. She stooped down, her knees groaning like a gate that hadn't been used in years, and ran her hand along the body.

Troy shivered and flipped over one of the pedals. Seeing her initials scratched underneath the pedal was anti-climactic. She already knew that this was her bike, but how the hell did she get here?

"So much for the accident theory. You look about as worn out as you always do, huh, girl?" Troy stood and placed her hands on her hips. Had she ridden her bike here? Maybe she had begun to feel ill and had decided to get herself checked out. No, that didn't make sense, either. She knew of at least two free clinics within riding distance. Whatever this place was, it didn't look free, which meant she couldn't afford it. Why would she have come here?

Troy eased Dite out of the bike rack. Her U-lock and chain were wrapped beneath the seat but had been left unsecured. A chill that had nothing to with the temperature settled over her. She could count on one hand the number of times she had been forced to leave Dite unchained in order to make a deadline. It didn't make sense that she would take the time to park Dite in a rack but neglect to lock her up. As unattractive and as hefty as Dite appeared to be, Troy treasured her. She provided her a means to make a living. She wouldn't risk losing her if she didn't have to.

A chill scraped long, jagged nails along the back of her neck, and Troy turned toward the hospital. The windows were like dark gaping mouths, she thought. Something flickered in one of them, and Troy gripped Dite's handlebars hard. She waited to see if the motion in the window would repeat itself. It didn't, but Troy felt the urgent need to be away from this place and out of the view of those windows.

"Freaking yourself out for no reason," Troy said, and swung her leg over her bike and began to pedal away. The headache was tolerable now, and the cool, damp air in her face made her feel almost human. It wouldn't be the first time a messenger was almost killed and the bike survived. Hell, that's how she'd ended up with Dite's current seat. Troy felt her shoulders relax. She was overreacting. Still, as she made a turn that would put the hospital out of sight for good, something told her that she had been right to leave when she did.

THE AIR CONDITIONING kicked on, although the room was already cool enough. Abe stood in darkness watching. "Magnificent," he thought. It was amazing the difference being awake could make in a human being. The woman, this Troy, moved as if she knew she was being watched. She was graceful, although not at all delicate. Asleep, she had been uninteresting, dull, just like any of the other thousands of people he was sure he would see when he left the hospital. But awake, she was power in motion.

Was it the fact that everything else was so still that made her so attractive? Abe tilted his head as she squatted and leaned in to look at the bike, her bike, as if it were the strangest thing in the world. Abe chuckled. He felt like a voyeur watching a woman sunbathe in her own backyard. The idea stirred him like his wife, Teresa, never could. Abe felt an odd thrill that he hadn't experienced since grade school. Teresa's skin was so pale that it made this woman dark in comparison. But then, hell, Teresa made Europeans look dark.

Abe watched Troy Nanson trace the bike's frame as if searching for a wire. Her biceps were more defined than his were. Teresa was so thin that she could be mistaken for a model but for the fact that she was in her mid-thirties. Troy was anything but thin. Muscular, but not at all mannish. Abe thought back to her chart that he was sure still lay at the end of her bed. She weighed a hundred and twenty-eight pounds, but she looked so powerful. "That's what it is," Abe decided. She looked like she could handle herself. Unlike Teresa, this woman wouldn't be afraid of anything he asked of her in the bedroom.

The thought caught him off guard. She was nothing—a plaything, a hamster in a cage. Abe watched as Troy swung her leg over the bike and settled on the worn seat. She sat there for a moment and then with a sudden movement turned toward the hospital. Toward him. Abe caught his breath. He almost hoped she *would* see him. No, that would ruin everything. *You're here to observe.* The though was enough to keep him rooted to the spot. She turned and began to pedal away. There was a rattling up above. Abe moved away from the window and frowned up at the ceiling. Had he left a window open up there? He returned to his position at the window just as she turned the corner and rode out of his sight. Abe straightened up and walked out of the room. No need to hurry. He knew where she would go. They always did—eventually.

EMMA AWOKE ON the inhale, eyes wide, body stiff with apprehension. She was able to cut the scream off before it came to fruition—before it, like many other waking screams and the memories that came with it, could haunt her for the rest of the day.

Her curtains billowed out and the world outside her window seemed to hold its breath until she released hers. She did, and relaxed against her pillows. She ran her hand through tousled curls. *Not so bad this time, Emma. Not so bad.* But it *had* been bad. They weren't all as detailed. Sometimes she woke up before she walked out into the parking lot. Sometimes she didn't hear the sound of—*stop it, Emma. It's over. It's been over for a long time.*

Emma sat up, groping for the end table before her eyes had adjusted to the dim light. If she turned her head to the right she knew she would have a clear view of her alarm clock, but she didn't need to look at it to know what it would say. Five-forty or five-forty-one. Perhaps even five-forty-five. Any later and she would hear the sound of traffic would be floating through her window. Any later and she would feel like she had gotten a decent night's sleep. Any later—Emma frowned and forced herself to focus on her end table. Her heart seemed to slow. Even half-comatose from sleep deprivation, she always left her cane in the same place—hooked on the end table where she could always reach it. Emma's knee began its slow, dull throb. *Don't panic. It's got to be here. It's got to be close; you wouldn't have gone to bed without it.* She took two deep breaths before looking over the edge of her bed. She reached down in desperation. Her cane blended with her wood floors in the darkness, but she had faith that it was there, and sure enough, her fingers found the smooth curved handle.

Emma closed her eyes and yawned. A soft breeze swept between the blinds and settled in her mouth as tangible as cotton candy. She wallowed in the peace and silence that she always felt before her neighbors began to stir. She rose from the bed and limped into the kitchen, looking forward to a cup of raspberry Tazo tea. Emma put a teapot full of water on the stove to heat and limped through the great room, as her mother called it, and settled onto the window seat. The great room was just that, a large room. Emma's only concern had been being able to walk through her own house without obstacle. Her intention had been to remove the wall between the bedroom, leaving the bathroom and the kitchen as the only walls in the condo. But that would have required workmen—or worse, she would have had to stay in a hotel until the work was done. She wasn't ready for that.

She wasn't sure she ever would be. Emma sighed and gazed through the rust-colored bars down to the street below.

The world was so quiet that Emma could hear the water in the teapot as it began to boil. She rose from her window seat without using her cane and limped into the kitchen. She had taken great care in deciding where she wanted the movers to place the desk, couch, and rug when she had moved. By positioning the back of the couch against the front of her desk, her mother had convinced her she would be able to gaze out the window from any of her three seating areas. Emma had agreed, because that was what one did with Darby Webster. You agreed in the hope that she would soon move on to "helping" someone else.

Emma was careful to only fill the cup halfway. Her gait on a good day was uneven, and past experience had taught her how painful filling the cup to the top could be. In moments, the streets would begin to bustle, and the scent of truck fumes and damp asphalt would drift up to her. The occasional car, running on bio-diesel, would go past and Emma would experience a fleeting regret. Not for French fries or Kettle Chips, but for the freedom to run out and get either of those things. She had been so wasteful. Eating half bags of chips and leaving them until they were stale, or ordering large orders of food and tiring of it after a few bites.

Emma leaned back against the pillows, brought her cup up to her nose and inhaled deeply. The sun would slide over the tops of the buildings soon and the first few cars would begin to line her street. She would watch distracted men and women get out of their cars. Sometimes she'd catch a whiff of perfume, cologne, coffee, or a breakfast sandwich from BurgerCity.

Other times she would catch an indistinct feeling of anger drifting up from them. She guessed it was because they had had to leave their warm beds and go to a job they felt no great enthusiasm for. Only once had she sensed excitement coming from someone on the sidewalk below her window.

Emma still remembered her. Pigtails, dyed an unnatural shade of red, poked from beneath a rainbow beanie cap. She wore a backpack—like everyone else in Portland—black jeans, thick heeled shoes, and a white shirt. She walked, no, she swaggered, as if she were in no great hurry, but Emma sensed that she was looking forward to something. Emma longed to know her story. Did she work at a used bookstore? A coffee house? Perhaps she was one of the many cooking school students who seemed to permeate Portland. No, she would be wearing the checkered pants and white smock if she were a cooking school student. Emma had watched her until she was no longer in view.

Emma blew into her cup and then sipped her tea. She loved being awake at this time of morning. It was as if the world was on hold, and then, almost to the second—it would begin to move, almost too fast for Emma. It was at those times that she would turn away from her window. She'd watch as the streets awakened. After that, she lost interest.

Emma glanced back at the wall clock her mother had insisted she have. It was the wrong style for the condo. It was as if her mother had bought the clock in order to point out the poor job Emma had done decorating. Emma had not planned her décor. The condo was a wide-open floor plan. Her furniture was understated and comfortable, in shades of browns and tans. The clock was gold, ornate—and like nothing else in the condo. It was, however, accurate to the second. That bothered Emma, because if the clock was to be trusted, it was just past six now. There were always two or three early birds plugging the meters instead of using a garage, and then trudging off into the cold morning to God knew what kind of desk job. Emma would watch them and tell herself that any one of them would change places with her in a heartbeat. But deep down, she knew that none of them would want to be what she had become.

Emma took a deep breath, picked up the quilt her great-grandmother had sewn, and wrapped it around herself. She wasn't cold, but sometimes the quilt was enough to push the anxiety away. *I'm safe. I'm safe. There's no need to be afraid.* Emma ignored the pain that shot through her knee and back as she drew her legs up. She placed her chin on her knees and closed her eyes. She hadn't felt this anxious since her mother's last phone call. So where was this coming from? Was it the nightmare? No, although she could guess the nature of the nightmare, she didn't remember it. Emma gazed at the bars that covered her windows. She could have had the bars removed when she moved in; most of the other tenants in the building had and would no doubt take up a collection for her to do so, too. The bars were an eyesore, she knew, but Emma gave her realtor the excuse that they added to the mystique of living in an old factory. If you got rid of the bars, it was just any other apartment-style home. But Emma was glad of the bars for other reasons. The unease wafted over her and settled. Something was wrong.

Emma swallowed and stared at the street below, looking for the root of the dread that was stealing over her. She would not panic. *What was it?* There was nothing there, nothing she could see that would be giving her this odd feeling of...

Where were the trucks this morning? There were always trucks. It wasn't a weekend or a holiday. There should be trucks delivering products to stores. Emma should hear men unloading and yelling things to each other from blocks away. She could never make out exactly what was said, but the sounds were always there in the background: doors slamming, brakes squealing, and the faintest smell of fumes. But today there was nothing but the wind. Nothing at all. Nothing.

Emma's heart quickened. She hadn't felt like this in... She stopped herself. That's what was making her so uneasy. This feeling of disquiet, this warning; she hadn't felt it in so long that it was making her jumpy.

"You're eighteen months too late, you fucker," she said, and then felt ridiculous at how angry she felt.

Maybe there was a strike or a parade. Emma's mother had complained that Portland seemed to have a parade for just about everything. Maybe that was the problem. Maybe they had the streets blocked off so that trucks couldn't get through and people couldn't park. Emma almost had herself convinced and raised her cup to her lips. She took a large calming gulp of tea that stung the roof of her mouth and the back of her throat as she swallowed. That would explain the lack of cars and even the lack of trucks. But not the complete silence. Emma leaned forward and listened harder than she ever had in her life.

She heard leaves rustling and the sound of small debris being pushed along the streets and sidewalk by a gentle breeze, and she could hear the sound of her own raspy breathing. But what she didn't hear was the one thing that a pending parade would not curtail.

"The birds. Where the hell are all the birds?"

Chapter Three

PORTLAND WAS DARK, cold, and too goddamned still. The latter bothered Troy the most. The last time the streets had felt this lifeless was when most of Portland had been glued to their TVs watching replay after replay of airplanes hitting the World Trade Center. Troy had watched it once before she hopped on Dite and rode until her legs burned as much as her chest and her tears had dried like spilled eggs at her temples.

She felt the familiar dueling emotions of joy and sorrow when she rode her bike through Southeast Main Street. She had regained her bearings as soon as she'd turned off the unpaved path leading from the hospital. In less than five minutes she could be at Mountain View Cemetery. What the hell was she doing so far past the cemetery?

Maybe I was making a delivery and I got into an accident over there.

No. Traffic was too light for it to be a weekday. Besides, Raife would never ask her to cross a bridge for a delivery when he could send one of the others. Mountain View's gate, overgrown with ivy and tiny pink flowers, called to her over the buzz in her head. She would love to go in there and lie on the grass for a few minutes, but the niggling feeling in the back of her head made her hook a left on Southeast Twentieth Street toward the Burnside Bridge.

She wasn't surprised when her legs began to feel rubbery and her fingertips started tingling. "Breathe, damn it," she told herself. She squeezed the handlebars every time her right foot neared the ground and she counted under her breath. "One, two, three, four..." Her voice sounded like she had been riding for several miles instead of just a few. "Twenty..." She blew out a deep breath and continued her count. Sweat dripped down the center of her back until the elastic waistband of the scrubs stopped it. She shivered and gripped the bars tighter. *Come on, just thirty more counts. Breathe.* She interrupted her count with the command and blinked several times to keep the sweat from her eyes.

At thirty, she felt the relief that always came at the end of the bridge flood through her, and by fifty her legs had regained their strength and the prickling at her fingertips had dissipated.

For the umpteenth time, she cursed complete strangers for forcing her to do this, and for the umpteenth time, she said, "See? It's getting easier."

It wasn't getting easier. Every time she crossed this bridge, any bridge, she felt the same knife-sharp surety that the concrete would disappear from beneath her tires and the water would reach up and pull her into its darkness.

With the exception of Raife, no one knew about the panic attacks. She had admitted it to him so that he would stop asking her to deliver on the east side. "Things will get better. You just need time to heal," he had said.

Time. She had too much time. Time to think, time to remember, time to hurt. And things still hadn't gotten any better. She hadn't begun to heal. She wasn't sure she wanted to if it meant she had to forget.

By the time she realized where she was going, the U.S. Bancorp Tower was already in sight. "Big Pink," as some people called it, had the friendliest security staff in the city. It wasn't unusual for Troy to find herself in the building at least three times on any given weekday. They would let her use their phone to call Raife. After he bit her head off for losing her cell, he would come pick her up.

Pedaling was second nature, as was her glance to the right as she made the turn onto Northwest Fifth Street. How many times had she made that same turn, only to have to throw on her brakes in order to keep from being hit by a car speeding through the yellow light?

But there was no Subaru to dodge. In fact, no cars waited at the light. She felt uncomfortable and exposed sitting in the middle of the empty street. She imagined an audible click as the light changed.

When she reached the front door of Big Pink, she lifted Dite on her shoulder. She had expected to get curious stares from people heading up to the numerous offices and financial firms that populated the building. A girl carrying a bike wasn't unusual, but one wearing scrubs and no shoes might be. But no one was hurrying through the doors. In fact, when Troy pulled on them they didn't budge. Whether it was a weekend, holiday, or a Presidential visit, those doors were always open between six a.m. and seven p.m. Even outside of those hours, a security guard was posted at the desk.

Troy cupped her hands against the glass, and peered into the darkened building. Something bad had to have happened for that many people to stay home from work. Troy tried not to notice the eerie quiet of the area, the lack of outside noise from the city. But her clenching stomach acknowledged it before she did. There was an explanation for all this. She just had to find it. She set Dite on the sidewalk and looked down at her bare feet.

Pioneer Courthouse Square. Benny and Toni F should be there right now, leaning against the wall, sipping coffee and eating something crappy.

They'll know what happened, she thought as she hopped on Dite and pedaled toward the square.

Troy coasted down Broadway and almost begged for a car to whip around the corner and come barreling at her. None did. The first people she came across were three young men crouched in the doorway of a stationery store. All three were leaned back, their eyes closed, and knees up as if they had been playing a game of jacks and had stopped for a nap. Troy stopped but didn't get off Dite.

People slept in doorways a lot in Portland. Doorways meant survival—from the cold, the rain, and from steel-toed boots looking for a soft place to land. With your back against a doorway you only had to worry about danger from one side. Three teenagers huddling in a doorway hadn't been an unusual sight in Portland in years.

But Troy knew in an instant that this was different. The store wasn't abandoned, for one thing. At least it hadn't been the last time she had passed it, no more than two days ago. If a homeless person were desperate enough to sleep in an occupied business' doorway, they would be sure to leave long before start of business to avoid being hassled by police. These boys' clothes looked too expensive for them to be homeless, though. And she could see from where she stood that all three were Asian. Most of the homeless youth that roved the city were white. Troy's eyes were drawn to three spots of red on the ground between one of the young men's feet. Two items she had mistaken for leaves stirred in the wind and Troy recognized that they were dollar bills. They hadn't been playing jacks.

"Hey, ya'll all right?" Troy called out, but no one stirred, and her voice sounded sharper and louder than it should have been. "Whatever." She rode hard toward Pioneer Square and blew through a red light as if it were green and right past a patrol car. She slowed and turned on Dite's seat. The balding head pressed against the car window glistened, but did not move as she rode past. She could no longer ignore her terror. She kept telling herself that there *was* an explanation, but she refused to think about what that explanation could be. Nor did she allow herself to wonder why she no longer felt the need to push her legs to the limit.

The Square had no fewer than ten occupants, not to mention several people waiting for the MAX train, all asleep and all very still.

Across the street, a red warning light blinked from the wall of the Fox Tower, although Troy could hear no car coming out of its parking lot. Troy rode up to a woman lying on the ground with a department store bag sitting upright next to her, as if she had just set it down before she herself ended up, inert, on the sidewalk.

Troy laid Dite down and squatted next to the bag and then moved closer to the woman. She hesitated, her fingers hovering just above the woman's neck. Cold air cut through the thin cotton pants as if she were wearing nothing. She shivered and placed two fingers on the side of the woman's neck. "Oh, thank God," she said as she found a pulse.

She stood up and knocked over the woman's shopping bag, spilling out what looked like exercise clothing.

"Not dead. They're not dead." The words made her feel better, but not by much. She checked the pulses of the people lying closest to her next. A high-school-aged boy had a strong pulse, as did the older man next to him. She tried shaking the older man, but she wasn't surprised when he didn't wake up. Troy ran to the short wall that separated the MAX shelter from the square.

"Hey, can anyone hear me?" she yelled, feeling stupid, scared, and cold. It was as if they had all decided to just lie down and take a nap. Another chill hit the back of her neck and she looked back at the people on the ground behind her.

Just as when she'd left the hospital, she half expected to see one of the lounging bodies move, unable to hold its pose, but not one did. She couldn't remember seeing one person moving since she had awakened.

"PLEASE CONTINUE TO hold. Your call will be answered shortly."

Troy pressed what had to be decades of ear grime onto her own ear, and she welcomed the contact. She even welcomed the sight of the brown paper bag that had been stuffed into a hole in the corner of the phone booth. For the last ten minutes, she had kept her eyes focused on a grayish wad of gum that had been placed so precisely on the top of the phone that she was sure its owner had intended to pop it back into his mouth after his call was finished.

"Hurry, please hurry," she whispered into the phone. There was a small click, followed by a buzz of static. "Hello?"

The frantic quality of her own voice scared her.

Troy rested her forehead on her free hand and let a sob escape. She had thought the day couldn't get any worse than waking up in a hospital.

"Please continue to hold..."

"Answer the call, goddamn it!" she yelled into the receiver. She was answered seconds later by the same monotone female voice repeating her promise that an operator would be with her shortly.

Dizziness swept over her and the familiar prickling began at her fingertips. She squeezed her eyes shit and concentrated on calming her breathing. It would do no good if she passed out. *Just think of something else.* The operators had to be dealing with thousands of calls from panicked people trying to figure out why their friends and neighbors were asleep.

"Please continue to hold. Your call will be answered shortly."

The emergency operator would be able to tell her what to do. She just had to do as they said and continue to hold. That's all she *could* do, right?

She would give anything for that bottle of vodka she had seen at the hospital. She had assumed more alcohol had been there at some point because, well, there just had to be. The punch bowl was still full, the present unopened. It looked like they had just gotten started. As wasted as those people seemed to have been, there should have been empty bottles all over the place, but there weren't. Just the one.

"Please continue to hold..."

"The one, almost-full bottle," she said out loud, and the recording paused as if being polite.

"Your call will be answered..." Troy stared at the wad of gum.

Five people didn't just pass out from drinking a half a bottle of vodka, did they? Maybe there were more bottles. Maybe they were in a trash can somewhere? *It's not like you bothered to look.* It made sense that they would hide the bottles. If someone saw them drinking on the job, they could be fired. Then why leave the one bottle sitting on the table if they were worried someone could come in and see them? Why not pour it in the punch and hide the bottle?

They must already know what's happened down here. Troy's mind went back to the sleeping cop in the patrol car.

"Please continue to hold..."

If they already know, where are they? Where are the sirens?

"Your call will be answered..."

They were being cautious. It made sense that they would want to know what they were up against before they sent in the guys in white suits. *Stop analyzing everything, damn it.*

"Please continue..."

The hospital staff, the cop, those boys in the doorway of that stationery store. Why had she ridden on by? Because that's what she did when something made her uncomfortable. Drunks, cops, and people huddled in doorways—whether they were homeless bums or thugs playing dice—were all to be avoided.

What if this was a bigger problem that she thought? Troy opened the door to the stuffy phone booth and stood, phone pressed hard to her ear, staring out into the city. She heard no far-off sirens, no birds chirping, no planes overhead. The phone clicked, and a buzz tickled her ear drum.

"Please..."

The receiver tumbled from Troy's hand and crashed into the shatterproof glass.

Standard, Oregon
August
Years ago

EVER SINCE THE Boy could remember, he had to have his birthday dinner at Bernie Ann's Corner Side Café. Pam, that was his mother, told him that she could remember going there on her birthday when she was a little girl, so he figured it had to be the oldest restaurant on earth. The oldest in Standard, Oregon, that's for sure.

He hated his birthday because of Bernie's. He wished it was in winter instead of the summer. He wouldn't even care if it was the same day as Christmas, like one of the girls in his class. He'd never forget to wear long pants if it was cold outside. Then his legs wouldn't feel so sticky or get scratched by the holes that were all over the seats from people dropping their lit cigarettes. Pam had fallen asleep on the couch with a cigarette once and he had watched the flame grow so high that he knew it would have reached the ceiling if she hadn't woken up and put it out. These seats must be better quality than their old couch.

Pam cooked when Hoyt made her. She would bang around in the kitchen for hours, and then he would always smell burning food. Hoyt would then go out for cigarettes and come back smelling like BurgerCity onions. Pam made him eat what she had cooked—as if it were his fault she had to cook. Pam's food didn't taste so good, but the food at Bernie Ann's made his stomach hurt.

He pushed his creamed corn under his mashed potatoes and wished it was BurgerCity French fries instead of the mess on his plate. He had learned on his fifth birthday that pushing the corn under the potatoes made it look like he had at least eaten something, and it also made the mashed potatoes look less runny.

He pretended to eat some of his chicken, but he spit it into his napkin when no one was looking. Last year he'd swallowed the mashed potatoes because they didn't taste all that bad. He'd ended up in the bathroom for so long afterward that his ass had felt raw for three days straight.

He could hear the slippery smacking noises that meant that Pam and Hoyt were being gross. He didn't have to look up to know that Hoyt had his fingers sunk deep in Pam's long blonde hair, and Pam's hand would be on Hoyt's crotch. He had overheard someone call Pam beautiful. She was tall, had blue eyes, and blonde hair, and long, red nails. She was kind of skinny because she sometimes didn't eat very much and smoked a lot of cigarettes. The waitress—she'd said her name was Amy—had to wait until they came up for air before she could give Hoyt the bill.

Pam snatched the receipt so fast that Amy had to jerk her hand back to keep from being scratched. Amy must have hurried away because The Boy heard her asking another customer if they "needed more syrups." He liked the way she put an "s" at the end of syrup. He poked at his chicken leg until a pool of grease grew on his plate.

"You going to eat that chicken, boy, or just play with it?" Hoyt sounded amused.

"Uh... Excuse me?" Pam sounded annoyed.

He stopped pushing at his chicken and looked up. He knew that tone. She was getting ready for a fight. She was always ready for a fight with anyone except Hoyt. With Hoyt, she always backed down, but never with anyone else.

"You hear what I asked you? You gonna eat that chicken or just play with it all night?" The Boy tore his eyes from Pam long enough to look at Hoyt and then down at the chicken leg.

Hoyt was in a good mood today, which made him feel sad. He was the one that should be in a good mood. It was his birthday. Why wasn't he allowed to pick where he wanted to go? He would have been happy with a kid's meal and a box of cookies from BurgerCity.

He smelled Amy's perfume when she returned to their table.

"If you'd of *asked,* you would know it's my son's birthday, so we don't have to pay for his food."

The Boy glanced up in time to see Amy look to Hoyt for help, but Hoyt was busy picking his teeth with a toothpick and staring at the chicken leg on The Boy's plate.

"The special's for kids five and under, ma'am," she said, just like she had last year and the year before that.

Pam leaned forward in her seat and jabbed her red nails in his direction. "He ain't but five, so he eats for free."

The Boy felt real bad for Amy. Pam was always mean when they came in and Amy still gave him a free scoop of vanilla ice cream for being the "birthday boy," even though the deal didn't include dessert.

Nobody said anything and The Boy prayed that Amy would not argue with Pam.

Hoyt reached across the table and snagged the chicken leg off his plate. A moment later, he heard a crunch and the heavy, appreciative breathing that meant that Hoyt was enjoying his food.

Amy still hadn't said anything. He stopped forking his mashed potatoes over his corn and waited. He closed his eyes tight and prayed for Amy. He could hear Hoyt's breathing increase. He hated that sound. He had heard it enough. The walls of the trailer were thin. Hoyt's excited breathing and other sounds made his tummy churn more than the thought of eating the stuff on his plate.

"Ma'am, I thought your boy turned five last year." The Boy dropped his head as if concentrating on his plate. He brought the fork beneath the table and jabbed it into the side of his leg. *Please God, please don't let her hit Amy.*

"You must be thinking of some other family, 'cause my boy is five. You trying to tell me I don't know when I gave birth to my own boy?" Pam's voice was tense, past the point where she would back down. Amy would have to, or Pam would hurt her.

He pressed the fork harder; tears burned the corners of his eyes. He wanted to help her. He wanted to yell out, "I'm seven, I'm seven," but he knew that that would mean pain when he got home. He would have to sit still and quiet and hope Amy would do the same.

"I'm sorry, my mistake." Her voice was soft like she was talking to a mad dog. He eased the fork out of his leg and looked up just in time to see Amy walking away, her back stiff.

"No tip for her today." Pam's voice was loud enough for Amy to hear, but The Boy relaxed. He brought the fork back up to his plate and began toying with the mashed potatoes again.

Soon, Hoyt would reach over and began scooping the corn and mashed potato mix into his mouth and they could go home.

Tonight he would whisper all that had happened into his grandmother's ear. He would also tell her how much he hated Pam and Hoyt. She would never tell anyone.

Amy came back with a new bill and set it on the table between Pam and Hoyt. Pam acted like she was Amy's best friend and told her that she should come by the nail shop and get her nails done. She'd even give her ten percent off.

Amy said something and was gone.

It had worked this time. No one was fighting or crying. The trick was to hurt himself enough that God would feel real sorry for him. Sometimes it worked, but most times it didn't.

Chapter Four

LIGHT FORCED ITS way through the trees and onto Troy's bare feet. Warmth from the sun kissed the part in her hair and the back of her neck, but she shivered. She was sitting with her knees drawn up, and her face pressed into her forearms. Her head and eyes hurt, but crying had felt good. No, not good, necessary. She needed to cry, and she could think of nowhere better to do it than with Patricia.

She had gone to her small cottage—the only place she had ever felt comfortable calling her own, once, and had stayed no longer than the time it took her to shower and stuff some clothes into her bag. Home reminded her of how lonely she had been without Patricia and of how wrong she had been in thinking things couldn't possibly get worse. Why return to that when the whole city was full of showers and clothes that didn't carry painful memories.

For the last two days she had ridden the city looking for any sign that there had been an evacuation, but she had found none. She would look more today, but she no longer held out hope that she would find anyone else awake. The only thing she knew for sure was that something had happened to everyone else and had missed her.

"So this is it, right? This is the price I'm supposed to pay for what happened." She didn't expect an answer. She hadn't gotten one in sixteen months, but sometimes she'd imagine that Patricia was still there with her, rooting for her to continue to live. Not today, though. Today, Patricia seemed to have deserted her, and the hurt of that seemed more tangible than the fear of being left alone.

"What am I supposed to do?" She spoke out loud for no other reason than to disturb the quiet. "I've tried calling...you name them, and I've tried calling. There's just no one out there, and I don't..." She stopped speaking and smiled. "You know, I used to think that I wanted something like this to happen. But I had something more exotic in mind.

"I read this story once about these two girls marooned on an island, and the whole time I was reading it, I kept thinking, you know, I would love that. I would love being alone with you, not having to worry about people bothering us." Troy laughed. "That would have driven you fucking nuts, wouldn't it?" She ran her hand along Patricia's grave marker and sighed, her eyes taking in the cemetery. Small and private, it got a surprising amount of sunlight for Portland. Which is why she had agreed when the Harveys had insisted Patricia be buried there. She hadn't cared at the time that she would have to cross one of the bridges to visit her, and she still didn't care.

Patricia's life insurance, and four hundred thirty dollars borrowed from Raife, had gotten her a "desirable" spot. Troy wanted to give Patricia the best. Something she could never do on her messenger's salary. Not that that had ever been an issue between them.

"I used to have this dream that someday I could save enough to buy in with Raife, and maybe we could buy us a small house in Mount Tabor. We would have the pick of the place now. Everyone is asleep there, too." Troy leaned back and studied the old-growth trees, the sky, and the clouds." Why is this happening to me?" Her voice sounded disjointed and curious, but not scared. "What did I do to you?"

She was so tired of it all. So tired of being sad and angry because the world kept moving when she would have preferred it all to stop. Now she had gotten what she wanted. The world had stopped, but it forgot to stop her with it. All of Portland was like this graveyard—everyone dead, at least, to her. What's the point of living amongst that?

It's only been two days. They could wake up, but what if they don't? What are you going to do? Keep riding through the streets yelling for people who can't hear you? And so what if they do wake up? You're just doing what you have to do to survive anyway. That's not living.

Troy straightened. Maybe she had been looking at this the wrong way. What if this wasn't a punishment? What if this was someone's way of telling her she didn't have to fight anymore?

"Even you wouldn't want me to be alone, would you? Not like this." Troy stood up, her heart pounding. She didn't need an answer. Patricia would not want her to be alone. Patricia had told her on more than one occasion that her worst fear was to die alone. Troy liked to think that she was unconscious when she died. But she would never be sure, and that fact haunted her.

Troy jumped on Dite and forgot to say her customary goodbye to Patricia as she allowed the argument to continue in her head. *Was she going crazy? Is that what this was? It would make sense.*

After Patricia died.

After you let her die.

That particular thought was familiar. It had tormented her since Patricia's death. She'd started taking the sleeping pills to get some sleep, but she continued taking them when she found that it also dulled her senses. She floated in a haze of bad TV and crying. She left the house to buy food, but even that was rare.

Lack of money and Raife were the two things that forced her to deal with the human race. Work helped with the debilitating guilt during the day, but it did nothing for the nightmares that robbed her of sleep almost every night. The nightmares that Troy had come to depend on to remind her of the promise she had not kept: to be there—as no one had been for either of them. Troy hadn't realized that she was pedaling faster until her legs were pushing against the pedals like pistons. She wanted every muscle in her legs to scream. She decided she would ride until she couldn't ride anymore, and then she would settle down in a nice drug store where she planned on taking every pill in the place along with a side of trans-fats. She would wash it all down with a Big Gulp and a bottle of spiced rum.

She didn't have to do this anymore. She didn't have to hurt or be alone. She didn't have to fight. Troy slowed her pedaling as she coasted onto the Burnside Bridge. The water was like glass, though gray clouds on the horizon told her there would be rain soon. A boat bobbed miles off shore, and Troy wondered about the people on board. What would become of them? How long could any of these people last in the elements? Pretty soon the city—all cities—would be a wasteland of decaying corpses. Something in Troy's core shuddered, and she pushed the thought from her head. *Drug store first. You can get all depressed and contemplative later.*

The sun was behind her when she noticed the first of four lawn chairs lined up along the bridge, each chained to the other, a rectangular space around them marked off with masking tape. Troy didn't want to slow down, but she couldn't help herself. She stopped and turned around. Several sets of lawn chairs lined the street. Most were locked together with a cheap U-locks and chains. "Abernathy" had been written with orange chalk on the concrete. Troy shaded her eyes attempting to see further down the bridge, but the shadows kept that area a secret. Back on her bike, she pedaled toward several small clusters of chairs. Johnson, Strasburg, Melville, Dr. J. Smith and family. The Smiths consisted of a man and woman in their mid- to late-thirties and a little girl. Troy pegged her at four, but she'd never been good at guessing the age of children.

Troy glanced at her watch: June ninth. In a halfway normal world, she would be sitting right in the middle of Portland's Rose Parade. This family was one of the odd few who didn't trust that their chalk marks would be honored. Maybe it was their daughter's first Rose Parade, but Troy could think of any number of things she would rather be doing then sitting in a lawn chair waiting for a float covered in wilting flowers and high school cheerleaders.

"Dumb asses." Troy got off her bike and approached the family.

The girl had on a hat with earmuffs and a pink coat. A pink umbrella was stashed beneath her chair. Troy picked up the umbrella and, feeling awkward and uneasy, opened it and propped it over the little girl's head. Dark, smoky clouds crouched over the water, and the boat seemed to have grown smaller against the slate backdrop. She looked back at the little girl and considered moving her. She shook her head. *Stop it, damn it. If the elements don't do it, the lack of food will.* Something inside of her wailed.

Troy rode away from the bridge, berating herself for the tears that she couldn't stop. She stopped in front of a liquor store that was situated mere feet from the homeless shelter on West Burnside. There were at least a dozen people sleeping on the sidewalk next to the shelter, but that wasn't unusual. A large, coal-black man wearing a plaid dinner jacket and a scarf sat with his back to the wall of the liquor store. He gripped an empty can in one of his ash-dry hands. His medicine-ball stomach supported breasts which looked like two wet baby seal pups lolling in the sun. *He looks like he's been breast feeding twenty kids with those things.*

Troy shuddered and dropped Dite on the ground, something she never would have done if the world hadn't gone to hell and then fallen asleep afterward. She unwound her bike chain from her waist and with the lock still clipped to the end she swung it at the window of the liquor store like a chain mace. The first crack to the door took a small chink from the glass. No matter. She had all the time in the world, didn't she? Of course, she could look for a liquor store that was open 24/7, but what would be the fun in that? She liked the idea of destroying something before she destroyed herself. There was a certain poetic resonance to it. The second and third blow to the door left little damage, but the fourth sent little cubes of glass flying across the sidewalk and all over Troy. Pieces of glass glinted in the cuff of her rolled up Dickies, but she ignored it as she crouched then scooted under the metal piece of the door and into the store. A young Asian man, perhaps thirty-two, very clean-cut and—of course—asleep, sat with his head resting on a brown box that had Frito-Lay printed on the side. Troy made a beeline for the numerous bottles beyond the counter. She dumped *Anna Karenina, The Known World,* and an empty cardboard canister from her burnt-orange and gold messenger bag and replaced them with two bottles of spiced rum. She grabbed a six pack of cola from the sliding-door refrigerators and was about to add a few bags of sizzling hot corn puffs to her stash, but decided against it.

That's all I need is to die with heartburn and have to live with that shit for all eternity. The thought made her smile. Patricia had always said she had a dry sense of humor. Now she would either be seeing her soon, or the pain of missing her would be over.

Troy found a bag of clear plastic cups and walked outside to enjoy the last of the sun. She took a swig from the bottle and eased onto the sidewalk, no more worried about the glass than she was about the three-hundred-pound homeless man with no shirt and titties as big as her head sitting not a foot away from her.

Troy frowned. B.O. and lilac emanated from the man like a cloud. She wondered if someone had given him hand lotion to combat the dry skin. It was the kind of thing Patricia would have done. Troy toasted the air. "Thanks a fucking lot for the fantastic company," she said before knocking back the drink. The slow burn in her chest reminded her that it had been a long time since she'd had a drink. The memory of a voice that could be both beautiful and cruel swept over her and caused her to let loose a choking cry. *Come on, Troy, you know you're a lot more fun when you've had a drink. You're too damn serious. Nobody likes to drink alone.*

Troy pulled another cup out of the bag and poured a healthy amount of rum and then colored it with cola. She leaned over and placed the cup in Mr. Big Titties free hand. She didn't need to put much pressure on his dry fingers for them to grip the cup. She looked at his face. Not an angry face. In fact, he looked kind, and not unhappy.

"You're welcome," Troy said, already feeling the effect of the alcohol working its way through her system.

Patricia had been right. Nobody likes to drink alone.

JAKE WAS MAKING up for the two days he'd wasted being afraid. Money was no longer a problem. His parents were no longer a problem. He could have anything he wanted. All he had to do was take it.

The first thing he took was a pair of jeans exactly like the ones Sully Tolliver wore on the last day of school. They were frayed, boot cut, and two sizes too big. Gold stitches on the pockets gave them that retro look. But unlike Sully, he knew how to complete the outfit. He found a leather belt that was so big it almost didn't fit through the belt loops. He was on his way to Toppers. Everyone knew they had the best caps, and then he would go in search of the new Aaron Austin sneakers that he'd been saving his money to get.

Jake thought about getting into one of the numerous cars with its owner still in it, but Dad had refused to teach him to drive until he was fifteen. He wasn't scared of hurting anyone. They all might as well be dead anyway, but he didn't intend to kill himself. Not now when he was free of *them*.

His parents claimed they weren't filthy rich. But he knew they could afford to buy him almost anything he wanted, but didn't. They said he needed to "learn the value of a dollar." Yeah, right. Like *they'd* had to. He knew for a fact that both sets of their parents had been rich, and that neither of them had ever wanted for anything. He was, he knew, an experiment to them. Just like everything else. They were insistent on doing it all by the book. "The book" said he couldn't wear colorful shoes or baggy jeans because people might confuse him for a gang banger. That same book said that he had to save his allowance for ten weeks in order to buy his ipod. By the time he'd bought it, there was already a newer, better model on the shelf. He clenched his jaw as fresh anger coursed through him as he remembered taking his brand new iipodpod to school to show it off, and then Sully Tolliver shows up with a better model the next day. He hadn't said anything to them about it. He'd just bided his time, and now, none of it mattered. He could pick up the new ipod after he got his shoes, if he wanted. Jake smiled as the cuffs of his pants swept along the sidewalk. Maybe he would pick up a frozen pizza and some beer while he was out.

Chapter Five

BY THE TIME Troy finished shoplifting from the drug store, her ears, lips, fingers, and toes were rum-numb, but her brain refused to fog. The messenger bag that had held everything from chocolates sent by apologetic husbands to a huge box of Maxi Pads for the CEO of a floundering dot com, now held Percadan, Paxil, Ambian and something she was pretty sure was just a sinus medicine, but she decided to take anyway.

She careened through the streets no longer bothering to look for oncoming dangers or to bother with the lights that seemed to turn yellow just when she reached an intersection. Her plan was to find one of those ritzy downtown restaurants that she had never been comfortable going to and pop pills and drink until the sun came up. And then, she hoped, she would sleep. Just like everyone else.

Troy's pedaling had slowed, and she found herself looking up at the brick facades of the buildings she passed. She wondered what kind of people had lived in them. She wondered if death would keep her from missing her rides along these streets. She didn't see how it could. A tear crept down her face and ended up at the corner of her mouth where it tasted a lot like spiced rum and cola. A flash of light caught the corner of her eye. Troy flinched and braked hard.

She had been blinded by sudden glares enough times to know that they could be caused by glass, mirrors, or anything shiny. The one constant was movement, and that was one thing, aside from a slight breeze that managed to snake its way down the city streets, she had not seen in four days.

"You're just seeing things because you want to see something," she said, but hope was already welling in her chest like the rum tears that had spilled moments before.

Ah, what the hell. Troy cupped her hand over her mouth and bellowed. "Hey, anyone up there?" Her voice sounded high pitched, scared, and drunk. She shivered and laughed. *You fool; you're seeing things. You haven't found anyone awake in days. It was the wind.*

"So, that's it then. Either I kill myself, or I go crazy." Troy's voice sounded thunderous in the silent city.

"Hey!" Troy called out again. This time, she heard the element of anger in her voice, and she welcomed it. Anything was better than just lying down, wasn't it? She got off Dite and stood glaring up at the window. "I know you're up there. I know you're up there, and you're looking out here thinking 'look at that loon,' but I'm not crazy. I just want to talk to you. I've been in an accident. I..." Troy's words hung in her throat. "Hey? Damn it, you could at least acknowledge that you're up there. Tell me to go to hell, or something."

The quiet was what would do it in the end. She *was* going crazy. She needed to stop this. She needed to stop feeling so alone. "Okay," she said to nothing in particular and began pushing Dite back in the direction she had come.

She turned the corner, propped Dite against the wall, and squatted. She waited as long as her curiosity would allow before peering around the corner. The glint was there, and this time it didn't disappear. A small, red mirror was being held between the bars of one of the windows. It hadn't been there before, and now it was, which meant someone was holding it. Someone was awake up there and holding a mirror looking for her.

Anger returned full force, and almost before Troy had uttered the words, the mirror was being pulled back inside. "I see you, you son of a..."

Troy heard a dull clang followed by a gasp and the sound of glass shattering on the sidewalk. She ran to the splintered remnants of the mirror and crowed up at the barred window. "Can't spy on people now, can you?" Anger felt good. She had someone to focus on instead of something she didn't understand. "So you're not going to say anything? You're just going to hide up there and not fucking say anything?" Troy waited, her fury growing as the silence continued.

She felt like she had been alone forever. And now she had found someone, except they didn't want to be found. "Well guess what, lady?" Troy paused and then repeated herself because she was sure the gasp had been from a female. "You don't want to talk to me? Fine. I was on my way to..." Troy stood up and ran around the corner to where she had left her bag. She ran back and sat down on the curb fumbling in her bag for the fourteen or so pill bottles she had stolen from the drug store. "I'm not going to be here for long, and then you can talk to your own damn self." Troy's eyes stung and her throat tightened. *What the hell am I doing?* "I'm going to do it right here where you'll remember my ass every time the fucking wind blows."

So someone doesn't want to talk to you, you decide to kill yourself in front of her window? What kind of shit is that? Why am I so angry?

"I don't suppose you'd drop a bottle of water down, huh?" No answer came from the window. Not even a glimmer of movement. What the hell was up with this chick? She had been delirious when she realized that someone else was awake. Maybe she doesn't care that everyone else is asleep. *Maybe she would rather be alone than be around you.*

Troy slumped forward and put her forehead in her hands. If I was up there in the safety of that condo I wouldn't let some drunk, crazy bitch in either. She *was* acting psycho, and it wasn't just the alcohol. She was just tired of feeling so...alone. She had been tired long before she woke up in that odd-ass hospital.

"If you're still there...please, listen to me. I don't know what's going on, but everyone I know, everyone in this city is asleep, and I'm scared. I don't want anything from you. I just need to know that I'm not alone.

"I'm not crazy. At least I don't think I am. Hell, maybe I am crazy. I wouldn't let me in, either. I just wanted to talk to you, see that someone else in this world is still awake." Troy swept the pill bottles into her bag and stood. She didn't look up at the window for fear her heart would start that desperate longing again. "I'm sorry if I scared you. I won't bother you again." She swung the bag over her head and adjusted it as she started toward the corner where she had left Dite.

"Wait."

Troy stopped almost too afraid to move.

"Don't go."

The voice was soft, frightened, and young. A kid maybe. Troy's lower jaw cracked when she opened her mouth to answer. "I won't leave, I promise."

Troy was startled at how relieved she felt. There was someone else awake. This was not a hell built for her. Well, if it was, it was a shared hell. There was someone else in it with her. Troy swung her bag from her shoulder and sat down on the curb, her back to the window. Lack of sleep, rum, and relief made her eyelids feel weighted. She leaned forward, wrapped her arms around her legs, and squeezed as hard as she could; there was someone else up there. She was alone, too, and no doubt terrified of the demented chick out front, but she didn't want to be alone anymore than Troy did. Troy let hot tears drift down her cheeks and this time they tasted like a warm sea.

EMMA HAD BEEN sitting at the window seat for over an hour when she spotted the monstrosity of a bike at five minutes past six. She had expected her earlier, not because of anything spoken between them, but because that's what time she had shown up the previous two days.

On that first day, Emma could do nothing but watch her sit on the curb and cry. Emma's head had begun to throb and her own tears flowed as she was drawn into the stranger's pain. She hated feeling so helpless. She was relieved to watch her get on that bike and ride away three hours later.

But the relief soon faded and fear settled in its place. *She's been sitting out there for two days already. What if she's tired of waiting and doesn't come back? What if she gets hurt again? What if she hurts herself?* The what if's shoved themselves into her waking moments and didn't let up until she returned on the second day, embarrassed, but not as sad and a lot more talkative. Emma learned that her name was Troy, that she had no family, and that she made her living as a bicycle messenger.

Emma watched as Troy disappeared, probably propping her bike against the building, before reappearing on the sidewalk below her window. *Winter clothes on that body would be a shame.* Emma flushed. It had been a long time since she had had a thought like that. Not since Sharon. Not since that night.

Troy placed her hand on her forehead to block the glare. "Hey, are you up there?"

Emma wanted to answer, but her throat constricted and choked off her planned response. Her "yes", when it came, was pathetic, but Troy must have heard because she grinned, sat down on the curb, and began rummaging in her messenger bag. She pulled out a yellow and green box and began to talk. Even hunched forward and with her back to the window Emma had no trouble hearing her in the absolute quiet. She watched the muscles flex in Troy's back and she wished she were close enough to see what she was doing.

"I bet you went to college, huh?" Troy asked, without looking up.

Emma leaned so close to the blinds that her upper lip brushed against the faux-wood. She opened her mouth to answer, but Troy was already speaking.

"I tried going to college, but I dropped out after a couple months. They wanted me to take classes that I hated, like math and science and shit." Troy's body seemed to go into a frenzy of motion.

"I mean, what the hell does a fashion design major need advanced math for?"

Emma smiled. She could remember saying something very similar to her parents when she was trying to convince them to let her drop out of college. Emma found herself wanting to ask Troy to go into more detail.

"I think about going back. I used to anyway." Troy stood up and moved to the side.

Emma's lips brushed against her blinds again as she leaned close to see what Troy had been so intent on drawing. She had drawn herself on her bike with wild hair, big wrap-around style glasses, shoes untied, and grinning like a mad woman.

"I ain't no Picasso, but I used to like to draw," Troy said as she studied her picture, and then Emma felt an overwhelming sense of weariness coming from her.

She's not sleeping. Maybe she's afraid she won't wake up, which makes two of us.

"I'll see you tomorrow," Troy said. She didn't look up at the window as she walked away, but Emma could sense that Troy was becoming weary of their one-sided conversations and was in need of something else.

"What if she doesn't come back tomorrow?" Emma thought, *No, she just said she would see me tomorrow, but what about the next day and the next? How long can I expect her to keep me company with nothing in return? But what can I give her? You can give her human companionship. That's all she wants.*

Troy had come back into view pushing her bike and with her bag swung across her back. Emma wanted to call out to her. She wanted to say, "Don't go. Don't hurt. Don't be afraid," but none of that came out. *Why can't I just talk to her? She's stood down there and let her heart pour out on the sidewalk, and you can't even speak to her?*

Troy was looking up at the window now, her hand still in the bag. When she spoke, Emma heard the desolation in her words.

"Can you just tell me your name before I go...please?"

Emma closed her eyes. *My name isn't important. I can't be what you need. I wish I could.*

"Why is it so hard for you to fucking talk to me? This is driving me nuts. I swear there are times when I'm sitting here thinking that I made you up."

Emma turned away from the window and the agony. Troy had a very expressive face, and her feelings were so acute that Emma could sense most of them, even from a distance. A loud crack close to her ear sent Emma sliding off the seat and on to the floor. Desperation overwhelmed her with so much force that it took her a moment to realize that the feelings weren't her own. She hesitated before standing and peering between the blinds. One of the fists that had been balled at Troy's side shot up in a gesture so violent that her bag swung out and knocked her bike over.

Emma gasped. Troy had just thrown chalk at her window and then flipped her the bird!

"Screw you, too, lady," she said low enough that she was sure Troy wouldn't hear her. Troy yanked her bike up and readjusted her bag across her body. In a few seconds, she would be on that monstrosity and pedaling off to wherever the hell she went when she wasn't sitting down there on the curb.

Emma stood up, telling herself to ignore the sick feeling in her stomach and the yearning she felt for the fierce young woman. *She's out there all alone and she's scared.* Emma found herself facing her front door.

What are you gonna do? Run after her? Yeah right, you couldn't run if you wanted to. The internal trash talk was as familiar as the fear. Both kept her rooted to the floor when she should have been trying to get back to the window to beg Troy not to go. She was already at the door before she realized it. Her hand went to the knob and then away from it, and then she went to the release button for the front door and pressed it. She kept her eyes closed. The buzzer seemed louder than usual. She sensed no surprise, no anger. She sensed nothing that she could attribute to Troy.

Had she already ridden away before Emma had made up her mind to let her come up to the condo? Or had she just realized it wasn't worth it, ignored the buzzer, and ridden away? Emma limped back to the window seat. Troy's self-portrait seemed to have grown larger in her absence. She was right, she was no Picasso, but she had captured what Emma felt from her—a wild joy with a nucleus of sadness.

Emma remembered how Troy had cried that first day. She had seemed so sad that Emma had been forced to speak to her for fear she would harm herself. Troy would have had to have been desperate to have sat on that sidewalk for two days straight in the hopes that Emma would talk to her.

Tears dropped down Emma's cheeks. She was surprised at how hurt she felt. Not so much for herself. She had been alone for a long time. If anything, she felt less afraid right now than she had in two years. Her hurt was for Troy and the utter loneliness that she must feel to consider killing herself.

"Please, don't do it," she whispered. The knock on the door startled Emma so much that if she hadn't been sitting she was sure she would have fallen on the floor. She stood, her hand reached for and found the cane, but she didn't make a move toward the door. Her leg ached, and even though she was expecting it, she still jumped when the knock came again.

"It's me. Troy."

Emma looked down at the blue jeans and white tank top she was wearing and then back at the door. Her hand went to her hair. She could feel Troy now. There was uncertainty, and, yes, that under-layer of sadness.

"You pushed the buzzer, so I figured it was okay to come up." Troy's voice sounded different now that she didn't have to raise it to be heard. Emma limped to the door, and she got the sense of someone holding her breath. Was it Troy? No, it was her. Maybe it was both of them. She slid the first latch back and then the second, followed by the lock on the knob. She stared at the door. Should she tell her to come in? Would she try the knob herself? She had to have heard her take the lock off. Emma gripped hard on her cane and felt more tears prickle her eyes. *Why was this so damn hard? It's because you're tired and hungry. No, it's something else and you know it.* Emma turned the knob and pulled the door open. Her heart slammed against her chest the whole time.

Troy was wearing a pair of fitted tan pants with pockets on the sides, shoes with no socks, and a thin, tight t-shirt. The strap of her bag cut across her torso, pressing the form fitting t-shirt even closer to her skin. Emma blushed as her eyes went once, twice, and then a third time to Troy's nipples. *Could I behave any more inappropriately?*

She watched as Troy took in her bare feet, the cane, and then rested on her eyes with so much honest curiosity that Emma had to look away. Her gaze landed on Troy's bare midriff and then skittered away to somewhere safe.

"Emma," she mumbled.

"You're a what?" Troy looked confused and Emma would have laughed in other circumstances. Instead, she shook her head and looked anywhere but at Troy's upper body. *Good going, Emma. You ask the girl up, you ogle her chest, and then you act like you don't have control of your tongue.* Feet were a good place she decided and settled on Troy's shoes. *I've never seen any quite like that. They must help her pedal faster or something. Of course with calves like that—.*

"No," Emma said out loud. She made herself meet Troy's eyes and was surprised by the compassion she saw there. *She thinks something's wrong with me.* "I was trying to tell you my name. It's Emma."

"Emma," Troy said and slanted her head to the side as if deciding whether she would allow Emma to keep her name. "You look like an Emma."

"Uh, thanks...I think."

Troy grinned. "You're welcome."

"You look like a Troy, too."

"Thank you."

"You're welcome."

"Can I come in?" Troy tried to look beyond Emma into the condo.

"No."

Emma expected her to look angry or at least surprised. Instead, Troy threw her head back and laughed. She held the bike as if it were a toy. Her bicep bulged, but didn't look the least bit taxed. Emma wondered why she had carried the bike up at all. According to her, there was no one awake to steal her bike. In Emma's opinion, it was doubtful anyone would have tried to steal the bike even before Portland fell asleep.

"Do you always make your visitors sit on the curb for three days and then not let them in?" Troy asked, the smile still playing at her lips.

Emma almost told the truth—that aside from her parents, she'd never had visitors in the condo. "I'm sorry," she said instead. Her eyes went back to Troy's chest. And then to the small necklace she wore around her neck.

Troy shifted from one foot to the other. She didn't say anything, just stood there. Emma looked down. *What now*? She couldn't tell Troy she had made a mistake by letting her up, but she couldn't just—let her in. Could she? But what if she doesn't come back? What if she—

Once again Troy's emotions were so clear to Emma that she thought they were her own. Utter loneliness, fear, desperation, desolation. She backed away from the open door. Troy didn't move right away. It was as if she was giving Emma the chance to change her mind before she stepped into the room and shut the door behind her.

Chapter Six

WHEN ABE BROKE in to sixty-three-year-old Desdemona Bernard's home, he hadn't expected that he would be spending two nights in the tiny cottage amusing himself by going through her correspondence and personal items.

He now knew that Desdemona stretched her paltry social security checks by organizing monthly bus trips across the Canadian border to buy prescription drugs. She had two daughters. One was in love with her jailbird husband and the other was contemplating whether or not she should have an HIV/AIDS test because of an unfaithful partner. Desdemona also had thirteen cans of cat food, but no cat hairs, cat toys or cat smells present in her home. Abe hoped she had been unable to bring herself to throw away the food because the cat had recently passed away, but he had a feeling Desdemona was forced to stretch her food budget in other unsavory ways.

Abe was sitting at her desk because the only other seating with a view of the window was occupied by Desdemona's sleeping form. Her luxuriant grey hair spilled over the arm of her sofa. Abe thought she looked as if she was napping. Desdemona may have been a beauty at one time, but, Abe guessed, a harsh life and the birth of her children had sapped all but the last residue of that away.

Although the desk chair offered no lumbar support, he had the perfect view of Southwest Bonita Lane. On either side of the street were cottages identical to Mrs. Bernard's. Abe guessed they had been built forty years ago as low-income housing and were still being used as such. In Abe's opinion, no matter what race of people lived there, poor neighborhoods always had one thing in common—they always lacked space. Although it looked cared for, this neighborhood was no different.

All the cottages on Southwest Bonita Lane crowded the curb, leaving a strip of sidewalk that would be too small for a grown man to walk on. They were grouped in sets of three, with the unfortunate soul in the middle having only views of their neighbors' buildings out their bedroom windows. Both Mrs. Bernard and Troy Nanson had middle units. Abe would bet money those were the least expensive. The advantage was that both had large windows bracketing either side of their front doors, whereas, the other cottages only had one small one. Someone had helped Mrs. Bernard push a large ancient desk up to one of her front windows. He wondered if it had been Troy.

He could picture Desdemona sitting at the desk and writing her letters while watching the comings and goings of her neighbors. He wondered what she'd thought of Troy Nanson. Since they lived across the street from each other, they had to have interacted. Did Desdemona bake her cookies? Or did she call the police if Troy so much as glanced toward her mailbox? Maybe they just waved to each other in the same "I don't want to get involved" way he and Teresa did with their neighbors.

Abe stood up, and his hand went to his lower back where he kneaded the tense muscles there. His stomach complained as it had done off and on for the last few hours. He wished that he had stopped to get food on his way in. Rather than risk missing Troy, he'd had to make do with the one edible thing in Desdemona's house, popcorn. Not the microwave kind. Desdemona just had the kind you popped yourself, using a pan or skillet. Besides, she had no microwave. He had read the directions twice, but still burned the first batch. The second came out white and fluffy. It was apparent that Desdemona worried about her salt intake because he had to settle for No-salt and unsalted butter. Still, he had to admit it was better than the microwave stuff he treated himself to when Teresa wasn't around to throw out comments about the small bulge that had appeared where his flat stomach had once been.

Abe grunted. He had passed the annoyed stage hours ago. Where in the hell was she? They always went home, didn't they? It made no sense to him that this Troy Nanson could screw up his study on his first outing—unless... He stared at the darkened cottage. Could she have come and gone while he was sleeping? He had dozed off twice and awakened to the sound of his own snoring.

Maybe she'd seen him. No, that wasn't possible. He'd been too careful. Even if she'd been home when he was breaking into Desdemona's place, he would have seen her leave by now. He had been watching for three days and in all that time there hadn't been any hint that she had ever come home.

This was not going as he had planned. Jake Ostroph and Emma Webster were not the least bit interesting. He thought for sure that Troy would be worth his attention, but he couldn't even find her.

"Where in the hell..."Abe left the sentence unfinished. Crying about it would do him no good. He would just have to find her. He had waited long enough. He walked out of Mrs. Bernard's house, and the woman who had been his sole companion—even though she didn't know it—for the last three days was dropped from his mind like the unimportant memory that she was.

The one person capable of holding his interest had been Troy. Why she had taken on a more important position than the others he didn't know. But there was something about her that intrigued him. He felt she was the key to the answers he was seeking. The others meant nothing to him now, backups, if necessary, but not worth the time it would take to observe them.

Abe tested the doorknob and smiled. Of course she hadn't left the door open. That would be too easy. He thought about putting his foot through it, but instead went around the side of the cottage to look for a less obvious way in. Like he'd done at Mrs. Bernard's. Troy's bathroom would be small and prone to mildew if not aired properly and, sure enough, as Abe rounded the corner and walked down the two foot walkway on the side of Troy's cottage, he spotted the open bathroom window. Also, like Mrs. Bernard, Troy's view was of brown siding that had seen better days twenty years before. The bathroom window was small, but Abe was tall, and contrary to what Teresa thought, still quite thin.

He landed with a thud on the floor and lay there, struggling to catch his breath. What if she was in the house and he had just alerted her, like an idiot, to his presence? Abe forced himself to lie still even though his elbow smarted and the small of his back felt like someone had just pummeled it. His raspy breathing sounded loud in the tight quarters. Abe pulled himself to his feet with the help of Troy's pedestal sink and opened the bathroom door. He heard the hum of an appliance, but nothing else.

As he had suspected, Troy's floor plan was the same as Mrs. Bernard's, but it was obvious that Troy was not a believer in making things homey. From where he stood, he could see the living room and most of the kitchen. The living room consisted of hardwood floors, a black futon, a chair, a TV and TV cart, and dark brown walls that had no evidence of ever having pictures on them. Desdemona had too much furniture and Troy seemed to have too little. His groaning stomach dictated that he find something to eat before he allowed himself to look around further.

A wet bar and a bank of cabinets were all that separated the narrow kitchen from the living room. The kitchen was a perfect rectangle. It had a gas stove at one end, and the refrigerator whined from its spot against the wall. The refrigerator was similar to one his nana had when he was a kid. By age fourteen, he could prop his elbow on top of it if he wanted to. Abe snatched an open bag of pretzels from the top of the refrigerator and wolfed them down as he walked into the living room. A bicycle frame leaned against a wall near the front door, and a poster tube leaned against another wall. Abe's eyes were drawn to the black futon again. He walked over to it and sat down, his lower back protested as he leaned back. A pillow and a folded comforter had been left at one end. *She'd sat here, maybe slept exactly where he was sitting.*

Abe sighed. "How depressing." His voice sounded sharp and cruel in the empty room. A pair of shoes, slim with some kind of rubberized spikes on the sole, had been left on the floor.

He was a bit disappointed by Troy's home. He had expected pictures or chatchkas that would give him more insight into her personality. *Ha, you think you know this girl from watching her for two minutes?* Abe stood up; there was no point in spending too much time dwelling on it. There were two other doors to look behind before he had to leave with his tail tucked between his legs. With any luck, one of them would hold a clue to Troy's whereabouts.

The first door led to a closet that looked like a graveyard of bike parts. Frames, wheels, and seats had been stashed in every available space. Four bike chains hung from the clothing rod and the scent of motor oil or something similar assailed Abe's nose.

He closed the closet and opened what he figured would be Troy's bedroom. He fought down his initial disappointment and walked in. Although her living room and kitchen were both neat, this room looked as if it hadn't been lived in. Abe looked at the bedspread, the two end tables, the bureau, the curtains, and then he looked back out into the drab living room. It was like a movie he had once enjoyed on cable TV where two kids were sucked into a black-and-white TV show. *This is odd.* Abe rifled in his pocket for a small silver box the size of a cell phone. *Did she create this, or is this how she lives?* Abe walked over to the end table and started to sit down on the bed. He paused and instead of sitting down, he slid open the small drawer on the nightstand. Troy had placed a paperback book, two rings, a small locket, a newspaper clipping, and a tri-fold flyer inside. The clipping was an obituary. Pictured in the obituary, Patricia Rose Harvey, age thirty, had her head thrown back and seemed to be laughing at something the photographer was saying. The tri-fold flyer was Patricia Harvey's funeral program, but it made no mention of Troy Nanson as surviving relative or friend, although it mentioned others. *But who was she? A relative? A roommate? Not with one bed—.*

Abe sank down on to the bed. "I'll be damned." He tried not to notice the disappointment, but it was there. But why wouldn't Raife Paterson mention that she was gay? Abe had assumed that there had been a relationship between the two. Abe closed his eyes. He had made the cardinal mistake. He had assumed. His stomach quailed and the pretzels he had consumed threatened to come back up.

His attraction to Troy Nanson had been so textbook that even he had known what it stemmed from. She was his creation, his triumph: walking, talking, strong, and beautiful. It made perfect sense that he would love her. So what if she looked nothing like the women he dated before and after his marriage? So what if she would never look at him twice on the street? Abe had felt something when he watched her flee the hospital, even though she hadn't known what she was running from.

And now this.

His anger startled him so much that he laughed out loud. So what if she's gay? *It's not as if you had any real thoughts of ever starting something with the girl.* Abe placed the obituary back in the drawer and noted the cemetery where Patricia Rose Harvey was buried. Abe stood and smoothed the wrinkles out of the bed. He had a feeling that Troy would know someone had been in her home no matter what he did, but he didn't want her to think he was some kind of pervert. He was anything but that.

SHE DIDN'T LOOK the way she was supposed to. Or at least not the way Troy had imagined her. Of course, she'd also assumed that when they met face to face, there would be eye contact, but she had gotten that wrong, too.

Troy felt unkempt. She always did when she met new people. The fact that this Emma, this woman she didn't even know, could make her feel like she wasn't worthy made her angry.

Emma glanced at her and then back at the floor. Her eyes are weird. Not quite blue, more a steely, grayish-blue and they look dilated. *Is she high? No, has to be a trick of light.* Troy thought about taking a step closer, but one look at Emma's frightened face told her that it was best she stay where she was.

"Sorry about your window." Troy hated how gruff her voice sounded.

Emma looked up at her then. Troy was so disappointed to realize that Emma's eyes were, indeed, normal, everyday blue that she almost didn't register Emma's words when they came.

"I don't have any food," Emma said.

Hot licks of anger warmed Troy's ears. *"I don't want your food. Is that why you think I came up here? To try to steal your food? Wake up, lady. Food is pretty much ripe for the pickings out there. Why in the hell would you think I'd sit on that damn curb for three days – ?"*

Emma stepped back to escape Troy's anger. "I meant," she said, her voice soft and steady as if she were talking to a rabid dog, "I meant to ask if *you* had any food?"

She's scared shitless. She wouldn't have let me up here if she hadn't been hungry. The realization froze any angry words before they left Troy's lips. "When's the last time you ate?" she asked.

Emma looked toward her kitchen as if it could give her the answer. "What day is it?"

"Why didn't you say something sooner?" Troy started toward her.

Emma's face went slack and pale. She held up her hands and took another step back.

"What's wrong with you? Oh, my God." Her laugh sounded harsh and mirthless. "You're not going to tell me you have a problem with black people, are you? 'Cause last time I looked, fifty percent of the viable populace of Portland is black," Troy pointed to her chest, "and the other fifty percent," she pointed to Emma, "has no right..." Troy stopped speaking as Emma's face went from shock to disbelief and then anger.

"I am not prejudiced," she said as if Troy had just accused her of being a Republican.

"Good," Troy let her bag slide to the floor, "glad to hear it." She stooped and fished around inside the bag. Her eyes burned, her head ached, and she felt like someone had punched her in the kidney. She set each item on the floor, one by one. A can of Slim Jims, a large bag of peanuts, a bag of potato chips, and two packages of cheese and crackers. She looked at the stash feeling like she had just asked a date to share her Kid's Meal. She picked up the chips and held the bag out to Emma. "Sorry, none of it's good for you. I wasn't thinking about nutrition when I took it."

Emma stared at Troy's outstretched hand. "You just—took all that?"

Troy looked from the junk food to Emma. *What is she, nuts?* "Yeah, I *took* it. Why didn't you...?" The rest of the sentence wedged in her throat as she took in the condo and Emma's appearance.

Although she did have a lot of books, they fit neatly on her bookshelves, and there were no towers of old newspapers, nor did she see or smell twenty-three cats or sixteen Chihuahuas. But from what she had just gleaned, this woman had not left this condo even after she had many clues that something was wrong outside. What would she have done if Troy hadn't ridden by?

Troy dropped her hand to her side. Emma was looking down at the snacks lined up on the floor as if she didn't know what they were. *Great. I find someone else awake, and she's a fucking nut.*

"I'm not crazy."

Emma's voice sounded so sad that Troy regretted the direction her thoughts had taken her and then felt silly. "I didn't say you were." Troy held out the chips. Emma looked as if she wasn't going to take them. But then her hand came up, and Troy pressed the bag into it. Her fingers brushed against Emma's soft palm. Troy met Emma's eyes and shoved her hands in her pockets. Emma parted her lips to say something but didn't. Her eyes were wide, but she didn't look scared.

"Why'd you wait three days to let me come up?" Troy asked before Emma could further protest.

"I didn't want to..."

"You didn't want to let me up. Right, I get that. Why'd you let me sit out there all this time if you never intended on letting me in?"

Troy expected her to rip into the snacks, but she hadn't. The chips seemed forgotten in one hand while the other hand gripped the cane so hard that her knuckles looked white and shiny. Her hands, like the rest of her, were slim, but she was by no means emaciated. Even if she was hungry now, Troy didn't think she had been for very long. "How'd you get food before?" She kept her voice quiet, her hands in her pockets.

A twitch began at the side of Emma's mouth. "Kirkwood delivers it to me. I placed two orders, but nothing came. I was going to try another store when you rode by."

"You didn't know the rest of the world was asleep until I rode by and told you?" Troy couldn't keep the incredulity out of her voice. "How in the hell could you *not* know?"

"I...suspected. I don't go out much." She held out her cane. Troy studied her, and Emma looked away. *She looks the way white folk look when they don't want to see themselves as you see them.*

"What are we going to do?" Emma asked.

"What are we going to do?" Troy repeated. *We are going to leave you to your suicide while I continue with my own plans.* "I don't know. Like I said down there, I have no idea what the hell's going on or why it's happening. I do know that, other than you, I haven't found anyone else awake in the last three days. "

"Did you try a phone?"

Troy nodded. "On the first day. I spent hours trying different numbers, 911, long distance, the international operator. No one ever answered."

"So you're saying...you're saying it's not just Portland?"

Compassion flooded through Troy. She'd had almost four days to digest what had appeared to have happened, and it was still a hard thing to swallow, but she had accepted it somewhat. Emma, it seemed, hadn't. At least not yet.

"There's no one?"

"Not that I've found. Just me. And now you."

"How about the newspapers? Maybe we should check a few weeks back—"

"Checked all that the day after I woke up. I was hoping to find some passing mention of, hell, I don't know, a gas leak in some third world country that ended up being worse then anyone realized, but," Troy shrugged, "there's no mention of anything out of the ordinary. What ever happened out there must have happened too fast."

Emma turned away from her and sat down on a built in seat beneath the window.

She sat there watching me. Troy should have been embarrassed, but she wasn't.

"All sleeping?" Emma asked again, mulling it over. Troy didn't say anything. She had told Emma as much days ago, but for some reason Emma just now seemed to be taking in the full ramifications.

"Did you see any accidents?"

"Accidents? What, you mean like car accidents? No, no, I didn't. I was so—" Troy paused as she relived the horror of finding the city comatose all over again.

"I understand," Emma said. Their eyes met and Troy had the feeling she did understand.

That's crazy. How could she, when she's been in her safe little hidey hole. Troy pushed away her resentment and asked. "When did *you* first notice things weren't right?"

"When my groceries didn't come the second time. I also noticed that the building cleaning crew didn't come on their normal day. Emma flushed again. "I wasn't sure, though. It's real easy to loose track of what day it is."

Troy wanted to ask how a woman Emma's age could be capable of loosing track of days, but she pointed to the desk in the center of the room instead. "May I?" Emma hesitated and then nodded. Troy walked over to her desk and picked up a pen and paper. "When did you say you noticed?"

"At least four days ago."

Uh, huh, June seventh. That's the day after I woke up in the hospital."

"You were in the hospital?"

Troy looked up. "Yeah, everyone in the place was out cold. I thought I'd been in an accident." Now it was Troy's turn to feel heat surface on her face. "I didn't have money for the hospital bill, so I skipped out."

"What hospital was it?"

"Small place out near Southeast Thirty-First Street."

Emma frowned. "Must be new."

Troy shrugged, "I don't know. All the staff was asleep. It was kind of creepy, so I left. I thought it was weird, until I found the rest of the world was the same. Man, I never knew it could be that quiet."

"That must have been hard to deal with."

Troy shrugged again. "It was what it was. I dealt with it fine," she said, and then wondered why she felt the need to lie to someone who was so afraid of her own shadow that she was willing to starve rather than leave her own home.

"What about fires? Did you see any fires?"

"Fires? No, no, I didn't. I see where you're going though. If people just fell asleep you'd think they would—I don't know—burn themselves up with cigarettes in their hand or food left on stoves or something. I didn't see any of that. If they had warning or time to turn off stoves, there would be something on the net or in the newspaper."

Troy got up from the desk, took off her scarf, and ran her fingers through her hair. She twisted the scarf into a tight rope in her hands. Instead of answers, Emma was creating more questions. Questions she herself should have thought of instead of riding around trying to think of the least painful, wussy-ass way to kill herself.

"I'll be back," she mumbled.

She already had the front door open when Emma asked, "Where are you going?"

Troy met her eyes and then looked away before answering. Her words came out slow and concise as if she were speaking to a child. "I'm going to break into your neighbors' places and steal whatever food they have, and then I'm going to come back here and give it to you. After I do that, I'm going to lie on your couch and get some sleep, because now that I know that someone else is awake, I might be capable of sleeping for more than half an hour. Is that all right with you?"

A low wail emanated from the area of Emma's stomach.

"I thought so," Troy said and pulled the door shut. She bit her lower lip. What would cause someone to wall themselves up in their own home to the point that they don't know when the rest of the world goes to hell in a hand basket? Worse yet, what would cause her to stay there, even after she knows something's wrong? Troy tested the first knob and continued walking down the hall. Her frustration was already reaching the boiling point. She would check one more door, and then she would go to another floor so that she didn't scare Emma when she went nuts on one of her neighbor's front doors.

Chapter Seven

Standard, Oregon
September
Years ago

THE BOY'S SHOELACES had worked themselves loose again. Shoelaces, at least untied ones, bothered Hoyt. Anything that bothered Hoyt usually earned a slap on the back of the head. So The Boy tucked his feet back beneath the chair and kept his body still. He knew he hadn't done anything to get in trouble. Not unless this was about the fight, but he couldn't see why getting his ass kicked would be reason to call his father in.

Unless, his teacher, Ms. Carter, was planning on telling Hoyt what a pansy he had for a son.

The idea of Hoyt finding out that he got chased as far as the Pump and Go Gas Station almost every day made The Boy's stomach cramp. Something trickled down the side of his leg. Sweat, he hoped.

Hoyt had worn his Sunday best. Not that his Sunday best had gotten use on any Sunday that The Boy could remember.

"Mr. Pokorney, it's nice to meet you," Ms. Carter said as she rushed through the door. She looked so beautiful that The Boy forgot that he should be afraid.

"Hoyt. You can call me Hoyt, Ms. Carter. The Boy's mother couldn't make it. She's having female problems." Hoyt's laugh made The Boy's eardrums tingle and the smile he put on turned The Boy's stomach. It was the same one he had used on Amy, the waitress at Bernie Ann's Corner Side Cafe. Ms. Carter returned Hoyt's smile, but it didn't reach her eyes like it did for him when he answered a question right. The Boy wondered what a black eye had to do with Pam's female problems.

Ms. Carter looked down at her folder. The Boy liked how she was wearing her hair and how neat and clean her desk was. Everything in its place, even the folder that he was sure Mrs. Orson, the school secretary, had handed her just before she walked in the door.

The one thing that The Boy didn't like about Ms. Carter was the way she got quiet sometimes. She would ask a question and after you gave her the answer, she wouldn't respond right away. It made him feel like he had said something wrong, even when he knew he was right. She was doing that now and it scared him because he knew Hoyt wouldn't like it anymore than he did.

"Mr. Pokorney," she began.

The Boy jumped as Hoyt cleared his throat. The sound was like the rat-tat-tat of machine gun fire in one of those old westerns with all midget actors that his Grandma liked to watch every Sunday.

"Hoyt," Ms. Carter said with the same smile she used when she didn't want to tell a student that their answer wasn't quite right. "Are you aware that your son has shown an affinity for math?"

Hoyt looked at The Boy and then back at Ms. Carter with the same smile he used on all women he was sure found him good looking. The Boy gripped his armchair and looked down at the floor and hoped Hoyt didn't call Ms. Carter a gal.

"Has he, now?" His tone made The Boy even more nervous. It was always like this at home. Before a fight. Hoyt always got gentler before things got real bad. The Boy's bladder was so full now that his leg began to shake.

He wanted to yell at Ms. Carter to get on with it. He didn't understand why she had called Hoyt here. His grades were good and he didn't make trouble.

"Yes, some of the other teachers and I have organized an after school program with courses that are geared more toward middle and high school students. We offered your son one of the spots and he refused. He said you needed his help at home."

"He said that, huh?" Again Hoyt looked at him, but The Boy continued looking down at the floor. His cheek cooled when Hoyt turned his gaze back to Ms. Carter.

The Boy slumped forward and began to fumble with his shoelaces. He squeezed his eyes shut. *Some-bitch Some-bitch.* He repeated the mantra over and over in his head. Pee eased out of his penis; he grabbed his ankles, pressed his tummy into his crotch to stop the flow, and prayed.

"He told you right. I do need him to help me with my work."

"Hoyt," Ms. Carter's voice had softened and The Boy heard papers shuffling. Neither of them seemed to notice that he was still bent over. He clenched and unclenched his stomach. The pressure was building so much that he had begun to rock. *Some-bitch Some-bitch.* Should he tell them he had to go? No, they'd make him stand up. He didn't know what was worse: peeing his pants in front of Ms. Carter or the beating he would get for embarrassing Hoyt.

"Do you know your son wants to be a doctor?" His penis felt like it had shriveled up into his stomach.

"A doctor," Hoyt said and then he laughed. "He's seven years old."

"It's never too early to start children toward their future. In ten years, your son will be ready for college. With grades like his and his sharp mind, he could be eligible for a full scholarship."

Hoyt sat with his heel propped back against the leg of his chair, pressing so hard that his calf muscles stretched the seams of his pants. Something dark and brown spotted his white sock and The Boy wondered if it were Pam's blood. He had seen old blood several times in his life. But Pam had been fine this morning, aside from the black eye. It dawned on The Boy that Ms. Carter had just told Hoyt that she thought he could go to college someday. She thought he could be a doctor. A doctor. He sat up and looked at her. His resentment was gone, along with his need to pee.

"If *my* boy wants to go to school," the emphasis on "my" made The Boy's fingers stumble as he tried to tie his shoes, "money won't be a problem."

It was such an obvious lie The Boy could imagine Ms. Carter's eyes bugging out of their sockets. He hoped they weren't. He hoped she didn't question Hoyt on anything, because that was never a good idea.

"Of course not, Mr. Pokorney. I was merely letting you know that I think your boy has a chance to do so, if he wants to become a doctor."

Hoyt's laugh rang out again. "You're back to calling me 'Mr. Pokorney' again." Hoyt's voice sounded odd. The Boy was embarrassed, as if he shouldn't be in the room. Ms. Carter wasn't moving; her eyes were glued to Hoyt. Watching him like anyone would who's keeping an eye on a dangerous thing. He wondered if she had seen it, if she had figured out what he had known all of his life. There was something missing in Hoyt. It was like those gorillas at the Oregon zoo. They seemed peaceful, but there was nothing in them that would make them feel bad if they decided to tear you apart.

"Thank you for taking an interest in my boy. I'm sure his mother will be real happy that a seven-year-old could make such an impression on his teacher." Ms. Carter looked as if she was going to correct Hoyt and then thought better of it. She looked at The Boy and he smiled at her letting her know that it was okay. He was eight years old, not seven. It didn't matter that his father didn't remember how old he was, but it did matter that she knew.

Hoyt stood up as if he'd realized he needed to be somewhere else, and Ms. Carter did the same. More words were said, but The Boy didn't know what they were, and then he was looking at the back of Hoyt's muscular body as he hurried to catch up. He didn't remember saying goodbye to Ms. Carter, but he hoped he had.

Once inside the truck, country music blared through the one working speaker in the passenger door. The engine caught on the first try and The Boy hadn't even muttered his prayer. He felt himself relax. The seat that he shared with Hoyt shifted and the music lowered until he could hear the truck's steady idle. The Boy closed his eyes and turned, as if looking out the window. It would start now.

"A doctor, huh?" Hoyt's voice was too calm.

"They said we had to put something."

"Why a doctor?"

"'Cause they help people."

"You sure you don't just want to look at naked women?" Hoyt sounded like he had just heard a funny joke. He sometimes sounded like that during football season and he'd already had the first of what would be several beers. The Boy almost liked him then. Almost.

"That's it, ain't it? You think if you become a doctor you get to look at girls' bodies and shit. Bet you'd get to do all kinds of nasty shit, too."

Heat started in his hands and radiated up his arms and neck and to the top of his head. He was getting angry, so angry that if he didn't know for a fact that Hoyt would hurt him, he would lie on his back and try with all his might to kick Hoyt's head through the window. Hoyt didn't know shit about being a doctor. He swore up and down that he had never even been to one. Doctor Rose had let The Boy use the stethoscope to listen to his own heart. He had told him about the operations he had performed. The Boy hadn't told him about his own operations, but he wanted too. He could be a doctor if he wanted to. And once he became a doctor, he would show Hoyt.

"I bet you think you're smarter than me, don't you, boy" The question was quiet, too quiet, and all of the anger that had been settled on the top of The Boy's head now eased down to his pelvis. He had to pee again.

"Naw, sir," he said out loud. But secretly, way in the back of his head, he was screaming. *Yes, you big dumb bag of shit on fire. I am smarter than you. Ms. Carter thinks I can be a doctor. You ain't even smart enough to go to one when you're sick. I am smarter than you and better than you.* All of this flew through his head at the speed of light with so much anger and power that it surprised even him. Up until that point, he hadn't realized that he hated Hoyt.

The first blow caught him by surprise. He rocked up against the door, but didn't utter a sound. Crying made it worse. He didn't look at Hoyt either; he just waited for the next one. The threat of it hung in the air between them the same way it had for as long as The Boy could remember.

"I WAS JUST thinking."

"About how much you suck at spades?" Emma asked without looking up from the copy of *Little Women* that Troy had "checked out" of the library for her.

"No." Troy still felt miffed at having lost to Emma. The smirk on Emma's face would have been annoying if she wasn't so damned cute about it. Troy was sprawled on the floor next to Emma's window seat. The copy of *Pride and Prejudice* that Emma had insisted that she read was between her elbows. She hadn't admitted that she was enjoying it yet, and she wouldn't for a while.

"No, you *weren't* thinking about how much you suck at spades or...?"

"I do not suck at spades." Emma looked up then, and Troy had to back down. "I really like that game," she said in a quiet voice.

A small dimple appeared at the side of Emma's mouth. "Yeah, but you suck at it."

"I taught *you* how to play!"

Emma gave her a perfect 'your point is' look which Troy had also taught her.

"Yeah, well you suck at Monopoly," Troy said, quite smug in the knowledge that she had beaten Emma the last three times they had played.

"We'll see who sucks tonight." The dimple disappeared behind the cover of *Little Women,* and Troy picked up her mug of tea and filled her mouth with the hot liquid to keep from laughing. Would she ever get used to being around someone so innocent? Emma would say things like that and not have the least idea how sexual it sounded. At least Troy didn't think she did.

"As I was saying, you rude little thing, if everyone was just asleep, wouldn't they be emaciated? Dying from starvation?

Frowning, Emma looked up from her book. The little dimple was gone.

"I can't believe I didn't think about that. Sleeping or not, it's been two weeks; they should all be either dead or dying."

"That's what I thought, too."

"Have you seen any dead people?"

Troy shrugged.

"I don't get close to them, Em. They're kind of creepy. But I think I would know, right? I mean, wouldn't there be a smell? "

"Depends on how long they've been dead. But yeah, there would be a smell."

Troy rolled onto her back and closed her eyes. It bothered her that she felt so content. It was almost like she was accepting what was happening. She felt she should be doing more, but for the life of her, she didn't know what else she could do.

Emma hadn't spoken in so long that Troy assumed that she had gone back to her book until her voice came out low and contemplative. "So they aren't sleeping, are they?"

It took Troy a moment to realize that Emma was asking a question, not stating the obvious. "What makes you say that?"

"If they're just asleep," her words were measured, as if she wasn't sure herself what she was trying to say, "they would still need food."

"Maybe." Emma was going down the same road she herself had gone down days before. She set her mug on the floor and reached across and touched Emma's hand to get her attention. Emma jumped, but Troy didn't think it was from fear, so she didn't remove her hand. "I know what you're thinking. But I don't know the answer. I know those people out there are breathing; they have pulses, they're warm.

"But how could they survive like that?"

Troy sat up on her elbows and looked at Emma. "I don't know. I just know they aren't dead."

"Then are we?"

"Now why in the hell would you say something like that?"

"Because nothing else makes sense."

"You're right. Nothing makes sense. And it hasn't since I woke up in that damn hospital. But why would you all of a sudden come to the conclusion that we're the dead ones? What, you think this is some kind of Armageddon, and God rewards the good folks by giving them the heaven of everlasting sleep out on the dirty-assed sidewalks?"

Troy stood up. The words dropped from her mouth like stones. "Or maybe you believe you and I are the ones in hell. One problem with that theory." Troy pointed to the bars on the windows. "I don't think this is your idea of hell. You've been in purgatory for what is it? Two years now? That's it, isn't it? You want to stay here. Nothing has changed for you. You used to hide in your plush little condo, and you still do. There's no one to bother you here. No one to scare you, right? That's not living Emma. That's just sitting around waiting to die."

Emma sat up, her face a tight pale mask. "Why are you saying all this? You know it's not true."

"Because I don't understand why you and I are here and she..."

The hurt and shock on Emma's face was like a dash of cold water.

"What were you going to say?"

Troy shook her head; she would not discuss Patricia with Emma. It wasn't any of Emma's business. She had to think. She'd blown up at Emma for no reason. She needed to get away before she said something so hurtful that she couldn't take it back. "I'm going for a ride."

"There's a storm coming in.

"This is Portland, remember? I ride in rain all the time." Troy felt most of her anger seep away, but Emma still reacted as if she had been slapped. She said something about going to bed, and left the room. Troy picked up Dite and realized as she pulled the door closed behind her that she was not looking forward to her ride.

Coming Through the Fire

GLORIA COPELAND

KENNETH
COPELAND
PUBLICATIONS

Unless otherwise noted, all scripture is from the *King James Version* of the Bible.

Scripture quotations marked *The Amplified Bible* are from *The Amplified Bible, Old Testament* © 1965, 1987 by the Zondervan Corporation. *The Amplified New Testament* © 1958, 1987 by The Lockman Foundation. Used by permission.

Scripture quotations marked *New Living Translation* are from the *Holy Bible, New Living Translation* © 1996, 2004 by Tyndale Charitable Trust. Used by permission of Tyndale House Publishers.

Coming Through the Fire

ISBN 978-1-60463-270-5 30-0574

20 19 18 17 16 15 6 5 4 3 2 1

Kenneth Copeland Publications
Fort Worth, TX 76192-0001

For more information about Kenneth Copeland Ministries, visit kcm.org or call 1-800-600-7395 (U.S. only) or +1-817-852-6000.

Coming Through the Fire

Living the Christian life is not a piece of cake. Anyone who says it is isn't telling you the whole story.

Although as believers we have victory in Jesus, although we have the power in Him to triumph in every situation, sometimes things get tough. Sometimes we encounter troubles and trials that drag on...and on... and on (despite our desperate prayers for relief) until we want to say what the Old Testament prophet Habakkuk said in the Bible: "O Lord, how long shall I cry for help and You will not hear? Or cry out to You of violence and You will not save?" (Habakkuk 1:2, *The Amplified Bible).*

Almost every Christian on earth has been tempted to ask such questions at one time or another. It might have been because they needed healing and prayed for it for weeks, months or even years without seeing any results. It might have been because they were struggling with family issues or financial challenges they couldn't seem to resolve.

In those kinds of situations, we can all make the mistake Habakkuk did. We can be tempted to give in to the pressure of the devil, point the finger of blame at God and say, "Why is this taking so long? Why aren't You helping me? Aren't You listening to me?"

But that is exactly the wrong thing to do.

The trouble in our lives is never God's fault. He is never behind it. When we can't seem to get answers to our prayers, He is not the problem.

The problem is always on our end.

Habakkuk can confirm it. He learned that lesson well when God answered all his questions with one simple statement. "The just shall live by his faith" (Habakkuk 2:4). Or, as *The Amplified Bible* puts it: "The just and the [uncompromisingly] righteous man shall live by his faith and in his faithfulness."

In a nutshell, that's where Habakkuk missed it. He'd been complaining up a storm to the Lord, pleading with Him to fix the mess around him, but he hadn't been operating by faith.

God works with faith and Habakkuk hadn't given Him anything to work with.

The same can sometimes be said of us. Whenever we aren't getting the results we want from God, it's not because God is failing to do His part. It's because we're missing it where our faith is concerned. We aren't doing our part to receive the victory He has already provided.

"But Gloria," you might say, "I've been walking by faith for years. I know how to do my part!"

That may be true, but no matter how much you know, you can let things slip if you don't stay on top of them. What's more, every one of us is still learning. No one has arrived yet. So taking a faith refresher course is always a good idea. Especially when we're facing various tests and trials, we want to make sure we're handling them the way God expects—not like Habakkuk did, but like Shadrach, Meshach and Abednego.

You remember those three, don't you? They went through a time of trouble the likes of which most of us will never experience. They were literally thrown into a raging inferno simply for refusing to worship a king's idol.

Talk about a fiery trial! Shadrach, Meshach and Abednego really went through it. But they knew what to do. They lifted up their faith shield and quenched all the fiery darts of the devil (Ephesians 6:16). They not only survived the fire, they came out of it unharmed. "Not a hair on their heads was singed, and their clothing was not scorched. They didn't even smell of smoke!" (Daniel 3:27, *New Living Translation*).

All because they lived by faith.

A Substance More *Precious Than Gold*

What, exactly, is faith?

It's believing what God says, regardless of what we might see, feel or hear in this natural world. It's believing His Word without compromise. It's being so confident God will fulfill His promises that no matter how much trouble the devil brings our way we can say like Shadrach, Meshach and Abednego did, "Our God whom we serve... will deliver us" (Daniel 3:17, *AMP)!*

According to the Bible, faith is:

- "The substance of things hoped for, the evidence of things not seen." (Hebrews 11:1)
- "The victory that overcometh the world." (1 John 5:4)

- A force so powerful it will move the mountains in our lives. (Mark 11:23)
- So valuable, it is truly "more precious than gold." (1 Peter 1:7)

But it doesn't become ours simply because we want it. You can't just decide, "I'm going to live by faith," and let that be the end of it. You have to back up your decision with action. You have to open up your Bible and find out what God has to say, because "faith cometh by hearing, and hearing by the word of God" (Romans 10:17).

Anyone who will spend enough time in the Word can be a faith person. I could give a Bible to a beggar on the street and if he would read it, meditate on it and act like what it says is true, he could prosper. By this time next year, his poverty trial could be over. He and his circumstances could be so completely transformed that he wouldn't even seem like the same person.

Such transformations don't take place, however, just because someone reads an occasional scripture now and then. They don't happen to people who just have an easy-going, take-it-or-leave-it kind of attitude toward the Bible. They only happen in the lives of people who are seriously committed to knowing and doing what God says.

"For thus says the Lord...Seek Me [inquire for and of Me and require Me as you require food] and you shall live!" (Amos 5:4, *AMP).*

This is the first key to overcoming any trouble you'll ever face. It's the primary secret to overcoming faith: Make God and His Word as important to you as the physical food you eat.

Most likely, you rarely go very long without eating natural food. You're very diligent about it. I am too. So is Ken. Every evening at 5:30, we are at the dinner table. If I'm not there, Ken wants to know, "Where are you? It's time to eat!"

That's the way all of us, as born-again believers, should be about the Word of God. We should be as loyal to it as we are to the dinner table. After all, God's Word is spiritual food! It nourishes our spirit just as physical food nourishes our body.

You can't go far physically without food in the natural and you can't go far spiritually without spending time in the Word. You need to be feeding on it every day!

Actually, when you're going through a fiery test or a trial, you should feed on the Word as often as possible all day long. Instead of wasting time watching secular television or doing some other silly thing, you should get into the Word and stay there. If you'll do that, you'll be well on your way to walking in victory, because when you require the Word the same way you require physical food, God says, "You shall live!"

Don't Take the Road of Least Resistance

"But I *have* been spending time in the Word," you might say, "and nothing has changed yet!"

Well, just stick with it. Don't quit now! If you quit you won't have any hope at all. So keep giving God something to work with. Stay in faith—and while you're at it, make sure your behaving matches your believing.

That's what Shadrach, Meshach and Abednego did. They not only believed God's Word in their hearts, they honored Him with their actions. They obeyed God's commands and became living illustrations of Isaiah 33:14-15: "Who among us can dwell with that devouring fire? Who among us can dwell with those everlasting burnings? He who walks righteously and speaks uprightly..." *(AMP).*

If you want to be a person who comes through the fire without getting burned, you must do the same. You must not only believe right on the inside, you must do right on the outside. You must be obedient to the Lord's commands.

"But I thought you said faith is what matters!"

It is—and obedience is inseparable from faith.

Think about it. If we believe what God says,

we're going to do what He tells us to do. We're going to walk uprightly and talk uprightly, even when we're faced with trying situations like sickness, poverty or persecution.

Don't misunderstand me. I'm not suggesting that as faith people we never stumble or miss it. I'm just saying that when we do, we are quick to repent. We don't try to hide from God or justify our disobedient actions. We just say, "Lord, I was wrong. Please forgive me. I plead the blood of Jesus and receive its cleansing power. I ask You to help me and give me grace so I'll never do that again."

Then we get right back on track. We go back to walking and talking in line with God's Word. As a result, when trials do come, we have the confidence we need to stand against the devil, who is the one behind them. We can shake our fingers in his face and tell him to get his hands off our health, our finances and our families in the Name of Jesus!

"But Gloria, I'm not sure the devil will listen to me."

Then you need to study what the New Testament says about the subject. It plainly teaches that as born-again believers we have authority over the devil, and when we resist him he flees from us (James 4:7). It also says that we're the ones responsible to keep the devil out of our lives and give him no place (Ephesians 4:27).

Of course, even Christians who know these things sometimes get lazy and fail to act on them. I was reminded of this a few years ago when Ken and I were on the road preaching. We'd finished ministering in Detroit and had arrived in Milwaukee where we were scheduled to minister again. When we got to the hotel on Saturday night, I was rather tired. So I got into my pajamas and climbed into bed. "I'm taking the road of least resistance!" I said.

As I spoke those words, I realized that's what many Christians do when it comes to dealing with the devil. They take the road of least resistance. When sickness tries to come on them or they're faced with some other kind of trial, they just put on their spiritual jammies, climb into the bed and let the devil run over them. They just hide under the covers and hope God will do something to help.

That's a recipe for failure!

The devil is the thief. He comes into our lives "to steal, and to kill, and to destroy." Jesus came that we might "have life, and that

[we] might have it more abundantly" (John 10:10). If we want to enjoy the abundant life Jesus has provided, we must receive it by faith, stand up to the devil and resist him.

We must say, "No you don't, thief! You're not coming into my family. You're not stealing from my bank account. You're not destroying my health. I will not tolerate you in any part of my life. In Jesus' Name, I cast you out! Now, GO!"

Do you know whose voice the devil hears when you say those things? He hears Jesus, because Jesus is the One who whipped him in the pit of hell. Jesus is the One who "having spoiled principalities and powers, he made a show of them openly, triumphing over them in it" (Colossians 2:15). Jesus is the One who stripped the devil of all his power and left him with absolutely nothing, and gave us His Name to use!

All the devil has to use against us now is lies! He doesn't have any power that we don't give him. So don't give him anything to work with. Don't give him your words. Don't give him your actions. Don't yield to him even one iota of your faith.

Instead, give it all to Jesus. Give God everything to work with in your life and give no place to the devil!

I will warn you though, in spite of the fact that the devil is a major loser, he does have one thing going for him. He is a persistent cuss. He's not triumphant but he is tenacious. So you have to be aggressive with him.

Ken used to illustrate this by describing how his mother would have reacted if an old slop hog had ever gotten into her living room. That was always easy for me to envision because Ken's mother was a bold woman and she had white living room furniture. If some filthy hog had ever dared to get near that furniture, she would have kicked it out of the house fast!

She wouldn't have talked softly to it. She wouldn't have gently asked it to leave. She would have gone after it tooth and nail. She not only would have shouted, she would have grabbed the broom and beaten the tar out of that hog.

We ought to be the same way. After all, spiritually speaking, we have a white living room, too. We've been washed clean by the blood of Jesus and made white as snow. Our lives have been put together by God and He wants us to live abundantly.

So let's do it! Let's live by faith, take authority

over the devil and triumph over every trouble. Let's come through every fiery trial like Shadrach, Meshach and Abednego—unharmed and smelling like a rose!

Prayer for Salvation and Baptism in the Holy Spirit

Heavenly Father, I come to You in the Name of Jesus. Your WORD says, "Whosoever shall call on the name of The LORD shall be saved" (Acts 2:21). I am calling on You. I pray and ask Jesus to come into my heart and be LORD over my life according to Romans 10:9–10: "If thou shalt confess with thy mouth The LORD Jesus, and shalt believe in thine heart that God hath raised him from the dead, thou shalt be saved. For with the heart man believeth unto righteousness; and with the mouth confession is made unto salvation." I do that now. I confess that Jesus is LORD, and I believe in my heart that God raised Him from the dead.

I am now reborn! I am a Christian—a child of Almighty God! I am saved! You also said in Your WORD, "If ye then, being evil, know how to give good gifts unto your children: HOW MUCH MORE shall your heavenly Father give the Holy Spirit to them that ask him?" (Luke 11:13). I'm also asking You to fill me with the Holy Spirit. Holy Spirit, rise up within me as I praise God. I fully expect to speak with other tongues as You give me the utterance (Acts 2:4). In Jesus' Name. Amen!

Begin to praise God for filling you with the Holy Spirit. Speak those words and syllables you receive—not in your own language, but the language given to you by the Holy Spirit. You have to use your own voice. God will not force you to speak. Don't be concerned with how it sounds. It is a heavenly language!

Continue with the blessing God has given you and pray in the spirit every day.

You are a born-again, Spirit-filled believer. You'll never be the same!

Find a good church that boldly preaches God's WORD and obeys it. Become part of a church family who will love and care for you as you love and care for them.

We need to be connected to each other. It increases our strength in God. It's God's plan for us.

Make it a habit to watch the *Believer's Voice of Victory* television broadcast and become a doer of The WORD, who is blessed in his doing (James 1:22-25).

About the Author

Gloria Copeland is a noted author and minister of the gospel whose teaching ministry is known throughout the world. Believers worldwide know her through Believers' Conventions, Victory Campaigns, magazine articles, teaching audios and videos, and the daily and Sunday *Believer's Voice of Victory* television broadcast, which she hosts with her husband, Kenneth Copeland. She is known for Healing School, which she began teaching and hosting in 1979 at KCM meetings. Gloria delivers the Word of God and the keys to victorious Christian living to millions of people every year.

Gloria is author of the New York Times best-seller, *God's Master Plan for Your Life* and *Live Long, Finish Strong,* as well as numerous other favorites, including *God's Will for You, Walk With God, God's Will Is Prosperity, Hidden Treasures* and *To Know Him*. She has also co-authored several books with her husband, including *Family Promises, Healing Promises* and the best-selling daily devotionals, *From Faith to Faith* and *Pursuit of His Presence.*

She holds an honorary doctorate from Oral Roberts University. In 1994, Gloria was voted Christian Woman of the Year, an honor conferred on women whose example demonstrates outstanding Christian leadership. Gloria is also the co-founder and vice president of Kenneth Copeland Ministries in Fort Worth, Texas.

Materials to Help You Receive Your Healing by Gloria Copeland

Books

* * And Jesus Healed Them All
* * God's Prescription for Divine Health
* * God's Will for Your Healing
* * Harvest of Health
* Words That Heal (gift book with CD enclosed)

Audio Resources

Be Made Whole—Live Long, Live Healthy
God Is a Good God
God Wants You Well
Healing Confessions (CD and minibook)
Healing School

DVD Resources

Be Made Whole—Live Long, Live Healthy
Know Him As Healer

* Available in Spanish

Believer's Voice of
VICTORY
VICTORY
Whatever
YOU NEED TO
DO

We're Here for You!®

Your growth in God's WORD and your victory in Jesus are at the very center of our hearts. In every way God has equipped us, we will help you deal with the issues facing you, so you can be the **victorious overcomer** He has planned for you to be.

The mission of Kenneth Copeland Ministries is about all of us growing and going together. Our prayer is that you will take full advantage of all The LORD has given us to share with you.

Wherever you are in the world, you can watch the *Believer's Voice of Victory* broadcast on television (check your local listings), the Internet at kcm.org, or on our digital Roku channel.

Our website, **kcm.org,** gives you access to every resource we've developed for your victory. And, you can find contact information for our international offices in Africa, Asia, Australia, Canada, Europe, Ukraine and our headquarters in the United States.

Each office is staffed with devoted men and women, ready to serve and pray with you. You can contact the worldwide office nearest you for assistance, and you can call us for prayer at our U.S. number, +1-817-852-6000, 24 hours every day!

We encourage you to connect with us often and let us be part of your everyday walk of faith!

Jesus Is LORD!

Kenneth & Gloria Copeland

Kenneth and Gloria Copeland

Chapter Eight

COLD WIND CREPT down the collar of Abe's jacket like the icy fingers of death. His knees were wet from kneeling in the dewy grass. He had returned to hide behind this same oak tree for the last two days. He had been so sure that she would show. If this Harvey woman had been Troy's lover, and instinct told him she was, Troy would spend time at her gravesite, especially if she perceived her world as falling down around her ears. But as he sat there pondering those things, it occurred to him that if Troy had not accepted her girlfriend's death, why would she go to her grave? Wouldn't that have to be a form of acceptance in itself? Still, she wasn't sleeping at home, so he had no other way to find her but to wait here like an idiot. And then he would not let her out of his sight again.

He shuddered as the smell of earth and manure drifted to him. He had always hated graveyards. Hell, he hated dead people. That was one of the reasons he had become a doctor, to retard death if he could; and now here he was, hiding behind a tree in a graveyard, waiting for someone who might not even be alive. The fact that this cemetery had flat plaques instead of the traditional tombstones should have made him feel better, but it didn't. Kneeling as he was, it would be easy to fool himself into believing he was looking out over a park or a meadow. The fact that there were plaques with the names of deceased men, women, and children nestled in the grass on all sides of him made it impossible for him to relax. *This is not your failure,* he reminded himself.

A low, ticking sound coming from the trees above his head alerted him before any moisture hit his skin. "That's just perfect," he said out loud and pulled the collar of his jacket around his neck, as if it could somehow protect him from the rain. He looked up at the gloom of the sky and silently cursed his inability to put up an umbrella. He looked over at the top of the bridge. On an evening such as this, the sound of cars running over the top of it would be heard from here. Today, there was nothing, of course, and that's how he wanted it. He would be able to hear her long before she reached the graveyard and follow her to wherever she was holing up when she left.

Over the next two hours, his annoyance and anger doubled. He had expected to be back in his office by now, and as the evening crept toward dark, his certainty that she wouldn't come intensified. He had relied on the wrong kind of people: three charity cases and a fucking hermit. He would have to go back with his tail—he cut the thought off because he heard a slight click and then nothing. He leaned into the tree, the bark cutting into the softness of his palm, and waited. Twenty seconds later, he blinked, and there she was, turning into the gate and avoiding the tire puncture grates as she must have done many times in the past. His heart picked up a beat and he grinned at the approaching figure. As he had assumed, she did not look left or right. Her gaze was riveted to the plaque. Still, he hunkered down behind the tree and leaned close, cursing himself for not thinking of watching the area sooner. She didn't linger, just rode her bike to the curb, jumped off, and carried the bike up the slight hill to Patricia's marker. She laid the dilapidated bike down and then sat down herself.

"Damn it, speak up," he said under his breath and then sat still. She had stopped speaking and was looking in his direction. If he'd still been crouching instead of sitting on the ground, she might have caught a glimpse of him. When she turned back to the plaque she seemed calmer. After a few long minutes, she stood and picked up her bike, and walked toward the street. She easily avoided the tire puncture grates and rode away as if unaware of the rain and in no particular hurry to get anywhere.

"Good," Abe said aloud when she was far enough away that he was sure she wouldn't see him. He crab-walked to a pile of leaves and brushed them aside until his hands hit the handle bars of the bicycle he had taken that morning. He thought it was called a beach cruiser, but he wasn't sure. What he was sure of was that it made no sounds when he rode it unless he hit a pebble or used the handbrake. The bike would allow him to follow Troy, and if he stayed far enough behind her and she didn't look back, he would be able to see where she'd been staying.

ONE GUTTERAL MOAN warned Jake of its presence long before it appeared around a corner. He let it grab him, let it bite his neck, let all but the last of his energy seep from his body before he began to fight. He raised his gun and fired. The zombie fell back and Jake fired again, this time right between its eyes. He watched it sink to the floor, and blood spilled from its body almost as an afterthought—as if someone had opened an artery in the thing. Jake smiled with vague amusement at the carcass. He had played this game so many times that he often had to let himself be drained of some of his energy in order to make it interesting. He watched himself—the female version of himself—limp down the hall of a mansion. He didn't bother to open any of the doors because he knew what was on the other side of every one of them. An elixir here, a gun there. None of it was any use to him. He was on a mission to make it through the game as fast as he could because at the end, he would be given the key. It was the one thing that would save the doomed citizens of the city from the disease that had turned them into the zombies. The microwave beeped and a low whine to his left bought him back to reality. The smell of buttered popcorn and rotting dog flesh permeated the air.

"Smells like we finally got some that didn't burn, huh boy?"

Malice stood up on thin shaky legs. He looked at Jake with soft, brown eyes and licked his lips, as if to say, "Yes, I'm hungry, too."

He pushed pause on the wireless game controller and stood up. He had found the dog eating garbage out of a tipped trashcan in the alley behind the shoe store where he'd gotten his Aaron Austin's. The dog—he had named him Malice because it sounded good—had followed him home without much coaxing.

Malice wouldn't let Jake near the wound on his head and, from the look and smell of it, it wasn't getting any better. He would have to do something about it soon, but for now, Jake liked having the dog around, even if he was unable to play fetch. There were dark droplets of blood on the light-colored carpet. Mommy and Daddy always said pets were dirty. Not that that mattered anymore.

Jake could hear the dog's labored breathing as he followed him into the kitchen. Malice whined as Jake poured the popcorn into a bowl for himself. He was careful to scoop any extras off the counter and back into the bowl.

"Okay now we have to find something for you to eat, right?" Jake rummaged around until he found two cans of corned beef hash in the cabinet and mixed it with a few things he found beneath the sink.

"You're going to love this shit, aren't you?"

Jake took the whimper to mean that the dog wasn't picky. The wound on Malice's head no longer seemed to bother him as he pranced from side to side and licked his lips in anticipation of his meal. Jake got down a large serving platter. His mother's mother had given it to her when she married his daddy. He dumped the can of hash on it and mixed the other ingredients in and, at the last minute, decided to add an egg from the refrigerator. He gave the mixture a cautious sniff. It smelled like what he imagined dog food would smell like, and he placed the platter on the floor. To his surprise, the dog did not leap forward. The only sign that Malice was even excited about the meal was his black, bushy tail swishing back and forth across the tile floor.

"What are you waiting for?" He felt a bit miffed that his creation was being refused. The dog had never turned it down before, and he had made this at least two times since bringing the dog home. "Eat it."

The dog just stared and Jake realized he wanted him to leave so that he could eat his food in peace. "All right," Jake said and walked away as if returning to the living room. He stopped after he had turned the corner and peered into the kitchen. The dog was looking at the platter, but still wasn't eating. He waited, his tongue lolling out every so often, as if tasting the air. He sniffed, and then sniffed again before taking a cautious nip at the food. Jake was beginning to fear he had added too many things to the concoction when Malice began to eat.

Jake smiled and headed toward his parents' room.

Both were positioned on their backs. Father's hand was in Mother's. Her hair had been brushed out across her pillow until it gleamed. Jake sat on the side of the bed closest to his mother. He wished he had thought to steal a digital camera. The one they had required the film to be developed. He reached across both sleeping figures for the cigarettes and matches on the nightstand. Daddy was always "finishing the last pack" so that he could quit and had been since Jake had known him. Jake lit one of the cigarettes and inhaled. He blew the smoke out and watched as it shrouded the bodies in a white fog. He needed to finish his game and maybe get some sleep. He left the room closing the door behind him. As he passed the kitchen he glanced in. Malice was still bent over the platter. His hind quarters quivered as he licked the platter so hard that it was moving across Mommy's terracotta floors with little scraping noises.

Jake grinned and drew more smoke into his lungs and settled in front of the TV. Just before he hit the "resume play" button on his controller, he heard a loud gagging noise and a sneeze. The game's eerie soundtrack killed any possibility of hearing more. Not that he wanted to. He had been right not to put any water down. Less mess to clean up that way.

Jake watched his female alter ego, a messenger bag filled with herbs and extra ammunition slung across her body, limp into the depths of the warehouse where she would have to fight her final showdown.

RAIN AND CLOUDS brought darkness sooner than it should have. Emma had decided that Troy would hole up somewhere until the storm passed. She had been dozing off and on beneath the afghan that Troy slept under. The sound of the buzzer ripped her from the warm embrace of a dream that did not end with a scream.

She sat up, uncertain whether the sound had been part of the dream. The streetlights had not flickered to life yet, which meant it was not quite half-past seven. She looked in the direction of the door just as the buzzer sounded again. Emma stood up, and foregoing the cane, walked as fast as she could to the door, said "yes" into the speaker as if she didn't know who could be at her door at that hour.

"Emma?" Worry colored Troy's voice.

"Yes?" Emma said, smiling at the speaker, then muttered, "Shit," and released the speak button so that she could hear Troy's response.

"Can I come up, or are you angry with me?"

"I'm not...." Troy was too far away for Emma to sense anything. She hit the release button for the front door and took a deep breath. She had come back. She hadn't doubted that she would, even if it hadn't been tonight. She removed the chains and the lock and moved back to the window seat. Emma had to find someplace to put her hands and settled on picking up her book.

"It's open," she called out and was surprised at how good she felt when Troy walked in, carrying her bike. Troy let her bag drop to the floor and stood there, dripping on Emma's hardwood floors. Emma took in all of her as if she hadn't just seen her that very morning.

"I'm soaked," she said. Her smile was apologetic.

Emma jumped up, ignoring her protesting knee, and went to the linen closet.

"I'll get you some towels." She pulled down two large fluffy towels and handed one to Troy, then stood there holding the other, unsure whether she should help or not.

"Sorry. I should have left my bike outside. Habit." Troy turned as if to open the door.

And deprive me of the pleasure of watching you bring it in? "No, you can leave it right there."

"It'll drip all over the floor," Troy said, her hand still on the doorknob.

"It's okay. I have a lot of towels."

Troy smiled and leaned the bike against the wall. She ran the towel through her curls, leaving them askew, and then began to dry the floor with Emma's best towels.

She had to be honest with herself. She was relieved that Troy had returned. Even if food weren't an issue, she liked having her there, even when she was asleep. Emma used the moment to give herself some distance.

"You must be cold. Why don't you get into a hot shower, and I'll put some soup on when I hear you getting out."

"That sounds good, thanks. Ah, shit, I forgot the food."

Emma laughed, and Troy ran her fingers through her wild curls. Troy looked as if she was considering going back outside.

Emma was surprised at the ache she felt in her chest. The fact that this woman would go back in the rain to get her food when she wouldn't even get it for herself made her feel so sad, but cared for. "I haven't eaten the stuff you gave me yesterday."

Troy looked surprised. "Why not?"

"I wasn't that hungry after you left." It was a lie. She had been a little hungry. But she wasn't sure when or if Troy would be back and she wanted to make the food last as long as she could.

Troy's body had become rigid. "You didn't think I'd be back."

Emma hesitated and then decided to admit the truth. "I wasn't sure."

Troy looked offended. "Look, I know we don't know each other, but I try not to lie. Sometimes I can't do what I want to, but my word is all I've got to offer, so I try to keep it."

Troy was struggling with something. Emma could sense it, but it was so deep and convoluted that she couldn't figure it out. The words meant more to Troy than what she felt comfortable saying. Emma understood. Troy was trying to tell her that she wouldn't lie to her, at least not on purpose. She was asking Emma to trust her. Emma met Troy's eyes, giving her a little smile—the "thank you" she couldn't manage to vocalize. To Emma's great relief, Troy accepted it and walked into the bathroom, shutting the door behind her.

The tears were as unexpected as they were immediate. It was as if the closing of the bathroom door opened another portal inside of Emma. She scooted back against the pillow of the window seat and pulled her knees up, ignoring the dull pain. She wrapped her arms around her legs, closed her eyes and let the tears flow.

It was relief. Pure, simple relief. She hadn't known she was lonely. Sure, she had been worried when the groceries didn't come, but more than anything, she was afraid that she would die as she had lived. Alone and scared. And now, Troy was telling her she didn't have to. The touch to Emma's shoulder was such a shock that she let go of her legs and began to fight. Troy caught her arms and held on to her until she was sure that Emma realized it was her.

Emma shook her head and tried to speak. The stern look on Troy's face told her she would not be shrugged off. Emma allowed herself to be pulled into a warm, but not dry, embrace. Emma sobbed into Troy's chest. She felt compassion sweep over her, and then a deep sadness that made her cry even more. It was a slow realization, but so steady that she knew that it was coming from so deep within Troy that she wasn't even aware of it herself.

Why would Troy blame herself? How could any of this be her fault? Emma struggled to catch her breath and allowed her arms to loop around Troy's slim waist. She squeezed her eyes shut and pulled Troy close.

"I hate this," she mumbled. "I don't even know you that well and here I am, snotting onto what's probably your favorite shirt."

"Nah," Troy said. "I stole this shirt to make myself feel better."

Emma leaned back so that she could see Troy's face.

"It was a hundred and fifty dollars!"

Emma continued to stare.

"I left an IOU."

"Nuh uh?"

Troy grinned and said, "I did. I figure if someone comes to get me, it would mean they all woke up. Couple months in jail would be worth that."

Emma laughed a little, but stopped because Troy was looking at her with such concern that Emma felt self-conscious.

"You all right?" Troy didn't pronounce the "l" in *all right*, giving it a lightness that didn't match the concern in her eyes.

"I'm fine."

Troy's arms loosened, but Emma stayed close, her nose and mouth pressed into Troy's stolen shirt. "You sure? 'Cause I'm stinky and soaking wet, and you don't seem to be in any hurry to get away from me."

Emma laughed. Troy *was* soaked, but she was also warm and had a slight spicy scent to her. Emma didn't find it the least bit unpleasant.

"Look, Emma. I know you're scared. I think someone hurt you, and if you ever want to talk..." Troy paused and looked so serious that Emma's heartbeat quickened. "If you ever want to talk, there's no one else here." She said and smiled.

Emma blinked and said, "That's not reassuring."

"What I mean is there's no one to overhear us. I know we're kind of thrown together here, but I want to be your friend."

"That goes two ways, Troy."

Troy opened her mouth to say something and then closed it. "What I'm trying to say is what happened this morning won't happen again. You don't have to be scared of me, and you don't have to be afraid that I won't come back when I leave." Troy looked away and Emma could tell that she was as surprised by her own words as Emma was. She was promising Emma that she would be there for her and they had known each other less then a month.

"Why?" Emma asked. Troy started to stand, but Emma put her hand on her arm to keep her seated. Troy's shirt made her feel clammy and she shivered, but Emma kept her hand there. "Why would you promise something like that when you don't even know me?"

Troy took a deep breath, held it and let it out. "Because I know."

Emma shook her head. "You know what?"

"I know it's more than not getting out much. I know you don't leave at all. I know, because even though I gave you food, you hadn't eaten in so long that you were almost sick."

Emma flushed, and her eyes began to get watery again. "I don't know what you mean."

"Don't be embarrassed."

"I'm not."

"You are."

Anger boiled up from somewhere that Emma didn't know she had. "You don't know anything about me."

"I know someone hurt you, and because of it you're afraid to go outside. I know there isn't a soul awake beyond those doors and you still hide in here. I know that much."

She's right, Emma. Until you can stop being so afraid, until you can walk out that door, until you can trust yourself, you'll have to trust her. Even before this craziness, you had to rely on someone. They didn't have a name, but they brought you food so you didn't have to put yourself out there. And now you have to depend on Troy to do the same thing. Emma felt as if her life had been turned upside down.

Troy stood up. "I better get to that shower."

"Yeah." Emma looked toward the bathroom and glanced at Troy. She was shivering and now Emma could see the raised flesh of her arms. Her clothing clung to her hips and the narrow curve of her waist. The t-shirt was so thin that Emma could make out a small hoop on Troy's navel just before Troy turned away. *I wonder if she has a tattoo. Yes. She has to have one. I wonder where? Oh geez, stop, Emma. Stop right now.*

"Oh, I came back out to ask if I could borrow some sweats."

"Yeah, sure. I have plenty." Emma stood up, took another glance at Troy's sheer shirt and almost tripped over her own feet.

"I can get them myself, if you don't mind me rummaging through your stuff."

"No, you don't know where anything is. I'll get them. Go hop in the shower before you freeze to death. I'll just leave them outside the door for you."

Troy needed no further encouragement and seconds after Emma heard the door shut, she heard two heavy thunks and a thwack as Troy pulled off her shoes, followed by what sounded like her sodden cargo pants.

The pipes squealed and then howled as water came crashing through them, and Emma heard the glass doors slide back. She could almost see Troy getting into the hot shower.

Emma felt like someone had just draped a warm blanket over her—so comforting that she felt the slightest tingling between her legs. "Whoa," she said out loud and did her best to tune out Troy to give her some privacy.

Chapter Nine

TROY WALKED INTO the living room drying her hair with a towel. Emma hadn't moved from the window seat, but now she was pretending to read. She didn't look up as she would have in the past. Didn't smile, didn't ask if she was hungry or wanted to play a board game. *Something's changed.* Troy finished toweling off her hair and stood with her feet apart and looked at Emma. Her mouth was forming the words before she even knew what she was going to ask.

"Do you know how to braid hair?"

The question must have caught Emma off guard because she blinked and answered immediately. "Yeah, why?"

"Because I don't know how, and I'd like my hair braided."

Emma set her book down and swung around so that she could put her feet on the floor. Before Emma could utter another word, Troy slid to the floor and scooted back until her back was pressed against the wood of the seat and both of her shoulders were bracketed against Emma's thighs.

"I'll need a..."

Troy held up a large red brush.

"Thanks," Emma said.

"Where did you learn to braid?"

"One of my volunteers taught me."

"Volunteers?"

"I ran a non-profit clinic." Emma paused, and then said, "Ida Glass Clinic of Burnside?"

Troy turned around and placed her arm on Emma's knee. "You ran that clinic? That's where I went when I got doored by a freaking Bug Be-Gone van. I felt well taken care of."

Emma grinned and Troy could see the pride in her face. She turned around and let Emma brush another section of her hair.

"You have a comb, too?"

"Uh huh," Troy said as she handed the comb back to Emma. *Pure heaven. This is pure heaven.* Troy felt Emma draw the comb through her hair before her nimble fingers were working Troy's hair into tight cornrows.

"You always come this prepared?" Emma asked.

Troy could tell by her muffled voice that she was gripping the comb between her teeth while she was braiding. Emma's teacher had been thorough.

"Yup, what's that saying? Come right, or don't come at all?"

Emma didn't answer and Troy was going to repeat herself, but Emma spoke first.

"Um, you know that's from a condom commercial, right?" Emma asked in a garbled voice.

"It is not." Even as she denied it, she heard a hip female voice intoning, "Tell him to come right, or don't come at all."

"Damn it, I will never sleep with the TV on again." Troy could feel Emma's body shaking. "Go ahead, laugh it up," Troy groused. Emma made a choking noise behind her.

Troy crossed her arms in front of her chest. "And why do you know the dialogue to a condom commercial, anyway? You don't even have a TV up in here," Troy said. That must have been the final straw for Emma because whatever restraint she had been employing broke and she dissolved into a fit of laughter. A warm hand rested on Troy's shoulder and any embarrassment she felt faded.

"All right, so we've established that I'm an idiot. In my own defense, I think there's subliminal programming in those damn commercials," Troy said but she was smiling. She loved the sound of Emma's laughter.

Emma's chuckles dwindled, and she ran her fingers through Troy's hair as if she had forgotten that she was supposed to be braiding it. Troy stifled a moan just in time.

"We had a carton of those condoms in the public bathrooms at the clinic." Emma's voice sounded wistful, and Troy wondered why she would stay away from something she seemed to enjoy. "I'd see that phrase every time I went in there. Always made me cringe."

"You know what's funny? If you and I had met, I don't know, at the clinic or wherever, you wouldn't have given me the time of day."

Emma slapped Troy's shoulder with the comb.

"Ouch," Troy yelped.

Emma laughed. "Oh, stop it. I didn't hurt you. And that's not true, anyway."

"So, you're trying to tell me that if I walked up to you at the clinic and said, 'Excuse me, miss? I'm having a bad hair day. Would you braid my hair?' You'd be like, 'sure, come snuggle up between my legs and...'" Emma popped Troy again.

"Okay, that hurt." Troy rubbed her shoulder and squirmed.

"That's what you get for being weird. Now, stop moving around so much."

"I like your tattoo, by the way." Emma's voice sounded close to her ear, and Troy's hand went to cover the two intertwined dolphins on her shoulder.

"Thank you."

"Does it mean anything?"

"Yeah, supposedly dolphins find one mate and that's who they're with for the rest of their lives."

"That's kind of sweet; I don't think I knew that."

There was a dark side to the story. Sometimes one of the dolphins died, and the other one was left swimming alone. She'd keep that part to herself.

"Emma?"

"Hmm?"

"Someone hurt you, didn't they?" She wanted to ask, *"How'd you go from running a clinic to being too afraid too leave your home?"* but she didn't want to hurt Emma's feelings.

Emma didn't answer right away and Troy wondered if she had already overstepped her boundaries. Just because you sleep on the woman's couch doesn't mean you have the right to know her life history. "I don't mean to get in your business. You don't need to tell me if you don't want to."

"No, it's all right. I was wondering when you would get around to asking." Emma stopped brushing and ran her fingers through Troy's hair. Her voice was low and shaken as if she hadn't expected Troy to ask even though she may have considered it. "I never thought of it as a secret, but I don't think I've ever had to talk about it with anyone. Everyone either knew or they didn't need to know."

Emma's fingers stopped moving, and Troy realized that maybe she wasn't ready to hear what had happened. The thought startled her so much that she spoke out. "If you don't want to tell me, I understand."

"I want to tell you." That was all she said for several long minutes. Troy could smell the raspberry tea she was having and it made her feel closer, almost protective, as she felt Emma struggling with her words.

"I was leaving the clinic late."

Troy tensed. She closed her eyes and willed herself to breathe.

"It was so cold outside that the locks on my car froze. Or maybe he put something in them." Emma's fingers had curled into a tight ball tugging at Troy's hair almost painfully. "The police never said anything, so I never thought about it either way."

"What happened?" *Stop, don't ask any more. You don't really want to know. No, that's not true. You do want to know...if someone's hurt her... Oh god, no.*

"He didn't rape me." The words came out like a whisper. No, more like a mantra, as if Emma were reminding herself of something and had been doing so for a long time. "He just ..."

"Beat the shit out of you." Troy finished the statement for her. She welcomed the anger over the fear that stole over her now.

Emma went on as if Troy hadn't spoken. Her fingers had tangled themselves even tighter in Troy's hair. "He used to come to the clinic every so often with bumps and bruises. If he'd have just asked me for my money, I'd have given him everything I had. He didn't even ask."

"Emma..." Troy reached up and placed a hand over Emma's clenched fist. Emma jerked as if Troy had hit her.

"Oh, sweetie, I'm sorry. Was I hurting you?" The endearment came out of nowhere, but it felt right. Troy thrilled at being called "sweetie." When she looked back, Emma's face had turned red.

"No, I just—it made me angry to think that someone would hurt you."

"He wasn't a bad guy. He was just sick and desperate and angry at one of the doctors. I was in the wrong place at the wrong time."

"If you say so," Troy said and turned around so that Emma wouldn't see her face. Emma was trying to tell her that this man wasn't responsible for his actions. That he was sick. But even a dog knew better than to bite the hand that fed him. Emma seemed to be apologizing for having pulled at Troy's hair by rubbing her fingers over Troy's scalp. Troy leaned back and forced the muscle in her jaw to loosen. Emma inhaled and Troy felt the soft breeze of her exhale touch her shoulder.

"Okay?" Emma asked.

Troy closed her eyes and squeezed Emma's thigh for an answer. She would try to figure out why she had been so angry later.

Emma massaged her scalp for a few moments more." How did you get this scar? Must've hurt."

"Which one?"

"This one." Emma ran the pad of her thumb over a small scar just above Troy's right earlobe.

"Ahh, some guy opened his car door without looking first."

"That happen often?"

Troy shook her head. "Not a lot. It's called getting doored. People look for cars, not bikes. See this one right here?" Troy separated her hair and pointed to a small bump on the right side of her head. "That happened because a guy walked in front of my bike. I stopped so hard I went right over the handlebars. And this one," she propped her arms up on Emma's thighs and leaned her head back so that Emma could see the scar buried in her right eyebrow, "was from a rock that popped up when a MAX train went by. You should have seen the gore. It looked way worse than it was."

"Your job sounds dangerous."

Troy straightened and shrugged. "I'd be on a bike whether I had the job or not. Besides I'm careful."

"Didn't your family worry?"

"I don't have any family."

"I'm sorry. I didn't know."

"It's okay. I've never had any. You don't miss what you never knew."

Emma went quiet and the lie hung heavy between them. Troy felt compelled to continue even though she could count on half of one hand the number of people she had shared her story with. "I was left on a pew in a Catholic church when I was about two months old. I don't know who my parents are. I know I'm mixed heritage, but I don't know what with."

"Does that bother you?"

"Sometimes. Not as much as it did when I was young. People want kids that look like them."

"I think that's changing, isn't it? People adopt babies from overseas that don't look like them."

"Yeah, but why? There are plenty of children in America who need homes."

Troy thought Emma wasn't going to answer her. She had to remind herself that talking about things like that sometimes made people uncomfortable. Besides, Emma was probably thinking. "What difference does it make now?"

"I don't know." Emma's answer was slow as if she had been pondering Troy's question. "I do know that if I ever have children, I won't care what they look like or where they come from."

"Me either," Troy said, and something hung at the back of her throat, and Troy cleared it. "What about you? Do you have any family out there? I could check on them next time I'm out, if they're in the area."

"I wish you could. My only close relatives are my parents. They live most of the year on a cruise ship."

Troy turned around, "You're kidding me, right? People do that kind of thing? Full time?"

"Yes, they do. I get an e-card from them every so often." A flicker of worry crossed Emma's face.

"I'm sure they're fine." Troy said, but even as she reassured Emma, she wondered how long a boat the size of a cruise ship could avoid running into land without someone awake to navigate it.

Emma continued speaking as if she hadn't heard Troy's attempt at reassurance. Or maybe she had heard, and her mind had traveled the same path as Troy's. "My grandmother died—almost four years ago." Emma sounded surprised as if she hadn't realized how much time had passed.

"Were you two close?"

"She was my hero." Emma's voice sounded wistful and sadder than Troy would have expected after four years.

"How did she...?"

"She had a heart defect none of us knew about. She was too busy taking care of other people to worry about herself. She just didn't come to work one day. I knew something was wrong when she was late. I was told she died, without pain, in her sleep."

"I'm so sorry, Em." Troy turned to look at Emma. "She must have been a great person."

"The clinic was her life. That's why I wanted to keep it open."

"I don't know what messengers would do without free clinics. It's not like any of us can afford health insurance."

"That's why she started the clinic in the first place." Pride and loss were both evident in Emma's eyes and voice.

"So, you took over the day-to-day of the clinic?"

"Yup. I wasn't the best person for the job. I'm not a doctor, but I think that's what Ida would have wanted me to do."

"Who's running it now?"

Emma looked uncomfortable. "I make most of the money decisions." She looked at the desk where her computer sat. "My assistant handles the day-to-day administration though. I trust her implicitly. She was like the daughter my grandmother wished my mother had been."

"It sounds like you might have been more like a daughter, too." Troy turned around so that Emma could continue working on another cornrow.

"Sorry, I'm kind of slow at this. It's been a long time since I've done it."

"S'okay." She turned back around and propped her arms on Emma's thighs. "I got no place to be." Troy sighed and Emma knew without looking that she had her eyes closed.

"Come on. You mean to tell me a gorgeous girl like you doesn't have anywhere else she can be on a Friday night?"

"Is it Friday?" Troy asked.

"I don't know. I'm just sayin'..." Emma said around the comb in her mouth.

Troy chuckled and shook her head. Emma mumbled something, which Troy took to mean 'sit still.'

"Yes, ma'am," she said, liking the way it felt to sit with her arms propped on Emma's thighs. "It isn't like I dated much before the whole world went on siesta."

"No girlfriend?"

Troy grinned but decided not to tease Emma about assuming she was gay. "No. I haven't dated anyone for over a year and a half." Troy was surprised to find that saying this didn't hurt as much as it had just months before. "I don't know many women who would be all that interested in dating a dusty little bike messenger."

"Here, hold this." Emma handed the comb to Troy and leaned closer. Troy could smell her shower gel. "I would think women would be breaking their legs to get to you. Besides, you're not dusty. You take more showers than anyone I know."

"I bet I sweat more than anyone you know, too."

"This is true."

"You know, you're not so good on the ego."

Emma snorted, but didn't comment.

"How about you?"

"How about me what?"

"I just figured you wouldn't have those magazines over there if you didn't like the ladies."

Emma went quiet. She looked as if she couldn't figure out if she wanted to blush or laugh. She must have settled on the latter. "I haven't seen anyone in...in a while."

"You know, *The Minge* went out of business last year."

"You're kidding? I had no idea."

Troy wondered if the subject of her sexuality was embarrassing to Emma. She herself had never had any hang-ups about being a lesbian. There were always so many other things to worry about. She knew not everyone felt the same way she did, though. She decided light teasing was the best way to put Emma at ease.

"So, would you have looked at me? Asked me out, I mean, if things weren't like they are?"

"I never asked anyone out. I think I'm too shy for that."

"Not even a coffee date? A coffee date isn't a real date, you know?"

"It isn't?" Emma frowned. "How is it different?"

"It's almost a date without all the awkwardness of asking. You could just say, 'Let's go have coffee.' Not, 'will you go out with me?'"

Emma laughed. "I've never asked anyone out for coffee, either."

"Me either, but I used to think if I ever did ask someone out, that was the way I'd go about it."

"So your last girlfriend? She was... African-American?"

Troy laughed. "Did you just stumble over that, or were you trying to figure out if 'black' was the proper terminology?"

Emma didn't say anything and Troy hoped she hadn't gone too far with her teasing.

"Don't worry. I have a hard time remembering what's PC and I'm at least half African-American, if not more. But, yes, she was. She had the most beautiful dark skin, and eyes so deep they just swallowed you whole. Her voice was just... I could listen to her speak for hours."

"She sounds beautiful." Was that jealousy she heard in Emma's voice? Troy dismissed the thought immediately.

"She was," Troy agreed. Patricia's beauty had taken an almost surreal quality now. She realized too late that she had left her self open for questions about Patricia when she had slipped and said "was."

"What happened to her?" Even though Troy had expected the question, it startled her when it came.

"She died in a car accident." It was easier for her to say than she'd expected, and because of that, the words felt like a betrayal.

"I'm sorry," Emma said.

Troy couldn't bring herself to say anything more, and Emma continued to braid Troy's hair in silence. Emma had told her so much about herself that she had every right to ask Troy about her life. Why had she given her that opening? Any other time, she had to remind herself that she no longer had anyone to share her life with. *It's not like she's around, is she? Even if those people out there sprang to life, Patricia would still be buried in that cemetery.*

"Are you all right? Do we need to finish this later?"

Emma's question startled her. "I'm sorry. Was I moving around too much? I guess I get antsy sometimes."

"Maybe you should go out for a ride. I can finish your hair later." Emma's hand was resting on her shoulder and Troy started to feel like the room had grown too warm.

"Nah, I guess I just want to do something normal and not worry about what's going on out there, or if it's going to happen to us, or if there are other people out there like us."

"I think this is pretty normal, don't you?" Emma ran her hands through the unbraided side of Troy's hair.

"Are you serious?" Troy closed her eyes enjoying the feeling of Emma's fingers running through her damp hair. "I don't think this is normal at all. I get the impression that you don't have many bike messengers as friends."

"No, but that's because you guys are kind of stuck up."

"Okay, now who's being weird?" Troy turned and was surprised by the serious look on Emma's face. "What's wrong?"

"Never mind." Emma kept moving her hands through Troy's hair. "Troy?"

"Yeah?"

"Would you like to go out with me one night?"

Troy wasn't sure if she had quite heard Emma right. "Are you sure?"

"Uh huh. We could go Dutch, of course," Emma said, but she didn't smile at her own joke.

"When? Now?"

Emma looked toward the window and back at Troy. Troy could see the erratic throbbing pulse at her throat. She realized her mistake. Emma's question had been rhetorical; she hadn't meant right that instant, she had meant one night, which was exactly what she had asked.

Emma saw Troy's disappointment because her words came out in a rush. "Let's go now before I get scared."

Chapter Ten

Standard, Oregon
August
Years Ago

"YOU DON'T NEED to know where I'm going."

Hoyt's voice couldn't have been clearer if The Boy had been in the same room with him. If it hadn't been raining so hard, he would have gone to see if Mr. Mayberry's nephew was visiting. The rain sounded like someone was dropping shovels full of little pebbles on the top of the house. Mr. Mayberry would never let his nephew out in that kind of weather, so he was sitting in the living room reading a book to his grandmother and trying not to hear Hoyt and Pam as they had another fight in their bedroom.

Today was his birthday.

"Why don't you worry about getting this house cleaned up for a change?"

The Boy ignored Pam's answer and turned the page in his Hardy Boys mystery. Grandma liked this one. He could tell, because she would show him her pink gums every time he got animated while reading it to her.

Grandma didn't talk. She hadn't for as long as he could remember. Pam said Grandma had hurt her head when she fell down the stairs when no one was home to help her. But their house didn't have stairs. He had asked Pam about that. He wondered if maybe they had lived somewhere else before he had been born. She just got mad at him and told him to go outside and play even though it was raining. There were pictures on the wall of Hoyt and Pam on their wedding day. There was even one with Grandma in it, too. Mr. Mayberry next door had told him he remembered taking it. Same house as this one and it didn't have stairs. None of the houses in the neighborhood did.

He liked to look at them in their funny looking clothes. It was hard for him to believe that those two happy people in the picture were Pam and Hoyt. They had never been happy. Not that he could remember.

But his eyes were always drawn back to Grandma. In the picture, she was taller than Hoyt. He didn't think people could shrink, but Grandma didn't look that tall anymore. He wasn't sure, because the only time she walked was when she had to go to the pot-chair and then she was always hunched over with her skinny fingers digging into his arm for balance. Her hair had been white back then, too, but it was brushed back nice and neat into one of those knot things some of the teachers at school wore. It hung down her shoulders now, a long limp dirty curtain that hid her face. She had been the only one in the picture who didn't smile, so he couldn't tell if she had teeth back then, but her face didn't look so skinny, and he could see her lips. Maybe lips shrunk, too, because she didn't have any of those anymore.

The sound of Pam's voice interrupted The Boy's thoughts. He couldn't make out what she said, but that didn't matter. He never listened to her anyway. Hoyt was the one who had to be listened to. He was the dangerous one. Pam was just the one that liked to make things hard on all of them. He couldn't blame Hoyt for getting mad at her. She *didn't know how to* cook or clean worth a damn. When Hoyt left, she would just make him do it.

"Goddamn it, I told you it's none of your—" Hoyt's voice boomed through out the house. The whole neighborhood would be able to hear them now. The Boy wondered why they even bothered to go into their bedroom.

He dropped the book face down on his lap and glared at Hoyt and Pam's bedroom door. "I wish he would hit her already." He said it loud enough that anyone in the house interested in hearing what he had to say could have heard. He wasn't worried. The only one who ever listened to him was Grandma. Her gums were showing in one of her soundless grins. Or was she crying? He could never tell with her.

"I don't give a damn if you loaded the fucking wash machine last week. I can't find one sock that matches the other, and why don't you use some bleach for once?" The Boy was always surprised when Hoyt's voice got even louder.

"Least I don't have to go to Bernie Ann's to eat," The Boy said, and his grandmother rocked forward as if agreeing. He had told her about how the food made him sick.

"Why don't *I* wash the clothes? Why don't *I*? 'Cause *I* am the one with a real job in this motherfucking house, remember? You think doing nails part time could even put clothes on your back? I put food in all three of your mouths, and now you want me to wash my own goddamn clothes so you can sit up in here and watch Oprey all day?"

"Oprey?" The Boy repeated the word and grinned at Grandma. "It's 'Oprah,' he is *sooo stupid*." He saw a flash of pink, and this time he was sure she was laughing. Grandma was the only one he could talk to. She listened when he had troubles and never made him feel like he was annoying like Hoyt and Pam did. He had even told her his most powerful secret. The one that could send him to jail if anyone ever knew. That is if Hoyt didn't kill him first.

He had been so angry when Hoyt had made him miss the opening of the show to get sodas. The hairs on his arm stood up and he felt heat at the top of his head when he handed them over, neither Hoyt nor Pam seeming to care that the cans were already open.

He sat down and leaned real close and whispered in Grandma's peeling ear. "I put bleach in both of them.

The Boy needed to go to the bathroom, but he sat still because he didn't want to miss what happened when they drank from the cans. Grandma and he watched as first Pam and then Hoyt took drinks from their cans. He had smelled the lids and didn't notice any strong odor before he brought the cans out. Nothing happened. No death, no hospital, nothing. Hoyt did complain of a stomach ache and went to bed without watching the Simpsons, but he was fine the next day.

The Boy put the book up to the side of his face and leaned in like he was telling a secret. He dropped his voice and squinted his eyes. "All I do is work day in and day out," he growled in an imitation of Hoyt's voice.

"All I do is work day...." Hoyt bellowed, and The Boy giggled. Hoyt was so stupid he didn't realize he said the same every time they had an argument. He hated him, and he hated Pam for picking the same fights that always ended with—

The sound, like an open palm landing on a side of beef and the whimper after should have been no surprise, but he jumped when it happened.

Pam didn't scream. They all knew better than to do that, even Grandma. Crying was okay, but things got worse real fast if you screamed. He didn't look at his grandmother to see if she had that jack-o-lantern look on her face, but he knew she would. The back of his neck prickled. He was afraid to look at her.

The bedroom door slammed back against the wall. Relief flooded through The Boy's body; he'd been scared this was going to be a bad one. The Boy pretended to read the book, but his back had stiffened. Hoyt had not stormed through the living room and out the front door like he usually did.

"It's your birthday, ain't it?"

He had to look up then. He had no choice. "Yes, sir."

Hoyt looked like he was sorry for having forgotten. For some reason that scared The Boy more than the possibility of the police coming to the door again.

"What's say you and me go out and celebrate on our own? Just us men."

It took him a moment to understand. "Just us men," Hoyt had

said. Was he a man? Or was Hoyt just kissing up to him 'cause he didn't even remember to get him a card. Nah, that wasn't it. He never remembered.

"Come on, boy. You coming or not?" Before The Boy could answer, Hoyt was already out the door. The truck would be starting any moment now, and if The Boy didn't hurry, he would be left behind.

He put the remote in his grandmother's hand and wrapped her boney fingers around it until she gripped it so tight that his fingers were imprisoned in her grasp. He heard the truck's engine start.

"Grandma, let go." Pink gums glistened, only this time her eyes were moving back and forth, and there was a long stream of spit going from her top gum to her bottom lip. The Boy heard the loud crack and the squeal that meant that Hoyt was rolling down the truck's window.

"Boy, you gonna' sit around cuddlin' with your grandma all day or come on here?" Hoyt yelled and gave the truck a rev so that The Boy knew he was losing patience.

The Boy leaned close and stared hard into her eyes. "Let—me—go—bitch." He said each word, hard and firm like he had seen Hoyt do. The claw loosened and her watery brown eyes moved to the TV, and it was like he wasn't there. It was always like that with her. So he didn't have to feel bad about what he had just called her.

He ran out of the house, slamming the door behind him. As he climbed into the truck, his mind started creating scenarios for where they could be going for his birthday.

"Put your seat belt on. You have dinner yet?" Hoyt asked before The Boy had both feet in the truck. He never had to be told to put his seat belt on. Not after the beating Hoyt had given him after he had gotten a two-hundred-and-fifty-dollar ticket.

"Yeah, I had dinner." That was a lie, sort of. He'd had some Frosted Flakes, or rather, sugared flakes; they weren't the real thing, but some cheap brand from the discount store. They tasted all right for dinner. Truth was he was still hungry. He was just afraid that Hoyt was going to take him to Bernie Ann's Corner Side Café.

"That's too bad. I could sure use some BurgerCity."

"Oh, I could eat," The Boy said, and his stomach growled loud enough to be heard over the truck's engine. Hoyt laughed and put his hand on the back of The Boy's head and pushed it forward. Warmth started in The Boy's chest and spread to his stomach. Maybe he had been wrong to try to poison Hoyt.

"All right, that's what we'll do, then. You and me gonna get us some dinner and leave the women folk at home. I just got one thing to take care of first, and then we'll get us some burgers and fries and maybe some beer. We'll sit up at the park and have a few. That sound good?"

The Boy agreed that it did sound good. Maybe Hoyt hadn't been kidding about the man thing.

He watched his school flash by the side window. He saw the wash house and the gas station and then he was in a neighborhood he didn't recognize. The sound of Hoyt's even voice faded into the background along with all the landmarks The Boy recognized. This didn't feel right. Why was Hoyt being so nice? Why was he telling him he was a man? He wasn't a man, he was a boy. What if he was going to leave him out here in the dark? How would he find his way home? The Boy gripped the door handle hard. He looked out the window for something he recognized. The turns, he would remember the turns.

"One left turn," he said to himself, *"one right."* He was able to remember six turns, but he lost track after that. Wherever Hoyt was taking them was not in town. The roads were too dark. The Boy figured they were in the Stix. The Stix was what most folks called the area on the outskirts of Standard where a lot of rich people had their second homes.

He wanted to ask where they were going, but he didn't because he was afraid of what Hoyt might tell him. Afraid that Hoyt might just stop the truck and put him out. He knew Hoyt never wanted him. He had heard it screamed through walls for as long as he could remember. He had seen Pam's bulging belly in their wedding photo. Was Hoyt done with him? Tired of feeding and clothing him? He wanted to cry out and tell Hoyt that it wasn't his fault. He wanted to beg him not to leave him out here. It was too dark and too far from where someone could help him. Tears stung the corners of his eyes before spilling down his cheeks.

"I got to pee."

"What?" Hoyt sounded surprised, like he had forgotten that he wasn't alone in the truck.

"I got to pee real bad," he said, trying to keep the sob from his voice. Hoyt was silent for a moment. He expected him to say something angry, maybe even hit him, but the truck began to slow. He gripped the arm rest, determined not to make Hoyt angry by peeing in his truck.

The moon peeked through the trees and the boy saw with great relief that they were on a driveway. If Hoyt left him here, he could go to the door and ask for help. The house was one of the biggest he had ever seen. Hoyt pulled the truck to a halt. The Boy had always thought of his father as handsome. Mostly because Hoyt had always assured him that he would grow up to be just as good looking as he was. But in that moment, in that light, The Boy thought Hoyt looked like a gigantic gorilla. His head hung forward as if it were too heavy for his neck to carry, his shoulders hunched as if to help support the weight.

"You just hold it. We're almost there, and you can ask the nice people in the house if you can use their bathroom."

"I...I can just go in the woods."

"Naw, you can't, either." Hoyt's voice sounded gruff and mean. "You and me are gonna go ask those people if you can use their bathroom, you hear me?" Hoyt got out of the truck and walked around the back of it.

"Yes, sir." He was already reaching for the door handle. He had to stand up. He had to move, or he would pee in Hoyt's truck. He already felt the smallest bit forcing its way out, but he clenched real hard and cut it off. He could hear Hoyt walking behind him, not trying to keep up but not letting him go too far ahead either.

The Boy was scared. He didn't know these people. Why would they let him use their bathroom? "Go ahead, ring the doorbell. I thought you had to pee so bad."

He rang the doorbell twice, switching from one leg to the other before a light flickered on and a man peered out of the window.

"Excuse me for bothering you, sir, but my boy and I are on our way back home, and he can't hold it no more." The man looked from Hoyt to The Boy and back to Hoyt again.

The Boy couldn't help it. His hand went to his crotch; he was about ready to explode. The man grinned. "Yeah, just a minute," he said, and within seconds, the door was opening. The man called to his wife in the den, "It's all right, Liv. It's just the handyman and his son needing to use the bathroom." He turned back to Hoyt and The Boy. "It's right down here," he said. The Boy followed him, gritting his teeth and holding on to his privates, not caring if it looked rude or if he was embarrassing Hoyt. He figured Hoyt would be a lot more embarrassed if he peed on this man's nice floor.

The man pointed to a door at the end of the hall and The Boy hurried past, still holding his crotch.

"What you say, boy?" Hoyt asked from down the hall.

"Thank you, sir," he said as he kicked the door to the bathroom closed behind him.

His fingers shook as he unfastened and unzipped his jeans praying that the little trickle of pee that he had been unable to stop would not turn into a flood. He sighed in relief as he began to pee. His held back a smile on his face. The fist clamped around his stomach released its grip. His pee sounded like Multnomah Falls as it hit the commode. He let his head loll back and closed his eyes. He hated having to hold it for so long. It made his tummy feel all crampy.

He opened his eyes and looked around the bathroom as his pee slowed. He was surprised. It was smaller than the one at his house, no bathtub or shower or anything. He was reaching for the flusher when he heard it. He'd heard that same sound so many times in his own home that he almost believed he imagined it, but then, as his urine trickled to a miniscule stream, he heard it again, followed by a woman's scream. Not loud. If it had been loud, he might have been more frightened. It was a soft scream. Just the one. He stood there transfixed, his privates in his hand. He shook it, then tucked himself back in. A wet circle darkened his underwear, but it wouldn't show through his jeans. He hadn't imagined the cry, he was sure of that, but he was afraid; he didn't know if he should flush the toilet or not.

"Boy?" He whirled around and faced the closed door. He put his hand out to open the door, but something told him not to. That same something told him to turn that little knob on the door so that Hoyt couldn't come in. "Boy, I know you hear me."

"I'm not finished using it." He tried to keep the fear out of his voice.

"That's all right." Again, Hoyt's voice was nice—too nice.

The Boy shuddered, his eyes focused on the knob. *Please don't turn; please don't turn.*

"Me and these folks got business to discuss, so you stay in this bathroom until I come and get you."

The Boy felt tears prick at the back of his eyes. He wasn't stupid; he knew that Hoyt was doing something bad. He knew he was hurting people, and yet he couldn't figure out why.

"You hear me, boy?" Hoyt's voice started to sound not so nice and The Boy thought he saw the door knob move, as if Hoyt was resting his big ape-like paw on the door. "You stay in here until I come get you." Hoyt's voice was rising, but not in anger. He seemed excited.

The Boy pictured the ape again, this time hunched outside the door, salivating. "Okay," he said, backing away from the door. He waited for a response, but there was only silence. He stared hard at the door. *Please stop this. Please someone stop this. Grandma. Grandma,* he cried out silently, but his grandma wasn't there. No one was. And although he didn't know what was going on the other side of that door, he knew that Hoyt was making someone cry. He put his hands over his ears so that he wouldn't have to hear any more and squeezed himself in the tight space between the toilet and the wall. Tears seeped down his cheeks and neck and were now pooling at the collar of his shirt. He slid down the wall and started to pray. He didn't believe in God any more than he believed in Santa Claus, but sometimes, if you said things out loud, it helped to make the bad things go away. With his hands over his ears his whispered prayers seemed to come from way from far off. He closed his eyes and rocked a little as he repeated his prayer over and over again. "Don't scream, lady. Please don't scream."

Chapter Eleven

THE FIRST PERSON she and Troy stepped over was an old woman wearing a flowered, yellow dress and clutching a shiny white purse that matched her shoes.

Emma found herself looking for the slow automatic rise and fall of her ample chest. After they had passed her, Emma couldn't help but look back to make sure she hadn't risen without them knowing. Her trembling had eased after Troy had taken her arm, but the fear was still there. Troy had tried to describe this, but she had done a poor job. The sound of their feet, her cane tapping on the sidewalk, Troy's attempts to distract her with uncharacteristic inane conversation, even her own breathing—all of it felt loud and out of place. Emma felt out of place.

"How you doin'?" Troy asked her for the third time.

"Fine," had become her standard answer, but it wasn't true. She figured Troy knew that, based on the fact that she hadn't released her arm since they had set out. What *am I so afraid of? Troy's right. There's no one here to hurt me.* Her ability to sense people's feelings wasn't infinite. She had to be close, but even the people they had to step over or walk around gave off no impression. She couldn't sense much from Troy, either, just a carefulness that she wasn't sure that she liked.

"This was my route until I inherited a different one when another messenger moved to L.A. See that sidewalk right there? I once had this old man just walk right off that sidewalk, inches in front of my bike."

"Really?" was all Emma could manage.

"Yeah, you wouldn't believe the number of elderly people that rely on their hearing to get them around. A bike doesn't make any noise." She shrugged. "One of the guys broke his collarbone after running into a pedestrian. He never rode again—said he lost the joy of it. Parceled out his bike and everything. That's how I got my current saddle. Best seat I've ever had."

"What happened to the pedestrian?"

"He died. Cops tried real hard to pin something on the messenger, but the pedestrian was at fault. Nothing ever came of it."

"Aren't you ever afraid?" Emma felt the muscles in her neck loosen; a mannequin in the window of a small boutique caught her eye. She decided she would keep the fact that she liked the shirt the mannequin was wearing to herself, just in case Troy was tempted to pull an IOU from her pocket.

"Of being hurt? Not really."

"I'd be afraid for you."

"Nothing to be afraid of now, though."

"You almost sound disappointed."

Troy shrugged. "What's a world without at least some fears?"

"Safe?"

"If I wanted safe, I'd have been satisfied with getting a degree in something I wasn't interested in."

"Is that why you became a messenger? Because of the danger?"

"Nah, I just love to ride. Being a messenger *can* be dangerous, and it's also getting harder and harder to pay the bills. Don't get me wrong, I don't have many. I figure if I can't pay cash, I don't need it. But people are using the Internet and fax for most things that don't require signatures. I started when I was twenty-one and I can tell a big difference in the number of calls I get."

"Twenty-one? That means you've been riding for...?"

Troy smiled. "I'm twenty-eight, Emma. If you wanted to know how old I am all you had to do was ask."

"I would have guessed twenty-five."

"Uh huh. Keep blowing smoke up my boxers and I might pay for your half of dinner."

"You're going to pay? No IOU?" Emma laughed at the exasperated look on Troy's face. It reminded her of how she looked when they played spades and Emma had taken all of her play money. "Do you miss it? I mean, now that there's nothing to deliver?"

Troy looked around the empty streets and then at Emma.

"Yeah, I miss it. I can ride, but it doesn't have a purpose. I'm not trying to get anywhere. When I come back to you, that's always worth something."

The timber of Troy's voice made Emma blush.

"I'm glad we found each other, Em."

Emma sensed what Troy didn't say, which probably was something like, "I'm glad I saw your mirror. I'm glad you let me come up to see you in your apartment. I'm glad I didn't kill myself."

"I'm glad too," she said, and looked down for fear her eyes would tear up. Leaving the condo had been a good decision. Troy needed this from her.

There was something else that Troy needed from her, but she refused to think about it. Maybe it would go away. Part of her hoped it wouldn't.

They walked in silence and when gentle raindrops first hit the top of Emma's head she tossed her head back and let them cool her heated face.

Troy laughed. "At least you don't have to worry about it being bird shit, huh?"

"Ida used to say there's always something positive in every shitty situation." The Ida quote made her think of Dr. Edwards and the night she had been attacked. She pushed the thought away.

They turned a corner and Emma could feel the slightest bit of fatigue starting to creep up around her knee. She would ignore it for now. She needed the exercise and she didn't want this night to end. She could tell that Troy didn't either.

"I'm not sure I agree, but I bet your grandmother and I would have seen eye to eye on a lot of things."

"Yes. I couldn't put my finger on it at first, but now I think I've got it." She studied Troy with a serious look on her face. "It's the cursing. You and she have that in common."

"I don't curse that much."

Emma looked at Troy with her eyebrow raised. "Um hmm. She used to say that, too."

Troy sighed. "All right, I'll watch it from now on."

"I was just teasing. You don't need to watch what you say around me." She stopped speaking because Troy was grinning.

"Okay, I won't."

Emma realized she had walked right into Troy's trap. Emma watched as a drop of rain fell onto Troy's cheek and disappeared beneath her jaw line. Emma's eyes were drawn to a pulse at Troy's neck, and then she was drowning in the feeling of arousal. She felt an answering tug in her chest and her crotch. *Stop it.* She looked down at the sidewalk and felt heat creep up her neck and around her ears. She was eavesdropping again. She needed to learn to control that better if she planned to stay with Troy. *Stay with Troy?* Of course she would stay with Troy, unless Troy tired of her. What if she does? *Then what will you do? You'll do what you've done for the last two years; you'll find a way to fend for yourself.* The idea of going back to the way things were made Emma's heart pound. Fear, she recognized.

Troy looked concerned, but she didn't ask any questions. "It looks like it might be about to come down hard out here. Do you want to...?" The end of Troy's question was drowned out by an uncharacteristic clap of thunder.

"Whoa!" They both shouted and jumped close together under what was fast becoming a torrential rain.

Troy looked around. "Come on over here."

Emma walked as fast as she could in the direction Troy had pointed. Troy tried to shield Emma with her body, but both of them were soaked by the time they reached the front door of BurgerCity. Troy pulled the door open. "After you," she said with a sweep of her hand. Emma could see the gleam of her teeth in the semi darkness.

Emma entered the empty, well-lit restaurant. "How'd you know it would be open?"

"I worked at one when I was in high school. Most of them are open 24/7 now."

Troy shook water from her hair like a wet dog. Emma burst out laughing.

"What?" Troy grinned, and once again Emma felt another pleasing burst of joy coming from her.

"Your hair. I only finished half of it. You look like a rooster. Here, let me."

Troy bent forward and Emma began undoing the rows that she had so painstakingly braided. Emma finished unbraiding the last one and ran her hands through Troy's damp curls, smoothing them out until they coiled around her head like black silk. Emma's smile faded as she realized that Troy was watching her face. Emma's hands stopped moving as Troy's hands went to her waist.

"There you go," she said and dropped her hands heavily to her side.

Troy looked like she was going to say something, paused, and then asked, "Are you hungry?"

The easy answer would have been to say yes or no. Her mistake was in looking into Troy's eyes.

"I asked if you were hungry." Her voice lowered as she leaned closer. She took a deep breath and, with a finger under Emma's chin, tilted her face up and kissed her. Troy's lips were gentle on hers. One hand pulled her close, but all Emma would have had to do was take a step back and the contact would be broken.

Troy broke off the kiss just as Emma was beginning to feel the first tumult of emotions coming for her. Troy pressed her forehead against Emma's and took a deep breath.

"You are so sweet, Emma Webster," she said, her voice a whisper.

Emma pushed back the need to lean in to steal another kiss.

"I'm going to wine you, dine you, and tuck you into bed. Maybe tomorrow we can talk about the way you're trying to seduce me."

Emma's mouth dropped as Troy walked toward the cash registers. All kinds of smart comebacks came to her mind, but Troy had already disappeared behind the counter and into the kitchen.

The moment had passed.

She'd file them away for later; there would be other occasions. Troy took great pleasure in teasing her. Not that Emma didn't enjoy it. And sometimes she gave as good as she got. Emma looked around the restaurant and slid into one of the booths.

"Hey, Em, you should see this guy back here. He's got a shit-load of girlie magazines, and I bet he was about to get himself off.

Bet this fucker doesn't even wash his hands after he does it," Troy called out.

Emma's stomach writhed and she told herself it was just a reaction to the idea of eating fried food for the first time in years. Over the next few minutes the loud popping of grease was flavored with the occasional muffled curse word. Troy was trying to take her mind off the attraction between them, hence the profanity and the information about the poor guy in the back. Emma bit her lip. Her own feelings mirrored Troy's right down to the small pulse of excitement. *Come on, Emma, it's not like you've never done it before. Done it? Great, now I'm acting like I'm a teenager. I might as well run into the bathroom and write "I'm about to get me some" on one of the stall walls.* Emma's right temple gave a warning throb. The idea of yelling out a heartfelt "fuck" seemed very appealing at that moment.

"You asleep out there?"

God, no, she thought before calling out, "I'm here."

"Okay." Troy came out holding two red trays heaped high with food. "Dinner is served, m'lady." She slid the tray in front of Emma with a flourish and sat across from her in the booth. Emma picked up her diet cola and almost choked on her first swallow as she got a good look at Troy's food. The hamburger was so tall it leaned at an angle. There were more French fries outside of the package than in it, and the cup that held Troy's shake was three times as big as Emma's diet cola cup.

"You're not going to eat all that?"

"Sure. Why not?"

Emma looked down at her own platter and then at Troy's. "It's a lot of food."

"Come on, don't tell me you're worried about getting fat."

"Yeah, sort of."

Troy began the arduous task of picking up her burger. "Go ahead and eat. There's only me, remember? And we see each other every day. I won't even notice when you get fat. What's that they say? 'More of you to love,' right?" Troy bit into her burger.

"That's very reassuring, but I don't want to die of a heart attack from eating all this fried food," Emma protested.

The amount of food in Troy's mouth made her smile look distorted. Emma had to wait for Troy to swallow before she could respond." I couldn't think of a better way to die, myself."

"Really?" Emma asked as she looked at Troy's arms, her neck, and the tensing jaw line that was no longer chewing. Emma became very busy with her own colossal burger. She could feel Troy watching her and it was making her nervous. She hadn't even managed to pick up the burger yet.

"May I make a suggestion?"

"Sure." Emma hoped Troy didn't notice how unsure the word

"sure" had sounded.

"The fries are nasty when they're cold. By the time you pick that hamburger up, let alone eat it, it'll be winter."

"Okay," Emma said, and without looking at Troy she reached for a French fry.

"Uh..."

Emma paused with the fry midway to her mouth. Troy was looking at her with the same expression her mother had worn almost every time Emma wore something she didn't approve of.

"What?" Emma let her eyes fall to the right of Troy's so she wouldn't have to meet them.

"You want me to show you how to do that?" Troy asked and reached across the table and took the French fry from Emma's fingers before she could answer. Emma released the fry as if she had snatched it out of the hot grease with her bare hands. Emma heard the sound of Troy's tray being pushed across the table and the sound of her rough work pants scraping against the pleather seats as she moved to sit next to her.

"You have to watch what I'm doing, Emma."

Emma shivered. Troy's arousal was almost tangible. Emma took a deep shuddering breath and forced her drooping eyelids open. When she looked at Troy she noticed for the first time how incredibly long Troy's lashes were.

"Yes?" Troy asked and Emma nodded. "Good. Let me school you on this, then. First, you have to make sure the fries are real hot and just a little bit salty. You understand?"

Emma's "uh huh" earned her a mesmerizing smile.

"You only want them slightly crispy. So you have to wait until they're just a little bit past done." She paused and tilted her head.

Emma said "yes," again as if she had been asked a question.

"And then you want to take the top of your marionberry shake...and Emma?"

"Hmm?"

"It has to be marionberry." She smiled, and Emma swallowed. "Are you paying attention? 'Cause this part is important."

Emma nodded again. Troy dipped the French fry halfway into her shake and pulled it out. Then, closing her eyes, she bit into it like it was manna from the gods. "And then, you enjoy," she intoned, her eyes closed.

Emma's face heated. This had gone past playfulness and it scared her.

"Your turn," Troy said. Her teasing smile was back.

Emma was already shaking her head. "No. I think—" she stopped speaking because Troy had already dipped the half eaten fry into her shake and was offering it to her. As if pulled on a string, Emma leaned forward and took the rest of the fry from Troy's fingers. Troy's thumb lingered on Emma's lips and Emma chewed with eyes closed as she used the moment to regain her senses. "Mmm, Troy?"

"Hmm?" Troy's voice sounded husky and more than a little aroused.

"This is really disgusting," Emma said as the oddities of flavors slapped her senses right back out of the gutter. Her eyes flew open in time to see that Troy was leaning in to kiss her.

"Then something must be wrong with the shake. Here, let me try," she said and began to nuzzle Emma's lips.

Emma felt her own breath hit Troy's upper lip and bounce back to her. *Come on, Emma. You haven't forgotten how to do this. Oh, yes, I most assuredly have.*

Troy deepened the kiss and left her floundering to catch up. Emma felt like she needed to press her feet into the linoleum in order to keep from sliding out of the booth. Her hand went up, settled on Troy's shoulder, and then moved lower over Troy's heart. And then she felt it: wave after wave of wanting that took her breath away. The depth of the emotions and the strength of her own need made Emma's stomach twist. A sharp intense pain started between her eyes and made her feel even more nauseous. *Not right now. Please, not right now.*

"Emma, what's wrong?" She felt Troy's hands on her upper arms.

She turned roughly away from Troy. "I have to stop," she said as she stood up and stumbled in the direction of the bathroom.

In the bathroom, Emma splashed water on her face. Troy had tried to hide her embarrassment as Emma had run from her. She had never felt this much emotion coming from one person before. She couldn't remember ever getting so wound up that it made her sick but she should have seen it coming. She should have left the table sooner so that Troy wouldn't be out there right now struggling to deal with confusion, shame, and embarrassment.

A sob coursed through Emma's body as she sensed Troy getting her emotions under control. Emma could sense her buttoning them up and hiding them behind a wall. By the time Emma put her hand up to push through the door, there was almost no evidence of the sexual tension they had shared.

"Sorry," she said when she reached Troy. She couldn't bring herself to look at Troy. The platters of food had already been removed from the table and Troy stood up.

"Rain's stopped. We should get back," she said and offered Emma her arm, much as she would have with an old woman she was helping cross the street. The walk home was quiet. Emma could feel Troy's embarrassment grow into anger and by the time she swiped her access key to open the lobby door and they were riding the elevator up to the condo, it felt as if they were two strangers who couldn't wait to get out of each other's personal space.

HER HEAD HURT and the room felt funny, like someone had forgotten to turn off the AC before they cranked up the heater. And what was that sound? The wind chimes, of course. Troy frowned. Patricia wouldn't have left the window open at night, though. How could she be hearing the wind chimes? The sound was rhythmic and slow. No, it wasn't wind chimes; it was water, dripping water. Spider webs brushed against her arms and then over her face. She opened her eyes, but a dark cloud blinded her, and something cold and soft lapped at her ear lobe.

She tried to call out and struggle, but her arms felt weighed down; something was holding her in place. Her heart felt like it was going to pound out of its cage, and then something breathed life into her. She struggled against it at first. She had forgotten something, left it behind. But the lips—soft, moist, and needful—opened on hers, welcomed her hunger, took what she had to give. So she gave in, allowed herself the pleasure, just for a moment. Patricia never let her control things like this, and it felt wonderful. Something tugged at her memory, tugged at her conscience, but she pushed it away. She didn't want to focus. Not yet.

For a few moments she was in heaven. She pulled the slight body atop hers closer. Moving her hips against her, feeling the arousal build quicker than it ever had. She thought she heard her moan.

She opened her eyes. Blue eyes, not brown, stared down at her. She watched them change from aroused to something else. Hurt? Embarrassment? Troy drew her arms away from Emma as if a button had been pushed to release a vice.

"Oh, my God," she breathed and stopped. "Oh, I am so..." Troy couldn't find the right words.

Emma scrambled to her feet, not looking at Troy. She didn't say anything, just shook her head. Her fingers went to her mouth as if to wipe it.

Troy covered her embarrassment with anger, "What the hell were you doing out here anyway?"

Emma could have responded with, "This is my place and you're sleeping on my couch," but instead she said, "You were calling out in your sleep."

Troy's face softened. "I'm sorry if I woke you up. I have bad dreams sometimes. I don't make a habit of grabbing people." She stopped speaking and looked down at Emma's knee. "I didn't hurt you, did I?"

"No, and you didn't wake me. I was already up. I need to explain what happened in the restaurant."

"There's nothing to explain. It's late. We both should get some sleep."

"I can't imagine you'll be going back to sleep anytime soon, not with the way you were screaming. Who's Patricia?"

Troy looked startled. "I was calling for Patricia?"

"Yeah, you were crying out for her when I walked in."

Troy looked pensive. "I think you should go to your room. We'll talk about this tomorrow."

"Why are you saying this when it's not what you want?"

"Because I need time to think, okay?"

"No, you don't," Emma touched her shoulder. *Who the hell do I think I am? I don't know how to do this. I've never known how to do this.*

Troy reared back. "I don't need a charity fuck if that's what you're trying to do."

Emma paused before replying. "No, what I'm trying to do is get myself laid by the one person capable of helping me out these days."

"Emma I—" Troy closed her eyes, ashamed at how aroused she was.

"I need to tell you something first. Remember, you said that you wouldn't lie to me?"

Troy didn't answer so Emma rushed on. "It wouldn't matter if you did. I'd probably know if you were lying."

"What are you talking about? Are you saying I lied about something?"

"No, that's not what I mean. God, I hate this. Hear me out, okay? I'm trying to tell you that I sense things. I always have."

"If you could read my mind, you'd know that I want you to leave me alone."

"I can't read your mind. And I hear you telling me to go away, but your body doesn't lie, and I can feel that you want me to stay."

"Not you," Troy said, and regretted the words the moment they were past her lips.

"Now you *are* lying. Is it just to me, or are you lying to yourself, too?"

"Go to bed, Emma."

"Did it ever occur to you that I might be the one that needs a charity fuck? That I might want to be close to someone?"

"Do you always get sick after kissing the person you want to get close to?"

Emma closed her eyes and spoke softly. "That's what I'm trying to tell you. It gets overwhelming. I wasn't sick because you kissed me. I did something today that I haven't done in a long time and, for the most part, I wasn't afraid. It was exhilarating, and I felt powerful and sexual and desirable. It was a lot to deal with emotionally. So I got sick. It happened on my first..."

"Stop. I'm not angry at you. It was probably good that it

happened. I can't just have sex with you." Troy's voice was cold and tight and her stomach was quailing. She had been right; Emma was a fucking nut case. She should get her shit, hop on Dite, and ride home. Even as she thought this, her crotch tightened and desire swept through her body.

Emma inhaled. Troy turned to look at her. That was it. The moments when Emma would look at her oddly, would somehow know what she was thinking. It was because, if she were to be believed, she had known exactly what Troy was feeling. Dread flooded through her body. She clinched her fists and turned toward Emma.

"You bitch," she said, but there was a look of calm surprise on her face. "This whole time you've been eavesdropping on me?" Troy lurched up from the couch and almost slipped on the quilt that had fallen to the floor during her nightmare. Emma reached out to steady her but she pushed her hand away.

"Listen to me, please. I don't eavesdrop; it's more like you broadcast."

"Oh, so this is my fault?"

"No. I shouldn't have said... I don't mean just you. It's like this with everyone. This is why I didn't want to tell you. I knew you wouldn't listen. I don't pick brains. I just sense feelings, not even all feelings. Just the strong ones. Those are hardest for people to control. Most of the time it's no secret anyway. Anyone would know it by body language or the look on their face. I can also sense it. Sometimes I don't even know if they're my feelings or someone else's." Emma stopped speaking, because Troy had stepped around her as if she were a cactus and was walking toward her bike.

"Don't leave like this. It's dark, not to mention it sounds like it's pouring out there. I'll go to my room, okay?" Troy felt Emma's hand on her bare shoulder and she reacted without thinking. She grabbed Emma's wrist and pulled her toward her. She hadn't meant the kiss to be a punishment, but her lips stung from the violence of the kiss.

Emma's body had grown tense and Troy forced herself to loosen her embrace. Emma was right. She didn't want her to leave her alone. She had been thinking about this all day. Her anger was because Emma had known all along.

Troy tore her mouth away and they leaned against each other breathing hard.

"Couch."

"Too narrow." She wanted to suggest they go to her room and would have, in her dreams. But that was too forward and she was still afraid that Troy would walk out the door.

The back of her knees hit the frame of the window seat. She hadn't felt herself being moved backward. Her hands went to the muscles in Troy's back and dug in, as if it were possible to be any closer. Troy kissed her again as they fell onto the narrow window seat. Emma was amazed at how well they fit. Troy opened her legs, stretching Emma's wide and then even wider. Without breaking contact with her lips, Troy raised herself up on her elbows and arched her body into Emma's center.

Emma pressed her hand into Troy's lower back and then, without hesitation, Emma allowed her hands to cover Troy's ass and squeeze. Troy's chest heaved and Emma squeezed harder, pulling Troy to her with all of her strength.

Troy began to rock into Emma's body, each movement becoming stronger than the last, until the seam of Emma's jeans was pressing hard into Emma's crotch. Emma arched her body to meet Troy, and one of them moaned, deep, low, and guttural. Emma's hands went to Troy's upper arm. Her fingers tingled where she felt the outline of Troy's tattoo.

Just when she thought she wouldn't be able to tolerate any more friction, Troy shifted, arching her body, increasing the pressure until Emma could barely move. The orgasm shot up the center of Emma's body and sent ripping shockwaves from her toes and up her back. Troy's steady rhythmic grinding began to slow down. Her heart was pounding so hard that Emma couldn't tell where her heart began and Troy's ended. Troy's body quieted and she whimpered in her ear.

Emma sank her fingers into Troy's curls and held her close. Troy buried her face in Emma's neck. Troy sucked in and Emma could feel every rib in her body as the orgasm slammed through her leaving them both breathless.

"WE SHOULD MOVE into the bedroom." Troy's voice was hoarse and distant.

The perspiration on Emma's body cooled at the words. Troy's arousal, now appeased, had been replaced by another strong emotion. Sadness. *She's sad about what we did.*

Troy lifted her body and rested most of her weight on her elbows. Emma couldn't see her face, but the sadness deepened along with another emotion. Shame.

She intended to order Troy off of her, but choked on the words.

Troy spoke first. "It should have been better than this."

"Better than this?" Emma repeated.

"I didn't want it to be so rushed," Troy said, and the shame was so strong that Emma was no longer sure if it was Troy's alone.

Troy moved herself off of Emma and sat on the floor, her knees drawn into her chest, her shoulders hunched. Emma lay there trying to understand what had just happened. She felt like a sixteen-year-old boy who had gotten a girl drunk so he could cop a feel.

Tears warmed her temples. She was so caught up in how horrible she felt that it took her a moment to realize that Troy was holding her hand. Her thumb was rubbing back and forth over Emma's wrist. Emma shivered and tried to swallow down the instant bloom of desire. She felt like she was being toyed with. One moment Troy regretted being with her, and the next she wanted her again. But damned if she was going to complain right now.

"Can we try this again, please?"

Emma marveled at the pleading quality of Troy's voice. *She thinks I might turn her down.*

"Come here," Emma said.

Troy knelt at Emma's side. "I'm right here."

"No, come back up here," Emma whispered.

"I'm not getting on top of you again. This thing is too hard. We should go in the bedroom."

Troy held Emma's chin gently, leaned over and kissed her lips. Emma reached up and tried to pull Troy onto her. Troy inhaled deeply and pulled away. Emma turned her head and captured Troy's finger in her mouth.

If she had thought about it, even for a split second she wouldn't have done it. But based on Troy's reaction, she liked to have her fingers sucked. Suddenly the finger was replaced with Troy's tongue, and Troy's knees were bracketing her hips. The kiss was no gentler than their first, though it was less desperate.

Troy lifted her head, "Damn it, Emma. We should be in your bed."

"I can't wait that long," she gasped as Troy's nimble fingers began unbuttoning her pants and were inside her panties before she could finish her sentence. She closed her eyes.

Once again, she found herself giving Troy complete access to her body, trusting that she would not go too far, but she was shocked at how far she could go without causing her discomfort.

Emma stuck her hands beneath Troy's shirt and slipped beneath her sports bra. She groaned when she was able to feel Troy's breasts. They were warm and soft and fit easily in her hand. She could feel Troy's heart pounding beneath them.

Troy broke the kiss again and Emma growled out a protest.

"Sit up," Troy directed.

Emma did so and allowed Troy to slip her pants and underwear off. She expected Troy to let her lie back down, but she didn't. She pulled Emma forward with her hands at her buttocks, holding her so close that Emma could feel every muscle in Troy's abdomen press against her clitoris as she breathed. She moaned. Troy was right; they should have gone into the bedroom. The moment she had enough air in her lungs to speak, she would suggest that they head that way. But Troy's mouth wasn't allowing her any breathing room. Troy's hands had made quick work of her T-shirt, and the bra went with it. Her mouth was moving from Emma's neck to her breast and any thought of actually walking was wiped from Emma's plans as Troy's tongue dipped into her navel. She leaned back against the pillows. "Hurry," she pleaded.

Inappropriately, in Emma's opinion, Troy seemed to regain some of her will when she realized how close Emma was to climaxing. Her mouth became torturous and teasing and her hands were firm, restricting Emma's movements. And if she sensed Emma was closer to climaxing than she wanted her to be, she slowed her down further, but never once did she increase the pressure.

It was the most frustratingly pleasurable thing Emma had ever experienced. She was determined not to beg. In the end, she not only begged, she grabbed Troy's head and held her exactly where she needed her to be. Moments later she called out Troy's name in a voice that would have been embarrassing if she had really given a damn. Which she didn't.

EMMA GROANED HER protest when Troy left her lying on the window seat, her legs and arms akimbo. She looked, she was sure, like a ready-rolled hooker, and she didn't really give a damn. She jumped when a light touch to her stomach signified Troy's return.

"Can you turn over for me?" The question was barely audible over the sound of the wind blowing through the blinds. Emma hesitated and shyness took the opportunity to creep back in. She turned over so that she could see Troy's hand glistening in the moonlight. The scent of coconut drifted over her and she turned over to let Troy rub the liniment into her skin. She wished she had taken better care of her body. There wasn't a memory of fat anywhere on Troy's body. She would probably always look like a college athlete, thanks to the riding. The thought made Emma feel flabby, feeble and—

"You are so beautiful," Troy whispered.

Beautiful? Yes, damn it, she felt beautiful. The only other person awake in the world thought so. So it must be true. She reached up and put her hands in Troy's lovely hair and stroked the side of her face.

"Why do you sound so sad, then?" she asked.

"I hope I didn't hurt you."

"You didn't. I feel fine."

"I should have been more careful." Troy moved her hand slowly, sensuously, without really being sensual, touched her hip and rubbed and kneaded some imagined ache.

"It wasn't the time for careful. I'll be fine. You don't need to do this, although I certainly won't stop you if you want to continue."

"Good 'cause I'm going to. This stuff is awesome for sore

muscles. I buy it down at Saturday Market. The walk we took and then me lying on you like that—it's bound to make you sore tomorrow. I have to do this for myself sometimes after I ride."

"I wondered what it was when I smelled it on you. Does the coconut help in some way?"

Emma could see the flash of white that meant Troy was smiling. "No, I just like the way it smells."

"This feels wonderful, but you don't have to treat me with kid gloves. The limp is from nerve damage. I don't baby it anymore than anything else."

Troy kept rubbing, her hands gentle but insistent, until Emma's body became as pliant as warm taffy. "I don't want you to pay for this tomorrow. So let me do this, okay?"

Her answering moan made Troy chuckle. Her figure was a shadow in the relative darkness; touching Emma, pressing into her flesh, working out soreness that didn't exist. Coconut and Burt's Beeswax lip balm drifted over Emma. Air from the ceiling fan cooled her skin for a second before Troy's calloused hands passed over her body, warming it again. Arousal had long been forgotten, and she allowed herself to be cared for in ways she had run from.

"I have dreams, too," she said as sleep pulled and Troy's hands pushed.

"Are they about me?" Troy sounded amused.

"No. Bad dreams about someone standing over me in the dark." Troy's hands stopped, and Emma tried to stay awake long enough to explain. "I'm not scared anymore. This doesn't scare me."

The hands were back, and lips, soft and sweet, pressed against hers. "No more pain, Emma."

Troy's sadness tugged heart Emma's heart.

"No more fear. There's no one here who would ever hurt you." And then the hands coaxed her into a deep sleep.

EMMA AWAKENED ON the left instead of the center of the bed. Her first thought was to reach for her cane. And then she remembered that it was on the floor near the couch, which was followed by thoughts of why it had been discarded there.

She opened her eyes and looked around the familiar room. The air held the subtle scent of coconut and lovemaking. She stretched her hands above her head. Despite what she'd told Troy, she was surprised at how little her body protested. She smiled and curled into a ball. The absence of pain was no doubt thanks to Troy's magic hands. She felt safe, relaxed, and somehow satiated when she hadn't realized she was hungry. Then she realized that she was alone, and the feeling of safety receded.

The sadness and regret in Troy's voice last night came flooding back to her.

She had assumed that Troy was sad because she was afraid her lovemaking had been too rough, but maybe it was something else. *Of course she regretted it you fool. She called out her dead lover's name in her sleep, for God's sake.* Emma turned on her side and curled into herself. *You pushed and pushed until she slept with you, and now you're upset because she didn't stick around for more. What the hell did you expect, Emma? You had sex. You should be glad she was willing to put your ass out of its misery. You could have ended up with a Christian soccer mom who insisted on reading the Bible to find an explanation for what was happening to your gay ass.*

Emma stop, just stop. You've drawn enough blood. She allowed herself to taste the pain and then she got angry. No, she got rip-roaring bitchy, like any woman would whose lover had just gone to visit another woman, regardless of the fact that the other woman was dead. The first thing she wanted to do was wash the smell of their lovemaking off of her body. Then maybe she could think.

Lovemaking? It wasn't lovemaking, it was sex. "Yeah, it was sex, and I loved it," Emma muttered and dragged herself out of bed and limped into the bathroom. She turned the shower nozzle as far toward the H as it would go and stepped inside.

She wasn't gentle with herself in the shower. She made sure not to linger over spots left sensitive by last night's activities. It hadn't been rough at all times. Troy's mouth had been excruciating and wonderful at the same time; so much so, that it had left her sobbing during her release.

Stop it, damn it. It isn't worth it. She's probably at her lover's grave confessing that she cheated with you. Damn, why did you let this happen? She told you she didn't want you, Emma. She told you.

Emma rinsed the shampoo from her eyes and remembered how it had smelled in Troy's hair while she was braiding it. Even her own shampoo had memories of Troy and it hurt that the woman had been able to weave herself into her life without her noticing. Emma turned off the shower and dried her skin. Two small red spots between her legs marked where Troy's hip bones had been.

She would not cry and she would not wait around like a puppy for Troy to come back. She needed to find out what Troy wasn't telling her. What tied her to Patricia so thoroughly that she would leave Emma to go to her?

She threw on jeans and a t-shirt and went in search of her cane and her library card.

Twenty minutes and several old wallets later she found her library card stuck in a backpack that she couldn't ever remember purchasing, let alone carrying. She hooked her cane on the edge of her desk, sat down, and turned on her computer, fastidiously refusing to look at the window seat across from her. She pulled up the Multnomah County Library website. She hit the research link and typed in her library card number for access. She was prepared for several hours of research, but she found the first article on Patricia as soon as she entered the keywords "Patricia" and "Troy Nanson" into the search engine.

She scanned the article, although she realized that she had already read about Patricia's death. **Woman Drowns in the Oregon River** said the headline. It had been the lead story on Yahoo news the day it happened. She remembered feelingly badly for the woman's family, but not much beyond that.

Emma's anger and jealousy intensified as she looked at the black and white photo of Patricia Harvey. She was beautiful, just as Troy had said. There was something about her, even in the flat two dimensional black and white picture. Her hair was billowing around her head, and the photographer had caught her mid-laugh. She looked as though she had just said something sexy. *I bet she always looked that way*. Emma could tell that her lips were as familiar with sexy words as hers were with inane conversation.

Emma wondered if Troy had taken the picture. Perhaps they had just finished making love. *This is not helping*. Emma reached for her wireless mouse and was about to click out of the article when her eye caught the last paragraph.

> The passenger, Troy Nanson, was released from the hospital with only minor injuries.

"Oh, my God." Emma reread the sentence and then began typing quickly, dread settling high in her chest like a bad meal. Troy had told her that Patricia died in a car accident, but she hadn't told her that she was in the car at the time.

She found two more articles. The first was about a proposed bill to raise the several million dollars needed to reinforce the Morrison Bridge. The second was the coroner's inquest into the death of Patricia Harvey.

Emma read the latter twice, trying to understand what she was reading. In so many words, the coroner had found that Patricia had been high at the time of her death and her body showed signs of long-term prescription drug abuse. Although there had been evidence of alcohol in her system, she was not legally intoxicated. However, the alcohol, coupled with the drugs already in her system, could have been the cause of Ms. Harvey's inability to avoid the accident. The article went on to mention that all legal actions against the city of Portland were dropped by Patricia's family. It didn't mention Troy at all.

She pulled up Patricia's picture again. The jealousy was gone, leaving nothing but pity in its place. She wondered if Troy had known about the drugs. Regardless, taking any kind of drug and getting into a car on a rainy night was suicide, and she had very nearly taken Troy with her. White hot anger spliced through her. *Why in the hell would she love you so much? Because she's loyal, because she keeps her promises, and because she probably refuses to believe.*

"Hey, you're awake."

Emma jumped and spun her chair around, knocking her cane to the floor. She had been so deep in her own thoughts that she hadn't heard the door open.

"You scared me." She was having a hard time meeting Troy's eyes. "How'd you get back in without me buzzing you up?"

As usual, Troy carried her bag strapped across her torso, her bike resting on her right shoulder. She was wearing green, fitted cargo pants, a black cropped top, and black shoes that had Velcro straps instead of laces. The outfit looked new, but Emma couldn't be sure. Troy sat the bag down and dropped the bike on the floor. She bent down, picked up Emma's cane, and hooked it back on the desk. She stayed in that position, her eyes going over Emma's body so thoroughly that Emma wished that she had taken more time with her appearance.

"I didn't want to have to wake you if you were still sleeping, so I took your keys off the hook in the kitchen. Was that all right?"

Emma nodded; she was left mute at suddenly having Troy in front of her.

"How are you feeling?" Troy asked, her words sounding measured to Emma.

Emma's heart quelled at her somber tone. "I'm fine. Better than fine. Please don't be sad about this. It makes me feel like you regret what we did."

Troy pulled the computer chair forward so that Emma had to open her legs so that Troy could kneel between them. Troy's bare midriff was hot against Emma's thin t-shirt. Troy wrapped both arms around Emma's lower waist and pulled her into an embrace that should have been awkward but wasn't.

"I don't regret what we did. Why would you even think something like that?" Troy's lips claimed hers and she was dropped right back into the fantasy of last night. Troy didn't try to hide her desire. The sadness was there, but the passion was for her and her alone.

Emma allowed her body to fall in to Troy's. She ended the kiss first and Troy wrapped her tight in her arms. They listened to the sound of their own breathing for a few moments.

"Wanna try the bed this time?" Emma felt a laugh bubble up in her throat as she made the suggestion. Troy's body grew rigid.

Emma eased back. Troy held her, but it was as if she had forgotten her arms were around her waist. The smile was still on her lips, but it didn't reach her eyes. Her eyes were cold. "What were you doing?"

"What?" Emma tried to look behind her as Troy released her and stood up. She followed Troy's gaze and immediately wished she hadn't. The screen saver, thanks to a blinking banner, hadn't popped up. Patricia grinned out at them from the screen as if to say, *who you pitying now, bitch?*

"You looked her up? Why?"

"I just needed to know what happened to her."

"I told you what happened to her."

Troy leaned around Emma, grabbed the mouse and clicked out of the article. Emma caught the scent of coconut oil and new fabric.

"Can we talk about what the article said?"

Troy moved away from her as if she didn't want to risk touching her. "Why would I want to talk about it, Emma? I lived it. I don't need to talk about it with you."

"I know you lived it—now. You didn't tell me you were in the car. You led me to believe that she was alone when she died."

"She did die alone. I wasn't there to help her. I got out of the car somehow, but she didn't."

"You don't remember how you got out?"

"No." Troy bit her bottom lip. "The dream last night—I have that one a lot. I think we were in the car and water was coming in and I could see her hair. I think...I think she must have already been dead. But I can't be sure."

"You can't feel guilty because you survived? You don't even know how *you* managed to get out. How could you have saved her, too?"

"I shouldn't have just left her down there."

"You don't know that you did. For all you know, you could have been thrown from the car."

"I watched them pull her car out of the river. The passenger door was closed. I had to have crawled out the window. I don't remember doing it, but I had to have left her behind." Troy was looking at her as if she couldn't stand the sight of her. "Why would you bring this up now? What's wrong with you?"

Emma swallowed down the hurt, pushed it away to be licked and mended later. "It was stupid. I was jealous. I guess I wanted to know what I was up against."

"Up against? Up against? She's fucking dead. What competition could she be to you?" Troy was yelling now, and Emma wanted nothing more than to back down, apologize, and make the whole thing go away. She wanted to, but she didn't.

"You were screaming for her last night." Emma was unable to keep the hurt out of her voice now.

Troy threw up her hands in frustration. "I told you, I was having that nightmare."

"When you made love to me, you were so sad. I could feel it. I could feel how much you hurt."

Troy went quiet. "Don't try to tell me how *I felt*. Stay the hell out of my head and out of my past."

"I'd like to discuss something I read in the article."

"What the fuck for?" Troy bit off each word and Emma toyed with the idea of dropping the subject, but for some reason, Troy's anger strengthened her resolve.

"Because you *need* to know."

"I need to know what? That the woman I thought I would spend the rest of my life with drowned when I was right there to help her? I was there, remember? I was the one who had to bury her. That's all I need to know."

"Then you knew she had been abusing prescription drugs?"

Troy's face was emotionless. "You shouldn't believe everything you read. We don't *all* abuse drugs."

"Don't."

"Don't what?"

"Don't start playing the race card with me. I don't deserve that." Emma could feel the shame, and she took the opening that it afforded her by making the last point she might ever get.

"You didn't do drugs. Patricia did." Troy's face gave nothing away, but Emma sensed what her words did to her, and she felt like a clumsy bully. Why was she doing this? It was as if she couldn't stop until she had finished breaking Troy's heart. "She abused prescription drugs. She was on them when she drove you off that bridge. Even if she was conscious when the car hit the water, the drugs could have made it hard for her to save herself. I just want..."

"How about asking me what *I* want? How about asking me what happened, not reading it in some damn paper? Did it ever occur to you that I already knew about the pain killers? The doctor prescribed them a few months before... she hurt her back when she tripped off a curb wearing some fucking high-heel shoes.

Emma shook her head. She had already come so far she might as well finish. "The coroner said..."

"I know what the coroner said. I read that article. I read all of them, Emma."

It takes more then a few months of usage to cause damage that would be classified as long term drug abuse. Emma reached out, but Troy stepped out of her reach. Emma was prepared for the feelings of sadness, betrayal, and anger, but what she wasn't prepared for was the resignation. Troy may not have admitted any of this to herself, but she had to have suspected.

"And you've based your expert opinion on what?" Troy pointed toward the computer, "Some damn article that you read on that thing?"

Angry tears were pouring down Troy's face now, and Emma's

heart twisted at the utter hurt, betrayal, and pain in her eyes. "I understand why you don't want to hear what I have to say," she said, "and I'm not trying to hurt you or hurt the picture you have of Patricia, but you blame yourself. I can feel that. Your guilt is making it hard for you to move on. I just wanted you to face the truth."

"You want to talk about facing truths? All right, let's do that. The truth is this has nothing to do with Patricia. This is about you and your insecurities. You are nothing but a scared little girl, Emma. You're so damn scared to trust this *ability* of yours that you've locked yourself up for two years. And I bet you don't even know why you do. Well, I know why, and I haven't even looked you up on the computer. It's because you're afraid. You're afraid you won't know if someone else might come along and try to hurt you."

Emma was shaking her head in denial, but Troy was pushing on. Her words were clipped and low. "Welcome to the real world, Emma. The rest of us don't have that option, either. Do you really think I would have let her drive across that bridge in the rain if I had had any inkling that she wouldn't make it?" A tear dropped from Troy's lashes, and Emma felt answering tears well up in her own eyes.

She didn't think Troy cried often, and it hurt that she was the cause of it. Saying "I'm sorry," was too trite, and it wouldn't cut it.

"I woke up alone."

"You've been waking up alone for a long time."

Emma accepted the verbal punch in the chest as her due, but she still had to gather herself before she went on. "You go to her grave all the time." Emma made herself meet Troy's eyes; what she saw there made her shiver.

Troy's only answer was to turn and pick up her bag. She dumped its contents onto the floor. A large tub of plain yogurt thumped to the floor, followed by two cartons of strawberries, a box of tea bags, and four huge bran muffins. "You didn't eat much of your dinner last night. I wanted to make sure you ate." Her voice sounded as dull and heavy as the tub of yogurt hitting the hardwood floor. Troy dropped her bag on the floor and picked up her bike.

"And for the record, my "*sadness*" wasn't because I was wishing you were Patricia. I didn't want anyone but you last night. I wanted you so badly that I lost all control. Something I was never allowed to do with Patricia. It was always her driving things, her dictating when and how we made love, and I realized last night that she never really gave herself to me. Not like you did. And yes, goddammit, it hurt to know that the woman I had given my heart to may not have been capable of giving me hers in return."

The door had closed behind Troy before Emma had even thought of a response. She heard the stairwell door open, and then slam shut, indicating that Troy had declined to wait for the elevator and had taken the stairs down instead.

Emma ran to the window. She gripped the sill and squinted against the sunlight. What if she rode off in the other direction? She ran to the front door and wrenched it open. The stairwell door was heavy, but she braced herself and pulled hard.

"Troy!" she called. She was answered by the sound of the door at the bottom slamming. Emma ran into the stairwell, her feet pattering on the stairs as she negotiated the stairs in record time.

"Damn, damn," she cursed her knee, but she reached the first floor moments after she had heard the door slam. She yanked it open and glared out into the sunlight.

"Troy?" Her voice echoed on the empty Portland streets. "Troy, please come back!" There was no answer, of course. Troy could get far away on muscle alone. Add anger to the mix, and well, Emma was sure she would be out of ear shot by now.

She stood holding the door waiting and hoping Troy would come back. Emma walked back into the stairwell. Her knee was aching now, and she didn't look forward to the three flights up. And not too far back in her mind, she couldn't help but think that Troy hadn't said she would be back this time. *She said she was going for a ride. She said she wouldn't lie to you. So trust that she won't.*

Emma grimaced as she took the first stair.

The problem was Troy hadn't said she'd be back after her ride.

Chapter Twelve

WIND TORE THE kerchief from her head two blocks back and was now whistling in her ears so ferociously that she couldn't hear the whisper of Dite's tires on the asphalt. *Why did she have to sneak around behind my back? If she had questions about Patricia, why didn't she just ask me? She did try to ask you, and you blew her off.*

Bullshit! Her pedaling slowed. It wasn't bullshit, and the moment Troy acknowledged that fact, her anger ebbed, and she recognized her emotions for what they were. She couldn't ever remember feeling this hurt and she couldn't quite place why. Emma had said she only wanted Troy to know that Patricia had been abusing drugs when she died. It was as if she believed she had to besmirch Troy's memory of Patricia in order for them to have a chance. She didn't want to believe that Patricia had purposely overmedicated herself, but she knew that Patricia wasn't perfect.

Or had she? It had taken her weeks to even tell Emma Patricia's name. Had that been some form of denial? *Did Emma sense how important Patricia was to me, even in death? Of course she's important to me. I loved her with all my heart.*

Then what does that leave for Emma?

The thought seemed to come from nowhere, and it shocked her enough that if her feet hadn't been clipped in, she may have stopped pedaling.

What kind of question was that? Emma wasn't thinking about her heart! For God's sake, they had known each other for what, a few weeks? Troy caught a glimmer of what turned out to be broken glass and came to a stop. She brought Dite to a stop in front of a store she could never afford to shop at when things were normal. She leaned her forearms on Dite's handlebars to rest. What the hell was she doing here? She turned her head and heard a Benson Bubbler. She closed her eyes. The sound of running water was soothing; she forced herself to relax her shoulders. She thought about the look on Emma's face right before she had walked out. *Why did I say those things to her?*

Because she hurt me, that's why.

Yeah, but how did she hurt you? She was repeating what the newspaper said. What you already suspected. Troy crossed her arms in front of herself and refused to let the sob take hold. *What she had already suspected.* Patricia was always emotional. Her ups were so high that Troy had a hard time catching her breath. Hadn't she asked her about it? Hadn't she wondered why, every time Patricia begged Troy to go bungee jumping, she had a hard time getting out of bed two days later?

Emma had exposed the part of their relationship that she had allowed herself to forget. Yes, she had been happy. Yes, she loved Patricia, and she believed Patricia loved her, too. Had it ever been perfect?

A sob clawed its way up her esophagus. Emma had hurt her because she forced her to admit that she had been saving herself for a woman who had, in all probability, been responsible for her own death. Emma had every right to want Troy to acknowledge the fact that Patricia wasn't perfect. But it didn't mean Troy had to like it, and it didn't mean that Troy had to accept it until she was ready. And she wasn't ready. Not yet. She might not ever be.

Those thoughts aside, Emma had been wrong when she accused her of thinking of Patricia when they made love.

How would she know that, though? You told her you had room for only one woman. You have nightmares about her; call out for her in your sleep. Even now, you refuse to talk about Patricia, and you leave Emma alone to come to her own conclusions after making love to her.

Had she really left to get breakfast? Was that all it was? She could have picked up breakfast and returned before Emma had even awakened. Instead, she had ridden the city aimlessly thinking. Thinking of what?

Of Emma, and yes, thoughts of Patricia were there, too. But Emma was wrong on one account. She hadn't gone to see her.

Why didn't I go to Patricia's grave? You know why. Stop blaming Emma for realizing the truth before you did.

You felt guilty for being with Emma, so you stayed away from Patricia's gravesite. Troy felt sick when she started to realize the truth. She had accused Emma of hiding out in the condo, but wasn't she doing the same thing? Only, instead of hiding behind walls and bars, she was using the pain of Patricia's death to avoid living life again.

What if she was wrong about Emma, too? What if she and Emma were just trying to distract each other from what was happening to them? What if two, three years from now, they grew bored with each other? *What if Emma finds out I cheat at Spades*? The latter thought made her smile, and for the first time when she pointed Dite toward the cemetery, it wasn't with a heavy heart.

How many times had she ridden down this path? More than a hundred, she was sure. In all the times, she never even considered riding past its ivy-covered sign. She had never noticed how green the grass was, or how the flowers smelled like perfume, and the wind through the trees sounded like clothes rustling on a clothesline. But she noticed those things now. Troy left Dite on her side in the grass and walked up the hill. Last night's rain had made the soil thick and clinging. She followed rain-filled footprints, leftover from her last visit, no doubt, to Patricia's marker. The ground was too muddy for her to sit, so she stood, awkward and nervous.

"I've been living in a dream world, Patricia." Troy felt tears in her eyes. "Damn, I haven't cried this much since you died." She took a deep breath. "I wonder if it will ever get easier to say that. Ahh, to hell with it," she said as her knees sank into the cool soil.

She ran her hand over Patricia's grave marker, clearing away small particles of dust and grass that had blown over it since her last visit. "I used to pray that one day you would open your eyes and see me standing there and feel like you could never belong anywhere without me. That's the way I felt about you. But it didn't work out like that. I was the one who woke up in the hospital, and they were telling me that you were dead, and there would be no more chances for me to make you happy. I wanted to believe you when you said the meds were for your back because I didn't want to believe that I could never be good enough for you. I could never make you happy." Troy swallowed. "I met someone, Patricia. I don't think you can fight this kind of thing. Just like, no matter what, I couldn't make you stay here with me. I loved you, and I'm so sorry you had to die so young. I would have spent the rest of my life trying, and maybe failing, to make you happy. But I would have tried. Oh god, Patricia, I didn't even know that I needed and deserved more than that. Maybe you knew, though." Troy's hand went to the marker. She traced the word "beloved" with her finger and stood up.

"It's been hard for me to accept that you were never happy in this world. I think you had to know that you were driving too fast over that bridge. Part of me has always felt like I should have been with you even when you died. I don't know why or how I got out, but I'm glad I did. I didn't want to die."

Troy picked a dandelion, clasped it between her hands and rubbed them together until the seeds went spinning off into the air.

She didn't have the energy to sustain her anger with Emma, but the hurt was there and would be for some time. She would sleep in her own place for the first time since meeting Emma. Over the last four weeks, she had found it easy to avoid going home. The horror of finding the world asleep had made the pain of Patricia's death seem as fresh as if she had driven off the bridge the day before.

She tipped Dite to the side and was about to hop on when she heard a low droning noise. In another lifetime, she would have dismissed the sound. Her ears strained to hear a repeat of the sound, afraid that she had imagined the sound or that the wind had been playing tricks on her, when the sound repeated she let out a small, unintelligible cry.

This was not a sound caused by the wind or anything else in nature. It was a car engine and it was getting closer.

TROY CLIPPED INTO Dite's pedals, took a moment to pinpoint the direction of the vehicle, and took off.

The sound was coming from a mile or so down the path. Toward the hospital. Of course. Why hadn't she thought to go back there? If she had awakened there, maybe someone else had, too. Maybe her reason for being there was more complicated than a header off Dite.

When the hospital came into view, she slowed and then stopped. She hadn't paid much attention to the parking lot when she had left three weeks ago, but none of the cars sitting there looked out of place.

The engine had been shut off before Troy reached the hospital. She stopped in front of the entrance and looked up at the darkened windows. When she had first ridden away from this place, she had felt like something evil was watching her. And now, she was going to just troop her ass right through the front door?

"No, I don't think so." She took a step back. The grass was too clumpy for her to just ride across, so she lay Dite down at the end of the wheelchair ramp and walked toward the side of the building. She peered in several windows before she found one into a room that was occupied. An old woman lay in her hospital bed, her head lolled to the side and her mouth open. *How long can a person lay with their mouth open without their tongue getting all dry?* Troy shuddered and peered into the next room. Empty. If the place wasn't so creepy, she might have gone in and closed the old lady's mouth. Troy shuddered again. Or maybe not.

The second-to-the-last room was occupied as well. A woman sat slumped in a wheelchair. Her feet were sticking out in front of her as if she had been lifted from the bed and dropped into the chair like a rag doll. Troy was about to move on to the last window when something about the scene caused her to take another look. She cupped her hands around her forehead and squinted. The woman's hospital gown and what little she could see of the floor were stained dark black. A faint but putrid odor drifted past Troy's nose, and she told herself she had imagined it. Troy's eyes were drawn to the woman's face and then reluctantly to the gaping wound in her neck. A slash of red crossed the woman's neck, creating a jagged, lopsided smile. The wound looked vicious; it did not look accidental. In fact, Troy thought it looked like someone had caught the woman unawares and had slit her throat from behind. Troy was having a hard time understanding what that meant. Had this happened before the sleep took place? She was in the hospital, after all.

At some point, she had become desensitized to seeing bodies strewn about the city like so much offal. But this—this was different. Even through the window, even from a distance, Troy could tell that this woman was not like the others. She wasn't breathing. Troy wasn't sure how long she'd stood there before a movement near the floor broke her concentration and caused her to look away from the woman.

A man was hunched on his knees scrubbing at some dark stains on the floor. His white shirt pulled tight across his back. She could see his profile now. He appeared to be wearing an apron and white gloves. He also had something tied round his face.

He's wearing a mask. Maybe I didn't imagine that rotting smell. She had no sooner finished the thought when he sat up, his hand going to his forehead as if to wipe away sweat. Their eyes met.

He reacted first. His hand came up, gloved and bloody, and snatched the surgical mask from his face. A small band of crimson appeared on his cheek, and his mouth formed a word so clearly that Troy didn't have to hear the order to "Wait" to know that's what he wanted.

She ran. Her heart was in her throat, and her eyes were focused on Dite lying at the foot of the wheelchair ramp. She envisioned the bloody apron dripping down the hall as he tried to catch her. She picked up Dite, ran three steps, and launched herself up and onto the saddle. She clipped her left foot in, but it took her three rotations to do the same with her right. The hospital doors slammed back and she swung her head around terrified that she would see a gun pointed towards her.

He was running, and for one terrifying moment, Troy felt like he might be running fast enough to catch her.

Adrenaline pumped through her legs until she imagined them firing like pistons on Dite's pedals. Her forearms ached from gripping Dite's handlebars, and she could hear little over the sound of her own heartbeat, but she thought she heard him yell something that sounded like "Wait, I need to talk to you!"

In that case, I'll stop for a chat, you sick fuck. She glanced back one more time as she cut through a small grove and came out on another road that ran parallel to the main one.

She had almost convinced herself that he wasn't going to try to follow her when she heard the sound of a powerful engine being revved. She made a sharp turn, and realizing that she would be forced to cross the Burnside Bridge with him on her tail in a car if she continued on this route, made another quick turn, instead.

Dite's tires ticked across the asphalt like the second hand on a clock. *How much time had passed since she had heard the engine revving? Five minutes at least. Maybe she had lost him. Maybe the last turn—*

She coasted into another turn and found herself face to face with a candy-apple red mustang. The dealership stickers on the windshield kept Troy from seeing the driver. Troy locked her jaw and continued toward the car. The driver rolled his window down. At the last moment, she veered to the right and down a narrow one way street. The Mustang weaved around parked cars, clipped one, and barreled closer to her.

"Stop running, damn it. I need to talk to you," the driver yelled.

Troy jammed on her brake so hard that her rear wheel slid out from under her. She put her foot down and rode it out, then forcefully dragged the bike back under her body. The Mustang had to continue down the narrow street before it could turn around in the intersection. She heard tires squealing as it made a U-turn, and then heard the roar of the engine as he sped up to catch her. He was behind her so fast that Troy felt herself start to worry that she might have a hard time losing him.

She wished she had picked up a bike helmet along with all the other things she had lifted over the last few weeks. A helmet might protect her, at least a little, if this psycho decided to take a shot at her. Troy kept her head down and hunched her shoulders

If he had a gun, he would have used it by now, right?

She risked a look back to make sure a gun wasn't aimed at her. She jumped the curb and rode through the entry way of an office building. The Mustang was picking up speed; the engine grew louder. Troy careened across Burnside, grateful that the busy street was as motionless as the rest of the city. *One car moving in the whole city and it's intent on mowing your ass down.*

The Mustang disregarded the red light, as Troy had, and roared across Burnside. She didn't look back again, but Troy imagined she could feel puffs of heat on her bare calf as the car eased closer and closer. She wouldn't be able to outrun a car on Dite. She had to get him out of that car somehow. She had begun to feel the first signs of fatigue brought on by fear when she spotted the ornate gateway leading into Chinatown.

She hadn't been on this side of town since the eleventh grade. She and an old boyfriend had found a condemned parking structure that was perfect for ditching math class, smoking cigarettes, and making out. She had found the parking structure, but the making out and the smoking cigarettes hadn't been her idea. She was praying fervently that the city hadn't torn the parking structure down when it came into view.

"Oh, thank God." The structure looked dark and dingy and no different then it had eleven years ago. Troy felt like she wanted to stop and kiss its pavement if she hadn't taken a quick look back to see the mustang turning the corner behind her.

"Come on, come on." She forced more speed out of her legs, and she could hear the Mustang speeding up behind her. She swerved down what had been the exit ramp to the parking structure and, although her heart was pounding, it sounded like the grill of the Mustang was seconds from plowing into her back. She braked hard, and despite her speed, it slowed her down enough that she was able to avoid the wooden arm and the large metal teeth sticking out of the pavement.

The lights and anything else valuable had already been removed from the structure all those years ago. If she hadn't known about the teeth, it would have been hard to see them in the dark. Troy had Dite back up to speed in seconds. She heard the Mustang hit the arm and then two loud explosions and a long loud sequel as the driver hit the brakes. Troy had a brief vision of a large, angry, wounded animal.

Troy was halfway up one of the ramps when she heard his car door open. She was tempted to stop to see what he was doing, but she didn't. She knew he would get over the surprise and come after her again. She had reached the second ramp when she heard the car door slam again and the sound of the engine being put into gear and then the thump thump thump of the car being driven on at least two flat tires up the ramp. *What the hell is he doing?* Gooseflesh raised on Troy's arms. She had expected him to give up. Or at the very least, follow her on foot.

You idiot. All you did was corner yourself and make him mad. He can still catch you even on two flat tires. He wouldn't care about ruining his rims. He didn't pay for them.

She didn't realize what she was going to do until she had reached the empty upper level and saw the short wall that she used to sit on tossing cigarette butts into the creek below. She slammed on her brake, torqued her hips as hard as she could, and once again, let the back tire slide out from under her. Only this time, it came to rest with a gentle bump against the five-foot high stone wall. As scared as she was, she couldn't help but think she couldn't repeat that move in a million fucking years. She threw herself off Dite and over the wall before she could talk herself out of it.

She dropped for what seemed like ages until she landed in some blackberry bushes. Her first impulse was to get up and start running but she was afraid he might follow her. Even with flat tires, he could abandon the car and catch her on foot. She rolled beneath the lip of the parking structure using the wall and the bushes to block her from view. Her shoulder and hip smarted, and she could feel the sharp sting of scratches on her arms and legs. She had to lie on her side to fit into the small space, and her face was pressed into the dirt and gravel. She heard him open the car door. He must not have shut it, because a few minutes later she still hadn't heard it slamming. She thought she heard him say something, but whatever it was was so low that she couldn't make it out. She wished that she could see him. Several yellowing cigarette butts lay on the ground, and she wondered how many other kids used this place to cut school.

There was a loud crash, and then a stinging pain just below her right eye, and then Troy was looking at the remains of her bike. He had tossed Dite off the structure. There hadn't been any time to do anything but leave her there. She had to save herself right? She had to. Troy reached up and touched the spot on her right cheek bone. In the shadow of the overhang, she couldn't see her hand, let alone discern if it were blood or tears on it.

Chapter Thirteen

Standard, Oregon
Years Ago

THE LAST TIME Hoyt had taken The Boy hunting, he had become so frightened that he had wet his pants. It wasn't the blood that scared him, he didn't mind that. It had been the sound of the gun firing. He had heard gun shots on TV and in video games, but neither of those prepared him for the ear-ringing sound, the sharp metallic taste of the air, or the feeling that something that was once alive wasn't any more.

Hoyt had made him wash himself in an icy stream before forcing him to ride home with his naked ass sitting on a towel that Hoyt used to check his oil. Everything about that hunting trip came flooding back to him now as he sat shivering in the dark. All of it was the same, the cold, the whispering of trees, and Hoyt's breath—a combination of caffeine and tarter, mixed with nicotine and milk, overpowered the more pleasant scent of green grass crushed beneath their boots.

"Look at her." Hoyt handed him the binoculars. "Beautiful ain't she, boy?"

"Yeah," The Boy said as he looked through the lenses. "Yes sir, she is."

"See how long her legs are? How she kinda prances a little when she walks? That one there ain't never had no kids. You see what I'm sayin', boy?"

"Uh huh."

"You sure you ready for this? You even awake?"

"Yeah, I'm awake," he lied. He hadn't been awake when he'd pulled on his camouflage clothes. He was still asleep when Hoyt had driven them to a dirt road behind a line of houses and had told him to 'get out and be careful not to slam the fucking door.'

His eyes were half closed as he followed Hoyt for what seemed like an hour, but was probably more like fifteen minutes, until they got to where they were squatting now.

He would not complain about being awakened only a few hours after he had gone to bed, nor would he ask questions. He wanted to, though.

There were things he didn't need to ask. Like why Hoyt liked to hurt people. He knew why. Hoyt's eyes gleamed when he read the newspaper reports about the things he did. He liked to hurt people because it made him feel good. The Boy figured it was a lot like how he had felt when he'd poured the bleach in those drinks. He had felt powerful, as if he could do anything.

"So, what you think, boy? You ready for your first one?" The Boy put down the binoculars; he could already hear Hoyt's breathing quicken. His skin crawled, but at the same time, his crotch tightened.

"Yeah, yeah, I'm ready."

"Remember, do it real gentle. Same way that little rat dog of hers does when he's ready to come back in."

"Okay." The Boy was shivering now, and it wasn't even cold outside.

"Now we're in this together. You're the same as me. If you ever tell anyone about this, even your friends, it'll get real bad, real fast. You understand?"

"Yeah, I understand."

"Good." Hoyt cupped the back of his neck and gave him a gentle little push. He walked hunched over toward the backdoor. He squatted down low and scratched at the door, about two feet from the bottom. He felt real bad about what Hoyt made him do to the dog until he remembered that Hoyt had said he would let him try to pick the lock on the next one.

He heard her get up from the table. "Where have you been sweetie? I had to keep your dinner warm."

He hoped this didn't take long.

TROY STARED UNBLINKING into the darkness. She hadn't slept, at least she didn't think she had, but she had drifted in and out of awareness.

He must have left the car up there, because she hadn't heard him drive away. She almost wished the car hadn't been disabled. At least then, she would have been able to hear the engine before he could get close again.

The fear that he might sneak up behind her on foot had kept her in her place longer then she intended. That, and the fact that she hated to leave Dite scattered on the ground in this place.

Something took flight from behind her as she scrambled to her feet. The lights in the parking structure had long since been knocked out by kids bearing rocks. She herself was responsible for destroying the one at the entrance ten years before. Shadows would have been welcomed over the utter darkness.

Sharp bushes grabbed at her arm and clothes as she pushed her way out of them and onto the dry creek bed. She heard the pinging sound of metal hitting rocks as she stumbled and then began to run. The moon and stars would have helped to light her path if they hadn't been cloaked by clouds. She knew the creek was fairly straight and would lead her to a street to the left of the parking structure. She could take that out through Chinatown and follow some of the smaller, less traveled streets back to the Pearl District, back to Emma. All she had to do was keep running.

The dark was so complete that she could have closed her eyes and been in no more danger of falling. Her mouth was dry and salty. Sweat? She ran her tongue around the inside of her mouth, and the sting of pain confirmed that it was actually blood. The impact of the fall had caused her to bite her tongue. *Don't think, just run,* she told herself, and for at least a mile, the mantra kept her from becoming crippled by terror.

What about Emma? What if she starts to worry? What if he finds her? I have no way of warning her. Why didn't I ask Emma for her phone number? Hell, does she even have a phone?

Troy let out a gust of air that could have been a choked sob as light began to cut into the utter blackness. Soon she was able to make out the edge of the creek bed. She scrambled out and paused long enough to make sure that he wasn't laying in wait for her before she began to run again.

She looked behind her several times, even going so far as to stop to listen for footsteps. *You're being paranoid. No, not paranoid enough. Remember the woman at the hospital? He tried to decapitate her. You have to be sure you don't lead that man back to Emma.* Her heart was slamming against her rib cage, and her throat felt raw. Her muscles were screaming in protest after lying in one position for so long and now being forced to propel her body so far and so fast. Her breathing became more and more labored as her fear added a twenty-pound weight to her back. No matter how hard she tried, she kept replaying the sight of the wounds to that woman's neck through her mind.

She tried to think of Emma, but that brought her to how they had left things. If that man caught her, Emma would be left to think she had simply chosen to walk out of her life.

The argument seemed stupid now. If she had simply talked to Emma, told her the truth, told her that yes, at one time, she had planned on spending the rest of her life with Patricia, that she had had a hard time moving on with her life without Patricia in it, but that she was ready—

Troy slowed her pace and came to a stop across the street from Bike Rite, a store she was familiar with, but would never shop at, even if she could afford its pricy garments. The two large, flat-panel screens that had been one of the store's main attractions were now broadcasting snow, and someone had thrown something heavy through the front door. But neither of those things were what captured Troy's attention. Troy's shoes crunched on the glass as she approached a man lying in front of the store.

The man was lying with his legs sprawled awkwardly out in front of him. His hat was several feet away from his outstretched hand. Troy squatted next to him, taking in his clothing: a pinstriped suit, an overcoat, and what looked like brand new, shiny black shoes. *Come on, what the hell are you doing? You're what? Maybe fifteen minutes from Emma's? There's nothing special about this guy.* Troy stood up, but she continued to stare at his placid face trying to figure out what, if anything, was wrong with him. He was unremarkable. So much so, that if she turned away from him, she doubted she could give an accurate description of him to save her life. Maybe that was what bothered her. She hadn't bothered to look at the others. It had felt too much like a wake—too much like viewing the dead, but this man's position had revived her curiosity.

All of the other people she had seen in the last few weeks looked as though they had simply lain down for a nice nap. Their peaceful positions made it easy for her to remember that they were all just sleeping. But this man looked like he had fallen... or maybe he had been disturbed after he had fallen. The thought caused Troy's fist to tighten.

Calm down; you know he's out there. The fact that he might have disturbed this man should be no surprise to you. He's far better off than that poor woman at the hospital. Troy squatted next to him again and hesitated, remembering her horror the last time she had touched one of the sleeping, and shook her head.

That was different. She had seen at least a hundred people just like this guy since then. Troy picked up his wrist. There was an even pulse, and Troy was about to put his wrist down when she noticed that the face of his watch was broken. "Eleven o'clock," she said aloud and looked at the man's face. That's what time the clock in the hospital had said, too. Chills formed on Troy's arm, and she stood up and backed away from the sprawled figure. She hadn't worn a watch since she was in elementary school. She lived her life based on how fast she could ride her bike from one side of town to the other. She rarely noticed clocks, but the fact that this man's watch had stopped at eleven, and so had the clock in the hospital, seemed like an odd coincidence. Troy backed further away from him and ran with renewed strength. Troy forced herself to ignore the sound of her shoes hitting the sidewalk like drumbeats in the dead, quiet streets.

EMMA HAD WATCHED from the window seat for the first three

hours before she moved to the couch where she read the same five pages over and over again until she had fallen asleep. When she next opened her eyes, thirteen-and-a-half hours had passed since Troy had left the condo. Emma gave herself permission to stop pretending she wasn't worried.

She was on her way to the kitchen to make her sixth cup of tea when the buzzer rang. The weight that had been pressing into her chest eased. She limped to the speaker and pressed the speak button.

"Troy?"

No answer. She's still mad. She came back, though, which means she must be willing to talk to me. Emma pressed the door release button and unlocked the bottom lock. She limped to the window seat. She would be able to keep her hands to herself much better if she sat down. Her face flushed, and she stood up again. Maybe the couch would be a better choice. She hadn't taken one step when a wave of nausea swept over her. Her eyes went to the door and she froze. *Something bad is coming. I need to lock the door.*

The feeling was acute, insistent, but she brushed it off as leftover emotions from her fight with Troy. *She's might be angry, but she wouldn't hurt me.* Even as she thought it, even as she told herself she was being ridiculous, she realized that what she was feeling had nothing to do with Troy. She scanned the room for a weapon and her eyes fell on her cane propped between the wall and the window seat. She needed something more lethal. A gun, no, a knife—she had knives. Her feet felt as though they had been encased in quicksand as she stumbled into the kitchen and reached for the hilt of the longest knife in the butcher block. *What am I doing? I should be hiding, not looking for a weapon.* She pulled the knife out of the butcher block and stood there looking at it. She would have to fight. There was no place for anyone to hide in the condo. She had made sure of that when she moved in. Just as she had made sure to have the extra security chains—the chains. Emma moved toward the front door as fast as her knee could take her.

She had turned the bottom lock and the deadbolt and had the last of the three security chains in her hand when the elevator chimed. She froze as she heard the elevator doors glide open. They would hear her if she put the last one in. *So what if they did?*

Her breathing was shallow as she willed the person to go away. She had been a fool. She should have made sure it was Troy before she pushed the door release. But who else would it have been? Troy had propped the door open earlier. And why not? She'd ridden up and down those streets out there. She said she'd seen no one.

A small scratching sound toward the bottom of the door startled her enough to cause her to take a step back. The chain jerked from her hand and landed against the door with a loud crack. There was complete silence before the scratching began again. This time there was no effort made to hide the fact that someone was on the other side of her door. They wanted her to know they were there.

Movement caught her eye, and Emma took another step back. Her doorknob was moving. Why were they turning the knob back and forth? Wasn't it obvious it was locked? Emma wanted to scream at them to make them go away. The scratching sound began again, and to her horror, Emma recognized the metallic sound that accompanied it.

She heard that sound every time she was forced to go out to the garbage chute or on the handful of occasions that the building manager brought her a package. She knew the sounds of her locks engaging, like she knew the sound of her own voice. *He's trying to pick the locks.* She continued to stare with horrified fascination until the scratching stopped and started again, this time on the deadbolt, and Emma told herself she should find someplace to hide. He didn't seem in any kind of a hurry. He wasn't worried in the least that he might be caught.

Emma gripped the knife hard and swallowed. The dead bolt began to turn. It hung up, as it always did, in the middle, and she held her breath. The lock turned one way, then the other and finally clicked to the open position. The door swung toward Emma, but the safety chains held and sent the door crashing back closed. Emma jumped back and held the knife out in front of her. The door slammed back against the chains again and again, and Emma had a vision of a small, enraged animal.

"Stop it! Go away!" she yelled. The frenzy behind the door escalated. "I have a gun." All movement stopped. The door stood open, the chains hanging limply, swaying as if resting up for the next test of their strength.

If she leaned to the left, she could probably see who it was, but she was afraid, and part of her was hoping that he had gone away. She knew he hadn't. The door was cracked, and she hadn't heard any footsteps. The point of a knife appeared in the door opening. Emma heard the clink of metal on metal as it fumbled for a moment before catching one of the links in the chain. The knife point rocked back and forth until, to Emma's horror, the chain fell, impotent against the door. The point of the knife began working on the last chain with the same amount of patient assurance, which meant she had seconds rather than minutes.

Emma threw her body at the door. She sensed his shock and then his fury, but by then she had already turned the bottom lock and was replacing the chains. All three of them this time. Something small and powerful hit the door.

The scratching began again, only this time it was more furtive and then she heard the elevator chime. Troy had come back. Stark horror followed elation as she realized that, at any second, Troy would be walking unsuspecting out of the elevator and into the path of a maniac.

"No!" Emma rushed the door again, only this time she was unlocking it and removing the chains. She heard the door to the stairs slam just as she opened her front door. The fluorescent light drained the color from the hall and there was a long moment when Emma stood there shaking until Troy walked out of the elevator and came to an abrupt stop when she spotted Emma.

Emma got to Troy as fast as she could and hugged her tightly. "Thank God," she said into Troy's shoulder.

"What's...?"Troy pushed Emma back gently. She spotted the knife and looked behind Emma toward the open door of the condo.

"Someone tried to break in. He ran down the stairs when he heard you coming."

It took Troy a second to comprehend what Emma was saying and then she was through the stairwell door, her feet thundering down the stairs before Emma could yell at her not to chase him.

Emma caught the door before it closed and rushed into the lit stairwell after Troy. She could see the top of Troy's head below her as she took the stairs, sometimes three at a time.

"Don't chase him. He has a knife!" Her knee reminded her with every step how much pain it could give her. She heard the door at the bottom of the stairwell open, and then the only sound was her own slow footsteps. She had the horrifying vision of Troy running out into the darkness and getting ambushed. She stumbled down the last three stairs, saving herself by grabbing the railing at the last minute. She opened the heavy door and leaned against the frame to catch her breath.

The streetlights did nothing to illuminate the area, but Emma could see Troy standing halfway down the block, her feet spread, her hands balled at her sides. Even from a distance and in poor light, Emma could see that Troy was furious.

Come back inside, Troy. We'll be safe inside, she thought, but then she realized she didn't know if that was true anymore. She had thought herself safe inside the condo, but he—whoever he was—had found her, had almost gotten inside, had tried to hurt her. The door had come to rest on Emma's back as she stood in the doorway.

"Come back, you coward. I'm right here. I'm not running anymore." Troy's words echoed down the empty streets.

"Troy? Please come back. Please." Emma was sobbing now. She was afraid for Troy; afraid that, in her anger, she would do something foolish.

"Go back inside." Troy's voice was authoritative, gruff, and angry, but Emma could sense her fear.

The tingling that signaled the start of a migraine began at the back of Emma's head. She swayed but braced herself with a hand on the frame of the door. She closed her eyes. *Not now. Don't do this now.* As if willing a reprieve for herself, the tingling receded and Emma opened her eyes.

Troy had started to walk, then jog, and soon she was sprinting toward her. She caught Emma up in her arms and carried her into the stairwell. The door slammed shut behind them.

Emma couldn't stop shaking. The dizziness had returned and her eyes were blurry. She blinked and tried to get her bearings. Troy released her just long enough to cup the back of her neck in order to pull her into a kiss that was more reassurance then passion.

"EMMA, ANSWER ME, damn it. Are you okay? Did he hurt you?" Troy stared into Emma's glazed, blue eyes. She hadn't meant to yell, but in her frustration and fear, her voice had risen.

Emma blinked and looked at Troy as if she had just realized she was there. "I'm fine. Just scared." Troy pulled her close and held her too tightly. "I'm fine, it's okay," she said right into Troy's ear.

Troy felt the listless arms around her waist strengthen, tighten, and she felt like Emma was holding her up, instead of the other way around.

"How did he find out about you?" Troy asked. "I was so careful. How did he get here first?"

Emma pushed away from Troy. "What are you talking about? You knew this guy was out there? Why wouldn't you tell me?"

"I didn't know. Not until I heard his car today. I followed the sound back to the hospital."

"What hospital? You mean the one where you woke up? You went back there? I thought you said it creeped you out."

"It did, but I heard a car engine, and I figured it had to be coming from there." Troy stopped, uncertain whether she should tell Emma what she had seen.

Emma looked at her long and hard. "What happened? Don't try to sugarcoat it. I'll know if you do," she said firmly.

"I think he killed a woman, a patient there."

Emma's face paled. "Are you sure she wasn't asleep?"

"You mean like the others? No, she wasn't sleeping."

"Maybe she killed herself. You know, because of how things are, I mean." Emma's voice was climbing higher. "You thought about it, too. Maybe she was just so afraid of being alone."

Troy shook her head slowly. "No, she couldn't have done that to herself. He did it. He chased me because I caught him cleaning it up." Troy felt the bile rising in her throat. "I can't figure out why in the hell he would do that to her and then clean it up."

Troy noticed that Emma's face had gone ashen. "Sit down." Emma didn't move. "Sit down," she said louder and pointed to the stairs. Emma's eyes widened. She looked behind her and eased down on one of the stairs. Troy sat down beside her. Emma's reaction to what she had just told her seemed off, but Troy couldn't pinpoint how.

"He chased you?" Emma seemed confused.

"Yeah, that's why I didn't come back until now. I was afraid I'd lead him back to you. I don't know how he got here first." She held Emma's cold hands between her own and tried to rub some warmth into them.

"I jumped over a wall to get away from him. I had to ditch Dite. He threw her off a parking structure."

Emma reeled back as if Troy had slapped her. She ran her hands all over Troy's body, her fingers finding all of the scrapes and bruises.

Emma pulled Troy close then, and Troy buried her face in Emma's neck. "We'll go back and get her when it's safe, all right?"

Troy felt both comforted and embarrassed by the fact that she didn't have to try to hide how upset she was at the thought of losing her bike. "How did he get in? How did he find you?"

"I ...I buzzed him in because I thought it was you."

Troy leaned back and looked at her.

Emma's hand went to the bridge of her nose. "I know. I can't believe I did it now. I move into a secure building because I'm paranoid about break-ins, and I just let him in without verifying who it was." Emma reached up and touched Troy's cheek. "I was so scared that you weren't going to come back that...."

"I just needed to cool down."

"That's what I figured, but you were gone so long. When I heard the buzzer ring, I tried to speak to you but...I don't know. I thought maybe something was wrong with the speaker, or you were still angry with me and didn't want to answer. By the time I realized it wasn't you, he was already getting off the elevator and I could feel something was wrong. How did he know which condo to ring?" Emma asked.

"Every city kid knows that one. But, how'd he know where you were once he got in the building? There's no numbers or anything on the buzzers down there."

"How did you know the first time you came up?"

"After all that time sitting down there yelling up at your window, it was pretty easy to figure out which door you were in once I was up here."

Emma closed her eyes and shuddered. "The blinds. I had them open. I was waiting for you to come back. I guess I must have fallen asleep because it was dark when I woke up." Her voice quivered as she continued to speak. "That bastard must have been out there watching me. How could I have been so stupid?

"Stop that. It's not like you knew anyone else was out there. Thank God you had the security chains on."

"I took them off when I thought you were on your way up." Emma looked down at her hands and then somewhere far off. "I felt him coming, so I put them back on before he could get off the elevator. How did you get through the lobby doors? "

"I still had your keys in my pocket from this morning."

Emma nodded, holding the bridge of her nose with her left hand. "Can you help me back upstairs?"

"Are you sure you're all right?" Troy stood up and saw the knife lying by Emma on the steps. She reached down to help Emma up. "You were going to fight him with that?"

"I'm fine. Just not used to a fifty-yard-dash down stairs." Emma raised the knife, point down. "It was either this or my cane. I thought about hiding, but I kept picturing you getting off the elevator and running into him out there. I couldn't let that happen."

Troy grabbed Emma's shoulders. "Listen to me. If anything like that ever happens again, you hide. You hear me? I can take care of myself."

Emma's expression was hard for Troy to read. "I couldn't just let you walk in to that. He could have hurt you."

"It wasn't worth the risk. You didn't even know if I was coming back, Emma."

"Yes, I did."

Troy noticed the apologetic quality to her voice. As if she had overheard something she wasn't supposed to.

"Or because of— you know?"

"Both. I hoped, and because I felt it right here." Emma touched he chest. "I'm sorry. We don't have to talk about this right now. I know it makes you uncomfortable."

"No," Troy interrupted. "Don't apologize. I mean, yes, it's—you know— embarrassing to know that you knew stuff about me before I even became aware of it, but I'm kind of glad about it now. I mean, if you hadn't sensed it wasn't me..." Troy started looking angry again, and Emma stood up and started walking up the stairs as if every part of her body hurt. Troy followed behind her, wondering why the fact that Emma was so attuned to her had ever felt so disconcerting in the first place.

Chapter Fourteen

THE BLOOD-SMEARED FLOOR was the only evidence left of Reba Stefani's murder. His head smarted where he had hit it on the side of the chair. She was a hooker; the years of abuse were as telling as a diary. In her case, she was still young, but she had suffered a lot in her young life.

Abe touched the back of his head and winced. He had misjudged her. How had he been so damn careless? He had spent so much time trying to figure out why they weren't reacting the way he thought they should that he had missed something important.

"Son of a bitch." He stood up and kicked the mattress. He kicked and kicked until he was out of breath and his foot was sore.

Gregory Shorenstein, his research partner, had been right. He should have allowed someone else to do the observation. Someone with less to lose if things went wrong. And things *had* gone wrong. He had to admit that now.

He glanced at his watch, an extravagant gift from his wife—make that ex-wife, once she learned he would be unemployed.

He was running out of time. He had to find them. It was time to end this thing.

"EMMA, WE SHOULD pick up the pace." Emma stopped in the center of the condo.

"I know," she said, but made no effort to move faster.

"Here, I'll help you pack a few things."

All right." Emma sounded sluggish and distracted.

She's stalling because she's scared to leave the condo again. Too bad. We can be scared after we're safe. We have to get out of here, now. I'll apologize later. "Emma, are you listening to me? We need to get going. That guy could be on his way back with a gun."

Emma nodded, but made no effort to move. The skin on her face looked thin and delicate.

Troy reached for her hand. "Hey, are you...?" Emma started to topple forward and Troy lurched forward just in time to keep Emma from crashing to the floor.

"Jesus, Em, are you all right?" Troy lowered her to the floor.

Tears were streaming down the side of Emma's face. "Em, are you hurt? Tell me what's going on? We don't have to leave right now. The doors are locked."

"It's okay. Just give me a minute."

Troy caressed her cheek. She felt too warm, almost feverish.

"Don't be scared. It's just a migraine. I used to get them all the time." Her voice was a whisper. Her eyes closed after each word, as if the very act of speaking hurt.

"Tell me what to do."

"I have some stuff in the medicine cabinet."

Troy looked toward the bathroom and then back down at Emma. "Are you going to be okay?" Emma's smile was nothing more then a grimace.

A headache couldn't possible cause this much pain, could it? Troy took a few steps and noticed that Emma was wincing at her every footfall. Troy took off her shoes and carried them into the bathroom. Emma's medicine cabinet caused her to flash back to the pharmacy that she had raided in her failed attempt at suicide. Emma had everything from herbs to two-year-old expired prescriptions. Troy grabbed as many bottles as she could and hurried back.

Emma's eyes were closed, but the tears had pooled in her ears. Troy brushed at her hair and felt tears prick her own eyes. She felt so helpless. "I forgot to get water." She would have stood, but Emma reached out and grabbed her wrist.

"It just needs to run its course."

"I'll get you some water so you can take something," Troy said, but Emma didn't release her.

"Can you dim the lights while you're in the kitchen?" Emma's eyes were slits of pain, but she opened them and looked into Troy's eyes. "Don't be scared, okay?"

Troy didn't say anything. It made no sense to deny that she was afraid. Emma could feel what she was feeling. "I'm trying not to be," Troy whispered, but Emma just closed her eyes. Troy hesitated and then forced herself to get up and hurry into the kitchen. She was careful not to slam the cabinet doors, and she only took her eyes off Emma for the second it took her to find a glass. She shut off the lights, grabbed a throw and a pillow from the couch, and kneeled at Emma's side.

Emma's hands were small, tight knots of pain. Chill bumps had risen on her arms. Troy draped the quilt over Emma's body. "I'm going to have to help you sit up so that you can take these, all right?

Emma's response was a hard clicking swallow.

Troy placed her hand beneath Emma's neck, so that she could slip her leg beneath Emma so that her head was pillowed on her thigh. She picked up the glass and waited; Emma's breath came out in a shallow release of air.

"Which one do you need?"

"Doesn't matter."

Emma sat up with Troy's help, swallowed two pills, and lay back down, all without opening her eyes.

"I'm so sorry." Troy struggled to find her words and settled for wiping the tears from the side of Emma's face.

"Not your fault. Had these since puberty."

"Where does it hurt?"

"Right side of my head."

To Troy's relief, Emma's labored breathing became more even as she stroked Emma's temple.

"Why didn't you tell me you didn't feel well?" She stopped speaking when Emma winced. "I'm so sorry for yelling at you before. I thought you were stalling," Troy whispered. Emma opened her eyes again, and Troy brushed a tear from her face. "And I'm also sorry I'm so scared right now. So you'll just have to get better, okay? Please?" Troy leaned forward and kissed her on the forehead.

"Don't say anything. Just let those pills work." Troy was whispering now, but Emma just stared at her as if she no longer understood what Troy was saying.

The knot in Troy's belly eased when Emma's pink-tinged eyes fluttered shut. Troy brushed the hair back from her moist brow and slumped forward.

Her back ached; the small cuts from her fall began to sting. She allowed herself to sit that way for several minutes until she forced her eyes opened. She needed to get Emma in bed and settled so that she could check all the doors downstairs. Emma was in no condition to travel. She would also need to find a weapon.

She leaned close, smelling Emma's shower gel. "Em...?" Guilt kept her from saying anything more, but she still hoped Emma would open her eyes. "We should get you on the couch. The floor's too hard."

Emma's even breathing continued. "Emma?" Troy said again, this time louder. She would feel awful if the sound of her voice made Emma's head hurt worse, but she hadn't stirred. "Emma, please don't..." Troy broke off and looked toward the window. "It's okay," she whispered. "I'm tired, too. You just go ahead and rest as long as you need to. I'll wait right here."

IF IT HADN'T been for the mirror-like finish on the back of his new ipodipod with video, Jake wouldn't have seen the man in the white shirt following him. He wasn't surprised to see him, per se. He had known about the others for a few days now. What surprised him was that the man had followed him home.

"What are you waiting for?" Jake said as he peered through the blinds at the large oak in the front yard. He had watched the man squat there half an hour before, and then, nothing.

Jake cut off the lights and had been kneeling at the window sill ever since. He could see him, now that his eyes had adjusted to the darkness. The man was crouching behind an oak tree that wasn't quite big enough to hide him.

Whoever he was, he knew how to wait on his quarry. And so did Jake. He had learned to be patient at a very young age.

The man in the white shirt hadn't seemed all that interested in speaking with him because he had made no effort to do anything but follow him home.

He's a perv. The idea that of all the people who could have been left awake, he would get himself a perv amused Jake. Jake grinned at the window and shook his head. If he was a perv, he would have tried harder to catch him, but he hadn't.

Now that Jake thought about it, why hadn't the man called out to him? It was almost as if he wanted to see what Jake would do. How he would react. Yeah, that was it. He hadn't wanted to catch him. He wanted to see what he would do. Jake understood that part. It was like dropping salt on slugs to see them squirm.

The idea made Jake angry. He didn't like being played with. He was the master of the game, not the other way around. Whoever this guy was, he had no idea who he was up against. Jake backed away from the window and headed to his bedroom. He was not content to let the man outside make the first move.

Jake pulled the bat that his father had purchased on his thirteenth birthday from its hiding place under the bed. His dad had given it to him in the hopes of luring him away from the TV set.

Jake hadn't been fooled. He had stashed the bat under his bed because he knew it would frustrate Father. Jake took a few practice swings with the bat. He thought he would have been a good baseball player, if he had cared to try.

With the bat slung over his shoulder, he walked barefoot to the sliding glass door. His heart quickened. Time to deal with the perv.

He circled wide around the house and approached him from the rear. He raised the bat high over his head. The man in the white shirt jerked and reached in his pocket. Jake paused. The man pulled out a stick of gum. The wrapper sounded loud in the quiet. As far as Jake could tell, the man never took his eyes from the house, as if afraid to miss something.

Curiosity burned in the back of Jake's head. He nudged the man with the tip of his bat.

"Son of a..." the man toppled forward and then rolled on his back. His looked at the bat and then at Jake's face.

Jake raised the bat an inch higher. "Who are you?"

The man held out his hand. "Hang on a second, son."

"I'm not your son."

"Listen to me. I'm here to help you."

"Help me? How?"

"It's hard to explain, but your parents sent me."

His curiosity got the better of him. "My parents sent you?" he asked, cautiously. "Why should I trust you? You followed me home."

"I know, and I'm sorry I did that. I just wanted to make sure you were safe. Listen, I know you have no reason to believe me, but I can get you out of here."

Jake stared at him, and then dropped the bat to his side.

"Really?" His voice sounded young and close to tears.

The man seemed relieved not to have the bat threatening him anymore. He stood without being told he could do so. "Yeah, I really can."

"How?"

The man looked at his watch. "In about twelve hours my associate will start the process. It's very difficult to explain, but by this time tomorrow, you and I will be home reading the funny papers."

Jake smiled. *Reading the funny papers? What century is this dumb ass living in?*

"I'm at home now."

"Yes, you are. I mean I can get things back to the way they used to be." The man's voice had taken on that exasperated quality that grown ups get when a kid asks too many questions. Jake tightened his grip on the bat.

"Back the way they used to be? You can do that? Is it because you're responsible for me being here in the first place?" Jake's voice had lost its dreaminess.

The man seemed dumbstruck. "Look, son, I'd be happy to talk to you about this on the way."

"Where are we going? You said we have twelve hours."

"Yes, but it's not safe for you to stay here."

"Not safe?" Jakes voice grew tremulous. "Mister, what's going on?"

"I don't know, son. I wish I did."

It was a lie. Jake knew it the instant the words were out the man's mouth.

"All right, I'll come with you, but I want to get a few things from the house first." Jake turned away before the man could protest. He carried the bat high on his neck. He could hear the man hesitate, and then follow behind him. Once Jake entered the house, he didn't turn around until he had reached his bedroom.

He watched the man through the crack in his bedroom door. The man had a look of disgust on his face as he stepped over the food wrappers and dirty dishes on the living room floor. Jake forced himself to wait, loving the way energy surged through his muscles. He rocked from one foot to the other. He would need to do this fast because he had to pee. *Come on, come on.*

Mr. White Shirt hesitated, perhaps two seconds, and then began walking toward the bedroom door. Jake had to take a step forward in order to keep him in his line of sight. Jake waited until the man had his hand on the doorknob to Mother and Father's room before he crept out of his bedroom. The man turned the knob, and the door swung open without a sound. Jake wished with all he had that he could see the look on the man's face when he caught sight of the bed. His right hand started for his crotch but he forced it back on the bat. He shivered as his need to pee reached just the right pitch.

"Hey," Jake whispered.

The man whirled around as if he had screamed the word, his eyes wide and his lips drawn back in silent horror.

Jake swung the bat as hard as he could. The resulting thwack would have made Father proud.

Chapter Fifteen

"EMMA?"

"She can't hear you, Darb." Her father's voice sounded tired and old.

"You don't know that. Emma, we want you to wake up, sweetheart. There's so much you've missed."

Emma tried to turn her head toward her mother's voice. What were they doing here? The last postcard she received was from the Fiji Islands.

"We're so sorry." Her father was talking to her now.

Sorry. What could they be sorry about?

"I know you don't want to wake up. I know you're afraid, but that man can't hurt you anymore. He's dead. They killed the bastard in jail." Her mother's voice had taken on an angry quality that Emma had grown accustomed to hearing after her grandmother's death.

"You shouldn't tell her that."

"Why the hell not, Mark? Dr. Dunham says this is all psychological—that she's afraid to wake up. Maybe if she knows he can't hurt her anymore, she'll feel safe enough to come out of it."

"You know it's not that simple." The tone of her father's voice told Emma that they had had this very same argument many times before.

"What would you suggest? You think we should just let her waste away in this damn bed?"

Her father's voice had risen with his frustration level. "I don't know. Maybe we should get another opinion." Emma heard the scrape of fabric and imagined her father standing up and pacing. "Where is Dr. Dunham? We haven't seen him in days. Are we supposed to just sit back and wait?"

Mom? Dad? What the hell are you talking about? The thought was there, but her mouth wouldn't move. Emma tried her fingers, then her toes; her throat tightened as she realized that she could neither move nor speak.

"Dr. Dunham is one of the best. If he says this might work, we have to at least try."

"He hasn't told us what *this* is, Darby. What if these drugs are hurting her?"

"And you don't think leaving her in this bed isn't hurting her? She would hate being stuck here all alone. Not seeing anyone. Not interacting." The anger in her mother's voice was obvious now, and Emma stopped struggling to speak and waited for her father's reply. His lack of one seemed to be all the validation her mother needed.

"Emma, wake up, darling. Your father and I are right here waiting for you."

A deep aching chasm in her heart seemed to open wider. How could they, the two people responsible for bringing her into this world, be so wrong? She *had* separated herself from the rest of the world.

They didn't know her any better than they'd know a stranger. Had that been her fault? Maybe her mother had been right to be jealous of the gift. Maybe she *had* spent so much time with her grandmother because they had that one thing in common. And maybe she had more in common with Troy than she thought. Maybe Troy wasn't the only one holding on to the best parts of herself for someone no longer living. A wave of anxiety flooded though Emma. Where *was* Troy? Why didn't she hear her voice? Feel her presence? For that matter, why couldn't she feel her parents' presence? Was she awake? Was this a dream?

"Please come back to us, Emma. We need you." Her mother's voice cracked and Emma felt the dig to her heart again. The one time she remembered seeing her mother cry was at Ida's funeral. She had looked like a little girl—a little girl who had just lost her mother. Not like the socialite, globe-trotting woman that Emma had grown to tolerate.

Damn it, this makes no sense.

"Honey," Mark said.

"No, don't '*honey*' me. I don't understand how she could just check out like this. Just leave us to worry."

"Darby, listen to what you're saying. You're getting yourself all worked up."

"Why shouldn't I be worked up? That's my daughter lying in that bed."

"She's my daughter, too," her father said.

"She should have listened to me. I told her to get rid of that damn clinic. It killed my mother and now it's trying to kill her."

"Your mother had a congenital heart problem. It had nothing to do with the clinic."

"And what about, Emma? Are you going to tell me that her being attacked had nothing to do with the clinic? She wouldn't have been in the same breathing space as that man if not for that *damn* clinic."

"Darby, she might be able to hear you."

"Good, I hope she does hear me because...," Emma heard a soft sob that clawed at her heart. "I just want her to wake up so I can tell her how much I love her."

"I know you do, and I wish I could make that happen for you."

Her mother's tears pulled at her. She had never remembered her mother sounding so tired. She wanted to open her eyes, tell her she was there, that she was fine.

But Troy needs me, too, and she's alone.

"Darby, why don't you go for a walk? I'll have you paged if she even so much as blinks."

"I shouldn't."

"Yes, you should. You haven't been outside in days."

"You'll have them page me?"

"Of course." There was a moment of quiet where Emma pictured them kissing goodbye. They never left each other without a kiss, but it was always on the cheek. She had never caught her parents in an impromptu embrace. Their relationship, like their kiss goodbye, was habit; only they hadn't admitted it yet.

"It's Daddy, sweetie. I hope you can hear me. Your mother—she's blaming herself because you two were never close." He paused as if trying to figure out what he would say next. Emma realized that those few short sentences were the longest he had spoken to her in years. "I don't know how anyone could be as close as you and your grandmother, but Emma, your mother loves you. We both do." He choked up then and Emma thought perhaps he was holding her hand.

"Emma?" The voice was soft, female, and scared. Finally, Troy was there.

"Emma, can you hear me? You don't have to be afraid, okay? I'm not going to leave you alone. I'm going to stay right here with you."

Alone? Doesn't she see my father?

"Your mother and I miss you, honey. She's just—"

"You should see the sunset," Troy was saying, her voice was deep and thick with tears.

Emma felt the misery settling over Troy. She was scared. More like terrified. Why couldn't she just wake up and tell them that she was okay? Why couldn't she just fucking wake up. She couldn't speak, she couldn't open her eyes, and she couldn't move anything. Terror ripped through her. Was this what was happening to all those people lying in the streets?

"I was thinking about maybe building you a bike. Would you like that, baby?"

The endearment sent a shot of adrenaline through her. Troy had never called her by an endearment before. She was doing it now because she thought Emma couldn't hear her. *I can hear you, Troy. I'm here, I'm awake.* She screamed it, but nothing came out.

Standard, Oregon
Years ago

THE BOY WOULD have been less surprised if his grandmother had been the one that came strolling through the door of the teachers' lunchroom. He had been expecting Pam, not Hoyt, and not carrying four pizza boxes along with a bag of clean clothes, either.

"Your teacher called and said you needed dry clothes. How'd you get that shiner?" Hoyt handed him the paper bag while glaring at his face.

The Boy told him the truth because he had overheard Ms. Carter tell the story when she had called his house. He had been beaten up and he refused to say who did it. He had wet his pants during the beating. What he didn't tell Hoyt, or anyone else for that matter, was that this wasn't the first time he had done either of those things. The difference was this time it happened at school, and he couldn't change out of his dirty (often pissy) clothes before anyone saw them.

When his story was finished The Boy expected Hoyt to get mad but all he said was, "Go change out of them clothes."

The Boy hurried into the small bathroom and began taking off his wet pants. He was shaking and it wasn't because of the clammy underwear he had just pulled off. He didn't want to make Hoyt madder by taking too long, so he dropped his wet clothes in the paper bag and shoved the bag beneath the sink. He did take the time to wash his hands before opening the door and walking back out to the teachers' lunch room.

Hoyt was standing in front of the long table looking down at the pizza boxes as if he were trying to make a difficult decision.

"What kind of pizza you like, boy?" He hadn't expected that. He expected Hoyt to beat the names of the bullies out of him. He kind of hoped he would. He wanted them to get in trouble; he just didn't want to be called a snitch. "Piss boy" was bad enough.

"Just cheese," he said under his breath, and waited for the look of utter disgust that always came across Hoyt's face when he didn't ask for pepperoni.

"That's what I thought." He opened a box and turned it toward The Boy. "How many can you eat?"

"Two, sir," he said politely, unsure if Hoyt was trying to trick him. Hoyt nodded. "Take three and put 'em on that plate there," he said.

The Boy was quick to do as he was told. He waited, unsure as to what he should do next. Hoyt placed four slices of combination on a plate and set it aside.

"All right, so this is what you do," Hoyt said slowly. His hand was going to his belt and The Boy looked away, tears coming to his eyes. He was going to get whupped 'cause he'd peed his pants. 'Cause he had embarrassed Hoyt. He cupped his crotch roughly. The pressure began to build.

"You're gonna go out there and invite those boys that beat you up in for a pizza party. Don't invite no friends, you understand me?"

"Yes sir." That would be easy; he had no friends.

Hoyt unbuckled his belt and he felt the first real prickle of pee come out. He shifted from one leg to the other. It would hurt more if his legs were wet. He knew that from other times.

"You got to pee again, don't you, boy?"

The Boy hesitated and told Hoyt he did have to go. He hoped Hoyt would let him go relieve himself before he whipped him. Wet legs only made it worse.

Hoyt chuckled and put his hand on the back of The Boy's head. "You're just like me. I always had a weak bladder. Your grandmamma used to try all kinds of home remedies to get me to stop wetting my bed. Even went so far as to invite the most popular boys on the block over to the house for a sleepover." Hoyt rocked back on his heels and the belt buckle clinked against one of the buttons on his Levis. "Nah, that ain't true. She went to their mommas and asked them. They came over kicking and screaming and you know why she did it?"

The Boy shook his head unable to picture his grandmother doing anything besides sitting in her rocking chair.

"She did it so they would tease me when I wet the bed. And I did wet the bed, and they did tease me. It didn't stop me, though. I didn't stop for another two years. Only then, I had to deal with wetting the bed and everyone and their momma knowing about it."

The Boy started to feel sorry for Hoyt. He knew how it felt to be teased and not be able to escape.

"I got her back. Got them all back. The boys who teased me and your grandmother." Hoyt's voice was so conversational that The Boy had almost forgotten that he was about to get a spanking until the clink of Hoyt's belt reminded him.

"See here's something you have to understand. You and me ain't big men."

The Boy's heart swelled even through his fear at being called a man again.

"There's always going to be someone bigger and stronger than us."

The Boy looked at Hoyt's muscular forearm. Hoyt was big. Not tall like Principal McDaniel, but he had lots of muscles.

"Stronger than you?" he asked with disbelief. Hoyt grinned at him again and pushed on the back of his neck.

"Yeah, sometimes stronger than me, too. See, here's the thing, I ain't never been beat." Hoyt's voice had an air of seriousness that made The Boy nervous. "That's what you let them boys do to you if you don't get them back."

"How do I get them back?" He had forgotten about the spanking because he liked the way Hoyt was talking to him—like he was a real man.

"You still got to pee?"

"Yes, sir."

"Me, too."

Hoyt grinned and The Boy's heart quivered with happiness. Hoyt began to unbutton his tight jeans and pulled out his penis. "The bathroom—" The Boy pointed and watched as motionless as a statue as urine arched across the table into one of the open pizza boxes.

The Boy looked at Hoyt too stunned to speak.

"Not too much. You don't want them to taste it before they get a belly full. Ya understand?"

Hoyt gave himself a little shake over one of the boxes, tucked himself back in his pants, and buckled his belt. The Boy kept his hand cupped over his crotch.

Hoyt picked up his plate of pizza, and then pulled a closed pizza box over and tossed the lid back. He took a bite of his own pizza and began chewing. "Best pizza in town," he said. "What you waiting for, boy? You gonna get even or what?" The Boy fumbled with the unfamiliar buttons on the jeans. He didn't remember the last time he had worn these particular jeans. Hoyt must have gotten them from the back of his closet. They were too tight and rode too high above his ankles. They would probably earn him another beating or at least some harsh teasing on the way home from school. Even nice kids couldn't resist teasing someone wearing nut-hugger jeans.

Hoyt dropped the crust of his pizza back on the plate. "It's just gonna be me and you what knows about this, right? Just like our other secret?"

The Boy nodded. His pee came out in drops like Hoyt's had. The urgency that he had felt seconds before had gone away when he realized what Hoyt had intended. Hoyt must have been satisfied, because he picked up his plate, leaned back, and put his cowboy boots up in one of the chairs.

"What you waiting for? I ain't gonna be here all day. Go get 'em."

The Boy started for the door.

"And boy? Make sure you hang on to your plate, unless you want a special topping on your pizza."

He could hear Hoyt cackling at his joke as he walked down the hall and out the double doors.

He was halfway across the playground before he realized that he should be happy. Hoyt wasn't angry—at least not at *him*.

He found Eric hanging by one arm on the monkey bars. The Boy had watched him do this many times from afar. He had tried it once himself, but he had never had the strength to stay up there for long. He bet Hoyt could stay up there longer than anyone.

The Boy braced himself and called out, "Hey."

Eric turned without changing his grip on the bars, saw who was calling him, grinned, and jumped down. "You changed your pants fast, piss boy. Your momma bring those to you or did you borrow them from one of the teachers?"

"I want to invite you and Sean and Andrew inside for a pizza party."

Eric looked suspicious, "Why? We ain't your friends."

Damn right you ain't my friends.

"My father is making me do it. He thinks you'll be my friends if I invite you to a party. I told him you wouldn't, but he said everyone likes pizza. He said you could have as much as you want, too." He told the lie so easily that he surprised himself.

Eric didn't know that neither Hoyt nor Pam gave a shit if The Boy had friends. Eric's parents threw birthday parties for him every year. The Boy could tell by his expression his face that Eric wanted to tell him to go to hell, but free pizza proved too hard for him to turn down.

"All right, I'll get the other guys, but," Eric moved so close that The Boy could smell the milk and cereal he had eaten for breakfast, "we ain't never gonna be friends. No matter what your faggity-ass daddy wants."

The Boy felt the air leave his body as if he had been punched in the stomach. He watched Eric jog off toward the tetherball court. The Boy felt so angry that he was tempted to yell out that Hoyt wasn't faggity, but he changed his mind.

Hoyt wouldn't like it if he got his assed kicked again, so he stifled his rage and walked back toward the building. He was almost at the teachers' lounge when he heard the loud footfalls and the giggles from Sean and Andrew, the boys who always seemed to follow Eric. Hoyt was on his second piece of pizza, he hadn't removed his feet from the chair, even though Ms. Carter was in the room now.

"This is a phenomenal idea, Mr. Pokorney."

"What can I say?" Hoyt was giving her his best smile. "I know boys, and what boy can turn down free pizza? I just hope this will help Junior get along better."

"He's a lucky boy to have such an understanding father." The Boy looked down at the floor and then at Hoyt. What if she smelled the pee or suspected what they'd done? What do they do to people who pee in other people's food?

"They comin', boy?"

"Yes, sir," The Boy answered. He had to move aside to avoid

being pushed up against the wall as the three excited boys raced into the room. The shortest of the three was two inches taller than The Boy. Hoyt stood up. He towered over them—at least he would for a few more years.

He gave them his Hollywood grin. "Have at it, boys. We don't want it getting cold."

Eric elbowed his way toward the pepperoni and picked up a large slice. The Boy picked up his plate and began eating as the other two boys picked up slices from the box with his "special toppings." The other three boys stuffed pizza in their mouth faster than they could chew.

"Hey now, slow it down, boys," Hoyt said and laughed loudly. "There's plenty of pizza for everyone. Take your time and enjoy it. This is good stuff, ain't it?" All three heads bobbed like the figurines they sometimes gave away at the Beavers' games.

Hoyt winked at The Boy and joy flashed through his heart. So this was revenge. He liked it. He liked it a lot.

"So, Ms. Carter," Hoyt was saying, "aren't you going to have a slice?" The Boy stopped chewing and sat up straight. What was Hoyt doing?

"No, I can't. I have to watch what I eat."

Hoyt looked surprised. "You do? What for? You look fantastic." The Boy felt ill. He didn't want Ms. Carter eating pizza that he and Hoyt had peed on. He liked Ms. Carter. He had told Hoyt that.

Ms. Carter laughed, but shook her head.

Relieved, The Boy took another bite of his pizza. He had two slices left on his plate, while Eric and Sean were already on their third.

"You know, on second thought that does look good. Maybe I will have some."

"Try that there combination. It's my favorite," Hoyt said, his mouth full of pizza.

The pizza felt thick and hard to swallow. He felt sick. He looked at Hoyt, but Hoyt was too busy smiling at Ms. Carter. Hoyt picked up his last slice and bit into it. The Boy dropped his half eaten slice back on his plate

"What's the matter, boy? You full already?"

"Yes, sir," he said. He could not tear his eyes from Ms. Carter, who had bitten into her pizza while listening to something Sean was saying. She chewed for what seemed like forever before taking another large bite.

Chapter Sixteen

HE AWAKENED TO a cacophony of gunfire. He was slumped forward, his forehead resting on his arm. He cut off a moan when white hot pain shot down his throat. His head and the back of his neck were so painful that he thought about just falling back into oblivion so that he wouldn't have to deal with it. He remembered the bat coming toward his face, and his eyes flew open.

He focused on his hands first. A girl he'd dated in college—he could no longer remember her name—had called them beautiful. He agreed with her. They were beautiful as hands go, but he had kept his opinion to himself. His hands hung limp and pale, encircled by a pair of silver handcuffs encrusted with dried blood—his blood.

More gunshots blared from a TV in the front room. He forced himself to straighten so that he could see through the open door. Reddish brown droplets marred the light-colored carpet along the hallway. He had misjudged the boy in more ways than one. He wouldn't have guessed that the boy's frail body would be strong enough to drag his dead weight into this room. He must not have been strong enough to lift him on to the bed, or he hadn't tried, because Abe half sat, half lay on the floor, both hands cuffed to the bed post. Judging from the ache in his shoulder blades he had been that way for a long time. Other pains besides the ones in his head and neck made themselves known, and he was finding it hard to concentrate.

The TV had not ceased its endless ricocheting gun fire. He craned his neck to see through the open door and down the hallway. The TV went silent, and the upper body of the boy, Jake, appeared as he leaned back on his elbows to look down the short hall into the room where Abe was held prisoner. Abe wondered how many time he had stared down that hallway at him while he was unconscious.

"You're awake." His voice sounded lazy and relaxed. Fear kept Abe from answering him. Jake stretched, stood up, and started toward him.

The swelling around Abe's eye made it impossible for him to see detail, but he could tell the boy was holding something in his hand. *A gun. Please tell me he doesn't have a gun.* Jake propped one boney shoulder on the door frame. He tapped something against his pant leg and Abe realized from the sound more than the sight of it that it wasn't a gun. He squinted until he made out the colored buttons of a wireless controller.

"Why are you doing this?"

"Because I can." Jake's answer was too matter-of-fact for Abe's liking.

Abe suppressed a shudder. What the hell had he done? Why hadn't he listened to Gregory? He had been too cocky—so sure that he could handle things. And now... now he could be about to lose his life.

"Son, did you kill that woman in my clinic?"

Jake held the game controller in front of him and began pressing the buttons as if he were sitting in front of a TV playing a game. It went on long enough that Abe wondered if he had forgotten he had been asked a question. Jake dropped the controller and slouched back against the door frame and said "Yep."

"Why?" Abe's throat closed around the word. He wanted to lay his head down on his arm. He couldn't care less about the hooker. He cared about his research and now thanks to a mistake—an oversight named Jake—he was finished.

Jake acted as if he hadn't heard the question and continued to study Abe. "Are you a doctor?"

Abe almost didn't answer, but he was too curious not to. "Yes, I am. I want to try to help you."

Jake slanted his head to the side. They could have been discussing football or some other mundane topic. The boy seemed unmoved by anything he had done. Abe's heart gave a hard thump. He had to keep him talking.

"I used to want to be a doctor."

"Why did you change your mind?" Abe was sure he was in shock, although his mouth seemed to making the right sounds. *What happened? How did it all go wrong*? He had checked the backgrounds of all of them, even the hooker. He had made sure that none of them would be a threat to the others.

Jake laughed and his genuine amusement sent cold fingers creeping down Abe's spine. "What difference does it make now? Everyone's asleep; who needs doctors?"

"Jake, why would you do that to your parents?"

Jake's thin body stiffened. "Don't fucking call me that." His voice held an icy threat. No, a promise. Abe felt off kilter, as if he had taken a wrong step and had realized it too late to save himself from a fall. He was very aware of his inability to protect himself. So he stayed quiet until Jake appeared to relax.

Abe kept his tone contrite. "I'm sorry I thought that was your name. What would you like me to call you?"

"You hungry?" Jake asked, once again ignoring Abe's question and asking his own.

Abe wanted to say "no." His stomach churned at the thought of putting anything in it. "Yes," he said. Eating would give the appearance of calm, and it would buy him more time.

Jake pushed away from the doorframe and stretched his arms above his head, fingers entwined. "You're not really hungry, are you?" he asked as he dropped his hands to his sides and let out a great burst of air that Abe was sure was meant to sound like a disinterested sigh.

"I haven't eaten in a few days." That part was true, he hadn't eaten in days and that wasn't helping his head any, either.

Jake looked like a typical bored teenager, but Abe wasn't fooled. He was a chameleon, capable of going from innocent to lethal in seconds. Is that how he had gotten to Reba Stefani? Had she been relieved when her door opened to reveal this frail looking boy? Abe wondered if she had been as afraid as he was now when she looked into those calm eyes for the last time. A shiver traveled through his body as he remembered lifting Jake's eyelid and shining a pen light into each of his eye. They hadn't seemed any different from countless other teen boys. They seemed evil and serpentine now.

"I'll make us something to eat, soon," he said. "First I want to know something." Jake walked into the room and squatted close to Abe. Abe forced himself to continue to breathe. "Did you do all this? Make everyone go to asleep?"

"Yes, I suppose I did." He could have explained more, and he would, if he had to kill more time, but for right now, his main objective was to get little Jake a safe distance away from him.

"Wow!" Jake looked around the room as if he were seeing the wallpaper for the first time. "I can't believe this shit. How much money they paying you?"

"They? They who?"

"Somebody's got to be paying you for this. Doctors make good money, right? I bet you're rich. Are you a surgeon?"

"Yes, I'm trained as a surgeon, but I'm not rich. I'm a researcher."

The look on Jake's face told Abe that he didn't believe him, and in truth, it had been a partial lie. While it was true that as a researcher his salary wasn't as high as a specialized surgeon, he was considered wealthy by most people's standards. He had, to coin a phrase, married well.

"How much are you going to charge the government?"

"Charge the government?" Abe caught Jake's look of exasperation.

"Yeah, you're going to make them pay for this, right?"

"It doesn't work like that. You have to prove that your research is viable first. And then you can get a grant."

"I bet somebody is going to pay you a lot for this."

"It's not about that. My research is supposed to help..." Abe stopped speaking because he could tell Jake wasn't listening.

"I can't believe anyone could do something this cool. It's like being inside a video game."

Cool? He had never been called cool before. There may have been a time in his life when he would have been flattered by a teenager's admiration. But that phase in his life had passed a long time ago.

"Like being inside a video game," Jake had said. It was as if he had no concept of the consequences of his actions, because none of it was real.

"I haven't been to the store. Peanut butter, okay?"

"What?"

"You eat peanut butter?"

"That's fine, thank you." Abe hated peanut butter, but he wouldn't do anything to piss Jake off. Jake walked away without another word. Every so often music from the video game Jake had been playing blared its mindless audio loop. Abe could hear cabinets and the refrigerator door being opened and slammed shut.

He had no idea how much time he had left. He did know that the longer he kept Jake talking, the longer he kept the boy occupied, the better. Jake returned carrying a plate of sandwiches and a glass of milk.

Jake sat down so close to him that Abe could smell the odor of Jake's unwashed body mingled with the peanut butter. Jake held the sandwich up to Abe's mouth, his face expressionless with the exception of the slight hint of boredom. Abe couldn't shake the unsettling feeling that he had done this before.

He leaned forward to take a bite. He tried to ignore the dirt-encrusted nails that held the bread. His stomach protested the food. Abe pushed the vision of Reba Stefani to the back of his mind. Had the hands that made this sandwich been washed after killing her? Would they kill him, too? He hadn't been wrong about this boy's parents.

They were good people who couldn't understand why their son was in a coma.

"I wanted to see if she would die."

Abe stopped chewing; peanut butter and white bread melded his tongue to the roof of his mouth.

"You saw Mother and Father?"

Abe grunted and forced the food down, thankful when the lump went down his esophagus after a scary pause. The boy offered him some of the milk. He drank it, not because he was thirsty, but because it was something to do, something to give him more time.

Jake put the plate on the floor next to the half-empty glass of milk. "I'm going to go finish my game." He stopped in the doorway, his head cocked to the side again. Abe thought he looked like a small mongrel dog that had grown lean and mean from years on his own. His left hand cupped his crotch.

"They left me in that place alone." His voice sounded young and hurt. "I had to walk all the way home and I found them *sleeping*. I cut and cut, but they kept breathing. No matter what I did, they kept breathing. That's why I cut her open. I wanted to see if she would keep breathing, too."

Abe inhaled, horrified.

When he spoke again, Jake's voice reminded Abe of a small child—perhaps a boy of seven.

"How come she stopped breathing? What did you do to us?"

I WON'T DO this to her. I won't leave her here alone.

She couldn't open her eyes or move yet, but she took a deep breath and inhaled the scent of coconut.

"I hear you, baby." Troy's voice had gone hoarse in its excitement. "You just have to open your eyes now."

"Troy."

"I'm right here, I'm right here." Her words sounded like a moan.

"Didn't leave." Emma forced out.

"I'm not going anywhere. I promise. You just open those beautiful eyes for me, okay?"

She was careful to keep her voice soft as she held her so close she could feel her breath on her ear. Peaches and coconuts enveloped Emma and she reached for it. Took it in to her core and used it as a tether to the present.

"I am so sorry that you got stuck here with a weak ass like me. I was so scared of you, Emma. Scared that I might have to let my relationship with Patricia go. I was a coward." Troy buried her face in Emma's neck. Emma realized then that they were both lying on the floor.

"Did I pass out?"

Troy was leaned forward as if her head was too heavy for her to lift.

"Look at me, please."

Troy sat up, and Emma could see her red, swollen eyes. Troy looked away first. "I couldn't wake you up."

Emma put her hand up to Troy's cheek, hating how contorted and pained her face looked. "Help me sit up, all right?"

Emma noticed that Troy's hands were shaking as she helped her sit up. Emma swallowed; the pain had receded a great deal but the dull ache between her eyes persisted.

"Is your head hurting?"

"Not as much as before. I'm a little stiff, though."

"I was too afraid to move you."

Emma searched Troy's face. "Stop blaming yourself."

"I'm not."

"Now you're not telling the truth," Emma said and she leaned back as if Troy had taken a swing at her. "Don't lie to me, please. I can tell."

"I forgot about that." Troy looked so abashed that Emma had to smile.

"Good," she said. "It means you're getting used to it."

"Do you think you can stand?" Troy looked toward the window seat. "You'd be more comfortable up there."

"In a few minutes I'll try, all right?"

Fear was rolling off Troy in fits and waves. So much so that Emma wondered if Troy had even heard her.

"I'm sorry I scared you."

Troy looked as if she wanted to speak, but nothing came out at first. "I was scared you wouldn't wake up."

"No, this happens sometimes. It's my body's way of dealing with the pain from the migraines."

Troy touched the scar on the side of Emma's neck. "I was so scared."

"Listen to me. I won't, of my own free will, leave you, unless you ask me to. All right?" Emma wished she could say more. There will be time for that after we're safe. A feeling of slow understanding overpowered Troy's fear.

"You don't have to say that."

"Yes, I do," Emma said.

"I'm the one who should be comforting you." Troy laughed. "Damn, look at me." She brushed hard at the side of her face with one hand but didn't release her grip on Emma's fingers. "I won't leave you, either."

"I know you won't. Now, you should help me up."

"Do you need more of the pills first?"

"No, I'm fine. How long was I out?"

"A little over four hours, I think."

Emma gasped. "I've never been out that long."

"I couldn't wake you. I kept thinking I had forced you to go out there and you'd gotten infected with something."

"I haven't had a migraine in over a year, so I didn't think to mention that it could happen." The memory of what triggered the migraine came flooding back to her. "I just need a few minutes and we can get going."

"We'll see how you feel tomorrow."

"He knows where we are."

"I won't risk having you pass out again."

"And I won't risk him coming back and finding us here. I think we should go."

Emma sensed Troy's apprehension before she asked, "Do you sense anything?"

Emma had never been asked that question before. Her answer was sharp. "It doesn't work that way. You were right when you said I was scared of trusting it. When I was attacked, it didn't warn me. I never even saw it coming. I won't trust your life to it this time."

Troy's eyes didn't seem focused. Emma grabbed Troy's hand. "Troy, are you listening?"

Troy stood up. "I'll help you grab a few things," she said. Her voice was soft and concerned, but Emma could feel coolness creep between them, like a door left open on a fall evening.

"TROY?" EMMA'S VOICE was sharp and close to her ear.

"Hmm, did you say something?"

"Yes, I've been speaking to you for the last couple minutes."

Troy's smile was apologetic. "I'm sorry, baby. I was thinking about something."

"That's obvious, although the 'baby' thing almost makes it better. You want to tell me what has you so deep in thought you weren't listening to a word I was saying?"

Troy shook her head. "Not right now. I'll tell you on the way."

"Where are we going?"

"That's one of the things I've been thinking about. I work—worked—in a building about a mile from here. It's not pretty, but Raife's got a state of the art security system in there. Not to mention it was a textiles factory before it closed during World War II. It's built like a tank. No one's going to get in there—not without us knowing it. And I know where Raife keeps a Hide-a-Key."

"Raife's your boss?"

"He's the owner of Quick Fast, the company I work for, and he's also my friend." Troy went to the window again, as she had about ten times in the last hour.

Jealousy pulled at Emma's heart. Aside from Patricia, Troy had never mentioned having anyone else in her life. And now she seemed so distant and preoccupied.

Even the endearment of "baby" earlier had been nothing more than a distracted slip of the tongue. Emma felt like she could have been anyone standing there talking to Troy. Troy hugged herself and Emma turned away to take one last look around the condo.

Hardwood floors, bright walls, small open kitchen, new looking appliances. Emma hadn't noticed how unlived in the place looked until now. She walked into her bedroom. Her comforter laid half on the bed and half off. The sheets looked more mussed than they ever had before. Emma walked over and picked up Troy's shirt. She was stalling, and she knew it, but this was her home and—

"You're afraid you'll never see it again." Emma jumped and turned to Troy.

"I didn't hear you walk up."

"I didn't mean to scare you." Troy wrapped Emma in her arms and held her close. Emma pulled out of Troy's embrace and picked up the burnt-orange day pack that she had never had reason to carry. She realized that the rest of her life—all of it—was packed in that one bag.

"I'm ready," she said with a bravado she didn't feel. She had left her home once in two years, and that was under the misguided notion that there was nothing awake that could hurt her. Now she knew differently.

"All right, I guess we're out of here, then."

Emma followed Troy into the living room. The backpack felt too light. *Of course it's light, you fool. There are only clothes in there.*

Emma motioned for Troy to walk out the door first. She took one last look back. She didn't pause or linger, she just reached inside and turned the lock to the locked position. She could see her keys sitting on the breakfast bar where Troy had placed them. She pulled the door closed without getting them. She would never be able to come back.

The elevator pinged just as the door latched shut. She hesitated again before turning around. Troy was holding the elevator door open. When Troy finally spoke, she sounded distracted. "Come on, baby." Troy's voice was soft, coercing her as if she were trying to get Emma to come outside and play instead of leaving her life behind. Emma wanted to strike out; she wanted to make Troy feel like she did. As soon as that thought came, she pushed it away.

Troy was just trying to protect her. Emma sensed when Troy emerged from her personal thoughts and realized Emma was having a hard time. Troy's face softened and Emma felt the empathy emanating from her. The elevator pinged a rapid protest at being blocked open. Troy didn't seem to notice. Her eyes and her attention were focused fondly on Emma.

"Come here," Troy beckoned. "I'll tell you what's bothering me."

Emma hesitated and then walked onto the elevator and into Troy's arms.

Chapter Seventeen

Portland, Oregon
Years ago

THE BOY'S TIE was too tight; his pants rode too high in the crotch and made a little swishing sound when he walked, and the gel in his hair made his scalp feel just like the time he had gotten head lice at school. He wasn't at school and he didn't have head lice.

He was in a courtroom with sixteen adults. All strangers, all staring at him, with eyes full of pity. All except one pair.

He sat with his hands folded and his back straight, as he had been instructed.

"How old are you, son?"

He leaned close to the mike, as he had been taught, and said, "I'm ten," so loud that it echoed throughout the room.

The woman in the black robe smiled at him and said, "You don't have to lean so close. It's very sensitive. It'll pick up your voice fine if you speak in your normal voice."

"Yes ma'am," he said, also as he had been taught to do.

"I'm sorry." Mr. Knightley, the defense attorney didn't look at all sorry. "How old did you say you are?"

The Boy didn't like Mr. Knightley's eyes. It was the way he looked at him, the way he looked at Hoyt. As if they were lower than toilet scum. He also wore so much cologne that when The Boy took a deep breath, he could taste it in his mouth. The Boy guessed it cost a lot of money, maybe as much as twenty bucks.

"I'll be ten, day after tomorrow."

"I see. Why would you tell me you're ten if you're nine?"

"'Cause I'm more ten than nine." The Boy looked at the woman in the black robe wanting her to understand. "Mrs. Sally said that I'm supposed to tell the truth, all the time. And I swore on the Bible. So I wanted to tell the best truth there was."

"So is that what you did when the police asked you about your daddy? Tell the best truth?"

"Your honor?" Mrs. Sally stood up and glared at Mr. Knightly.

The Boy thought she looked beautiful.

"Mr. Knightley, save the dramatics for some other time."

"Yes, your honor." Mr. Knightley walked toward the table where Hoyt sat, writing something on a piece of paper. Without turning around he asked, "Hoyt Junior, do you understand why we're here?"

"Yes." The Boy didn't move, even though his insides felt jittery. He kept his eyes on Mr. Knightley, and he did not, as he had been instructed, look at Hoyt. He had made the mistake of doing that at the beginning of Hoyt's trial. Hoyt had smiled at him. It wasn't the smile that frightened him; it was the way Hoyt had reached for his crotch and gripped and twisted it until The Boy felt as if it were his balls being twisted, even though Hoyt was standing on the other side of the room. The smile never left Hoyt's face.

"They asked me if I had seen my daddy do bad things."

"And what did you tell them?"

The Boy didn't answer at first.

"You have to answer the question, son," said the woman in the black robe.

The Boy looked at Mr. Knightley and, forgetting he didn't have to, leaned close to the microphone and said, "I told them that I hadn't."

"You changed that story later, right?"

"Yes." The Boy left the sir off the end on purpose.

"Why'd you change your story?"

"Because I saw..."

"Your honor?" Mr. Knightley turned to the judge, but she ignored him and instead leaned over to speak to The Boy. The Boy could tell she was getting a little tired of Mr. Knightly. Good! So was he.

"Mr. Knightley doesn't want to know what you told the police. He wants to know why you changed your story in the first place. Right, Mr. Knightley?" The Judge's tone was stern, sort of how Ms. Carter got when the class was being too loud.

Mr. Knightley acted as if the judge hadn't said anything and repeated her words.

"I was scared that I would get into trouble, too."

"Now, why would you think you would be in trouble?"

The Boy felt angry with Mr. Knightley. He was trying to get him to say that he was lying. He knew that, but he didn't understand why. He was just a kid. Hoyt made him do that stuff. It was all Hoyt's fault; he was the parent, the father. *No one knew he did bad things, right? Unless*—he looked at Hoyt—unless Hoyt had told this man the things he had done.

"Because I was there sometimes."

"When were you there?"

"I was there when Hoyt did bad things."

"I see." Mr. Knightley turned and walked away as if he was going to sit down, and The Boy felt a small amount of pressure lift off of his chest. But Mr. Knightley did not sit down next to Hoyt. Instead he turned around and looked at The Boy as if he had just remembered an important question. "Hoyt Junior, who let you into Ms. Carter's house?"

"Nobody."

"Who told you to go inside?"

"Nobody."

"Did your daddy tell you to go into the house?"

"No."

"So why were you there?"

"I wanted—I wanted to see her things."

"You wanted to see Ms. Carter's things? What were you planning to do with those things?"

"Nothing."

"So, you just broke in to see her things." Mr. Knightley looked at the jury and then back at The Boy. "Why did you urinate on Ms. Carter's bed?"

The Boy flushed and looked at Mrs. Sally. "I didn't mean to. It was an accident."

"So, you *just so* happened to be near Ms. Carter's bed when you had to go so bad that you couldn't hold it?"

"Yes," The Boy said.

"Thank you, Hoyt Junior. You've been very helpful."

The Boy wanted to yell out in anger because he didn't like this man. He didn't want to be helpful; this was all Hoyt's fault. Mrs. Sally had said so. All he had to do was tell the truth, and everyone would know it.

Mrs. Sally stood up. "How are you doing, Hoyt Junior? Do you need a glass of water before you continue?"

"No ma'am, I'm fine," he said, remembering this time not to lean too close to the microphone. She smiled, and he felt good that he had remembered.

"What did the police ask you about your father?" She asked.

"They asked if I had ever seen Hoyt do bad things."

"And what did you tell them?"

He hesitated. He considered telling a lie, and then remembered what she had told him earlier that morning. "I told them that I had never seen my daddy hurt anyone."

"And was that the truth?"

"No, ma'am."

"When was the first time you saw your daddy hurt somebody?"

"I saw him hit Pam."

"Who's Pam?"

The Boy looked at her like she was crazy, and then remembered that the other people might not know. "Pam is my mother."

"How old were you when you first saw your father hit your mother?"

"I don't know. I was young because I was wearing the pajamas with the feet the first time I remember it happening. I'm not sure how old I was, though."

"That's okay. That gives us a good idea." Mrs. Sally smiled and The Boy felt warmth in his chest for having said the right thing.

"Anyone else?"

He thought real hard now; he didn't want to disappoint her. "I saw him hit a man who had given him the finger in the Freddy's parking lot."

"Anyone else?"

"He broke into peoples houses and took their stuff. He hurt them, too."

"Did you see him do this?"

The Boy nodded.

"Remember, you have to speak out loud so that Beverly, the woman typing on the keyboard over there, can take down your statement. Do you understand?"

"Yes ma'am. Sometimes I saw. Sometimes I just heard."

"Did you ever see your father break into people's homes and hurt them?"

"Yes, ma'am."

"When?"

The Boy told of the attack on the woman with the little dog. He didn't tell what he did to her dog and then to her. He made it sound like he had watched and not done anything, but that wasn't true. He was being extra careful not to look at Hoyt.

"So why did you tell the police that you had never seen your father hurt anyone"

"Because I was scared."

"What were you scared of?"

"That he would do the same thing to me that he had done to them."

"Who were you scared of?"

"Hoyt." He looked in Hoyt's direction and then away.

"You mean your father?"

"Yes, ma'am."

"Where did you first meet Ms. Carter?"

"At school. She's my teacher."

"Do you like her?"

"Yes, ma'am, she's real nice."

"What kinds of things do you like about her?"

The Boy didn't know what to say at first. "She thinks I could be a doctor." He looked at the judge. "I used to want to be a judge for a long time, too. I changed it to a doctor. Ms. Carter told Hoyt that she thought I'd do good in math and sciences."

"And what did Hoyt do?" Mrs. Sally asked as if he had not already told her this.

The Boy shrugged and then remembered he had to answer out loud. "He laughed and said I just wanted to look at naked girls."

"Did that make you feel bad?"

"No, he always laughed at me."

"So, you liked Ms. Carter because she believed you could be a doctor."

"Yes, ma'am."

"So why would you break into her house if you liked her."

"School was out. I didn't get to see her no more."

"So you broke into her house?"

"Yeah."

"How did you get in?"

"She left a window open in her basement, so I crawled through it."

"Had you done this before?"

"Yeah... uh no...not by myself. Just with Hoyt."

"Did Hoyt show you other ways to get into people's homes?"

"One time he had me act like I had to pee real bad, and one time I acted like I was a dog scratching at the door. Another time I acted like I was lost." The boy frowned. "Oh, and he started showing me how to pick locks. He said if I practice every day, I could be as good as he is in a few years."

The Boy forgot that he wasn't supposed to look at Hoyt. He froze when their eyes met. *He wants to kill me. If he ever gets out, if he ever escapes, he's going to try to kill me.* The Boy looked away, swallowed, and crossed his legs. He wanted to look up to see if Hoyt was staring at him again, but he didn't.

"Why did you urinate in Ms. Carter's bed?"

"I...I didn't mean to."

"Why were you in her bedroom?"

"I just wanted to see where she lived."

"Why?"

"Because I used to pretend that Ms. Carter was my mother."

Ms. Sally leaned close. "Why would you pretend something like that? Didn't you tell us that Pam was your mother? Why would you pretend that Ms. Carter was your mother if you already have one?"

The Boy was confused. They hadn't talked about this and he didn't know what he was supposed to say. He thought hard before he answered. "Ms. Carter is nicer to me. She doesn't curse at me, and she thinks I'm smart. Pam says mean things to me and hits me sometimes. She also says I'm just like Hoyt."

"Do you think you're like Hoyt?"

"No ma'am," The Boy answered before Ms. Sally had finished talking. He saw the corner of her mouth turn up and he felt warm inside.

"So if you like Ms. Carter why *did* you urinate in her bed, Hoyt Junior?" Mrs. Sally asked.

The Boy looked at Hoyt and then at the judge; he felt a soft sob escape his chest. He was tired. He wanted his grandmother. Even Pam would do, but neither of them was in the courtroom. He hadn't seen them since the police had taken him from the house. The judge's eyes looked kind. The women in the jury looked sad to see him cry, so he didn't feel like a stupid little kid when the tears rolled down his cheeks. He wasn't at all surprised when the familiar need to pee came over him. He closed his legs tight against it.

"Why did you urinate in her bed?" She asked again, her voice was soft this time.

He let out a sob. "I got in her bed because I wanted to feel close to her. Like she was my mother, only I fell asleep and I...I wet the bed in my sleep. When I heard her come in, I ran away but she saw me."

It was a lie, of course. He didn't wet the bed. He had peed on Ms. Carter's bed because being in her bedroom had made him have to go real bad.

He looked at Hoyt then. Hoyt's eyes looked like those shiny black rocks he found in the quarry sometimes. He should have been afraid, but he wasn't. He felt more powerful than he ever had. He had taken Hoyt's secret and made it his own. He didn't feel like a weak little boy anymore. He had all the power. He put his hands over his face. Through the slit in his fingers he could make out some of the jury. Their faces were concerned and full of pity. He could also make out Hoyt's murderous stare. He was pretty sure the jury saw that, too.

Goodbye, Hoyt.

"I SAW SOMETHING when I was on my way back here after that guy chased me. There's this little store that has these monitors in the window. Not monitors, really, they're more like flat-panel TVs."

"Really? Is it a new store?" Emma asked in an effort to push down the anxiety by focusing her attention on something else.

"It's been there for a few years. They have these big ass flat-panels in the window with cameras on them. They film people as they walk by and play it back on the screens. Sometimes they play a tape; sometimes it's real time. Anyway, I noticed someone had busted out a window.

That caught Emma's attention. "You think he broke in?"

"He must have. If it had happened—before this thing, then they would have had to hire a guard or something. A store like that would have been robbed blind with a window busted out and no security."

"What kind of store is it?"

"It's a poser messenger store. One of the guys at Quick Fast threatened to sue them, because they recorded him riding by on his route and played it on those screens. He claimed it made it look like he endorsed the store."

"They stop doing it?"

"Nah, they just changed it so that they recorded everyone, not just messengers.

Anyway, none of us could afford to shop in that store, not that they needed us to. They got plenty of money from rich kids who wanted to look the part without the risk and the crappy pay."

Emma looked at Troy. "One of the first things I noticed about you was how you dressed. You have a great look."

Troy seemed embarrassed by Emma's compliment.

"Thanks, but with the exception of that one hundred-fifty-dollar shirt that I, um, borrowed, I get most of my stuff at Goodwill."

"You do?"

"You sound surprised."

"I am, sort of. Your clothes...fit like they were made for you." Emma couldn't help the glance she took at Troy's pants. Cargos that followed the curve of her backside as if they were made for her.

"You learn to be good with a needle when you grow up poor. I didn't make much money as a messenger either."

"Money's nothing more then paper and metal now. Your skills with the needle might be the new form of barter. I'd much rather have a 'Troy-Goodwill special' than something out of a trendy store."

Troy laughed. "Kids eat that shit up like popcorn, which is too bad, because it's expensive, and most of it is just cheap fabric thrown together in some sweathouse. But that's not what's got me thinking. The TV screens were all snow, as if the tape or DVD or whatever they use, had run out."

"Those things only last a few hours, right?"

"I would guess they would have to last at least eight hours, since they leave them running all night after the store closes. But there was this guy lying out front. His clothes were kind of spendy looking, but his watch was cracked and stuck on eleven. A guy like that wouldn't be walking around wearing a busted watch. So I'm thinking he busted it when he fell. I figure this thing—what ever it is—must have happened at eleven."

"Okay." Beyond that one word, Emma was silently mulling over Troy's story. "Oh, so you're thinking that if the cameras were recording at eleven, whatever happened, it would have been recorded."

"All we'd have to do is find the tape. The store's not that far from here." Troy looked at Emma. "You think you can walk another half-mile or so?"

Emma seemed confused by the question. "No problem."

"Did you forget your cane?"

"I left it."

"Do you want to go back and get it?

"I left the keys inside and locked the door. I don't want to go back there."

Emma became conscious of her body and of Troy's concern. Although she would always limp, she felt no better or worse for not having the cane. "I don't think I've needed that cane for a long time."

"Are you sure? I can go back and get it."

"Not without me. Besides, that cane was nothing special. I could always 'borrow' a new one if I needed to."

Troy grinned. "If you're sure."

"I'm sure." They walked for a few minutes in silence.

"Wow," Emma said. "I don't use a cane anymore."

"Wow," Troy echoed, and if not for the adoration that flowed from her, Emma might have thought Troy was making fun of her.

Emma took a deep breath. "I might get tired a bit easier, though."

"You just let me know when you're tired, and we'll stop, okay?"

"I promise I will."

Troy smiled and pointed with her chin. "The store is just up the way here."

THE MAN IN the overcoat and pinstriped pants lay in the exact same position on the sidewalk in front of the store. The glass on his jacket was no longer as noticeable, but the snowy monitors and the hole in the window were just as she remembered. The hole in the window was small, but big enough for her and Emma to squeeze through.

The store hadn't been looted, but someone had left a black backpack on the floor near the cash register counter. A shoe had been left in the middle of the floor, and several pairs of jeans and shirts had been left draped over clothing racks.

Troy picked up the shoe, flipped it upside down, and looked at the soles. "I wouldn't steal these shoes either. These soles wouldn't stick to glue." Troy left the shoe on the counter while she searched behind it for a recorder of some sort.

Emma picked up the shoe, and then a pair of jeans and a shirt.

"Troy, what did that man look like? Emma held the jeans out in front of her. The one who chased you?"

"I don't know. Just some white guy—dark hair, dark eyes, thin."

"How thin? How tall? Did he look like he would wear these kinds of clothes?"

Troy shrugged. "I don't remember what he was wearing, but he was five-eleven or six foot, maybe." Troy shrugged. "Average, why do you ask?"

Emma held up the shoe looking pale and confused. "This shoe is small, I couldn't fit it, and I bet you couldn't either."

"Maybe that's why he didn't take them, because they were the wrong size." But even before Emma answered Troy knew that that didn't make sense.

"They would all have to be the wrong size. Those pants are a twenty-eight. Twenty-eight, which makes them too small for the man you described."

"There's someone else awake." Troy said in amazement.

"I'm guessing it's a kid," Emma said.

"Shit." Troy snatched the scarf off her head and started twisting it. "We can't leave until we know for sure. Especially if it's a kid."

"Even if it isn't, we have to at least let them know that a psycho is out there."

"Let's find the recorder. If we're lucky, we'll get a look at who we're dealing with."

It took them ten minutes to find several recorders in a cabinet in the manager's office. It took them several more minutes to find the remote and a way to feed it to the monitor. And then it took almost an hour to get the tape to the time stamp right before eleven o'clock.

"All right, here we go," Troy said. They both stared into the small viewing screen. People walked by, looked into the screen, smiled and continued on their way for the next five minutes.

"Ten-fifty-nine, p.m." Emma sounded as if she were waiting for the ball to drop on New Years Eve.

"Hey, look." Troy pointed at the monitor. "There's Mr. Overcoat." The upright and walking version of the sleeping man out front looked at the camera, smiled at himself, and then the screen went to snow. "What the hell?" Troy said as she looked at the time stamp, it was eleven o'clock, on the dot...

"Troy, look," Emma said in a hushed voice. The monitors had picture again, and the man in the wool coat was lying on the sidewalk in front of the store the time stamp read 11:01 pm.

"Why would the tape stop right before it happened?"

"I don't know," Troy said as she picked up the remote and fast forwarded the tape. They sat in silence for what seemed like an eternity. If not for the small wrinkle that wiggled across the screen, it was as if they were watching in real time. Troy jumped and stopped the fast forward when a figure appeared in the frame. They both watched a boy of about twelve, maybe a little older but not by much, stood with his hands pressed against the window. The time stamped at the bottom of the screen read 4:45a.m.

"Look at him. He doesn't even look scared. He looks like he's window shopping," Emma said.

"It's shock. I was like that after I woke up in that hospital."

"What's he doing out so early in the morning?"

"Why not? Who's going to tell him to go to bed?" Troy felt a kinship toward him as they watched him walk away and return a while later with what looked like a heavy lead pipe. It took him several attempts to break through the window before he was successful. They could no longer see what he was doing once he disappeared into the store. The tape ran out before they saw him come back out, but they could see how the boy had amused himself by trying on clothing that he had probably either been unable to afford or not allowed to wear.

"How are we going to find him?" Emma asked.

"It'll be near impossible unless he comes back downtown to do some more shopping. Hey, did you notice the bag he was carrying?"

"I think so. What about it?"

"It was a black Jansport. I think I saw one out front." Troy was already walking out of the small office. "Come on."

"You think he left his bag?" Emma asked.

"Why not? If he traded up for a new one, what would be the point of taking the old one home?"

"The black Jansport was propped up against the cash register counter as if the boy had set it down and forgotten about it. Troy had the zipper open and was riffling through the bag. She pulled out a small wallet with a Multnomah County library card and a student ID inside.

"His name's Jake Ostroph," she told Emma. "Ostroph can't be a common name. There's bound to be a phone book around here."

"You think his parents are listed?" Emma sounded doubtful. "I didn't know that people did that anymore."

"Don't know, but it's a place to start."

Chapter Eighteen

DITE WOULD HAVE made the trip to the Ostroph house from downtown in about fifteen minutes. Alone, she could have made it in about forty-five, but with Emma and her knee, it would take them over an hour. Troy was surprised to realize that she was fine with the slower pace.

"How you doing?"

"It feels good to walk." Emma said, her voice had gone shy and Troy wondered how much of her thoughts were transparent to Emma.

Troy smiled at her and went back to scanning the streets and darkened windows of buildings two blocks ahead of them. She would have liked to have left Emma somewhere where she would be safe, but she had promised not to leave her, and she'd be damned if she was going to break that promise.

There's something happening between us, and I think I like it. She glanced at Emma. Troy realized she had been waiting for signs that Emma was getting tired so she could suggest that they rest. But Emma's breathing seemed no more elevated than if she had been walking from her kitchen to her window seat.

Troy felt her face flush as she thought about the window seat and the last time she had been on it with Emma. She pretended interest in an old colonial home that had been converted into several small apartments. Two signs in its windows reported that the colonial had both "Rooms Available" and that you could "Rent by the Week." *I wonder if they have rooms with window seats.*

Emma laced her fingers with hers. "What are you thinking?" Emma's voice was soft, seductive.

"I'm thinking you should stop talking to me in that sexy voice or we might have to take them up on their offer." Troy pointed at the "Rooms Available" sign. It didn't take Emma long to catch on and she laughed.

Mid-year's resolution: get her to do that more often. Troy looked behind them to make sure they weren't being followed before she turned to look at Emma.

"You're very quiet. Are you sure you're okay?"

"I was just thinking that you could have been there and back by now on your bike."

"Sure, but I'd be worrying about you the whole time."

Emma didn't say anything and Troy glanced over at her. She loved the way her hair had started to curl over her ear in the light mist.

"I hate that I'm already starting to slow you down."

Troy tried to catch her eye, but Emma was staring straight ahead.

"You're not slowing me down. I mean, yes, I could have gotten there faster on a bike, but faster isn't always better."

"Sometimes it's all right, though." Emma said, and Troy could hear the smile in her voice. It made Troy think of sex. It aroused her and then embarrassed her because she knew Emma sensed what she was thinking. Emma laughed again and Troy thought it was almost worth being the brunt of Emma's teasing.

"I'm sorry," Emma said.

"Liar."

Emma nodded. "I'm totally lying."

Damn it. The world's gone to hell, my bike is gone, some guy is out there killing people, and I'll be damned if I don't feel incredible. "Almost there," Troy said to distract herself.

"Why do you suppose he didn't answer the phone?"

"We're making an assumption he went home in the first place, Emma. Hell, I haven't been to my apartment since the second day, and even then, it was just to throw some things in my bag."

"I assumed you stopped by your place when you were out on your rides."

Troy tried to hide her embarrassment. "No, I was doing a lot of riding around looking for other people, but I'd go see Patricia a lot, too."

Emma didn't say anything.

"Let's rest over here." Troy led Emma to a small stretch of grass in a center median and they sat down on the park's solitary bench. "How's your knee?"

"I'll be sore tomorrow, but right now, it feels good to walk. Thank you for being so patient."

"Emma, I won't lie to you. I was in love with Patricia. I wish she had never died. I know that she had issues—problems. But I didn't see any of that when we were together. Maybe I was just young and ignorant, but I was happy when I was with her."

Emma tried to smile, but gave up. "I understand that, Troy. I wasn't trying to make you not love her anymore. At least, I hope I wasn't."

Troy put her hand on Emma's leg. "Let me finish before I chicken out, okay?"

Emma sat stiff, with her head down.

"Even with all this shit that's going on, I can tell we have something special. I'm scared. I was scared when I started to realize what was happening between us. For the longest time Patricia was the only connection I had to the world. When she was alive, my main goal was trying to make her happy, and after she died, my goal was trying to live without her."

"You don't have to explain."

"I want to. I accepted that Patricia was gone a long time before she died. I didn't know about the drugs, I just knew she was never as happy as I was. She was always searching for something that I couldn't give her. I was so sure that one day she would figure things out, and I would be all she needed."

Emma wasn't looking at her now, so Troy finished in a rush. "I was at the cemetery when I heard the car engine."

"You went to Patricia's grave," Emma said.

"I was telling her goodbye."

Emma did look up at that.

"It was just kind of symbolic. But it felt right, like I was being released. I was going to tell you when I got back, but that guy was trying to break in, and then you got sick."

Emma searched Troy's face.

"Thank you for telling me." Emma leaned forward and kissed her. She felt Troy's longing and happiness in that kiss.

Or was it her own?

"I am so glad I met you," Emma whispered against Troy's mouth. "So damn glad."

Troy couldn't say anything. They sat smiling at each other. Emma broke contact first by turning her face up as the light mist turned into a fine rain.

"We always seem to be getting rained on."

Troy turned her face up as well. "I think summer's just about over." She stood up and offered Emma her hand. "We should get going."

Emma stood up. "Oh, yeah. I'm going to be very sore."

"I could rub you down once we get settled somewhere."

"I thought you'd never offer."

They were quiet for half a block before Troy said, "Do you think we should leave Portland? I mean it's a big place. We might not see that guy again."

"I never thought I'd ever leave Portland." Emma looked around. "I love this city, but half of what I loved about it was the people." Emma chuckled. "I loved the people so much, I had nothing to do with them for two years, and now they aren't here anymore." She shook her head. "I worried every time you went for a ride, Troy."

Troy squeezed her hand. "And I worried every time I was away from you. Which means we can't stay here."

"Where would we go?"

"We could go anywhere we wanted. I've been avoiding the whole car thing for too long, I've been thinking about us borrowing one."

"Not on my account, you won't." Emma's tone was firm.

"No? Funny, I can't think of a better reason."

"What about this boy, Jake? What if he doesn't want to leave his parents?"

"All we can do is tell him what's going on and ask him what he wants to do. It's his decision in the end."

"We can't leave him alone here. Not with that man on the loose."

"He's been on his own for a while now, Em. I think that makes him capable of making his own decisions. We need to let him know about the guy at the hospital. If he doesn't want to leave town with us, we won't force the issue."

"And if he wants to?"

Troy looked at Emma, unsure where she was going with the question. "Then we bring him with us. I went nuts before I found you. I wouldn't wish that kind of isolation on my worst enemy, let alone a kid."

Emma squeezed her hand and Troy had to remind herself that she and Emma hadn't known each other long. "Should be just around the corner," she said because Emma's breathing had become more labored.

The Ostroph house was on the corner. It was large—four bedrooms Troy guessed from looking at it. It had three enormous old oak trees in a thick, green yard that looked as if someone—a gardener, no doubt—had spent many hours tending it. Troy wondered what it would be like to grow up in a house that size.

It looked as though every light, including the one outside the front door, had been left on.

Troy started toward the front door, but was brought up short because her fingers were still linked with Emma's, and Emma hadn't moved.

"What's wrong?"

"Let's wait a minute. Come over here." Emma pulled Troy behind a tree and kept her eyes on the house. In a few minutes the boy passed in front of the window, holding a bottle of what looked like beer.

"Is he drinking a beer?" Troy asked.

"Could be a soda."

"Could be a beer," Troy insisted and remembered her own reaction to not finding anyone else awake when she came to in the hospital. "Let's go ask him." She stood up and started toward the door.

"Troy, no. Wait, please." There was urgency in Emma's voice

now. Troy turned to look at her in the fading light.

"Emma, what's going on? I thought we agreed that we need to at least tell him so that he knows there's a lunatic out there."

"Yes, I know, but there's something wrong."

Troy studied Emma's face. "What do you mean?"

"I just know it feels wrong. I sense pain and fear, disorientation, and I don't know but..."

Troy was about to tell Emma she was over-reacting, but then thought better of it. "All the more reason to check in on him. Stay here. I'll be right back," she said, and before Emma could protest, she jogged, hunched over, to the front porch and peered in the window.

She could feel Emma's eyes on her back as she watched the boy, Jake. He had brown hair and eyes and a skinny chest. He was staring fixedly at the TV set. His shoulders relaxed as he moved his thumbs back and forth over a game controller. He picked up the beer and sipped it.

Troy jogged back to the tree. "He's drinking a beer and playing a video game. He didn't look afraid."

"I don't know. I just get a sense of fear and...pain." Troy could see the frustration on Emma's face.

"I don't get it. He doesn't look like he's in any kind of pain, but if he is, we need to help him."

"Don't you think I know that?" Emma closed her eyes, "I'm sorry. I don't understand it, either."

"We have to let him know we're here."

"He didn't answer the phone. He probably won't answer the door, either."

"Maybe he was out getting food or games or something. Do you want to wait here? I can call to you if it's safe."

"No, I'm coming with you." Emma stood up and took Troy's hand.

This is nuts. It's just a kid. But even as she walked toward the door, Troy felt uneasy. Emma seemed to be spot-on where her feelings were concerned, but if this boy was hurt or afraid, that made it even more necessary to make contact with him. She knew how it felt to believe that everyone in the world was asleep except you.

She put her finger on the doorbell and, after a brief hesitation, pushed. Emma stared straight ahead, not looking at her, but not releasing her hand either.

The door swung open and The Boy stood there looking at them. He did not look surprised. In fact, there was no expression on his face at all.

"Hi," he said as if greeting a door to door salesman.

"Troy?" Emma gasped.

But Troy had already seen the gun and the empty look in The Boy's eyes.

"HEY LOOK." TROY released Emma's hand and held both hers in the air. "We aren't here to hurt you. We just wanted to make sure you were all right."

Emma kept her hands curled into fists at her side. Why hadn't she listened to it? It had tried to warn her that there was something wrong here. Why hadn't she insisted that Troy come away from the house?

The Boy, his Multnomah county library card said his name was Jake, was looking at Troy strangely. He seemed almost in a trance. Emma followed the boy's gaze to Troy's arms. Her biceps were readily noticeable. Carrying Dite was probably all the exercise she had ever needed to keep her upper body toned. The boy Jake stared at Troy's arms a second longer, and then finally Emma sensed something coming from the boy that she could recognize: admiration and envy. It seemed so inconsistent with the situation that Emma gave her head an almost violent shake.

Troy glanced at her, her concern so immediate that it soothed Emma's nerves.

"How did you find me?" Jake's voice was deep, not quiet baritone, but deeper than should have been possible from such a frail body. Deeper than it should have been. Emma looked at his thin chest, at the way he held the gun, and at the lean, whipcord muscles on his arms. His voice was not that of a ten year old. He was closer to fifteen or sixteen than ten.

"We aren't here to hurt you. We...." Troy's voice lowered as she looked into his eyes.

"What do you want, then?"

"There's someone else awake. A man."

Jake cocked his head to the side, and Emma sensed confusion and then amusement radiating from him. The last emotion sent freezing-cold apprehension through her veins. She reached for Troy's hand and squeezed hard.

"We're sorry to have bothered you," Emma said and began to pull at Troy's hand.

"I already knew about that guy."

"Good. We just wanted to make sure. We'll go now." He hadn't asked them what they knew and he hadn't seemed scared. Emma couldn't sense much of anything coming from him and that scared her more than the gun.

Emma backed away, pulling Troy with her. The gun followed their movements, stopping them in place. Jake was so calm that his chest barely moved.

"You're too late. He got here before you did." Jake's features melted, seemed younger, his voice slightly higher.

"He's in shock," Emma thought, but something held her back, even as the gun dropped to his side.

"That's why I got this," he raised the gun again so that it was in front of their faces. Troy's body tensed visibly.

"Come in, please."

"Why don't you put the gun down first? Before you accidentally hurt someone."

"I'll put it down when I'm ready. What made you think I needed your help?"

The question was odd, considering the circumstances outside. He gestured for them to come inside. His emotions, or lack of them, told Emma they had no choice.

This person—boy, teenager, whatever—would shoot them if they didn't do as he asked. She walked through the door the house, with Troy behind her.

Shock. He must be in shock. The thought felt hollow and unlikely. *He's crazy. That's got to be it. That's got to be why I can't feel his emotions. Maybe I have some kind of built in safety mechanism that keeps me safe from…*

"I knew about the man before he got here. I was expecting him. I knew about you, too." His voice was filled with pride and disdain.

"How did you know?" Troy's confusion engulfed Emma, holding on to her. "Did you wake up at that clinic, too? Look... Jake. Your name is Jake, right?

He didn't answer. In fact he showed no response to the name at all. Finally he asked, "How did you find me?"

"You left your bag at a store downtown. Your wallet was inside." He looked as if he hadn't heard Troy's answer.

Jake took a deep breath. "In there," he said, looking across the living room toward a closed door.

"What?"

"Look in there," he said softly.

Troy took Emma's hand.

"No, she can stay here," Jake said, raising the gun again. This time he pointed it at Troy, probably dismissing Emma as no threat.

"No." Troy's voice had an edge to it. "She's coming with me."

Emma fought the need to laugh as Troy stared Jake down as if he didn't have a gun. It was Jake who broke the silent struggle first. "If she tries anything, I'll shoot her. If you try anything, I'll shoot her." Emma sensed anger rolling off Troy in waves, but there was fear too.

"Let me guess, you got that dialogue from one of your games, right? Why don't you just tell us what you want us to know so we can go? Save the corny ass Dirty Harry shit for someone who gives a fuck." Troy felt Emma's fingers tighten around her own. She was trying to warn her against provoking Jake.

"I want you to look in the room first, and then I might let you go," Jake said through gritted teeth.

"Fine," Troy said, as if appeasing a child. She sighed and

stomped toward the door. But Emma could feel her terror as evidenced by the tight grip on her hand.

Emma didn't take her eyes off Jake until Troy's free hand was on the door knob. She opened the door slightly and peered inside. Emma tried to look over Troy's shoulder, but Troy had already backed up, pulling Emma roughly with her.

"What is it?"

"Come away from there, now," Troy commanded.

But Emma had already released Troy's hand, and pushed the door open so that she could see into the room. Her nose was assailed with the smell of old urine. The only light was from a closet door; the rest of the room was cloaked in gray. But she could make out two people lying supine on a bed stained almost completely magenta with blood. The skin on their chests had been pulled back and pinned to the bed with long, metal stakes with loops at the ends.

Both their chests moved up and down in unison.

In a macabre impersonation of domesticity, a dog had been placed at the foot of the bed. Its scalp had been peeled back like an orange and pinned to the bed with the same metal skewers.

Shish kebab skewers, Emma realized.

Bile shot up Emma's throat and she did nothing to stop it. Troy pulled her back into the hallway and shut the door just before Emma began to retch against its threshold. Tears rolled down her face. She took the kerchief Troy handed her and began to wipe her mouth with it.

"Did that bastard do this to them?" Emma heard Troy ask Jake.

A demented kind of anger hit Emma with a force so hard that she whipped around to stare at Jake's red face. She kept the kerchief over her mouth as she stared at Jake in horror.

The boy was almost shaking with the force of the emotions that he no longer had to keep in check. He was clutching his crotch with his left hand while, and the gun shook in his right hand.

"You see that? Did you see it?" His voice had gone up so high that Emma was afraid he would pull the trigger in his excitement.

"Yes," Emma said. She felt Troy's revulsion when she realized what they were dealing with. "We saw it."

"Do you know who did that? Do you?" Jake held his pants bunched as his grip tightened around his testicles. Emma imagined his hand tightening around the gun.

"You!" She whispered. Her throat muscles constricted around the word.

"That's right." His eyes had glazed over and his voice took on a dreamy tone. "Those were mine." As he spoke, a slow, dark stain ran down his pant leg as if drawn with a Sharpie.

Chapter Nineteen

Portland, Oregon
Five Years Ago

"HOYT?" THE BOY jumped when he heard the name. He realized that Mrs. Sally was talking to him and not to his father.

"Did you hear what I said?"

"You said I did a good job today," he said, and Mrs. Sally smiled. He really did like her smile. He wondered if he would see her again after he got to go home.

"Yes, you did perfectly. Did you hear what I said after that? About your mother?"

"What about her?"

Mrs. Sally cleared her throat. "I'm afraid she's having a hard time making ends meet. She lost her job when the news came out about your father. She's also been sick."

"Sick?"

"She can't afford to have you come home right now."

"But what about my grandmother?"

"From what I understand, your grandmother would have a hard time feeding herself, let alone a nine-year-old boy. I believe your mother had to make her a ward of the state, too."

"What does that mean?"

"It means that she gets to sleep in a nice room, and she'll have people come to see her whose job it will be to take care of her." Mrs. Sally was shaking her head from side to side as she spoke, and it confused him. "She'll get three square meals a day. They'll buy her clothes, make sure she's clean and getting the proper medical attention and exercise. Doesn't that sound nice?"

The Boy, Hoyt Junior, considered what Mrs. Sally said. It did sound like she might be in a better place. All she did at home was sit in that rocker and stare at the TV. When Pam did give her a bath, she was always real mad about it. Sometimes he wondered if Pam scrubbed too hard. Grandma would have tears in her eyes when she was put back in her chair, all pink and smelling of Johnson and

Johnson lotion. He didn't mind kissing her cheek when she didn't smell like mashed peas, applesauce, and spit.

"You said if I told the truth everything would be okay. You said I would be able to go home!"

Mrs. Sally stood up, came around her desk, and kneeled in front of his chair. "I know I did, and I'm sorry." She put her hand on his leg to stop the rocking. "But you don't really want to go back to that place, do you? You don't want things to go back the way they were."

"Yes, I do. I want to go home," he sobbed.

"Oh sweetie, no, you can't possibly want to go back there." She leaned close. "Listen. I had a friend of mine pull some strings to get you into a good home. I know it's hard right now, but trust me; this is going to be for the best. And when she's better, your mother can go to the state and tell them she's ready to have you back home."

"When will she be better? When will she come get me?" He was scared and suddenly very sorry he hadn't kept his mouth shut. Hoyt was right. This was bad and it was all his fault.

"I don't know, Hoyt. Your mother will need to start feeling better and then she'll need to find a new job." Mrs. Sally stood up. He thought she looked tired.

"When will she be better? When will she come get me?"

"I don't know, but until she does, I have a friend whose job is to help good boys find nice places to stay until they can go back home. I talked to her yesterday, and she told me she had already found a very nice couple for you to stay with. They specifically requested a boy. They've seen your pictures, and they know how hard it's been for you. They live in a nice, big house where you could have a big room of your own. Doesn't that sound nice?"

A big room of his own *did* sound nice.

"Now, there is one thing. I need you to be real grown up about something that might be hard for you to understand. Can you do that for me?"

The boy shook his head and tried to stop sobbing.

"Remember when you told me how you got beat up all the time at school?

How would you like to go to a new school? With new kids that you could have over to your new house?"

Mr. and Mrs. Ostroph—that's the family you'll be staying with here in Portland—think it might be better if you used a different name. You and your father are both named Hoyt Pokorney. Your father did some very bad things. It might be better if you came up with something else to call yourself—just until your mother comes to get you. You could pretend you were acting in a TV movie."

The boy had stopped sobbing. He could name himself anything he wanted. He didn't have to be The Boy or Hoyt Pokorney, Jr., anymore. He could have any name he wanted.

"The Ostrophs suggested 'Jake.'" Ms. Sally leaned back in her chair. "But only if you liked that name. It's your choice, of course. They will want you to use their last name so that you'll be like a real family. Would that be all right with you?"

"Jake." His voice was garbled from snot and tears, but he said it again to make it real. "Jake." He liked it. It sounded like the name of a construction worker or a fireman. It sounded like a name a big man would have. "I like the name Jake."

"Hello, Jake Ostroph. It's very nice to meet you." She held her hand out like he really was a big man already.

He hesitated before shaking it as if they had never met before. Jake Ostroph? It was better then Hoyt Pokorney, Junior.

Anything would be better than that.

"HURRY UP." JAKE had a stoned, excited sound to his voice that scared Troy more than the gun pointed at her back.

She and Emma were being herded toward a room with an open padlock on the door. Emma stumbled and Troy reached for her elbow. She didn't want to be locked in this room either.

"She's walking as fast as she can, all right?" Troy snapped over her shoulder. She didn't look back for fear that she would see him pull the trigger. Jake didn't say anything else until they reached the door.

"It's unlocked, open it," he said. Troy hesitated and then turned the knob. This was her fault. She should have trusted Emma. She should have let her keep them away from this house. The light rain must have stopped because sunlight was forcing its way through dark blue curtains.

This is a boy's room. Must be Jake's. No, the furnishings are too juvenile or maybe it was decorated when he was younger and it hasn't been updated.

A faint ammonia-like smell hung in the air, but it was quickly pushed to the far reaches of Troy's brain as her eyes focused on the figure huddled on the floor next to the bed.

"Oh, my God," Troy cried.

Dry blood had crusted the side of his face and his right eye had swollen shut. Emma tried to push her way past Troy. Troy was shaking her head. "No, Emma. I think he's dead." She stopped and turned to Jake. "There was a woman at the hospital. She was cut open like your parents. Was that one of yours, too?"

The look on Jake's face was the same surly one she could remember placing on her own face when confronted.

Troy released Emma's arm so that she could step over the blood puddle on the floor and bent to look into the man's bruised face. "He's breathing," she said.

Jake laughed loudly. "They're all breathing. Didn't you notice?

Troy looked at Jake, shocked. She'd thought she had imagined it, but maybe she hadn't.

"Your parents? They're still breathing even after…."

"Yeah, isn't that fucking sick? You can't even kill people any more. I put a knife right through this cop's chest over on Northwest Taylor, and he fucking went right on breathing." His words had bravado to them that his eyes didn't.

"Why are you doing all this? What did the cop do to you? What did that woman at the hospital do to you? Did you even know her?" Anger and desolation swept through Troy as she spoke. This boy was crazy. He had no problems hurting people, and she had led Emma right to him. She hadn't protected her; she would be responsible for her death.

"What difference does it make? I told you," Jake said blankly, "I didn't kill them. You saw. No matter what I do they keep breathing."

"Jake..." Emma stopped speaking as Jake's dead eyes turned on her.

"That's not my fucking name. Stop fucking calling me that."

"What's your name, then?" Emma asked her voice gentle and cajoling.

"Hoyt. Hoyt Pokorney." Troy recognized the name, but struggled with placing it. A murderer. The kid was taking on the name of a murderer. The memory sharpened until a face, like Jake's, but older and more sardonic, came to mind. Her fear doubled and folded onto herself. She could see Emma's body rock as she, too, placed the name.

"Your library card said your name was Jake Ostroph. That's how we found you." Troy's voice dropped to a casual, conversational level.

"That's *their* dead son's name. He was hit by a car when he was three. He would have been the same age as me," he said with disgust.

"You were adopted?" Troy asked.

"No." Jake's tone had taken on a defiant petulance that Troy recognized and latched on to. This she understood.

"Foster kid?"

"What's it to you? "

Troy shrugged. "I just know how fucked up that is. I was a foster kid, too." Troy wanted to add, *but it wasn't in a nice house like this, you spoiled demon spawn*, but she kept her eyes turned toward Emma and leaned casually against the wall, as if she was just visiting a friend. She finally had his attention.

"How long?" His curiosity was grudging.

It was always like that with kids brought up in foster care. An immediate camaraderie that, in this case, made Troy feel like she had licked a public toilet seat.

"All my life," she answered lightly, and he grunted as if she had confirmed what he already knew. He mimicked her pose against the other wall. Troy pictured herself diving for the gun, but Emma was squatting right in his line of sight. She didn't dare risk it.

"How many houses?"

"Just one," she said.

"Me, too. Just this one."

"They made you change your name because of what your dad did, huh?"

"*Fuckers* made me think I wanted to change it. By the time I realized she'd tricked me, it was too late." Jake's voice dripped with self loathing.

"That's messed up."

"They make you change your name?" the boy asked, looking hopeful.

Troy shook her head. "Didn't have to. If I had a name before, I never knew it. I was left in a church when I was about six months old...by my mother probably, but I don't even know that for sure."

"That's messed up, too."

"Ain't it, though?"

Emma's shoulders looked tense as she pretended to focus all her attention on the injured man. "I think he's waking up."

"See? Told you I didn't kill anyone."

"Can I have some water for him, please? Maybe a little sewing kit?" Emma's voice was soft and respectful, not confrontational or accusing.

Good, Emma. Good. Don't make him mad. Troy looked at Jake and raised her eyebrow in what she hoped was a "What do you think?" gesture.

"I don't have a sewing kit," Jake said in a petulant voice.

"The water, then? And some towels?" Emma pressed.

Jake seemed to consider the request before turning to the door without speaking. He stopped and pointed the gun in Troy's direction, causing her heart to leap violently.

"You need to get over there with them." He waved the gun for emphasis.

Troy moved toward Emma and the man on the floor. The boy backed out into the hall and asked casually, "You want a beer or something?" He only looked at Troy when he asked.

Troy started to say no, but then changed her mind. "A beer would be great. Hey, you got any food? We haven't eaten all day."

He gave a small grunt and pulled the door shut, not taking his eyes from Troy as he did so. Troy heard the padlock click into place. She squatted down next to Emma.

"How is he?" she asked.

"He's awake," Emma said. Troy's stomach roiled as she got a

closer look at the deep gash.

"Can you talk?" Emma asked softly. He seemed to have trouble speaking, probably due to the swelling of his mouth.

"Yes." The 's' in "yes" sounded as though he were sucking on his own blood.

"Who are you? What are you doing here?"

"Dr. Abe Dunham. I came..." His body jerked in an effort to contain a harsh phlegmy-sounding cough. "Oh God, that hurts," he wheezed.

"Maybe we should turn him over," Troy suggested.

"I thought about that, but the cuffs are too short. We'd need the key." Troy noticed that Emma looked more concerned then she had before.

"He's got some internal damage. He's been worked over pretty good."

"I can see that," Troy said, somberly. "He was fine last time I saw him." She leaned closer. "Why in the hell were you chasing me?"

Emma looked from Troy to Abe and back again.

"I thought you killed Reba Stef...the woman back at the hospital."

"Why in the hell would I do something like that?" Troy asked.

"It had to be you," he labored on each word, "or the boy." He looked at Emma, "I knew you didn't leave your home. His parents never told me about his history. I didn't even know he was a foster kid. When you just showed up while I was cleaning up the mess, it just seemed obvious."

"Nice call, idiot. You could have killed me."

"I thought you were a murderer. I was trying to stop you."

A floorboard creaked, signaling Jake's return.

"Keep him talking. Keep making him think you're on his side. Use me as the scapegoat if you have to. If you see a chance to get that gun away from him, take it." Abe's voice was so low that Troy almost didn't hear him, but she could hear the desperation in his voice. "If we stay too long, it won't matter, anyway. We'll be stuck here, permanently."

Abe looked as if he wanted to say more, but the padlock was being removed from the door. Jake walked in carrying the gun in one hand and four sloppily-made peanut butter and jelly sandwiches in the other. He gave the sandwiches to Troy and walked back into the hall where he had left the towels. He gave those to Emma and finally returned with two frosty bottles of beer. The exchanges were made in silence. Troy took a bite of her sandwich and leaned against the wall.

Emma put the two sandwiches she was given aside and began wiping Abe Dunham's face with a light gray towel. Troy looked away, wondering how the man had managed to stay alive. *All right, focus on keeping you and Emma alive.*

"So, I got to ask," Troy said, careful to keep any accusation from her voice, "what's with the padlock? You put that on because of him, or what?"

"Nah, the Ostrophs did it a few months after I moved in. They said it was because I sleepwalk and I might hurt myself."

Troy took a sip of her beer and looked at the bottle. She lifted it toward him, as if offering a toast. "Not bad," she said after she swallowed. He had taken a sip of his own beer when Troy asked, "Do you? Sleepwalk, I mean."

"Nah," he said. But Troy had a feeling he did. She had a feeling the padlock was more for their protection than his. She stifled a shudder; it would be hell having someone you were afraid of sleeping in your house every night.

"So, is that why you killed them?"

"That wasn't my fault." He pointed to Abe, "It was his."

Abe was already shaking his head. "I had nothing to do with this."

"You're trying to tell me that woman I saw isn't dead," Troy said, looking at Abe.

"No. I think she's dead." Abe said before he dissolved in a fit of coughing. It sounded to Troy as if every word he spoke left the door open for more blood to flood into his windpipe. "I didn't—cut her open."

Jake seemed unconcerned by Abe's unspoken accusation. "I didn't think she would actually die. The others didn't."

Troy nodded, as if what Jake had said made perfect sense. Then she turned back to Abe. She closed her eyes for a split second and hoped she could continue to tolerate being close to something so evil. "The point is she wouldn't have been there if you hadn't done whatever it is you did to us. You're responsible for her death. Just like Hoyt said. What about those people sleeping on the street? What did you do to them?"

Emma was pretending to treat a wound on Abe's face but Troy could tell that she was listening to every word that was said. Troy raised the beer and hoped Jake didn't notice how the bottle quivered before she took a swallow.

"The people out there aren't dead. They aren't anything. They don't exist. His parents aren't cut up. Look, all of this? It isn't really happening. It's taking place in your head. You were all given an experimental drug and a hypnotic suggestion."

"Who gave you the right to do any of this...to play with our lives?" Emma demanded.

Emma's voice was calm, but Troy could see the tension in her body. *Don't forget what we're trying to do here, Em.*

Jake's body language was relaxed and unthreatened; he seemed fascinated by the exchange.

Good, Troy thought. *Just keep that damn gun at your side.*

"I *gave* you back your lives."

"Gave us—? You arrogant bastard. You aren't God." The words dripped from Emma's lips like venom. Troy stifled the urge to go to her. She might not get another chance like this.

Abe was attempting to sit up. Emma had scooted away from him and tossed the bloodied towel into a corner. Jake was sipping absently at his beer now, watching the exchange among the people in front of him like it was a soap opera.

"None of you had a life before I gave you this. You were..."

Emma opened her mouth to say something, but Troy spoke first.

"We were like them," Troy said softly. "Something happened to us and we were asleep."

"Then how did you get here?" Emma asked Abe.

"Coma can be induced."

"But what happened to *us*?" Troy asked. But she could guess what happened to herself even though she had no memory of it.

"The boy shot himself in the head, probably with that gun or one very similar. His parents said it was an accident, but who knows." The boy's expression didn't change.

"You were hit over the head by a meth addict as you were leaving work one night," Abe said to Emma. He held Troy in his gaze. "And your girlfriend drove you off a bridge. Your injuries healed, but something in your minds kept you from waking up. That's how we picked you. All of you were in a coma but shouldn't have been. I was the last hope for each of your families. It was either me or waste away in some care facility for the rest of your lives."

"I don't have any family. Who's paying for all this?" Troy asked.

"You have a lot of friends. I believe the folks you work for took up a collection. Messengers around the world sent in money, I was told. They were able to raise quite a lot of funding. It wasn't enough, of course. They had to rely on charity for the majority of your medical expenses. *My* charity."

"You used us like lab rats." Emma's voice had lost all of its fire.

"I didn't use you. You took part in a very successful experiment. You're talking right now because of me." A fit of coughing shook his body, and Emma placed her hand on his chest, but her face had turned a dull red. Troy only hoped Abe's words were having the same effect on Jake. "You all should be thanking me." Then Abe looked directly at Jake. "Especially you."

"What are you talking about?" he sounded bored, but Troy knew he was paying attention.

"The Ostrophs returned you to the custody of the state so they wouldn't have to keep you on life support." He canted his head toward Troy. "At least *she* had friends that tried to pay for part of her treatment. But you...you, you were nothing but a charity case." Once again the effort of speaking seemed to be too much for Abe and his body was racked by a fit of coughing. He leaned away from Emma and spit a large glob of frothy looking blood.

"You're lying!" Jake screamed.

Emma jump as Jake's beer bottle crashed against the wall. "The Ostrophs wouldn't have given me back." His voice softened. "They were going to adopt me." Bits of beer bottle and foam crawled down the wall and seeped into the baseboard.

Abe glanced at Troy. It was a brief look, but she picked up on it.

Here we go. Troy thought and took a slow deep inhale, careful not to draw Jake's attention from Abe.

"That's not what they told me. They said they were scared of you. They said the only way they could sleep in this house was to padlock you in."

The boy's thin body was ramrod straight now. He seemed to have forgotten about the gun.

Abe began to cough again.

Please keep talking, Troy felt nauseous from both fear and the overwhelming smell of beer and the bloody clot that Abe had spit onto the floor.

"They told me they were happy when you shot yourself. It was an easy way to get rid of you without their friends having to know they had brought a murderer's son into the neighborhood."

Troy saw the thin arm tense just before he raised the gun. He yelled something unintelligible, and Troy leaped on him just as the gun went off. She slammed the heel of her hand into the boy's nose twice, and he slipped to the floor.

Troy caught sight of Emma kneeling over Abe's leg. "Emma?"

"Right here. I'm okay, but he's been shot. Are you all right?"

"Fine," was all Troy could manage as she bent down and picked up the gun. She replaced the safety, and dropped it into a side pocket of her pants. Her ears were ringing as if someone had set off a bottle rocket close to her head

"Damn it." Abe said through gritted teeth. The unpleasant phlegmy quality had returned to his voice.

"Hand me that towel over there," Emma said.

Troy glanced at Jake one more time before reaching across his splayed form to retrieve the towel for Emma. Their eyes met briefly before Emma turned away and pressed the towel into the wound on Abe's leg.

Troy folded her arms in front of her and tried to get her breathing under control.

"He has the key to the cuffs in his back pocket," Abe said.

Troy was loath to touch the boy again, but she checked his pulse. She found it strong, and flipped him over on to his stomach. She handed the key to Emma, and Emma removed the cuffs. Abe tried to look at his watch, but his eyes were swollen shut.

"Can you tell me what time it is?" he asked Emma.

Emma looked at Abe as if he were a bug under a microscope.

"What time is it?" he said louder. "I can't see my watch. Tell me what time it says!"

"It's ten past ten."

"All right." He took a deep breath and fresh blood oozed from the gash on his head. "All right. I want you two to leave me and the boy here."

"What are you going to do?" Emma asked.

Abe smiled. "If I'm lucky, I'll be dead before he wakes up."

"Dead?"

"I've been bleeding for some time. I doubt I can survive all the damage this little sadistic fucker has done to me. If Reba's any indication, if we die here, we really die. At least our mind thinks we do. You have about fifty minutes before my partner starts bringing you back."

Emma looked at Troy in astonishment. "So you were telling the truth? This isn't real?"

"It's real. You created it. You created your own private hell. Mine too since I won't be making it back."

"But how did you do it?"

"Your guess is as good as mine. None of you made very good test subjects."

"What do we have to do?" Troy interrupted.

"You need to go back to where you were when you woke up."

"The hospital?" I don't want..."

"You have to. I don't know what will happen if he tries to bring you back and you're in a different place. Now go on. Leave him here with me."

"Are you going to kill him?"

"No, I'm going to keep him here where he can't hurt anyone else."

"Let us take him back. He was at the hospital too, right?" Troy felt the clock ticking as she looked at Jake's prone figure.

Emma gestured at Abe. "When are you going to stop playing God?"

"When I die," Abe said, his eyes snapped with anger. "Do you understand that if we let him go back, he *will* wake up? This boy is a murderer. What are you going to do? Wait around until he kills people in the real world? Are you really willing to take that chance? You don't have time to deal with him. You need to get back to the hospital," he said to Troy, "and you need to get back to your condo."

Emma was incredulous. "My condo? Why there?"

"Your parents took you home after about a month in the hospital. They wanted you amongst your things."

"I'm not leaving her alone." Troy said.

"You have to. If you're not back in your hospital room when my partner induces you, you might not make it back."

"I'm not leaving her." Troy's tone was final.

Emma closed her eyes and pressed a thumb to the bridge of her nose. "What if he's telling the truth?"

"What if he's not? What if he's just trying to get us to split up?"

"Lock us in with the padlock," Abe said. "The bars will slow him down. Go now. You're wasting time." Troy backed toward the hall, pulling Emma with her. Abe was holding on to the frail boy as if cradling a baby.

"You told us you didn't know he was a foster kid. Why would you say something like that to him?" Troy asked.

"I said what I had to. Did you see what he did to his parents? They might have been better off if they had sent him back."

Troy shook her head. "All I know is that boy needed help from the day he was born. He didn't need someone diddling with his brain, and he certainly didn't need to be dropped into a world with no human contact. I saw what he did to his parents. But it makes me wonder if he was crazy before you put him here or if your little dream world was the last straw. I don't see how you can live with yourself."

"I won't have to." The words were spoken with the assurance of a person who had seconds to live.

"Troy," Emma pulled at Troy's arm, "we should go." Troy gave a little start and turned to look at Emma. Emma's eyes had reddened and her face had the same pained, dazed look she had had when she had fainted in the condo.

Troy let Emma pull her out in the hallway, but she never broke eye contact with Abe." I hope he doesn't wake up before you die," she said and shut the door.

"Should we put the padlock on?" Emma asked.

"Yeah, put it on."

She waited for the padlock to click home before pulling Emma into her arms. "We have less than forty-five minutes. It took us over an hour to get here."

"That doesn't give us enough time." Emma said as Troy released her from the hug.

"We'll have to make it enough time." Troy's face was set in a grim line of determination. "Come on, let's get out of here."

Neither of them looked toward Mr. and Mrs. Ostraph's room as they left the house. Once outside, Troy jogged over to a Honda sitting in the driveway next door and pulled at the handle. "Shit." She started back toward the Ostraph's house, stopped and backtracked. A large hose and sprinkler head had been left in the middle of the Ostroph's grass. She had already unscrewed the sprinkler head by the time Emma had reached her side.

"We can make it in time if we drive," Troy said as Emma covered her hand and Troy realized it had been shaking until Emma had steadied it. Tears began spilling down her cheek and she hated herself for not being stronger for Emma. "We have to try, don't we?" She knew the answer; of course they had to try. But she needed to say the words out loud because it would be so easy to just finish life there. But she knew they couldn't—not without trying to get themselves back to reality. If they didn't fight—if they just gave up—this world would become a larger version of Emma's condo, nothing more then a safe prison.

"I think we both have to stop hiding. We have to try to get back, and if we can't, we'll live the best life we can here," Emma said with quiet determination.

"All right then, move back," Troy ordered. When she was sure Emma was clear she sent the nozzle slamming toward the window. She cleared a hole big enough to stick her hand through and unlocked all the doors with the flip of a switch. "Get in," she said.

Emma slid into the passenger seat and watched as Troy fumbled under the steering column.

"You know how to hot wire a car?" Emma's voice sounded incredulous.

"Used to know how. Old boyfriend taught me."

"Boyfriend?" The words were out of Emma's mouth before she could stop them and Troy looked up and smiled.

"I was fourteen. All he wanted to do was smoke cigarettes and make out. Those two things don't mix, in my opinion, so I—" Troy paused and gritted her teeth. "Damn it. That's not it," she said under her breath. "So I broke it off. It's a heart wrenching tale of shattered dreams and teen angst. I'll have to tell you all about it over coffee someday."

"Coffee?"

Troy sobered. "Yes, coffee." Her hand went to Emma's cheek. "If we're able to get out of this, I hope you'll want to see where this leads us."

"Every day, for the rest of our lives."

"That could be a long time," Troy said, smiling.

"I hope so," Emma said.

Troy smiled again, looking relieved. "Let me get going on this. It shouldn't take that long. These things are as easy as picking an old U-lock."

Emma was beginning to think Troy had spoken too soon when five minutes later they were still sitting in the driveway. "Troy maybe we should..."

The engine coughed, sputtered, and grumbled to life. Troy pumped her fist in the air and shifted the car into reverse.

Emma expected to feel excited, but her dread deepened as Troy backed out of the driveway.

"How much time do we have?" Troy asked as she put the car in drive and, with her eyes riveted on the road, pressed her foot to the floorboard and sent the car gunning down the narrow street.

"Thirty-eight minutes." Troy drove in silence. Her forearms bulged as she gripped the steering wheel. A muscle along her jaw line appeared and disappeared at random intervals and once she said something to herself. Emma thought it sounded as if she were counting.

"How are you doing?" Emma asked after what seemed like several long minutes of silence. Many of Troy's emotions were as apparent to her as if they had been written on paper. But she would much rather hear her voice than sit in pensive silence wondering if they would make it on time.

"I'm pretty sure I'm going to puke."

"Me too." Emma said.

Troy glanced at her. "Why are *you* going to puke?"

"Because you drive really badly, Troy."

Troy said nothing at first and then she began to laugh. "I'll tell you what. When we get back, I'll let you give me driving lessons. Hell, I may even get an actual Oregon drivers license."

Emma was holding on to the armrest with her right hand and her left was gripping Troy's thigh. She gasped and tore her eyes away from the road long enough to gawk at Troy. "You have got to be fucking kidding me?" she said. Troy doubled over trying to both steer and control her laughter. Soon Emma was laughing, too.

The laughter subsided, and Emma forced herself to relax her grip on Troy's thigh. There was so much she wanted to say to Troy, but if she said it all now wouldn't that be like admitting she wouldn't have time to say it later?

Too soon and not soon enough Troy was pulling the Honda toward the curb in front of Emma's building. She got out of the car with the engine still running and went around to passenger side. Emma had already opened her door and was getting out of the car.

"Okay?" Troy asked.

"Yes," Emma said but everything was not okay. She hadn't planned to come back here, and she hadn't planned to separate from Troy. Emma found herself standing outside the lobby doors. She punched in her code with trembling fingers and they walked through the quiet foyer. The ride up the elevator seemed quicker than Troy remembered. Emma's hand felt so small. Troy wanted to tuck it into her own pocket to keep it safe. When the elevator pinged at Emma's floor they both jumped.

"Ready?" Emma asked. Troy squeezed her hand and they stepped off the elevator and into the hallway.

It took Troy six minutes, with the help of a fire extinguisher, to break the knob off Emma's front door

Nothing had changed in the condo, but something about it made Emma feel uncomfortable. She felt like she had already said her goodbyes and now she was back. They stood in the center of the condo facing the window seat.

Emma looked at the clock her mother had bought her and thought how much she hated that clock. "You have twenty-seven minutes."

"That's plenty of time." Troy pulled the gun out of her pants pocket. "Here, you keep this. You won't need it, but I'll feel better."

"What about you?"

"Don't worry, I'll be careful." They stood looking at each other. "I am not going to say goodbye to you," Troy said sternly. "If this doesn't work, I'll come back for you. If it does, I'll come for you. No matter what, I'll come for you. You understand?" Emma was unable to answer.

Troy pulled her close and kissed her, holding her so tight that Emma could feel her body shaking with the effort. Emma welcomed it and as their lips met, she felt Troy's love hit her with so much force that her body jerked. Troy deepened the kiss.

She loves me. She might not realize it yet, but she does. That would be enough to get her through the next twenty-six minutes.

Troy broke off the kiss. "I better go. Put the chains on." Without looking back, Troy walked out the door, slamming it behind her. Emma limped to the door to put the three safety chains on. She heard the ping of the elevator, and an instant later, the faint whoosh of the doors sliding shut.

She limped to the window and looked down at the Honda. Troy came jogging out of the building and Emma put her hand to her mouth to keep from calling out to her.

Troy stopped just before getting into the car and looked up at Emma. Again Emma felt how hard it had been for Troy to leave her and she held on to it.

"Emma?" Troy called out.

"Troy, you need to go."

"I will, but you remember what I said, okay? I mean it." Troy wanted to tell her that she was falling in love with her, but she couldn't. That would be too much like a goodbye. But then, maybe she already knew. Troy found the thought comforting and with bleary eyes she jumped in the car and pulled away from the curb. Twenty-five minutes would be plenty of time.

Troy pictured Emma sitting on the couch in the condo, alone and scared. She wished with all her heart that she could be with her. She hoped Emma could sense what she hadn't had time to tell her. She found her heart reaching for Emma, wanting to feel her quiet trust, to feel her passion again. She was halfway across the bridge before she realized it. The car's clock said she had twenty minutes left.

Almost there, baby. Don't worry. Just close your eyes, and when you wake up, we'll have the rest of our lives together. Almost there.

Chapter Twenty

I'LL COME FOR you. No matter what, I'll come for you. Emma could hear Troy's voice deep inside her.

"Emma, can you hear me? Please wake up, sweetheart. Momma and Daddy are right here. We're right here. You don't have to be afraid anymore. No one's going to hurt you ever again."

Pain. White-hot and intrusive shot through her forehead, down her neck, and into her arms, back, and legs. Her throat felt full and ragged. She opened her mouth, closed it, opened it again, and then a train ran through her brain pushing her faster than she was ready to go.

"Keep talking to her, Darby. I think she's coming out of it."

"Emma, we're here. Please come back to us. We need you."

Wet tears moistened crusted ones and formed a seal. She forced herself to open her eyes despite the pain. Lights, harsh and bright, scorched her corneas and sent a shooting pain to the back of her head. She blinked and the world sharpened. Her mother was dressed in shockingly casual jeans and a pinkish-grey sweater. Her father wore a tan sweater and khakis. Both looked rumpled, tired, scared, and joyful. Emma's heart hurt for allowing herself to grow distant from them.

"Emma," her mother sobbed, "that's it, sweetheart. Wake up."

She opened her mouth and sucked in air. She couldn't smell anything; her tongue was heavy, so heavy that talking felt impossible.

"Where...?" A hot poker of pain shot all the way down her throat. More tears filled her eyes, blurring her parents' tear-stained faces. Somehow, her mother must have understood that she was trying to ask a question.

"You're at home. You've been hurt. The doctor should be here soon."

"Troy?"

"Toy? I don't understand what you're trying to say."

"Troy?"

"Troy?" her mother was shaking her head. She looked at her husband for help and finally back at Emma. "I'm sorry but I don't think I know a Troy." Emma looked at her mother desperately and then to her father.

Emma tried to speak, but this time, nothing came out.

"Don't try to talk, Emma. Just let the doctors help you. You've been hurt. Things were pretty touch and go. We flew in as soon as we could."

A man in a white lab coat walked in and introduced himself. Emma was having a hard time focusing. She needed to ask him something, but she was beginning to forget what it was. Emma didn't take her eyes off her mother; a soft, sorrowful joy swept over her from both her parents. Joy at having her alive and sorrow at how much she had been hurt.

"Doctor? I think she might be trying to ask for something or someone. She seems pretty upset."

The doctor looked up from Emma's charts. "Ma'am, she's been through a lot. Her brain will need time to recover."

"Can't you give her something so she doesn't hurt herself?" Her mother's breath smelled of coffee and spearmint gum.

"We need to let the other meds get out of her system first."

Emma reached up and caught the doctor's wrist before he could pull away. She held it as tightly as she could. She said Troy's name again but very little sound came out.

He gently pulled his wrist from her grasp. Emma could read his confusion and wariness but nothing else. If he was trying to deceive her in any way, she would have known. She closed her eyes; a ragged painful sob escaped from her throat. *Where is she? Where the hell is she?* Tears began to gather in the back of her eyes.

"I think she's having trouble breathing." Her father's voice sounded high and scared.

"Ms. Webster, are you all right?" Emma shook her head pushing his hand aside.

Idiot. Of course I'm not all right.

She felt the prick before she could do anything to stop it. "Easy now. We are just going to calm you down a little. All right. We can't have you getting too excited right now. You've been through a lot," he said as he removed the needle from her arm.

"Thank you, doctor," her mother said. Dr. Shorenstein said something else to her, and then turned toward a figure that Emma hadn't noticed before.

"Keep an eye on her. If it starts to..." Emma felt as if she was being moved away from the voices hovering over her. She tried to hold on to her anger, but it, too, faded away, and she began to forget why she was so upset.

"Will Dr. Dunham be in to see her? We want to thank him, too."

That's it. Now she remembered. Dr. Dunham was the one. He was the one that had done this to them. He was the one she should be angry at.

"I'm afraid I have some bad news. Dr. Dunham suffered an aneurism a few days ago. He died in his sleep."

Emma heard a quick inhale of breath and then silence. "He was so young," she heard her father say, but she couldn't make out the rest.

"It was quite a shock. Just a wife...no kids...brilliant future."

She was struggling to stay awake and although the anger was there, she didn't remember why.

No. I remember. I remember. I don't know where Troy is. What if she didn't make it back?

Emma glared at the youthful face of the doctor until he cleared his throat and turned to her parents. "She needs some rest, so I suggest you two take a break for a while." He cleared his throat again and left the room.

You bastard. What did you do with Troy? I saw the look on your face when I said her name. I didn't dream her. I didn't make her up. A warm hand on her forehead pulled her from thoughts that were fast becoming disjointed.

"Sweetheart, the nightmare is over. You're here with Daddy and me. We won't let anything happen to you."

She felt like she was moving through space without a tether, and really, she just didn't care anymore. Her mother was right; she was tired, and maybe it wouldn't hurt so much when she woke up next time. Then she would find her. She wouldn't forget. It wasn't a dream. She would find Troy.

Her name is Troy and she is not a dream. Not her. Not that part.

She felt soft hands wipe tears from the side of her face with a Kleenex. "Go to sleep, sweetheart. Things will be better tomorrow."

EMMA WATCHED DR. SHORENSTEIN go through the motions of checking her vitals every day for the next week. He had said that she needed to be observed 24/7. She had been moved from her condo to Oregon Unified hospital, where both Dr. Shorenstein and Dr. Dunham, according to her mother, were on staff. The ride from the condo to the hospital had been quiet. Emma had spent much of the time trying to remember why she had felt so sad until she had finally fallen into a deep sleep.

Dr. Shorenstein had been in her hospital room when she had awakened and although she wanted to quiz him about Troy's whereabouts, intuition told her to wait and watch.

Her parents might be fooled, but she wasn't. Dr. Dunham had said his partner would bring them out. Although he avoided her eyes, she could sense his excitement every time he was around her. Excitement, coupled with fear and shame.

One thing Emma was certain of: He couldn't know what had happened to them in that other place. And although Dr. Dunham had called him his partner, she was sure this man was no more than a flunky. With Dr. Dunham gone, he was probably dreaming of the prestige this would bring him. Emma was pretty sure that without Dr. Dunham, whatever had been done to them would lack all credibility. All he knew was that she was awake. She didn't ask about Troy again, and she answered his questions with as little information as possible. Her parents' arrival saved her from answering any more. She listened to the small talk between them and the doctor until one of them saw fit to acknowledge her.

"Hello, sweetheart. You're looking much better today. Have you walked any?"

Her walks were not quite walks yet. But they would be. She was determined to get back the use of her legs. She would not rely on the cane either. She would not become what she had been. She wouldn't let herself.

"Daddy, did you find anything?"

"Find what?" Her mother asked as she sat on the foot of Emma's bed.

He cleared his throat and sat down in a chair. "I did find her. It wasn't as hard as I thought it would be."

"Tell me."

He frowned. "How do you even know her?"

"Know who?" her mother was looking from her husband to Emma.

"I'll explain later," Emma said to both questions. "Is she all right? Where is she?"

"She was in an accident. She's in a small hospital on the east side. Emma, I'm afraid she's in a coma."

Emma stared at him bleary-eyed, "That can't be right. No, she should be out now."

"Out? No, she's been in the hospital about as long as you have."

Emma's heart writhed. "Take me to her."

"You haven't recovered enough to go out yet. Tell her, Doctor."

"Ms. Webster, I'm afraid that would be too much for you right now." His anxiety had increased. She was done playing games with him. She was done lying around wondering when Troy was going to come.

Emma forced herself to sit up, tears pouring down her face. She welcomed the pain that racked her body; she welcomed it, but it didn't take away from the utter desolation and fear. Had Troy become stuck in that place? Was she alone and scared? Had she not made it back to the hospital in time?

"I will check myself out of this hospital and your care right this minute if you try to stop me. I know what you did. What you tried to do and I will tell the press and anyone else who'll listen. And I'll make sure you can't put all the blame on Dr. Dunham." She felt it when he became almost overwhelmed with shame. Emma realized that this man seemed to be nothing like Dr. Dunham, not yet, anyway.

Dr. Shorenstein's eyes grew large at the threat. "I'm sorry, ma'am." He was talking to her mother as if Emma wasn't there. "I can't force her to stay here if she doesn't want to." He left the room before her mother could utter another protest.

"What is she talking about?" Emma's mother said in that no-nonsense-accepted voice that she used on everyone from children to adults. "What did he do to you?" she demanded, but didn't pause long enough for an answer. "This is just ridiculous. You can't go traipsing all over town to see some friend. You just came out of coma."

Emma ignored her mother and focused on her father. He met her eyes and his shoulders slumped. *Help me daddy. You've never stood up for me. Do it now.*

"I need to see her. I need to help her," Emma said to him. She was struggling trying to find the words to make him understand.

"Don't be silly. How can you help her if she's in a coma?" Emma was used to hearing disparagement in her mother's voice, but today it rankled.

Emma gritted her teeth and directed her words to her father. "I need to be with her." She held her hand out. "Please, Daddy."

"Emma, you need to calm down. Maybe you should get the doctor, Mark. I think Emma's becoming hysterical. Maybe he'll give her something to help her calm down."

"Daddy?" Emma flinched as her father turned and walked out the door without answering her.

"Emma." Darby's voice had softened now that she believed her orders where being followed. I know how much you care about those...those people that come to your clinic, but you have to watch out for yourself now.

Emma tuned her mother out and kept her eyes on the empty doorway. *What did you expect? It's not as though you haven't been guilty of giving in just to shut her up. Why would he be any different? Hell, he's had more years than you have to learn how to deal with her.* No, Darby was hard to argue with, but she had hoped that when she really needed him, her father would stand up for her.

Emma realized that Darby was sitting on her bed when she reached across and grabbed her hand. Emma looked up in time to see her shaking her head. "You are too much like your grandmother—look what happened to her."

"She had congenital heart failure." Emma closed her eyes. It was an old argument and it was making her weary.

"She worked herself to the bone and those people broke her heart at least once a day. Look what one of them did to you. This Troy is just going to do the same."

"You don't even know her."

"I know the type."

"You don't even know *me*. How can you know *Troy* or her type? And as for my grandmother..." Emma was almost speechless at her mother's audacity.

"My mother, Emma. Don't forget that she was my mother."

"That's right, she was your mother. But you didn't know her. If you did, you'd know that the people she helped at the clinic gave her life meaning."

Her mother stood up and looked as if she was about to leave the room. Emma kept speaking because, if there was one thing you could count on with Darby Webster, it was her need to have the last word. "You're right, sometimes things broke her heart. When a baby she had given care to came in pregnant fifteen years later. Or a boy she had known all his life ended up in prison for life. But you didn't know how happy she felt when she was able to help people feel better who had been sick for years but couldn't afford health care."

"Where were all those people when she died, then?" Darby was glaring at Emma now her fists furled into tight little knots of displeasure. "I didn't see any of them at her funeral. I didn't see one damn person who wasn't family or friends of Mark's come to pay their respect. She gave her whole damn life to these people, and when all was said and done, she died alone." A sob came out of Darby's throat and Emma felt horrible for having caused it. Emma raised her hand toward her mother, but wasn't surprised when Darby just folded her arms and turned away. "I don't want that for you," she said, refusing to look at Emma.

Emma understood it now. All of the anger, the need for control, all of it stemmed from jealousy. Darby felt that the time Ida had spent at the clinic had been stolen from her. And she was afraid that Emma would be headed down the same path.

"I'm not planning on dying anytime soon, Mother."

"I know that." Darby sniffed. The anger was back. "But you're too young to not have a life outside of work. You should be out with friends, maybe traveling. Hell, I don't know."

"You're acting like I'm a twenty-year-old kid." Emma smiled to soften her words. "Maybe I have been burying myself at the clinic too much, and I don't have as many friends as I should, but I do have one close friend. She's more than a friend actually." Emma saw the "I don't want to talk about this" look on her mother's face as she turned away to look out the window. Emma pushed on because she needed to express what she was feeling. "I miss her so much it hurts, and Daddy just told me that she needs me. Can you understand how I feel?"

She had expected something other than the silence that settled on the room. *I wonder why I keep being disappointed by her. She's always been this way. Available only for the non-emotional things. Why would I expect anymore than that?* Emma knew what would happen next, as if she had read the script beforehand. Her mother would continue to stand there as she was, arms crossed, looking out the window, and then she would excuse herself and return with coffee or a sandwich that she wouldn't eat and armed with a safe line of conversation.

Emma looked away from the rigid back and slender figure when she heard a sound at the door. Her father stood in the doorway hunched over the back of a wheelchair as if for support. There was a silent exchange between her parents that made Emma's chest ache. She could feel the sense of loss and fear coming from her mother and a soul-shattering feeling of sad resignation coming from her father. His disappointment mirrored her own when they both watched Darby squeeze between the narrow space between the bed and the wheelchair and walk out of the room without so much as a glance in his direction.

"I'm sorry for bringing you into this, Daddy," Emma said after getting over her shock.

"You're my daughter," he said. She could feel that deep down, what she had said had hurt him. And what her mother had not said had hurt him even more. How had she missed the pain in their relationship?

He loved her—loved her with a fierce, burning desire that she recognized. She hurt for her father. She would hurt for him more when she had time to think, but for now she was consumed with thoughts of getting to Troy.

Dr. Shorenstein came rushing in, and her mother trailed behind him.

"I'm sorry, but you can't do this. She hasn't been released yet."

Her father turned dark, burning eyes on the young doctor. "My daughter has something she has to do. I'll bring her back after she's done."

"I'm sorry, sir. I can't allow that."

"Let me tell you something, son. For two months she lay in that bed, and I didn't know if I'd ever hear her voice again. But she just told me that there's some place she needs to be. I'm going to make sure she gets there and you don't want to be in my way."

The last part was said with a thread of steel that was strong enough to encompass the young doctor and her mother. Neither of them offered to help as her father assisted her as she slid into the chair. Emma had already forgotten about them. Her mind was on Troy.

Dr. Shorenstein had to hustle to avoid being run over as they wheeled through the door and out into the hallway.

Emma barely noticed when they passed through the halls of the hospital. Why hadn't Troy awakened as she had? She remembered Dr. Shorenstein telling her parents that Dr. Dunham had died. What if he'd been wrong? The patients didn't know anything about the drugs they had been given.

"Ready?" her father asked.

"One, two, three." She counted along with him under her breath, and for once, she did not brace herself for the pain. The wheels of the chair whispered as they moved through the halls. Emma kept expecting someone else to try to stop them, but they were barely given cursory glances as they reached the entrance of the hospital. A cool breeze passed through her hospital gown, and she shivered. Across the street, a boy sat against a streetlight with a bag thrown across his back at an angle, a girl stood on the sidewalk waiting to cross, and a woman walked by with a black West Highland Terrier on a leash. The light changed, and as they walked across the street, Emma inhaled and shivered. She briefly set aside her worry for Troy and tried to feel the city.

"Emma, did you hear me? I need to pull the car around. Will you be all right if I leave you here alone?"

"Sorry, go ahead. I'll be fine." Emma assumed her father had walked away, but her eyes were riveted to the pedestrians on the street until they had disappeared and were replaced by others. She watched people awake and moving in their everyday lives until the long line of her father's black Lexus blocked the street from view.

He buckled her into the passenger seat and shut the door behind her. She watched him through the side mirror as he struggled to fit the wheelchair in the trunk. His hair was full and dark brown, but she knew he had begun coloring it several years before. He had worn sideburns, even when they weren't popular, but Emma thought they made him look stylish. He was a handsome man, and Emma felt proud of him for reasons she would need to explore later. He sat down in the driver's seat and put the key in the ignition before slamming the door.

"Thank you," Emma said, "for this, I mean."

He smiled. "You seem surprised."

"You and I have never been the 'I'll-break-you-out-of-the-hospital' type of close. Mother and I neither, for that matter." Emma winced, wondering how much of that was her fault. "Thank you for understanding how important she is to me."

Emma watched the emotions play across his face as he struggled to find words. Confusion, sadness, and the need to say what he was feeling made the car quiet as he drove onto Interstate 5.

Come on, Daddy. Tell me what you're thinking.

"You've never asked me for anything," he said.

Emma looked at him sharply. "Are you kidding? I always asked you for stuff."

"No, you asked your mother."

Emma frowned. "That can't be true."

He looked away from the road long enough to look at Emma. "It's true, and I'm not blaming you. It was easier that way for me, too."

How could that be? How could she go through her life—of course it was true, she realized. Even at a young age, she had known who ran the household, and it was never her father. She had asked her mother if she had known what it was to feel needed. Perhaps she had been asking the wrong parent.

"Who is she?"

"Her name is Troy Nanson."

"Does she work at the clinic?"

"No, she's a bike messenger here in town."

"Dangerous job."

"Yes, but she loves it."

"Is that how you feel about the clinic?"

"Yes," Emma said, looking at her father in surprise. "I thought I..." How could she tell him about the life she had led in her self-imposed dreamland? "I thought about what life would be like if I didn't have the clinic. It was empty and without direction. I think I was waiting to die."

Her father seemed to understand, and perhaps he did. Perhaps that's the conclusion he had come to when he contemplated living without her mother.

"Almost there," he said.

Emma found herself rubbing her hands across the front of her thin hospital robe. They exited Interstate 5. Emma watched the people on the streets in a daze. *Troy lived close to here,* she thought. She leaned her head back, closing her eyes, wanting to be there, yet not wanting to be there. Her father made a left turn onto a tree-lined road; a sign to the left of the road was almost obscured by trees and was so worn that it made it hard for her to read the writing. She didn't have to though; she knew that it would be Multnomah cemetery—the place where Patricia was buried. Her father drove for another mile or so and pulled in to the driveway of a small, colonial mansion that had been converted into an adult-care hospital.

"Please help me out," Emma said, her breath coming in short bursts. Her father was already out of the car and opening the trunk to remove the chair. Her legs trembled as she stood and allowed herself to be guided into the chair.

As he pushed her through the parking lot, she noticed a bike chained to a pole. "Daddy, push me over there." A sob hung in the back of her throat as she struggled with her own warring emotions. On the one hand she was happy to see Dite intact and not destroyed as Troy had described. She reached up and touched Dite's bars, her seat, and the duct tape on the handlebars. She was also ecstatic that everything, right down to the different colored rubber bands that Troy had daisy-chained along its frame, was as she remembered it. But on the other hand, it confirmed what she already knew. The things that she remembered, the time she had shared with Troy—the scary ones and the wonderful ones—had not physically happened.

Troy's bike in all its glory.

Someone had placed a plastic bag over the seat, and there were little notes taped all over the bike. Emma flipped one back so she could read it. *Come back to us, Troy. Dite's waiting for you.* She remembered Troy telling her the story about the messenger who had died in a traffic accident a few years before. "We chained his bike near his grave, and it had stayed until the city removed it."

"You ready to go in?" Emma swallowed and released the note. She looked up at the windows of the hospital and felt the fear Troy had described when she had caught Abe cleaning up the room. She wondered which one of these windows was that room. Reba Stefani's name had stuck fast in Emma's mind. *At some point I'll find out what happened to her in the real world, but I need to see about Troy first. What if he had come upon Troy's room first? What if...stop it. You can't play this game. He didn't find her first. She is alive. It may take her a little longer to wake up, but she is alive. That's all that matters.*

Emma gripped the armrest of the chair hard as her father pushed her up a ramp and toward the front doors of the hospital.

Fear crept like ice water into her veins. When her father hit the little blue button that swung the doors open, she had expected the sadness, the weariness and the feelings associated with people being ill, but it didn't make it anymore easy to deal with.

The walls were painted white, though they looked like they were in need of a few new coats. Four chairs sat across from a large reception desk. The woman manning the desk smiled at them and pointed to the phone glued to her ear with her free hand.

The top of the desk was lined with birthday cards from what looked like friends and coworkers. There was one drawn with crayons the adorable little stick figures on the front. It made Emma think of Troy's self portrait with the sidewalk chalk.

"May I help you?" She had been so wrapped up with her memories that she hadn't noticed when the receptionist ended her call.

"My..." *What was Troy to her?* Emma's stomach lurched. "My friend is here. Troy Nanson. I'd like to see her."

"Are you family?"

Tears filled Emma's eyes at the thought that she might not be allowed to see Troy. "She doesn't have any blood family that she knows of."

"Please," Emma's father said, "my daughter's been in the hospital for two months. She didn't know her friend was here until today."

The woman looked at Emma. She noticed the pallor and the bandages and the hospital-issue robe and wheelchair. "You'll need to sign in first." Emma watched as her father printed both their names in his neat, precise handwriting. By the time he had written the time, the purpose of visit, and the patient they were visiting, Emma wanted to scream and snatch the pen from his hand. "She's in Room 117, but there's someone in with her right now."

Emma's father was already pushing her in the direction the nurse had indicated by her glance down the hall. He threw the nurse a dazzling smile. "Thank you, ma'am" he said, and Emma had the briefest thought that her father could probably have his pick of any number of women, but it wouldn't matter. He, like Emma, fell in love once in a lifetime. Emma pushed the thought away.

"Here it is. Are you ready to go in?"

Emma looked at the door. *Was she ready? How could she ever explain to her father that she had been ready for years?*

"Let's go in," she said, and her father pushed the door open and began to wheel her into Troy's room. A man, perhaps her father's age, sat slumped in a chair. He jumped up when he heard them push through the door. He was short; perhaps five three, maybe a little less. What was left of his wispy jet black hair was tasseled about his head. His bleary eyes flew to Troy's bed and then back to Emma and her father. Her father topped him by at least ten inches, but he looked prepared to defend Troy if he had to. Emma liked him on sight.

"We're sorry to disturb you. My daughter here is a friend of Troy's." The man seemed to relax when he heard Emma's father say that.

"And here I thought I was her only friend," he joked, but his words dropped off unconvincingly.

"You must be Raife," Emma said.

"Yeah, I'm Raife."

"She said you were all the family she had."

Raife pressed his fist against his mouth. His eyes told Emma how choked up he was by what she had just said. Emma realized she had been avoiding looking at Troy. "Push me closer, Daddy."

Troy's mess of curls was all over her head. Her skin seemed pale, not golden brown like she remembered it. "She looks so thin." Emma choked on her words.

"They've been feeding her intravenously, but she just—I don't think she's getting any better..." The words broke off, and Raife looked away.

Emma reached out and put her fingers in Troy's hand. She felt the calluses that had created such an electric sensation when they had touched her body. She closed her eyes. Her heart ached at the thought that she and Troy had never actually made love, but there had to be something to her memories of it. After all, even though Troy looked a little different than she remembered, how could she remember Dite? How would she know how her hands would feel? It had not been a dream, not at all. She and Troy had grown close because of that shared horror.

"How long has she been like this?" Emma asked.

"Seven weeks, two days. I'm surprised you didn't hear about it. It was all over the papers. Messengers from all over came to help out with the medical bills for her." Emma could feel Raife's pride in how Troy's "family" had come together for her.

"She said she didn't have many friends." It was a statement, not a question, from Emma.

"She kept to herself a lot, but once you knew that about her, it was all right. She has friends. Hell, she has a family."

Seven weeks? I was in a coma longer than Troy? What does that mean? Emma bit her bottom lip. A dull ache had begun at her temples and threatened to break her concentration. *It means I didn't read about her accident in the paper and somehow pull her into my world. I couldn't have. I've never set eyes on her until today. No, that's not quite true. I know too many intimate things about Troy for us not have known each other.*

"What happened to her?" Emma asked.

The look on Raife's face told her that he had told the story many times and it hadn't gotten easier for him yet. "She was in a car accident. Her girlfriend was driving. You know about Patricia?"

"Troy told me some. But I don't know much about her."

Raife sighed. "Patricia didn't make it. I don't know how Troy did, but when they found her floating in the river, her heart wasn't beating. They were able to resuscitate her, but they aren't holding out much hope."

Tears fell down Emma's cheeks.

"Hey, don't cry now." Raife grinned at Emma. "If you know her like you say you do, you know she can be real stubborn. She got lucky being so close to this place. They got a specialist on staff here. Abe Dunham, he specializes in people with brain injuries like hers. If anyone can fix her up, he can." Raife said the words with the slow steady cadence of a man who had repeated the very same thing to himself and several others so many times that he wasn't even aware he was saying it.

"Dr. Dunham..."

Emma placed her hand over her father's to stop him from speaking just as he was about to tell Raife about Dr. Dunham's death. She wouldn't take that hope from him. Troy needed all the strength she could get.

Emma laid her forehead on Troy's bed and closed her eyes. *I've found you Troy. I'm here.*

Chapter Twenty-one

THEY HAD A routine now. Emma would be dressed and ready by nine-forty-five every morning. And her father would pick her up, help her to the car, and then drive her over to Troy's hospital, where she would sit with her until three o'clock. Raife would come in around that time, and they would sit and talk, about Troy for the most part, but sometimes about life in general. Her father would return around five and take her back to the hospital. Today she had changed the routine by asking him to make an unplanned stop.

Curiosity rolled off her father in waves. Somehow, he refrained from asking questions that Emma could feel crashing around inside his head. Questions like: Who was this woman he had been driving her to visit for the last eight days? What or who was she to Emma? And last, but not least, why were they sitting in the car at the graveyard?

Why are *we sitting in a graveyard*? Emma asked herself.

"Daddy, will you help me? The grass looks uneven."

"Of course sweet..." He was out of the car so fast that she didn't hear the last part of the endearment.

She had refused to use the walker as soon as she was able, and she had flat-out nixed the use of a cane. No one could understand her fear that it would become a crutch, but she had stuck to her guns, and her physical therapist was amazed at how fast her legs regained their strength.

As much as Emma adored his attentiveness over the last few weeks, she hated that it stemmed from guilt. She sensed that he felt that he should have been able to keep her from being hurt. Irrational though the guilt may be, his fear worried Emma more. She didn't have to work hard to guess what he was afraid of, even though she was determined not to turn into that scared woman who had hidden in her home for two years. There were long periods filled with fear and panic that grabbed hold of her and refused to let go. She fought through them, though, and she hoped that they would become fewer as time went on.

"Do you know someone here?" His words were careful, like the hand he had on her elbow. Emma concentrated on walking for a moment before answering.

"She was Troy's girlfriend. She died in the car accident."

"This is a big place. How will you know where to find her plot?" he asked.

Once again, Emma marveled at her father's willingness to help her while asking only minimal questions. "Raife gave me some idea. We should be getting closer. Oh, she's right there," Emma said, unprepared for the suddenness of seeing the name Patricia Rose Harvey in front of her. Somehow, she seemed more real. Not just a figment of Troy's dream world, but a woman who had once breathed, laughed, and made love to Troy. The latter thought made Emma want to turn and walk away.

"I'm going to walk a little down the way here. Do you want me to help you sit down?"

"Yes, the ground should be dry enough. Thanks, Daddy." He helped her sit down. She could feel his curiosity, but again he refrained from asking any questions, and again she was grateful.

"Take as long as you need."

"I shouldn't be long," she said as he started walking away. She wouldn't be long because she was there for one reason. To ask a favor.

"Hello, you don't know me, but I'm a friend of Troy's." The words sounded dry and silly. "I'm here because I think she might be having a little trouble finding her way. I was hoping you... you could send her the right way. No matter which way she chooses, I just don't want her in limbo anymore." The wind stirred around her like the softest sigh, and Emma stood up and waved to her father who was just a short way down the path. She was going home today. Back to the condo where she remembered making love to Troy. It hurt to think that she might never hear her voice again.

"Where to now?"

"I think its time for me to go home. To the condo."

"Did the doctor release you?"

"No, but I think he's done what he can for me. The rest is up to me."

SHE WOULD NEVER get used to the sound of her phone ringing. Emma lifted her head and looked at the digital clock on her nightstand. Half-past four in the morning. *Who in the world would call me so early in the morning?*

"Hello?"

"Emma? Emma Webster?" The male voice sounded drunk or excited or perhaps fearful.

"Who—"

"It's Raife. She's awake, Emma. She woke up! The hospital called me. They're working on her now, but she—"

"Oh my God." Emma said. "Patricia."

"What?"

"Nothing, I'll be there as soon as I can, all right?"

"Yes, hurry." Raife slammed the phone down in Emma's ear and she sat up, eyes wide, in the darkness. "Thank you," she whispered. "Thank you. Thank you."

She was grateful now that her father had insisted that she put their home number into speed dial after she had moved back to the condo. She didn't have to waste time getting up to turn on the light so that she could dial.

"Hello, Momma?" Her mother was either too sleepy or too annoyed by being awakened because she didn't ask Emma why she was calling at such an hour. "Just a minute," she said, and Emma heard the sound of the phone being fumbled.

Come on, Daddy. Hurry up, damn it.

"Hello?"

"Daddy? She's awake."

"I'll be right there," he said, and for the second time in as many minutes, Emma found herself listening to dead air.

She's awake. Oh my God, she's awake. Get going, Emma.

Emma limped to her chest of drawers and pulled out a pair of jeans. She had lost a little weight. Okay, too much weight, but she was eating better. *Don't get self conscious, Emma. I'm sure Troy won't be worried about how your jeans make your ass look flat.*

It felt like an eternity before her father got there. He looked groggy. He wore a T-shirt, pajama bottoms, and slippers. A leather jacket was the only thing that protected him from the frigid morning air. He helped her to the car as a gentle wind swept his hair up until it was pointed like a steeple. Emma gave him a quick hard hug and a kiss on his stubble-crusted cheek.

"What's that for?"

"For being here for me."

"I'm your father."

"I know. But it doesn't mean I can't say thank you."

He grunted and Emma thought she saw a light pink around his ears. She turned her gaze back to the awaking world of Portland—damp, sleepy, and a tick past chilly.

The reception area was deserted, so Emma hurried past without stopping to sign in. Her father hung back; she no longer needed his arm to keep her balance, but she found herself longing for his support now.

She took a deep, steadying breath before entering Troy's hospital room. Raife and a man in a white coat were standing next to Troy's hospital bed blocking Emma's view of Troy. Dr. Shorenstein glanced back at the door, then back at his clipboard, and then back at her again. She could see the wheels turning in his head, the question as clear on his face as if he had written it on the clipboard he was holding and passed it to her.

"What are you doing here?" She knew why he was there, but she was tired of pretending that she didn't know that she and Troy had been lab rats to these people. She really just wanted them all to go away so that she could be alone with Troy. Raife turned at the sound of her voice and stood up. The look on his face made Emma sick inside.

"Emma, wait." Raife's voice held a sadness in it that froze Emma in her place. Something was wrong with Troy. She could see it in his face.

"We should talk first." Raife put his hands on Emma's shoulders. "Let's talk outside, okay?"

"Raife, no. I need to see her." Emma ignored Dr. Shorenstein and pushed Raife's hands away. "Hey, you decided to wake up, huh?"

The men in the room ceased to exist as she met Troy's alert brown eyes. She kept waiting for the smile, the spark of recognition, something. When she did sense Troy's feelings, the force of them almost bowled her over.

"What's wrong?" Emma turned to Dr. Shorenstein. "What's wrong with her? What did you do?"

He looked at her and stood up.

She started toward Troy's bed, but was stopped by Raife's hands on her upper arms. "Raife, what..." The look on Troy's face made it impossible for her to finish her sentence. Emma turned to Dr. Shorenstein, glaring at him. He hadn't said a word to her since he recognized her. She didn't need him to tell her what was going on. She felt it when she looked at Troy

Troy was afraid, confused, and so sad that she seemed unable to process it all. But worst of all, Emma had no impression of happiness when their eyes had met. There was just utter confusion and fear. She let Raife push her gently from the room. Dr. Shorenstein had followed, his clipboard at the ready, as if to document the conversation.

Emma ignored him and focused on Raife. "What's wrong with her?"

"Nothing, as far as we can tell. Dr. Shorenstein says she'll be fine." Raife's words were clipped as if he didn't want to say any more than he had to.

"You're lying." She started toward Dr. Shorenstein, and Raife put a hand on her arm. "Tell me what's wrong with her," she demanded, but Dr. Shorenstein was shaking his head. She sensed his confusion mixed with his excitement, but he offered her no answer and she could feel herself becoming hysterical.

"Emma? What's going on?" Her father walked up carrying a

Styrofoam cup of coffee in one hand and a donut in the other. He glared at Raife's hand on her arm until Raife removed it.

"I don't know. They won't tell me anything." Emma wanted to run to her father like a small child.

"Look, there's nothing to tell. She woke up. She's having trouble talking, but she seems fine." Raife's words continued to be cautious, as if he had been coached in what he could and could not say. "She doesn't remember what happened, and she's grieving for Patricia. I....I told her you had been here every day waiting for her to wake up and ...she, uh..."

"She doesn't remember me." The words alone should have hurt, but she felt void of any emotion.

"No. She doesn't remember you at all." She sensed his confusion and suspicion.

Emma moved toward the seats that were lining the far wall and stumbled. Raife and her father got to her before she hit the floor and helped her into a seat. Tears were streaming down her cheeks by the time they got her seated.

Raife's suspicion had faded to pity and compassion.

"Ms. Webster, I have a few questions. To start, how are you and Ms. Nanson acquainted?" Emma forced herself to focus on Dr. Shorenstein's face.

"You have some nerve." She spit the words out as if they were lava in her mouth.

"Emma, what's wrong?" Her father's voice was confused but close, and she thought she felt his hand on her shoulder. Her anger began to build until she felt she might leap out of the chair and beat Dr. Shorenstein with his own clipboard. She looked down at the floor and forced herself to breathe.

"Dr. Shorenstein, I don't ever want to see you again." She kept her words slow and deliberate. "If I see you again, I will make things bad for you and everyone involved in this thing. Do you understand?"

They met each other's eyes, and Emma could feel his excitement build as he realized that she, unlike Troy, did remember something. Emma kept staring at him until she felt understanding dawn upon him, followed by his slow steady disappointment. It didn't matter if she did remember. She would not be telling him anything.

Dr. Shorenstein began to walk away, but stopped. He raised his pen up in the air as if he were about to hail a cab "If you plan on implicating people, you'll want to start with your mother. She's the one that signed the consent. There was nothing unethical about what we did."

"You keep telling yourself that," Emma said, but her anger had already begun to ebb away.

"If you should change your mind—"

"Never," Emma said and turned away from Dr. Shorenstein, pushing him from her mind like a terrible secret better forgotten. The hallway was quiet and Emma found herself wanting to talk.

"How could she not remember?" Even though she spoke out loud, she was asking herself the question, but it was Raife who answered.

"Doctor Shorenstein says that it might be because of the head trauma caused by the accident. He did say sometimes they regain—"

"Sometimes. I know. He told me the same thing. *Only I was lying about not remembering because I didn't want to be his guinea pig anymore. But Troy isn't. She didn't recognize me. She had no more feelings for me then she had for Dr. Shorenstein standing over her with that damn clipboard.*

"Will it upset her if I go in to say goodbye?"

Raife looked uncertain.

"Please." Emma was unable to stop the sob that came out. "I just want to know that she's okay."

"She's fine." He handed her a Kleenex from a box sitting on the built-in table next to her. "Clean up before you go in to see her."

Emma wiped her eyes, closed them, and took a deep breath. She pasted a smile on her face. "Okay?"

Neither of the two men gave her the impression that her smile was convincing, but she kept it in place. She had hoped for time alone with Troy, but Raife followed her into the room. She told herself she would have done the same thing in his position, but it still rankled.

Her father entered the room. "Go ahead and talk to her, Emma." He looked at Raife. "We'll both wait here."

Emma saw the quick flash of anger cross Raife's face, but he didn't seem interested in a confrontation, because he said nothing.

"Thanks, Daddy." Emma hoped he heard the unspoken thanks for everything in her voice.

Troy turned her head when she heard the voices. Emma felt awkward in her baggy jeans; she felt like she would never get to Troy's bed side. And the eyes—the sharp, brown eyes followed her every move. Saw the limp, saw everything about her, and there was not one pulse of recognition in them.

Emma hesitated and reached for Troy's hand. Her fingers were limp at first and then tightened. "Hi there." Emma continued to speak before the confused look on Troy's face could turn into discomfort. "It's okay, Raife told me. I wanted to see you anyway. I know you don't remember me right now. The doctor said that it might come back to you, but I just wanted to say thank you. Thank you for being my friend."

Troy's fingers tightened around hers and one of Emma's tears dropped on her own arm. She kept the smile plastered on her face.

She felt it when Troy started to feel agitated and uncomfortable. She released her hand.

"I'm...sorry..."

Emma shook her head. "You never have to be sorry. Not for me." Emma closed her eyes. She wanted to say more. She could have said a lot more. "I'm going to leave so you can get some rest, all right?"

Troy didn't say anything and Emma released her hand, although Troy didn't seem agitated by it. Her father must have convinced Raife to leave the room because they were alone. Emma took one last look at Troy. She wanted to tell her she loved her, but what good would that do? "Goodbye for now," she said, but Troy just continued to stare at her. Emma sensed curiosity and surprise but nothing else. "I'll send Raife in," she said and walked out of the room as quickly as her knee would allow.

Her father and Raife stopped talking when they saw her. She spoke to Raife first. "Will you let me know if... if anything changes?"

He hesitated. "You could still come and check on her from time to time."

Emma shook her head. "I make her nervous. I don't want to—." She stopped. The idea that her presence would scare Troy hurt more than Emma knew how to express.

It was no consolation that Raife's suspicion seemed to be fading because Troy didn't know who she was. She didn't remember.

How could she not remember?

Emma turned away and fell into her father's arms. She could hear Raife talking to her back.

"I'm sure she'll remember soon. You just need to give her time."

The sobs rocked through Emma's body. Did it really happen if she was the only one with the memories? What if there was nothing for Troy to remember?

Epilogue

EMMA HADN'T HEARD from Raife since just after Christmas, and here it was, nearing May, so yes, she was surprised when Dana gave her the message to meet him in front of the federal courthouse at noon. "Don't be late," the message read. Emma looked at her wristwatch; she had about a minute to spare.

She hadn't been surprised when Raife's calls had gone from weekly to monthly to even less frequent. Their last conversation had been between Christmas and New Year's. She had laughed until she was in tears over his description of Troy's attempt at cooking Christmas dinner.

They had grown silent during that phone call and Emma had sensed that there would be few, if any, others. She liked Raife, but any mention of Troy would always carry a bittersweet pain. She would never deny her memories of the time they spent together, but knowing she was out there somewhere, living, breathing and awake, yet inaccessible, would always hurt.

Through Raife she had learned that Troy had shown up at Quick Fast two months after being released from the hospital and sat there until he was forced to send her out on a few calls just to appease her. Within a month, she was back to riding her old route. The danger involved in the job worried Emma, but she would have expected nothing less from her. Troy was continuing with her life as best she could while coping with the loss of a loved one.

Emma had done the same.

She felt nervous and fidgety. Her eyes were drawn to the train windows with every street sign that they passed. She found herself studying the faces of her fellow passengers. Their annoyances, pleasures, and pains flowed around her with the occasional strong feelings getting her attention for the seconds it took her to push it out of her conscious mind. There was a time, even before the attack, when the "noise" associated with being around so many people bothered her. Now it made her feel alive. It made her aware of the lives around her. She cherished every minute of it.

Emma started as she realized she had unwittingly been staring at a woman sitting across from her—olive skin, dark seductive eyes, and a wonderful smile. Emma smiled back, feeling the prick of pride at the woman's interest.

She had spent the last year rehabilitating her body. She felt and looked lean. The limp was hers for life, but she was told that it wasn't noticeable unless you knew what to look for. She had even purchased a mountain bike. She had been too shy to do more than a few trails with the athletic group she had joined, but she was getting there.

She felt a surge of excitement mixed with apprehension as the train slowed for her stop. Emma hopped off and swung her day pack over one shoulder as she checked the sidewalk for Raife and then looked across the street at the park. Lunchtime meant the park had its usual assortment of homeless and business people. There was an unwritten, unspoken rule in Portland. While in the parks, the homeless could be trusted not to beg. And the business people with their bagged lunches and take-out cartons could be trusted to waste food, leaving a smorgasbord for anyone in need of a good meal.

Emma sat down on the stone stairs of the courthouse and started rummaging in her pack for the sandwich she hadn't had time to finish in her rush to meet Raife.

She saw her shoes first. Then she saw her muscular calves and the rolled-up black Dickies that always seemed two sizes too big for her. She had leaned Dite against her hip and was pulling off a light rain shell.

Emma's heart slammed into her chest. *Troy doesn't remember me. It'll only make her uncomfortable. And I was just starting to make peace with the situation. Did Raife send her on a bogus pick up so that we could run into each other? Why would he do that? He did it because you're too scared to do it, that's why.*

As Troy draped her jacket over the handlebars of the bike, Emma's eye was drawn to the tattoo on her shoulder. Her fingers pulsed and the ghost of a memory of how the tattoo felt materialized in her mind. She had almost convinced herself that the memories were a side effect of the drug. She had tried to tell herself that it was a dream so that she could move on, but even though it might be possible for her to have dreamed up a woman that looked, sounded, and acted like Troy, she couldn't have created memories of Troy's bike, Troy's tattoo, and even Troy's feelings about Patricia. Not without knowing her.

"I'm thinking about getting it removed." Troy said in a casual voice that threw Emma's body into turmoil. She felt her heart beating and air passing through her nostrils, her parted lips, but everything else seemed to have slowed to a near stand still. The buzz of emotions from the nearby park inhabitants—even from the woman in front of her—was suddenly cut off. It was as if someone was giving her something to savor before they snatched Troy away for good.

"I don't understand." She had dreamed of this moment often for the first few weeks after Troy had awakened, soothing herself with the possibility that she and Troy did live in the same city and that they might someday run into each other. But she hadn't believed it. Portland wasn't that small and she had never believed in coincidence.

"Oh, I thought you were looking at the tat." Troy looked embarrassed and turned to look behind her in a gesture that Emma almost recognized, but didn't quite. The Troy she knew had not been shy. But things had been different then.

Emma smiled trying to hide the fact that she was feeling slow and stupid because she sensed nothing from Troy. No nervousness, no curiosity—nothing.

"I'm in your way." Emma moved to the side so that Troy could get by.

Instead of walking up the stairs Troy gestured toward Emma's leg. "Does that hurt you?" Troy asked.

Emma glanced down at her leg and expected to see a splotch of mayo or something just as embarrassing. She realized that Troy had picked up on the limp. She couldn't have picked up on it from just those few steps, could she?

"How did you—"

"Your limp was worse when you came to see me in the hospital."

Emma looked at the ground so that Troy wouldn't see how elated she felt at her words. *She remembers me coming to the hospital. That was something, right?*

"I forget about it sometimes. I don't know what causes it. They think it's nerve damage, but," she shrugged, "it's hard to say. It seems to feel better as long as I use it a lot." Emma forced herself to shut up when she realized she had begun to babble.

Troy didn't say anything, and Emma worried that she was making her uncomfortable again.

"You're probably busy," Emma said, giving Troy a way out of the conversation. She couldn't rely on her senses this time to know if she was making Troy uncomfortable.

"No, I'm not busy."

"Business slow?"

Troy looked embarrassed again. "No, it's not too bad. I meant I won't be busy until Raife sends another call my way."

Emma figured that Raife wouldn't send her on another call if he had gone to so much trouble to get them together.

"I know you kept in contact with Raife and I've wanted to talk to you about what happened, but I don't know where to begin."

Emma looked away from Troy. Over the last year she had been certain that the way she was handling the situation was right. Troy didn't remember her or what they had shared and one day Emma would be able to accept that. But the fact that she had gone out of her way to avoid her would always hurt.

"I should...you're going to be late for your..."

"Uh, Ms. Webster?"

"It's Emma," she said too loudly. Then more quietly, "You can call me Emma."

"Emma...don't go yet. Please."

Emma turned to look at her then, surprised at the sadness she felt coming from Troy. "Why not?"

"I don't know. I've gone through so many feelings and I don't know why I'm feeling half of them. Do you think you'd like to maybe have some coffee?"

Wait, did she just ask me out? What was that she said about asking someone out for coffee? "It's exactly like a date without all the awkwardness of asking," Emma said aloud.

"What did you just say?"

Emma recognized the look on Troy's face. She'd probably been wearing a similar one when she'd realized who was standing in front of her.

Emma flushed. "I didn't say anything."

"You said, 'Exactly like a date without all the awkwardness of asking.' Did I tell you that?"

"Yes, you did," she admitted. She was afraid, but she was also tired of avoiding the issue. She and Troy had been through a lot together; the tattoo and her own feelings were all she needed to tell her that it had been no dream. She expected to feel some relief, but instead all she felt was an intense longing. The sex—although magnificent—had been too brief, but she missed her friend most of all.

Troy was searching her face with such intensity that Emma had to fight not to look away. "Raife told me that you came to sit with me everyday when I was in a coma. He said you told him that we were friends, but I think we were more than that. Weren't we?"

"Yes, we were more than that," Emma said. She was afraid of where the conversation was going, but she was also ecstatic that they were having it. Even if Troy was still having trouble with Patricia's death, even if she didn't believe any of what Emma had to say, it was time to put it out there.

"So what do we do now?" Emma asked.

"I think we were going for coffee."

"We can go another time if you think Raife will need you," Emma said, and could have kicked herself in the ass for suggesting it. She had waited a year for this very moment and now she was offering to postpone?

"He won't." Emma recognized the determination in Troy's voice.

"I asked him to call you. There's a coffee place down the street." Troy swung her bag over her head and started pushing Dite down the sidewalk.

Emma watched after her grinning like the village idiot and then had to hurry to catch up to her. *Calm down, girl. She asked you to coffee. She isn't going anywhere. Now, you just have to make sure you don't mess this up.*

"Want me to carry that while you push the bike?" Emma asked in order to cover her growing excitement.

Troy smiled. "I wouldn't do that to you. I have a ton of stuff in here." Emma smiled and wanted to say she knew that, but she couldn't. Not yet; maybe not ever.

"The coffee shop is a few blocks up. Are you okay with the walk? We could take the MAX if it starts to rain.

"No, I'm fine. I like the rain."

They continued their walk in silence. Troy seemed to be at war with herself about something, but Emma couldn't get a clue as to what it was. The skin over her knuckles was lighter as she gripped her handlebars of her bike. Emma's eyes went back to the tattoo again as the muscle beneath it bulged. She remembered seeing those arms poised above her, while those brown eyes—eyes so far off from her now—had watched her every move, even when she had succumbed to an orgasm.

Troy caught her looking, and Emma tried to cover. "You said you were going to get it removed. Why?"

"I don't need it to remind me anymore," Troy said as she looked up at the sky and then over at Emma as soft mist began to fall on them. "Do you want to wear my jacket?"

Emma glanced at Troy in surprise. "It's not raining that much."

Troy looked embarrassed and continued to stare straight ahead. The rain began to peck at the rain jacket laid over Troy's bike and they kept walking. Emma felt a sense of deja vu as people walked around them as they made their way toward the café to get that coffee.

"A few days after I woke up, I started to have these—dreams," Troy blurted out.

"About what?" The two words felt heavy on her tongue.

"About you. About us...about a strange time. I didn't know what to make of it. I knew I had seen you the one time, but I was dreaming of whole conversations, and they seemed so real." Troy's words were carefully selected and she wouldn't look at Emma. But Emma could sense that she was confused.

Oh, thank goodness! She had decided from the beginning that she would never tell anyone what she believed happened to her and Troy, in part because she couldn't be one hundred percent sure what was imagined and what wasn't. Emma couldn't help think how easy it would be to blurt everything out now that Troy admitted to having dreams. All she had to do was ask her what she dreamed and fill in the blanks for her. She would just be completing the picture. *No, I can't do that. I can't put my memories in Troy's mouth. Either she has to remember on her own or not at all.*

The thought that Troy might never remember hurt so much that Emma stumbled. Troy reached out to steady her, almost dropping her bike in the process. Emma looked up into Troy's concerned eyes. With her braids tied back she should have looked younger, instead Emma thought she looked exhausted—as if she hadn't slept through the night in some time. But worst of all, she looked sad.

"I just remember being with you." Emma couldn't leash a sharp barking laugh that escaped her mouth as she realized what Troy was trying to telling her. *She's remembering! She may not remember all of it, but her soul remembers what we shared.* A fleeting look of hurt flashed over Troy's face before it was replaced with a smile so fast that Emma had just registered the change.

"I remember your laugh. You didn't do it enough, but I remember." Troy's words were spoken so low that Emma wondered if she had sensed the words rather than heard her speak them.

Emma felt as if a door had opened to her. All of the things Troy felt inside began to tumble out for Emma to see, like a cupful of wishes folded into little triangles for her to unfold and read.

A bead of water fell from a curl of hair at Troy's temple and was held captive on her eyebrow. Emma reached up to capture the drop with the tip of her thumb. Her thumb moved as if of its own accord and brushed along Troy's eyebrow until she was cupping Troy's cheek. The back of her hand looked so pale against the dark gold of Troy's skin. Emma met Troy's eyes.

Everything around them seemed to pause, as if waiting. And then Troy's palm was covering Emma's hand, pressing it against her own cheek. Her long lashes swept down, and she sighed. Emma heard the murmur of conversations and felt the fleeting curiosity of strangers. Bagels, coffee, and wet asphalt—the scent of downtown Portland—hung in the air and Emma felt something inside of herself exhale, stretch, and unfold itself.

Troy released her hand, and Emma's heart plummeted when she felt Troy's confusion and discomfort. "I'm sorry if I make you uncomfortable."

"You don't," Troy said, but her emotions betrayed her. I don't know how to tell you this, but I dream about your touch." Troy looked up at the sky letting the rain hit her face. "My dreams are...pretty vivid." Troy met Emma's eyes again and Emma felt her fear seep away. "We should go get that coffee." Troy strode away so quickly that Emma had to work hard to keep up with her. Neither of them spoke until Troy stopped in front of a non-descript blue building and busied herself locking up her bike. Emma stood above her, wanting to run her hands across the back of her wet shoulders, wanting to take the bag, which she knew would be filled with books from the library, from Troy's back.

Troy stood up and Emma swayed forward as if pulled by an invisible force. All of the pain and longing of the months without Troy crowded into Emma's heart until she felt as though she wouldn't be able to think. Now that she had Troy in front of her—where she could touch her, smell her, feel her presence—the thought of having to live without her was unbearable.

Unable to help herself, Emma risked doing something she had thought about doing since she had first realized it was Troy standing in front of her at the court house. She reached up, hesitated, and then removed the tie that held Troy's braids back. She pulled a few of the braids in front of Troy's shoulders. Her fingers lingered as she admired the neat plats. "Who did these for you?"

"I did them myself."

Surprise made Emma speak without thinking. "You told me you didn't know how to braid your own hair."

Troy's lips parted in surprise; she took a deep breath and leaned closer, as if afraid someone would overhear her confess a secret. "It was all real?" she whispered, no, begged.

She wants it to be true. And even as she thought it, Emma felt all fear of rejection, all the pain of being alone disappear.

"I don't know. Maybe it was, but I remember, too." Emma was shocked to realize that the words came out as a half sob. "It's been so hard to let you remember on your own, but I had to. I wasn't sure if it was all just me...wanting you. I didn't know if what we had there was because there was no one else."

"I lied." Troy's face looked as if it had been dipped in a plaster cast.

"You lied?" Emma repeated.

"I wanted to be close to you. So I lied and said I didn't know how to braid my own hair. I remember sitting between your legs. And I remember—I think I remember—other stuff, too."

"Other stuff?"

"I remember making love to you, Emma. I remember how stupid I was the first time."

"You weren't stupid."

Troy continued as if Emma hadn't spoken. "I don't remember everything about it, but I remember being afraid. Not of you, someone else."

Emma felt almost dizzy with relief at having Troy share the onslaught of emotion that she had been dealing with for the last year without her.

"I remember enough to miss you and I spent a long time feeling guilty."

"Because of Patricia?"

"Yes. I felt like all my heartache should be just for her, but you were there, too."

"How do you feel now?"

"Confused, hurt, guilty...happy." Troy struggled with trying to put words to what she was feeling.

Emma reached out and put her thumb over Troy's lip.

Emma pulled Troy's neck forward until Troy's mouth hovered just in front of hers. Her own feelings echoed the fear coming from Troy until their lips met. Her answer was wordless. Troy's mouth opened and their tongues greeted each other like long lost friends. Emma heard Troy's bag drop to the ground then felt Troy wrapping her arms around her, pulling her close, deepening the kiss.

Emma's legs—the good one and the getting-better one—gave out beneath her. A passerby laughed and Troy loosened her embrace and eased the ferocity of the kiss, but not before returning to Emma's lips twice, as if promising that their separation was only temporary. When Troy released her, Emma stumbled back. Troy reached out as if to steady her, but didn't make contact.

Emma blew out air and pushed her damp hair back off her forehead.

"Okay?"

"Mmm hmm."

Troy dropped her hands to her sides. "I think we blew past the first date stage a long time ago, but if you want to go in, I'm game."

Emma bit her bottom lip, and looked up at the sky. "I don't like being inside much anymore. Would you mind getting a little more wet?"

Troy started to speak, paused as if to rethink her answer before saying, "It would be my pleasure."

Emma had to run the sentence over in her head twice before she figured out the innuendo. A flush darkened Troy's face.

"What are you thinking?" Emma asked.

"I was thinking that you know so much about me, but I don't know anything about you. I feel like an amnesia victim."

"I don't know as much as I would like to about you either. We weren't together that long. We were just beginning to learn about each other when we were..." *When we were what? How should she refer to it? When we were sleeping, comatose? How could we have been either of those things when I remember so vividly?*

Emma was tempted to tell her what she knew, what she had begun to feel, before everything was turned on its ear. She gathered her courage and said with careful determination, "I know this is going to be hard for you to understand, but I need to let you remember on your own."

Troy shook her head. "It's taken me almost a year to piece together the little bit that I can remember!"

"You have no idea how hard—how unbelievably heartbreaking—it's been for me not to come to you. I needed to let you remember us, because I wasn't sure if 'us' was just a figment of my imagination."

"But now you know it wasn't."

Emma felt Troy's frustration mingle with her own. Why was she punishing herself? So what if she told Troy a few things? She wouldn't be putting her words in Troy's mouth if what she told her was true.

"I know what I felt was real. I can't speak for you."

Can't I? I know exactly how Troy felt about me because I felt it. Emma pushed the thoughts away. That was a different time—a fairytale dreamscape where the real world was not around to point out their obvious differences.

"But what if I never remember it all?"

"Then I'd like to start over. Get to know each other all over again, if that's all right with you."

The tension left Troy's face and the smile she gave Emma seemed resigned. "Are you up for a walk down to the waterfront? I don't know if I feel like being inside right now."

"A walk sounds great. I'm sure we can find some coffee down there, too, right?" Emma teased. She and Troy would have to re-learn each other. She knew deep within her soul that they would be all right. There would be some bumps, but that would be no different then any other relationship.

"There's a cart on the way. He has pretty good coffee."

"Okay, that sounds good, but you have to let me carry your bag." Troy hesitated before handing Emma the heavy bag and bent to unlock her bike.

Emma, seeking to lighten the mood, asked, "Whatcha reading?"

Troy face looked pained as she said, "Jane Austen."

Emma smiled, but forced herself not to laugh. Troy was acting like she had been caught grinning into the pages of a Barbara Cartland bodice ripper.

Emma sighed. Troy might not ever remember everything, but she remembered some of it. And the feelings that were coming from her now were strong: curiosity, fear, attraction, and even deeper was a need to reconnect.

Emma had been dealing with that pain since she had walked out of Troy's hospital room. Her soul was suffering from the phantom pain of having Troy removed from her life. She had gone on with her life, had laughed, and had even had fun on several occasions, but sometimes she awoke crying. Sometimes she would sit at her table eating dinner and find herself remembering a snippet of something Troy had said. She would find herself in tears while working on the numerous invoices the clinic had amassed. Even though she had gone on with her life, she ached for Troy whether she was busy at the clinic or sitting at the window seat reading a book.

They began to walk toward the waterfront. Emma was holding Troy's bag and Troy was pushing her bike. They walked a few feet in silence before Troy spoke. "This feels a little bit scary to me. It's like all this stuff is just now clicking into place for me and here I thought I had been awake for over a year."

Emma knew how she felt. If Troy never remembered anything more than she already had, she could be happy—as long as they were together.

"We can slow this down," Emma said.

"You can try," Troy replied." but don't count on any cooperation from me."

Emma laughed and let the sense of joy and belonging flow through her as she and Troy walked toward the waterfront, alive and forever awake.

FORTHCOMING TITLES

published by
Quest Books

IM

by Rick R. Reed

A gay thriller with supernatural overtones, *IM* is the story of a serial killer using a gay hook-up website to prey on young gay men on Chicago's north side. The website's easy and relatively anonymous nature is perfect for a killer.

When the first murder comes to light, the first detective on the scene is Ed Comparetto, one of the police force's only openly gay detectives. He interviews the young man who discovered the body, Timothy Bright, and continues his investigation as the body count begins to rise. But, Comparetto hits a snag when he is abruptly fired from the police force. The cause? Falsifying evidence. It turns out that Timothy Bright has been dead for more than two years, murdered in much the same way as the first victim Ed investigated.

The case becomes a driving force for Comparetto, who finds more and more evidence to support that the person he first spoke to about the murders is really dead. Is he a ghost? Or, is something even more inexplicable and chilling going on? As the murder spree escalates and Comparetto realizes Bright is the culprit, he begins to fear for his own sanity...and his own life. Can Ed race against time and his own doubts to stop the killings before he and his new lover become victims?

Available May 2007

Tears Don't Become Me
by Sharon G. Clark

GW (Georgia Wilhelmina) Diamond, Private Investigator, dealt in missing children cases—only. It didn't alter her own traumatic childhood experience, but she could try to keep other children from the same horrors. She'd left her past and her name behind her. Or so she thought. This case was putting her in contact with people she had managed to keep a distant and barely civil relationship with for fifteen years. Now the buried past was returning to haunt her. When Sheriff Matthews of Elk Grove, Missouri, asked her to take a case involving a teenaged runaway girl, she believed it would be no different from any other. Until Matthews explained she had to take a cop as partner or no deal. A cop who just happened to be the missing girl's aunt.

Erin Dunbar, received the call concerning her niece from an old partner, Frank Matthews. It should have been from her sister, but their estrangement, compounded by her having moved to Detroit, kept that from happening. Now she would have to work with a PI. One had nearly killed her and Frank years ago; she expected this one would be no different. Matters were only made worse by discovering it was a "she" PI—a Looney-tune one who gave new and literal meaning to: "Hands Off." For the sake of her niece, Erin would put up with just about anything, until...GW seemed to be strangely affected by this case and Erin, to her chagrin and amazement, was strangely affected by her.

If Erin could solve GW's past, give her hope, could they have a hope of finding her niece?

Available May 2007

More Gabrielle Goldsby titles

Wall of Silence

It was supposed to be an average bust. Minimal backup. Minimal trouble. But everyone has their limit and Foster Everett has just reached hers.

In a blinding rage Foster makes the first mistake that she can't talk her way out of. A cover-up ensues, and Foster's guilt is left to fester. Ultimately, the death of a close friend proves to be her undoing and Foster begins numbing herself at a neighborhood bar. There she meets 26-year-old Riley Medeiros, the one person strong enough to see Foster's painful secrets and not turn away. And when Foster is forced to run, it's Riley who offers her sanctuary. A small cabin on the California coast becomes Foster's safe haven, and it is there that she begins to get to know the extraordinary woman that is Riley Medeiros. But, like all secrets, Foster's will come back to haunt her. And like even the most carefully built walls, the ones surrounding Foster will eventually crumble and she will find that not all secrets are what they seem.

ISBN 1-932300-01-5
978-1-932300-01-7

Available at booksellers everywhere.

The Caretaker's Daughter

Amidst the backdrop of a nineteenth century English country estate, two women struggle to find love—and the truth that could either bind them together or tear them apart.

ISBN 1-932300-18-X
978-1-932300-18-5

Available at booksellers everywhere.

OTHER QUEST PUBLICATIONS

Gabrielle Goldsby	Wall of Silence	1-932300-01-5
Trish Kocialski	The Visitor's	1-932300-27-9
Lori L. Lake	Gun Shy	978-1-932300-56-7
Lori L. Lake	Have Gun We'll Travel	1-932300-33-3
Lori L. Lake	Under the Gun	978-1-932300-57-4
Helen M. Macpherson	Colder Than Ice	1-932300-29-5
Meghan O'Brien	The Three	978-1-932300-51-2
C. Paradee	Deep Cover	1-932300-23-6
John F. Parker	Come Clean	978-1-932300-43-7

Gabrielle Genean Goldsby grew up in Oakland, California. At the age of nine, a childhood illness left her confined to bed for weeks. It was then, thanks to her mother's efforts to save her own sanity, that Gabrielle discovered a love of reading.

After receiving a Bachelor's Degree in Criminal Justice Administration from San Diego State, she spent time as a Gang and Drugs Prevention Counselor, a Flooring Specialist for a large home improvement store, a Facilities Manager inside some of San Francisco's largest and most powerful law firms, and an Administrative Assistant for a finance company. These varied occupations have become the basis for many past and future writing projects.

Gabrielle is the author of several short stories and two other novels. Although *Wall of Silence*, issued in 2003, was Gabrielle's first published novel, it was written two years after the completion of *The Caretaker's Daughter*, published in 2004.

Gabrielle currently resides in Portland, Oregon, with her partner of eight years, Melissa. She can be reached via her website: www.gabriellegoldsby.com

Printed in the United States
74571LV00003BB/323